SHE WASN'T EXACTLY WHAT HE WAS EXPECTING WHEN HE WAS SENT TO CATCH THE YANKEE SPY . . .

"The Decline and Fall of Ancient Greece," Jared read. "Unusual reading material for a spring afternoon," he commented as he handed it back to her. "And what do they say brought about the fall of the Greeks?"

"I don't know. I haven't read that far." Pippa was on her guard as she studied the perfect, sensual features of the rebel she was certain had come to arrest her.

"I believe you'll find this particular author ascribes their decline to slavery. He feels it weakened an otherwise glorious society to a point where the barbarians could sweep through and plunder at will."

Pippa met Jared's glinting blue eyes evenly. Though her heart quailed in fear, she forced herself to smile. "A tragic day," she said sweetly.

"More than a day," commented Jared. He eyed the stack of books awaiting shelving.

"I was organizing Aunt Charlotte's collection," she explained as Jared lifted one of the novels. "Arranging Aunt Charlotte's books isn't as easy as you think. See, there you've placed the works of Miss Charlotte Bronte beside Mr. Keats. They'll have to be separated."

Jared was mystified. "Why is that?"

"They aren't married," replied Pippa, "as I found out when I attempted to do the same. The Brownings, however, may reside together." She took the volume from Jared and placed it on the shelf.

Jared's eyes glinted. "What of Lord Byron?" he asked. "Surely there are several lady writers with whom he might happily be paired."

"I doubt very much that Aunt Charlotte would approve of that," said Pippa, but Jared saw her veiled smile.

"Probably not," he agreed.

STOBIE PIEL

REBEL WIND

PINNACLE BOOKS
WINDSOR PUBLISHING CORP.

PINNACLE BOOKS are published by

Windsor Publishing Corp.
850 Third Avenue
New York, NY 10022

The P logo Reg U.S. Pat & TM Off. Pinnacle is a trademark of Windsor Publishing Corp.

First Printing: March, 1995

Printed in the United States of America

To my husband, Gordon Voltin.
Thanks to you, I'll always believe in love at first sight.

And to our children, Natasha, Sophia, and Garrett, for making life wonderful and interesting.

To my mother, Barbara Piel, for listening to every story I ever told.

. . . But if instead
Thou wait beside me for the wind to blow
The grey dust up, . . . those laurels on thine head
O my Beloved, wilt not shield thee so,
That none of all the fires shall scorch and shred . . .
—Elizabeth Barrett Browning
"Sonnets from the Portuguese"

Prologue

No night wind rustled the leaves, yet the misty air seemed filled with activity. The small band of horsemen on the bank of the Rappahannock River held their mounts in check as their leader hurried down the narrow path to join their group.

"She's crossed," he told them. His great black horse broke into a controlled canter. "We must hurry."

The group leapt into a gallop, but they couldn't overtake their leader. The horses plunged into the river, crossing in great bounds. They surged up the bank on the far side, but there they stopped.

"Damn! We can't let that Yankee witch get away this time, Captain." The furious rebel rode up to address his officer. "What are we waiting for?"

"Do you know which way she has gone?" asked the captain. "Does she ever ride where you expect? I intend to catch her this time. Riding blindly into Yankee territory doesn't strike me as the best way to do it."

"She'd go straight on," began the angry man. "Where else? If we get going, we'll catch her. That big old horse of hers may be sure-footed, but it's not fast."

The officer made up his mind. "You all go straight. I'm going to ride up along the ravine. It's only wide enough for one horse. If she's there, I won't need any help retrieving her."

The others departed. The captain turned his horse and navigated the treacherous path along the bank of the swollen Rappahannock. Unseen tree limbs slowed his way. Often he crouched low to pass, but as he moved along, the captain knew his pursuit was not in vain. Up ahead, distinctly, he heard the heavy hoofbeats of a large horse. He had found the path of the woman he wanted.

The big horse picked its way with skill and agility. The young woman astride only needed to cling fast to assure her own safety over the unstable footing. She checked the horse's stride and listened with ears as sharp as an Indian scout's. She heard the following rider closing behind. Her heart leapt into furious activity, and she urged on her horse.

"Hurry, old friend," she whispered, "or I'll find myself hanging from a rebel noose. You'll be pulling artillery carts, so it's in your own best interest to get us out of this."

Despite her precarious situation, excitement overrode the girl's fear. Even as she considered her fate, her heart surged with the thrill of the chase.

"He'll think I'm going to the bridge to cross," she speculated to the horse, "but he can only be judging my position from the sound."

The heavy fog was parted by her soft, clear laugh. The girl turned the big horse from the path and headed him down the bank. She had utmost confidence in his ability, and as always, his sure-footed agility served her well.

She reached the far side, but instead of turning back, the girl rode onward, still heading for the bridge she no longer needed to cross. To her right, the ravine widened and the drop fell off over rocks and boulders even her agile mount couldn't traverse.

Though he could hear the horse ahead, the captain saw no sign of the rider he was pursuing. Gradually, the truth began to dawn on him. As he brought his horse virtually alongside the other rider, he realized his mistake.

The ravine was draped in fog, but the captain could see his enemy. She brought her horse to a standstill across from him, and they faced each other silently. The clouds parted and the moon sent shafts of soft light through the trees, illuminating the woman's figure. She sat astride the horse, her long legs clothed in a man's trousers, a hooded cloak draped across the horse's sides.

The woman's hood was flung back to reveal dark hair that fell like a cloud about her shoulders. Her image was pagan, and it occurred to the captain that in another time, such a woman might have been named a witch.

Despite the moon, it was too dark for a sure shot from his revolver. The captain's long-ingrained chivalry prevented such a recourse anyway. The war didn't necessitate the murder of a woman, however irritating her practices might be.

"It seems you've been led astray, rebel," she called across the ravine, and her voice was filled with laughter. Though it provoked his anger, the sound provoked something else in the captain as well.

"I congratulate you, lady," he answered. The girl in the shadows was surprised more by the faint English inflection in his voice than by the customary gallantry of a Virginian.

"It was well done," he continued, "but I warn you, my men are already in pursuit of you beyond the river. It may be more than you can handle to escape us all."

The girl laughed. "I think not, sir. In fact, I'm just where I wished to be. I doubt your men will find me on the road I plan to take. You rebels don't take defeat easily, but you will never catch me."

The captain laughed, too, but a curious welling rose in his heart as he met her defiant challenge. "Tonight at least, my purposes are thwarted. But I warn you, spies and agents of the North do not fare well in Virginia. I would curtail my activities if I were you." He paused, and his voice grew low, both caressing and threatening to the ears of the girl who listened.

"We will meet again, you and I. And I will have you then, my little witch. That is a promise."

The girl didn't answer at once. She felt a shiver of apprehension at his words. Far overhead, beyond the mists, the moon rose above the trees and broke through the clouds. It glinted upon the golden hair of the tall man across the ravine, and though he couldn't reach her, the girl felt a tremor of fear.

"You are arrogant and too sure of yourself, sir." She paused. "You may hold our army at bay for a time, but an army that can't catch one little woman on an old carriage horse is hardly likely to sever the Union in the end."

With that, the girl spun her horse around to head off through the woods. She lifted her arm and waved to him, and he lowered his saber in salute. Though they were on opposite sides of the new war, the captain had enjoyed their brief encounter a great deal.

The War for Southern Independence was little more than a year old, and after the Yankees' pathetic showing at Manassas, the captain doubted the Union would long resist secession. Still, he admired the girl's daring ventures to the Union encampments in Northern Virginia.

He knew she had been running messages almost at will to Yankee operatives since early in the war. She had damaged his cause on more than one occasion, and though he had every intention of removing her from service to her country, the captain looked forward heartily to their next meeting.

"Did you see her?" asked the returning rebel when the group reunited with their leader.

"I did, but she outsmarted me, I'm afraid," he told them without shame at being bested by a woman.

"The woman is a witch," said the thwarted rebel with conviction. "Think how she always moves about in a fog. She's a Yankee witch."

The captain sighed. "She is magnificent."

"You must be more careful, Pippa."

The dark, misty night was lit with the glow of lanterns, and Philippa Reid's heavyset cart horse stood steaming with sweat as she dismounted. She faced the tall man who greeted her with a shake of his dark head.

"Don't be silly, Byron," she replied lightly. "I had no trouble evading the great Southern defenders."

"You don't take them seriously enough, girl," he chided her, but his warm Southern voice was filled with affection.

"I haven't been caught yet. I know what they did to you, Byron," she added more seriously, and took his hand. "It's for you, and for Jefferson, that I must do this. I can't sit idle, any more than you can. You came South to fight. I can't fight, but I'm not without use in Virginia."

"What would your father say if he knew the danger his daughter is in, that I have put you in?"

"He shouldn't have left me in the care of a Virginian," replied Pippa with lingering resentment of her father's hastily considered arrangements. "I can't imagine what he was thinking."

"I don't believe your father expected to die, Pippa," said Byron softly. "A year ago, you were sixteen. He believed you needed the care of your family. Since your only family is in Virginia . . . Like everyone, North and South, he believed the war would be soon over."

"You never thought so," Pippa reminded him.

"No, but I know the rebels," Byron told her quietly, speaking as if to himself. "No one knows the master better than the dog," he added.

"Don't say that, Byron! You are so far above those, those . . ."

"No, I'm not," said Byron. "But I am no less, as they'll learn if I'm allowed to take up arms against them." Byron's handsomely sculpted face hardened. "There's one rebel who will answer with his life if I ever find him."

Byron was rarely angry, though Pippa was aware of his intention to one day confront his former master. But Pippa understood his quest to join the Union Army. She, too, had dreamed of aiding its cause before a way opened.

"Someone will let you fight, Byron. They'd be fools not to."

Byron sighed, his mood softened. "That's my hope. Jefferson is in Washington, with the same hope. But until that day, I can do some small part here. I assume you have a message?"

"I do indeed," replied Pippa as she withdrew a small crochet purse. "Here." She handed Byron the crumpled paper.

"It comes directly from the President's household, though it passed through many hands before mine."

Pippa sighed with a trace of frustration. "I wish I was closer to things. If only Aunt Charlotte would move to Richmond, but until our side proves itself threatening . . . Richmond! Think of what I might learn living there."

"You are close enough as it is, little one," replied Byron. He perused the note. "So Jeff Davis has a spy in his own White House, does he?"

"Gray House."

"This should be of value," concluded Byron. He looked at Pippa with misgivings.

"Pippa, it may be time for you to curtail your activities. If the rebels should catch you . . ."

"They'll never come close," she replied, but she remembered the rebel's vow as he stood across the dark ravine, and her heart trembled.

Byron glanced at the old horse beside her, its sides still heaving with exertion, its nostrils flared as its breath warmed the night.

"You arrived in a hurry, as if you were followed by an army. Or have you no better sense than to wear down this old horse for your pleasure?"

Pippa paused. "I came closer to a band of rebels tonight than I'd wish," she admitted with reluctance. "You needn't fear, Byron. One Yankee girl is worth a dozen Southern gentlemen."

"I thought the rebels were arrogant!" teased Byron. "I can't help thinking your father would want you to handle yourself with more decorum."

Pippa tossed her head, her long hair tumbling wildly about her shoulders. "No," she said. "Father would understand. I'm doing no less than his daughter should do. Father died for this. How can I sit among our enemies and do nothing, when so much is to be done, Byron? How can I? Some say the freedmen should stay out of the fight, yet here you are. It's your war, and it's mine, too. It's my world, and I won't see this injustice reign forever."

Byron sighed deeply. "You sound like your father. But I do understand. I doubt very much many of your kind would. Still, should your aunt learn . . ."

"She will never know," interrupted Pippa. "Aunt Charlotte believes women are not thus disposed. At least not well-bred women. It never occurs to her that I might be less than a perfect lady."

Byron smiled. "No doubt you've convinced her that you are, and dozens of young rebels, too. How heartsick they'd be to learn your sweet heart burns with the fire of abolition!"

"They are fools," she said. "It has been no effort at all to deceive them. Shy smiles, averted eyes, and they look no deeper."

"You don't know them, little one," said Byron. "These young sons of planters, they have an appeal to women."

Pippa shook her head vigorously, but Byron laughed. "Even you may not be immune to one compelling young rebel, Miss Pip. You haven't allowed yourself to know them. If you do, you may find a temptation you hadn't expected."

"That's impossible," replied Pippa assuredly. "No swaggering rebel could change my opinion of their kind. They're only braggarts, Byron. I've outsmarted them at every turn!"

"You underestimate the rebels, Miss Pip. As a Maine girl, they're bound to be suspicious of you sooner or later. Take care."

"I always do," she replied. "To that end, I must go or I'll never make it back before dawn."

Rising on tiptoes, the slender girl kissed Byron's cheek.

She mounted the large horse and rode away, melting into the warm, wet night. The tall former slave stood staring into the night after Philippa had disappeared.

"I fear for you, little one," he whispered. "Young hearts bear unexpected fire."

Part One

Northern Virginia

Gather the north flowers to complete the south,
And catch the early love up in the late.
                    —Elizabeth Barrett Browning

One

"Philippa Reid?" Jared Knox looked at his friend, and his brow furrowed as he observed the smitten expression on Edward Carlton's serious face.

"An unusual name," he said.

"She's called 'Pippa,' " replied Edward. Edward had a smile upon his lips, but Jared was unimpressed.

"I don't remember that Charlotte Reid had any daughters besides Agnes. As I recall, she was fairly lacking in charm," remarked Jared. He set aside a copy of the *Richmond Examiner* and drank the last of his makeshift coffee.

"Miss Reid is Charlotte's niece. I assure you, Jared, she isn't lacking in anything," replied Edward. He lifted his own coffee to his lips, but then he frowned and set the cup aside.

"I wish we could get around the embargo," he mourned, but Jared shrugged.

"It's hurting the Yankees more than us, Edward. It's costing them."

Edward nodded. "Finances. That's what matters most to the Yanks."

"Let's forget the Yanks today, Edward," suggested Jared. "We're on leave, after all. Tell me about your Miss Reid.

I'd be interested to know who could distract you from the ministry."

"Philippa is nineteen years old," began Edward enthusiastically, but Jared stopped him.

"Nineteen? Why haven't I heard of her?"

"Well, she's only been here a year or so," Edward told him hesitantly. "She came South to live with her aunt when her father died."

"Came South?" exclaimed Jared. "Do you mean this girl is a Yankee?"

Edward frowned. "Well, yes. Philippa was born in Maine."

"Maine!" Jared sat back in the broad-armed chair and laughed. "A New England Yankee! What do you know!"

"Pippa is nothing like a Yankee girl," Edward said hurriedly. "She has the sweetest manners, the kindest heart, the dearest personality, and she is lovely . . ."

Jared's abrupt laugh interrupted his friend. "No doubt it's the latter which has distracted you, Edward. Her beauty has made you blind to the obvious."

"What are you talking about, Jared?" asked Edward with mounting suspicion. "You can't mean to imply that Pippa . . ."

Jared leaned forward, his eyes gleaming. "Can't I? Dear God, Edward. A Yankee girl has been living here for a year and no one's thought to wonder if she might have some connection to the spy ring?"

Edward was aghast. "Jared," he said, trying to maintain his pastoral calm. "You haven't met Miss Reid, or you'd never say such things."

"Blasphemy, no doubt," agreed Jared. "We'll soon correct that," he added as he rose from his seat. "Come, take me to Charlotte Reid's home, and you may introduce me to this angelic creature."

Edward sat stubbornly in his chair, glaring about his father's study with displeasure. "Not if you intend to accuse the sweetest girl I know of spying."

"I'll do nothing of the kind," Jared reassured him unconvincingly. "I'll be a perfect gentleman, I promise you. Now come along."

"I know you're especially at odds with the Yankees, Jared," said Edward in a controlled voice, much as he hoped to utilize from the pulpit.

"I don't blame you, of course," he continued. "If they had sacked and looted and burned my family's home, I'd hate them even more than I do. But Philippa Reid had nothing to do with that."

"If she's the girl I'm after, she damn well did," replied Jared as Edward's frown deepened.

"She isn't," Edward maintained. "She couldn't . . ."

"She's too beautiful and sweet. So you've said. We'll see. If she is the same, she's quite capable of deceiving a smitten boy into believing anything she wishes."

"And you think I'm going to allow you to meet her?" asked Edward with a shake of his head.

"Either that, or I'll go alone. I'd think you'd want to be there to protect her if I learn she's the one responsible for that night."

Uncertain whether to believe Jared's threat or not, Edward reluctantly rose from his chair. His long face was etched with displeasure. Once he wouldn't have believed Jared Knox capable of any ungentlemanly act. But now his friend's fair face was hardened by nearly three years of war and hardship.

While Edward had been assigned the pleasant task of guarding Richmond, Jared had been in every battle the Army of Northern Virginia had seen. Granted leave together, Edward had accompanied Jared to Northern Virginia, site of his family's burned plantation. Edward knew, however, that Jared's main reason for returning was to find the spy responsible for the estate's destruction.

"We will go," Edward agreed at last. "But you must give me your word to do Miss Reid no dishonor, Jared . . ."

"I wouldn't think of it," Jared replied, but Edward looked at him doubtfully.

"Promise, our visit will be a pleasant call. Nothing more."

Jared's eyes rolled heavenward but he sighed in agreement. "You have my word. Shall we go?"

The two officers were met at Charlotte Reid's Georgian mansion by a servant girl. Seeing her bewildered face, Edward turned to Jared.

"Lucy is . . . simple," he explained without the effort of lowering his voice. "Lucy," he began, directing his words slowly toward the servant. "Would you tell Mrs. Reid that Major Knox and I have come to call?"

"On Missus Charlotte?" asked Lucy impertinently, and Edward blushed.

"Rather perceptive, despite being dim, isn't she?" observed Jared.

Lucy directed them to the sitting room. Within moments, Charlotte Reid appeared to greet her guests. As a neighbor and, of late, a frequent caller, Edward was on familiar terms with Mrs. Reid. She greeted him warmly before she turned to Jared.

"Major Knox, how lovely to see you well," she said, as she took in the tall, strong form of the young officer.

"I haven't seen your dear mother since . . ." Charlotte paused, not liking to touch on the delicate matter of the once fabulous Knox estate. "Well, since the difficulty with the Yankees last summer. But I understand she'll be at our ball tomorrow night. I'm so pleased. She must be grateful to get out of Richmond."

"She is," said Jared.

"Caroline must be delighted to have her son home. Will you be staying long?" asked Charlotte. Such information was often useful when conversing with one's neighbors.

"I have nearly two weeks," replied Jared, but there was a weariness in his voice that only Edward noticed.

"How lovely! Are you staying with Edward?" Charlotte inquired further.

"He is," answered Edward. "We were fortunate enough to gain furloughs together. It's lonely here, I'm afraid, without one's friends. I, for one, shall be immensely glad of the ball tomorrow."

"I'm so pleased to hear you say so!" said Charlotte. "We've been planning it for ages. To alleviate the strain of . . . our situation. And to accept donations for the Cause."

"It's a capital idea," agreed Edward. "Will Philippa be attending?"

Charlotte smiled. "She will indeed. I suspect it's to discuss the matter that you've come by today?" she questioned pleasantly. Edward blushed.

"Is she available?" he asked.

"I'd imagine she is," replied Charlotte, and she patted Edward's arm. "Come, we'll find her."

Charlotte led them from the greeting room toward the living room. The bell rang again and she was distracted by the arrival of several ladies on her planning committee. Jared continued down the hall, but Edward felt obliged to greet the women. The prospect of further polite conversation didn't intrigue Jared, and he passed into a darkened room to await Edward.

The curtains of the small library were drawn but for one. In the light of the open window stood a young woman. Her amber-brown hair was bound in a loose chignon that made an accurate comparison to the figure burned into Jared's memory impossible. The window through which the girl gazed faced north, and a slow smile crossed Jared's lips.

"You look to the north. Can it be that your heart lies beyond the horizon?" he asked, but Philippa's blood froze at his voice.

She knew that voice, the faint hint of mockery in the English inflection. That voice had haunted her dreams for two years, but that he stood behind her. . . . The open book she held dropped to the floor, but Pippa couldn't move. She knew the man behind her. Knew him before she dared turn to face him. As her heart had stopped when he spoke, it now raced in blind terror.

Remain calm, she told herself, and she clenched her hands into tight fists as she fought to control her fear. Pippa made herself turn, her teeth sinking into the soft flesh of her lip. The man who met her frightened gaze was not at all what she expected. He was younger than she had imagined, though the gray and butternut of his uniform showed signs of long wear. He was tall, with a strong, lean body that radiated a controlled power.

A Confederate saber hung at his side, reminding Pippa that this man was her enemy. Yet the rebel's face was beautiful, with full, firm features and intelligent blue eyes. Eyes that looked into the depths of Pippa's soul. The thought was unnerving and she bit her lip harder.

If Pippa was surprised by the handsome, blond officer, Jared was more so by the girl who faced him. She was frightened. He could see that plainly, and it was expected from a spy thus cornered. Nothing else about the delicate beauty before him fit his image of a destructive Yankee spy.

Wide eyes lined with full black lashes met Jared's. They were a haunting shade of green. Eyes as green as northern evergreens reflected in a forest stream. Jared fought the direction of his thoughts, but he saw the soft curves of her face, her delicately formed nose, the small, full lips parted as she looked at him.

Jared's eyes cast reluctantly across her body. Though slender, she was formed to draw the eye of the most sophisticated gentleman. Without question, Philippa Reid was the most beautiful, innocently beguiling woman he had ever seen. He had been mistaken to underestimate the power that charmed the staid Edward Carlton.

Without a word, Jared approached Pippa, aware that she didn't draw a breath as he came near. He bent to retrieve the book she had dropped. Pippa forced a quick breath as his dark blue eyes met hers, but she dared not speak until he had declared his intention. Apparently he was in no hurry to do so.

"Miss Reid, I presume?" he asked. Pippa nodded, but she didn't speak. "Forgive me for startling you."

"Not at all," she replied, but at the sound of her small, soft voice, an expression of doubt crossed Jared's face.

"Perhaps I should introduce myself," he offered gently. "I'm Jared Knox."

Pippa's brow furrowed as she studied the perfect, sensual features of the rebel she was certain had come to arrest her.

Jared closed the book Pippa had dropped and examined the cover. *"The Decline and Fall of Ancient Greece,"* he read. "Unusual reading material for a spring afternoon," he commented as he handed it to her.

Jared smiled. As her eyes rested upon his full, curved lips, Pippa felt a curious stirring in her heart. His blond hair had missed its due cut, touching his collar with a slight curl. Pippa fought a mad impulse to brush it from his forehead.

"And what do they say brought about the fall of the Greeks?" Jared asked.

Pippa was on her guard. "I don't know," she replied. "I haven't read that far."

Jared's smile deepened. "I believe you'll find this particular author ascribes their decline to slavery. He feels it weakened an otherwise glorious society to a point where the barbarians could sweep through and plunder at will."

Pippa met Jared's glinting blue eyes evenly. Though her own heart quailed in fear, she forced herself to smile. "A tragic day," she said sweetly.

"More than a day." Jared's expression was unreadable as he glanced toward a stack of books awaiting shelving.

"I was organizing Aunt Charlotte's collection," Pippa explained as Jared lifted one of the novels.

"I'll help you," he said. He began to slip books into convenient slots, but Pippa stopped him, a tiny smile tugging at the corners of her lips.

"I'm afraid that won't do at all, Major Knox."

"Why not?"

"Arranging Aunt Charlotte's books isn't as easy as you'd think," she explained. "See, there you've placed the works of Miss Charlotte Bronte beside Mr. Keats. They'll have to be separated."

Jared was mystified. "Why is that?"

"They aren't married," replied Pippa, "as I found when I tried to do the same. The Brownings, however, may reside together." Pippa took a volume from Jared and placed it on the shelf.

"More complicated than I realized," agreed Jared. His eyes found Philippa's and she saw his bewilderment, though she didn't understand it.

"I had tired of the procedure," Pippa confided with a sigh. "There aren't that many married authors, who can comfortably reside on the same shelf."

Jared's eyes glinted as he studied her face. "What of Lord Byron?" he asked. "Surely there are several with whom he might happily be paired."

"I doubt very much Aunt Charlotte would approve of that," said Pippa, but Jared saw her veiled smile.

"Probably not," agreed Jared. As he stood beside her, his heart was moved by a feeling he didn't welcome, yet he was powerless to resist its force.

Edward entered the room and saw Philippa standing close beside Jared. A shy smile lit her lovely face, and Edward's heart sank. Edward sighed audibly. He had foreseen this turn of events, despite Jared's earlier intentions. It occurred to Edward that it was probably best if a girl as tempting as Philippa Reid was otherwise occupied, lest he forget his own calling.

"Your aunt tells me you'll be at the ball tomorrow night," ventured Edward as he sat opposite Pippa in the Reids' music room.

"Yes," said Pippa quietly, but her eyes went to where Jared stood and he smiled. Pippa's heart fluttered, and she looked away.

From the next room, the voices of the planning committee raised in excitement. Edward reasoned this was a good time to leave, before the meeting broke up, and he stood to bid Pippa farewell. Pippa led them to the foyer, and Edward glanced nervously in the direction of the ladies' meeting room.

Jared, however, was in no hurry to be parted from Pippa. Edward headed down the wide stairs to their horses, but Jared took the girl's hand in his. Their eyes met and Pippa drew a quick breath as he gently kissed the back of her slender fingers.

"Until tomorrow, Philippa," he said softly.

Pippa was unable to speak as she watched him depart and mount the black thoroughbred. She stood alone by the door long after the two rebels disappeared from her view.

Pippa remembered Byron's words of warning: "You don't know them, little one. These young sons of planters, they have an appeal to women."

How truly he had spoken! Pippa sighed deeply and went back to the library, but she was unable to read. She longed to discuss the matter with someone she could trust, either Byron himself or Jefferson Davis, the other runaway slave who had found refuge at Gordon Reid's home.

But Byron had returned to New England to join one of the new Colored Regiments, and Jefferson had found his place in a Massachusetts company. How ironic, she reflected, that her two closest friends were men of color, both at war against the handsome rebel who troubled her heart.

"I half expected to be bringing Philippa back in irons," ventured Edward as the two men rode across the Carltons' vast cotton fields.

Jared smiled. "That wouldn't seem . . . necessary at this time."

"Indeed not," laughed Edward. "Maybe you plan to interrogate the lady further at Mother's ball tomorrow?"

Jared laughed, too. "That, my friend, is an excellent suggestion." He urged his great horse forward into a gallop. The two men raced across the rolling fields, their exuberance at odds with the dark lives they had led for the past years of war.

Pippa stood with her hands on the windowsill as Emmaline tied her corset and adjusted her stays. She paid little attention to the preparations, but her attendance was vital and she accepted her duty. Emmaline helped her to dress, fastening her crinoline neatly and arranging her elaborate petticoats with care.

"You're the prettiest flower in a meadow, miss," said Emmaline as she stood back to survey her work, but Pippa only glanced at her reflection in the looking-glass.

The dress was ivory and green, brocaded handsomely, and it suited her well. Charlotte had taken great care to present her niece with a wardrobe fitting for a young Virginian lady, supposedly to brighten Pippa's downcast spirits after the death of her father.

Pippa suspected that Charlotte's reasons were more personal, lest her Yankee niece prove an embarrassment with her somber wardrobe and straightforward manner. The clothes, at least, were in the aunt's power to control.

"Thank you, Emmaline," said Pippa as she sat for Emmaline's attentions upon her hair.

Pippa couldn't deny that Emmaline had a special gift for decorating hair. Artful strands of escaping tendrils framed her small, shapely face, and Pippa smiled slightly as she viewed her reflection. It wasn't like her to care for her appearance, yet this afternoon it seemed more important than usual. Unbidden, the compelling, fluid expressions of Major Jared Knox's face filtered across her mind.

The shadows were lengthening across the wide front lawn of the Carltons' mansion. Wide pillars of dark shadows fell from the tall Grecian columns lining the double-tiered portico, and carriages covered the lawn leading to the grand home.

Charlotte and Pippa arrived later than the other guests. Charlotte's nephew, Burke Mallory, had arrived unexpectedly and insisted on escorting the ladies. Pippa had met Burke before and liked him, though his dispassion where abolition was concerned kept her from true fondness.

"Not much like New England, is it, Pippa?" said Burke pleasantly as the Reids' carriage pulled up behind another.

"No."

Burke's brown eyes narrowed as he looked around the expansive estate with admiration and a suggestion of something else that Pippa couldn't identify.

"You'd never guess they're in the middle of the bloodiest war this land has seen, would you?" he ventured.

"It's just beneath the surface, always," stated Charlotte. "But we put our finest face forward, even now, when the Yankees are pressing at our door."

"You seem to have no trouble crossing back and forth," said Pippa, looking at Burke with curiosity. Her own adventures North had been increasingly harrowing over the past year.

"When it comes to business, the rebels are as interested as any Yankee, despite what they pretend," replied Burke derisively.

"You're going to Richmond, Burke?" asked Pippa with disguised interest.

"Yes, my business is there. Why?"

"I just can't imagine too many care about building new hotels now," Pippa replied.

"No, but selling, that's another thing."

Charlotte turned angrily toward her nephew. "I hope you're not considering making a profit from the suffering of others," she said with disgust.

"Of course not, Aunt Charlotte," Burke said quickly. "But such sales are of dire necessity to those beleaguered owners."

Charlotte wished to be reassured, and she was. But Pippa thought it was very shaky reasoning.

As Pippa entered the wide foyer of Edward Carlton's home, she saw the mingling guests with a dispassion and distance that set her apart. Her feet touched exquisite marbled floors, but the moment had the quality of a dream, unreal to the raging and anguished world at the outskirts of the crumbling civilization.

Burke seemed to be looking for someone, and he left his aunt when Parson Frederick approached. The parson greeted Charlotte and Pippa as they joined the other guests. He was an old friend of Charlotte's husband, and often visited Charlotte's home.

"Well, well, Miss Reid. I'm glad to see you here," he said cheerfully. "You should venture forth more often," he added with a laugh. Pippa's green eyes twinkled at the parson's secret joke.

"Charlotte! How pretty you look!" beamed the parson as he took Charlotte's hands.

Lucy walked past them carrying a tray, and the parson glanced at her. "Isn't that your maid, Charlotte?" he asked.

"Yes, Elspeth felt she needed more help, so I've loaned Lucy's services for the night. Lucy is adequate. She looks well in a uniform, anyway. As long as she doesn't talk too much," confided Charlotte.

Beside her, Pippa's eyes met the parson's, and the two exchanged a knowing glance.

"Philippa!" A high, pleasant girl's voice called from across the hall, and Pippa turned to see Fanny Woods waving.

Among the local girls, only Fanny had offered the Yankee girl friendship, and Pippa liked her. Fanny's blue eyes were glittering with excitement, and she hurried to Pippa's side.

Fanny grasped Pippa's hand in a conspiratorial gesture. "Edward is back," she whispered. "And Jared Knox is with him!"

"Yes, I know," said Pippa. "What of it?"

Fanny was aghast. " 'What of it?' Philippa, you can't have met him, or you wouldn't ask!"

Pippa frowned. "As a matter of fact, I met him yesterday, with Edward. I still don't understand . . ."

"Philippa, Jared Knox is the most beautiful man anywhere! Except for Edward, of course. You must be blind."

"I'm not blind," replied Pippa.

Fanny shook her head impatiently. "He's distinguished himself in battle from the first days of the war. He enlisted as a private, but he's been promoted faster than anyone."

Fanny missed the faint frown upon Pippa's face as she breathlessly continued. "Then he was injured, or sick or something, after Gettysburg. Anyway, it was rumored he had died!"

"A false rumor, I would say," Pippa injected with a detachment she didn't feel. The thought of Jared Knox having died was disturbing.

"Four girls went into mourning," Fanny continued, but Pippa forced herself to ignore the hint of scandal in Fanny's voice.

"Prematurely, it seems," Pippa said rather coldly. Fanny's eyes widened at the Yankee girl's lack of sentimentality, either genuine or feigned.

Fanny caught her breath and grasped Pippa's arm tightly. Pippa turned to see what had distracted Fanny. Across the hall, Jared Knox stood watching her. Even from the far side of the room, Pippa felt the power of his piercing blue eyes. She saw his lips form a slow smile, and a wild wash of heat coursed through her, a tide she could not stem.

Jared came to her, moving through the milling crowd without ever taking his eyes from her. Pippa awaited him as if transfixed. Whether it was with fear or enchantment, she couldn't guess. Fanny's presence at her side faded away, and Pippa's heart labored beneath her breast as he came to stand before her.

"Miss Reid," he said. "I hoped to see you tonight." His eyes cast briefly down the trembling length of her, but Pippa couldn't speak.

"You're even lovelier than I remembered," he said lightly, yet there was a feeling behind his words that belied the casualness of his flattery.

As if realizing this also, Jared turned to Fanny. "You, Miss Woods, grow more fetching each time I see you."

Fanny blushed, but Pippa was less moved by his easy words. She felt that Jared was teasing them, that he didn't take the esteemed role of ladies in such deadly earnest as did other men. While that realization disturbed her, she also found it a formidable quality. Such men were not easily deceived.

Burke Mallory came to stand at Pippa's side, and she hoped he would break the strange tension between herself and Jared Knox.

"Major Knox," said Burke. Burke extended his hand, which Jared shook, but Jared didn't look pleased to see Charlotte Reid's nephew.

"We met last year, if you recall," Burke reminded Jared. "Although I know it was a particularly difficult time, with the tragic loss of your father's estate. You may not remember me."

"I remember," replied Jared.

Burke didn't seem aware of Jared's mood, and he turned to Pippa with a wide smile. "Well then, little cousin, they're dancing in the next room. Shall we put on display in this hostile setting the grace of our beleaguered Yanks?"

Pippa felt it necessary to be kept from Jared lest his blue eyes see more than she intended, so she gratefully accepted Burke's offer. But as she accompanied him to the ballroom, she was intensely aware of those eyes upon her.

As Burke led Pippa away from Jared, Lucy came around the corner and bumped into Pippa. The tray the servant girl carried clattered to the floor, and Lucy bent to retrieve it. But it was Pippa who apologized.

"Oh, excuse me," said Pippa hurriedly. "Let me help you." She took the tray as Lucy picked up the hors d'oeuvres that had fallen.

Lucy completed her procedure and placed the useless hors d'oeuvres again upon the tray. Briefly, her dark eyes met Pippa's. As she took the tray, she slipped a small piece of paper into Pippa's fingers. The two women exchanged a fleeting glance, and Lucy again lowered her head as she hurried for the kitchen.

The red glow of sunset had faded, and as Pippa slipped from the Great Hall, the first stars appeared in the eastern sky. The veranda was lit with paper lanterns, but as the night was chilly, the Virginians preferred to stay inside.

Pippa made certain no one was in the immediate vicinity, then hurriedly withdrew the note Lucy had given her.

"Agent detained. Alert the parson. Not tonight."

Pippa put the note back in her crocheted bag and sighed deeply. She looked over the railing, leaning forward to see the northern star. It comforted her when she was missing her far-off, coastal home, but this night the swift clouds obliterated its presence from her view.

"Again you look north."

Pippa whirled around and saw Jared Knox standing close behind her.

"I seem to be making a habit of surprising you," he said with a smile, but Pippa's heart leapt wildly in her breast. In the soft lamplight, his beautiful face glowed with unearthly power and his golden hair glimmered. Pippa felt weak with his impact.

She had avoided looking his way throughout the evening. She had fought with herself for caring as he danced with Fanny and numerous other blushing young ladies. *He has this way with girls,* she reminded herself firmly. *I'm no different, and I mean nothing at all to him.*

With this in mind, Pippa forced herself to meet his eyes. Her detachment was feigned with every ounce of her will.

"I think startling me must please you in some way, Major

Knox," she ventured daringly, but instantly Pippa regretted her comment.

Jared smiled, the change in his expression a physical tug at Pippa's light veneer of composure.

"Oh, yes, Miss Reid. It pleases me immensely."

Jared paused, his eyes boring into her with a heat like fire, but Pippa didn't breathe as he moved closer to her.

"For, you see, you are disarmingly beautiful when you're surprised."

Pippa couldn't speak, but her heart raced so swiftly that she wondered wildly if she might actually faint. Jared knew how she reacted to him. Pippa realized this with acute discomfort as she saw his smile deepen, the trace of gentle mockery glinting in his eyes. She knew he was deliberately provoking her, but Pippa couldn't resist when he held out his hands to her.

"Dance with me," he said softly. Pippa's breath came in a soft gasp at his gentle command.

"I can't hear the music," she replied, her voice small and without force.

"There's no need."

Jared drew her into his arms, leading her slowly in a mesmerizing waltz. Pippa was helpless in his arms, and her reaction to Jared Knox overpowered her warring emotions. Her wide eyes met his, held there perfectly by his lingering gaze. Pippa thought blindly that she was losing herself in those warm, blue depths.

There was in Jared a strange quandary of feelings that Pippa recognized—it was so like her own. Partly, he seemed to be teasing her, yet there was a curious vulnerability in his eyes that aroused her sympathy. The combination was compelling, and she had no idea how to resist her reaction.

Distant strains of music reached Pippa, soft and low and

heart-piercingly sweet. Jared's eyes searched her face, looking for something to seal his opinion, but it wasn't to be found. Pippa's wide gray-green eyes shone with a light he recognized, and Jared knew he was losing his better judgment to her mystical appeal. It was too easy to forget everything when he held Philippa Reid in his arms.

The music stopped, but Jared didn't release Pippa from his arms. She made no move away from him.

"I've wanted to dance with you all evening, Philippa," he said, his voice soft and low. "I thank you for giving me such a sweet opportunity."

Pippa's lips parted, but she had no idea what to say. Her heart thundered in her breast, her breath came with effort, and feelings she had never known raged in her body. She was certain her wild need to be close to Jared was unladylike. But Pippa knew her reaction pleased Jared. Frighteningly, it was all that mattered.

"One opportunity leads to another," Jared continued huskily.

Before Pippa was aware what Jared intended, he bent and kissed her soft mouth. Gently at first, but when a small gasp escaped her parted lips, Jared felt a rush of need and he deepened the kiss.

Pippa felt the urgent pressure of his lips, the light tease of his tongue against her mouth, and her insides turned to flaming liquid. She should pull away, she knew, and blush at the indecent liberties this man was taking.

Instead, Pippa's small hands went to Jared's broad shoulders, then her arms were around his neck. She pressed close against him, returning his kiss with a passion she had never dreamed possible. The need to be close to him was overwhelming, obliterating all else, and the strength of his arms about her waist told her he felt the same.

Jared broke the kiss. Pippa's arms slid from his neck, hung imply at her side. She didn't flush. Nor did she quail at the indecency of what she had allowed him to do. Instead, she just stared at him, disbelief over what she had done written plainly across her face.

Jared placed his hands on her slender shoulders. "Perhaps it would be wiser if you and I continued this dance inside," he said with a widening grin. Despite herself, Pippa smiled, too.

"If I were wiser, I wouldn't be here at all," she responded, but Jared wondered if she meant at the Carltons' ball or in the land of her enemy.

Jared held out his arm, and Pippa fitted her small hand there to walk beside him back to the crowded hall. When he led her in yet another dance, Pippa knew the fires of her wild heart were not so easily cooled.

They danced together for the remainder of the evening, and Pippa was unaware of anything but the tall, handsome man beside her. Her fear of him dissipated, replaced by interest, a yearning need to learn about him, to know him.

"Sometimes you sound like an Englishman, Jared," she stated as he sat telling her the history of the Carltons' home, built during the Revolution to store arms.

"So I've been told," he replied. "I'm not aware of it myself, but I spent many years in England, so it's possible."

"Did you?" asked Pippa. "What were you doing there?"

Jared hesitated briefly before answering, and Pippa's brow furrowed as she considered what this might mean. But Jared's smile drove away her disquiet, and she forgot the vague discomfort his words had provoked.

"My father was educated in England with his brother, and

felt I should follow likewise. My cousin, Garrett, was also in Europe at that time," he told her with an enigmatic grin.

That sounded respectable enough, but something in Jared's eyes gave Pippa the faintest trace of suspicion.

"Is your cousin here also?"

"No, you won't find Garrett Knox at any Virginia dances this season. Garrett is, I'm afraid, a faithful Yankee, as was his younger brother, Adrian."

"Oh," replied Pippa. "That must be difficult for you," she ventured carefully.

"Garrett was like my own brother," Jared told her. "No war could break our friendship."

Pippa hesitated briefly before pressing the matter. "Do you know if they're well?"

"Adrian was killed at Fredericksburg," Jared said sadly. "But Garrett was well the last time I saw him, at Chancellorsville. I hear of him on occasion, so I know he lives."

"You saw him?" asked Pippa. "Chancellorsville was hardly a friendly occasion, Jared."

"That's true. Yet at every such occasion soldiers of North and South meet, under flags of temporary truce. It's a strange thing, because the battles are no less bitter for the friendships exchanged."

"Was he well?" Pippa asked, but Jared sighed.

"He seemed so, though there was a sadness in him that wasn't there before. Garrett always considered it his duty to protect those in need. When we met, he was accompanied by an impertinent young soldier, albeit a devoted one. My cousin is a man who inspires great loyalty. He's a fine officer, and it saddens me to stand against him in war."

Pippa sensed that Jared didn't enjoy the direction of their conversation, but it pleased her to think that Jared had a Yankee relative of whom he was obviously fond. Perhaps his ties to the South weren't strong, especially if he had spent the better part of his youth in England.

"Your son seems to be enjoying the company of the Yankee girl." Margaret Woods leaned over toward Caroline Knox and spoke loudly to be heard over the music.

Caroline Knox met the other woman's gaze serenely. Only the sudden clenching of her carefully folded hands gave any indication of her true feelings.

"Jared has always been . . . kind-hearted. Charlotte's little niece was probably lonely, and he recognized that. It must be hard to be a Northerner in the heart of Virginia."

Mrs. Woods was unimpressed. "Philippa Reid is a companion of my daughter. That young woman is not lonely, Caroline, I promise you. Edward Carlton rarely lets a day pass that he's home from Richmond—too frequently, to my thinking—that he isn't hovering around Charlotte's home. No, Philippa Reid has no shortage of admirers. I suspect your son is one of them," she added with undisguised glee.

Caroline Knox was immensely dignified, still beautiful at forty-six. As she had been as a young woman, she was still the envy of her peers. Her fair face showed little sign of age, her golden hair was rich and shiny, and her composure had never suffered any cracks, even through nearly three years of war.

"I wonder what David would think if he could see his son courting a Yankee girl," continued Margaret Woods.

"I hardly think they're courting," replied Caroline with a light smile.

"I don't know," considered Margaret. "I've rarely seen

Jared so taken with a girl, if ever. Even from this distance, one can easily see how distracted he appears."

Caroline smiled patiently, and sighed as her eyes fell upon Jared as he sat in a far corner beside Charlotte Reid's niece.

"Jared is twenty-seven," said Margaret. "It's high time he married."

"Oh, for heaven's sake, Margaret. He's barely met the girl. Jared is in the midst of war. I can't believe he has time for a courtship."

Margaret nodded knowingly and glanced back to where Jared sat close by Philippa Reid's side. He was smiling, as was Philippa, and he toyed with her ivory satin sash as they spoke.

"It seems your son has forgotten the war."

"As it should be," said Caroline softly. She hadn't forgotten the weeks her son was missing and feared dead. No, marrying a Yankee girl wasn't the worst thing she could imagine after all.

"Shall we go for a walk?" asked Jared as he gazed into Pippa's shining eyes. "It's warm inside tonight."

Pippa felt a faint tremor of apprehension, but she had long since given in to her pleasure in Jared's company.

"Yes, thank you, I'd like that," she replied, and she took his arm as she rose.

Jared led Pippa back to the veranda, and they walked through an arched lattice gate into the garden. Spring brought a special beauty to Virginia, with bright flowers fragrant in the humid evening air. The stars were clear and bright, the quarter moon rising amongst them like a queen, and Pippa sighed.

"Virginia is lovely tonight," she said wistfully.

"She is indeed," said Jared.

As they walked out of sight, he drew her into his arms without preamble. Jared kissed her mouth tenderly, savoring the taste of her sweet lips. He drew back to kiss her face as he brushed a wisp of wavy hair back from her forehead.

"I thought I couldn't feel this way. I thought myself incapable after so long, so long . . ." he murmured, but Pippa stopped him with a slender finger upon his lips.

"Don't think of that now," she whispered, her heart filling with tenderness and sympathy for a man who should be her enemy.

But Jared smiled as she spoke and slid his hands about her small waist. "This time is for us alone," he told her. "We won't speak of the time before our meeting, nor what lies ahead. These days to come are too short, and I wouldn't have them marred by any darkness."

Pippa nodded, and they were bound in an agreement neither fully understood. "Then I'll see you again?" she asked, but Jared laughed as he pulled her close.

"Nothing in heaven or hell could keep me away from you, Philippa. I promise you, you will see me again."

Jared's words were hauntingly familiar to Pippa, but now they brought comfort rather than fear. Again she wound her arms about his neck and moved close to him.

"Tomorrow," murmured Jared as his lips brushed hers. "It shouldn't be too difficult to convince your aunt how necessary it is that I take you for a buggy ride."

He drew her tighter against him, and took her mouth in a full kiss; gentle, yet with hidden force. Like an ocean, raging with untold power beneath the calm surface. Every feeling in Jared was passed to Pippa as the sliver of the moon rose high above Virginia.

Two

"Did you enjoy yourself last night, Philippa?"

Charlotte Reid peered over the rim of her teacup as she awaited her niece's response. Pippa sat gazing off at nothing, idly running a long finger around the edge of her cup. With effort she forced her attention to her aunt.

"It was a perfect evening, Aunt Charlotte," she responded, her voice wistful and far away.

"I imagine Major Knox would say the same," guessed Charlotte.

"Where is Burke?" questioned Pippa, none too artfully changing the subject. "Has he left for Richmond already?"

Charlotte was temporarily distracted, and she appeared vaguely troubled. "Burke left at dawn," she said with a sigh. "He'll be back tomorrow."

"Is he still going to the President's office?" asked Pippa, and Charlotte nodded regretfully.

"I don't feel certain that Burke's activities are appropriate. I'm pleased, of course, that he isn't fighting with the Yankees. Naturally, his business requires such meetings. My dear sister married a successful man, and Burke is only furthering his father's affairs, I know . . ."

Charlotte's voice trailed off, and she sighed heavily. Pippa knew Charlotte didn't approve of her sister's aggressive husband, fabulously wealthy or not. But her loyalties to her nephew knew no bounds. Pippa's father had thought his brother's wife a fit guardian for his daughter, but it had taken Pippa a long while to adjust to her aunt's disregard of reality.

"I'm certain Burke will handle himself graciously," Pippa reassured her aunt. "He always does."

Charlotte smiled gratefully, and Pippa returned to her little room. She hadn't mentioned Jared's invitation for a buggy ride, though she doubted her aunt would deny the request. Once, such an invitation would require weeks of chaperoned meetings, but the war had changed much in the manner of courtship.

Pippa located her seldom-worn carriage dress and tried it on, just in case. She examined herself in the looking-glass and liked the slimmer lines of its design, especially since a crinoline wasn't necessary. The burgundy fabric suited Pippa's soft complexion and she bit her lip to contain a giddy smile.

Pippa twirled about as she imagined an afternoon spent in the company of Jared Knox. Lucy entered the room and laughed.

"Didn't you have enough of dancing last night, Pippa?"

Pippa sat on the edge of her bed and placed her hands upon her forehead.

"Oh, Lucy. What am I doing?" she groaned.

Lucy came to sit beside Pippa, and patted her shoulder.

"Nothing that countless others haven't done throughout time, I expect."

"But I shouldn't . . . care. Not this way."

Lucy sighed. "And yet, we do. We do," she said quietly, her eyes looking far into the distance to one whom Pippa could not see.

"Lucy! Do you have a lover?" asked Pippa in wonder.

She had never known the diligent slave girl to be distracted from their task.

When Lucy answered, her voice was so small that Pippa could barely hear her. "There was a man, long ago," she confessed. Telling her secret, Lucy's voice grew in strength, and her eyes were bright when she looked back to Pippa.

"He was tall and strong, and handsome as a god," Lucy began. "He was a slave, of course. On the plantation where I was born. I loved him since I was a small child," she added with a sigh.

"He was older than I." Lucy sighed again. "Now he would be twenty-seven."

"Where is he?" asked Pippa.

"Gone. He ran away years ago."

"Why didn't he take you with him?"

Sudden emotion crossed Lucy's face and her lips tightened as she fought her surge of feeling. "I begged him, but he refused. He thought I was a child, that it was too dangerous."

Lucy paused, regaining control of herself. When she continued, it was with the pleasure of her cherished memory.

"I was young, but my heart was a woman's, though he didn't see that. I knew he was leaving. He was a man who couldn't be a slave. I saw the fire in his eyes, the anger, and I saw the power that came when he made his decision."

"What did you do?" questioned Pippa with fascination. "Did you try to stop him?"

"No, but I couldn't let him leave without giving him my heart, myself." A small smile crossed Lucy's face as she spoke, and Pippa leaned closer as she listened to the other girl speak.

"I followed him to a secret little house. He was getting a small pack ready, and I knew he had chosen that night to leave. He always looked by me, as if he didn't want to see the love in my eyes. When I entered that little house, he did the same, treating me like a child.

"But this night, I wouldn't allow that. I was no child. Where my courage came from, I don't know, but I had nothing to lose. At that time, I believed I could convince him to take me with him."

"What happened?

Lucy took a long breath. "He saw me standing there, he looked away. I let my clothing fall, so that I was naked before him."

Pippa gasped, but her eyes were glowing with admiration. "What did he do?"

"He didn't look beyond me this time," said Lucy with satisfaction. "I saw the fire in his eyes. He told me I should go, but his voice was shaking. I went to him and touched his chest. His heart was racing like a captured bird's, and I knew I had won. I kissed him, and beneath my hand I felt every muscle in his body grow taut."

Pippa's mouth opened, and she bit her lip as the scene was described to her so vividly.

"He couldn't deny me," said Lucy. "That night, he was mine and I, his. I've lived on that memory for many years."

"How could he leave after, after . . . ?" began Pippa, but Lucy stopped her.

"We didn't complete the . . . act," she said sorrowfully. "He didn't wish to get me with child, and perhaps he was right—this is no world to raise a baby in."

Tears welled in Pippa's green eyes as she thought of Lucy's thwarted love. She swallowed hard as she remembered how many other lives had been altered by slavery. She thought of Byron's clear, intelligent mind, and of Jefferson with his gift for music. How long they had been denied their rightful place among humanity!

But Lucy smiled, a teasing light in her dark eyes as she looked over at her innocent friend. "There are other things a man and a woman may do together."

"What things?" asked Pippa. The conjugal act itself was somewhat vague in her understanding.

"Things that don't lead to intercourse," began Lucy, but Pippa blushed furiously at the reference to such an intimate act.

"Yet the pleasure is . . . similar, I believe. What one does to the other can yield great satisfaction," said Lucy, and she grinned when she saw Pippa's look of horrified embarrassment.

Lucy sighed and continued. "But the night passed, and he was gone. Mrs. Reid isn't unkind, and I've been spared the indignities many of my sisters are forced to endure at the hands of white masters. But I can't rest, not knowing what might have been had my love not been driven from me."

Lucy sighed, her heart lightened by the telling of her story, and her face was set in resignation. She stood up and gazed out the window, both loving and hating the only world she had ever known.

"At times, I weary of this pretense of idiocy. But when I see the affected mannerisms of the ladies, as last night, I wonder if what I'm doing is so different."

Pippa nodded. "I, too, long for a time when I don't need to watch my words," she said. "With Jared, I thought . . ." she began, but then she stopped. "Of course, I must be more careful with him than anyone."

Lucy looked back at Pippa intently. "Yes, it would be dangerous for you to reveal too much of yourself to him."

"Jared Knox is an unusually intelligent man. It's plain he's taken with you, but I doubt he would take kindly to your true loyalties."

"He's spent much time in England," began Pippa hopefully. "Perhaps the Cause means less to him than others here."

Lucy hesitated before shattering the other girl's wistful illusions. "Jared Knox is a good man. I know that he doesn't think well of slavery. But he's a Virginian, Pippa. Never forget it. Robert E. Lee didn't believe in secession, yet he leads one of the finest armies the world has ever seen. Jared is much the same."

Pippa sighed miserably. "Then it would be wiser if I didn't see him again," she said, as pain constricted her heart.

"It probably would," laughed Lucy. "But there isn't much chance of that, I fear."

Pippa looked at her questioningly, but Lucy pointed out the window and smiled as Pippa joined her. "See, there's your handsome Major Knox. Already he's easily convinced your aunt how perfect it is for you to spend the afternoon in his company. He can be a most persuasive young man."

Pippa didn't answer, so loudly was her heart pounding in her breast. "What am I going to do?" she asked wildly, gripping Lucy's arm.

Lucy shook her head. "I expect you'll be going buggy-riding."

"But I can't, I can't," moaned Pippa.

Lucy nodded. "You cannot choose who moves your heart, Pippa. If it were possible, do you think I'd love a man I'll never see again?"

"What should I do?" Pippa whispered.

"Go to him, Pippa. You may not get another chance. Love, as I've seen for myself, is too fleeting. Go to him."

Lucy said no more and left Pippa standing alone, but in moments Pippa heard Charlotte calling to her. As if in a trance, she descended the stairs. When she reached the second landing, she lifted her downcast eyes to see the perfect, smiling face of Jared Knox.

"Major Knox would like to take you for a carriage ride, Philippa," Charlotte told her with a sparkling smile. "I see you are not unaware of this chance," she added when she saw Pippa's appropriate attire.

"The matter was discussed last night," Jared admitted, and Pippa felt her heart flutter when she saw the pleasure in his blue eyes.

"Shall we depart, Miss Reid?" he asked. Dreamlike, Pippa went to him and took his strong arm.

"Where are we going?" asked Pippa as Jared directed the Carltons' dappled gray carriage horse off the road and down a barely visible path.

"Lesser worn roads often lead to the sweeter places, Miss Reid," he teased. Pippa blushed, though she wasn't completely certain why.

To be at Jared's side was in answer to her heart's dearest wish, and Pippa felt a contentment she had rarely experienced in her life.

"Oh!" exclaimed Pippa.

Down a slight slope, they rounded a turn. Before her eyes glistened a swift-flowing stream lined with giant willows and scraggly hickory trees. Bright flowers peeked from beneath the tall spring grasses like stars in a green heaven. Pippa felt Jared had led her not to a place at all, but to another time where only they two existed.

Jared stopped the horse, who was already much intent on

the rich grazing afforded, and he helped Pippa to the ground. "What do you think?" he asked as she gazed about in wonder.

"It's a perfect spot," she said. "Where are we?"

"At the far western border of the Carltons' estate. It's been unused for several years, though horses were pastured here before the war began. Those are in service or dead now, and the field has overgrown. Not without effect, however."

Jared paused and took her hand in his. "I'm pleased you like it. When I lay thinking of you last night, I thought of this place and how well you would look among the flowers."

Pippa's heart leapt and she knew all Lucy's warnings were in vain. There was no choice. Her heart had taken its direction and there was nothing she could do to prevent its course, or its ending.

They walked to the edge of the stream. Jared placed a blanket on the grass and they sat together. Pippa wished they had brought food, even if lunch had passed. Anything that might distract her from the overwhelming urge to be again in his arms.

"To think you've been living here more than a year, and I've known nothing of you," said Jared as he gazed into Pippa's eyes.

"Nor I of you," she replied.

"I would have taken leave far sooner had I been aware of your presence," he told her, and to Pippa's joy, he leaned to her and gently kissed her mouth.

Resisting the temptation to pursue the kiss, Jared released the gentle touch and lay back on the blanket, propping himself up on one elbow. The position was curiously compelling to Pippa, and she looked away lest he guess what was in her heart.

"I'm curious what brought you to Virginia in the middle

of a war," Jared asked. Pippa glanced quickly at him, but she saw no trace of suspicion in his eyes.

"My father left me in the care of my aunt when he died," Pippa replied.

"It seems a strange choice, considering the circumstances," he continued, obviously unsatisfied with her answer.

Pippa shrugged. "Possibly, but Aunt Charlotte is my only living relative," she told him. "When Father died, the war had just begun. He didn't believe it would last very long."

"Few did," agreed Jared.

Their conversation was disturbing and Pippa made an effort to redirect it. "How long have you been back in Virginia, Jared Knox?" she asked pleasantly. "You told me you were long in England."

Jared allowed the conversation to drift, though he didn't miss Pippa's discomfort with the subject.

"I'd been home a year when the war began," he told her.

"A year? You must have passed school age, Jared."

"I went to live in France for a time, with Garrett. I studied architecture there."

"And you came home to war?" she asked.

"I did."

Pippa studied Jared's face, and she knew he was shutting away part of himself.

"Why were four girls in mourning for you?" she asked, but Jared grinned devilishly.

"Now, how would I know that?" he teased.

Pippa's delicate brow rose and her small, bowed lips curved upwards. "I expect you know very well."

"Apparently they believed I was no more," he answered.

"That much is obvious," replied Pippa.

Jared's smile faded, and Pippa saw that memories he didn't welcome had returned to him.

"I was separated from my company during the battle of Gettysburg," he told her. "They believed I was lost, and reported so to Richmond. It was a difficult time for my family."

"And for you?"

"Few days have been darker," Jared answered, and he lay back to look at the blue sky.

Pippa didn't dare ask him what had happened, but with the door thus opened, Jared found himself telling her.

"I was with my men in a peach orchard, and then in the hills where the fighting was heavy. We were separated from the rest, and many were killed. We couldn't move, nor do anything but keep the Yankees from overrunning our position.

"As we withdrew, seven of us were separated. Five were killed instantly when a shell exploded through the trees. A young lieutenant, Liddell, was badly wounded and I was struck on the head. When I woke, it was deep night, and Liddell lay dying."

Jared stared at the sky, allowing the intensity of his memory to return. With Pippa beside him, he could face the bitter vision, but his voice was taut with emotion as he continued.

"Liddell had lost a leg," Jared told Pippa. "His arm was half severed. But he never said a word about it, Pippa. He didn't complain, though he was in agony."

Jared paused, and Pippa reached to touch his hair. "He must have been very brave," she said, but inwardly she fought the image Jared described.

It was Yankee boys that died tragically, not rebels. She reminded herself that the rebels had willfully defied the Union and arrogantly defended slavery. But looking down into Jared's beautiful face, Pippa found she couldn't summon the old anger against his people.

"Before he died, he gave me his letters," Jared remembered sadly. "He lived not far from here, in Fredericksburg. He wanted me to tell his parents he died easily. All that mattered to him was that they not suffer over his death."

"How did you escape?" Pippa asked. She couldn't bear to hear any more about the brave rebel boy. Compassion for one's enemy could be a dangerous thing.

Jared sighed. "I didn't expect to escape," he admitted. "But when the battle ended, the Yankees just pulled back."

Pippa frowned slightly. Gettysburg. Had General Meade been a leader of sterner purpose, the war might have ended with that battle. But he let the rebels go, and the war raged on.

"I went in search of my army, hoping to hell the Yanks weren't interested in searching out wayward rebels for prisoners. Apparently they weren't interested in much more than regrouping, and I made my way to Virginia."

"By yourself?" asked Pippa in amazement. "How awful!"

"That wasn't the worst," said Jared grimly. "I returned here, to this stream in fact, and followed it to my home. On the horizon south," he told Pippa as he pointed in the direction of his childhood home, "there I saw a great red glow, and I knew my house was on fire."

"I remember that," she said. "What happened?"

Jared frowned as he stared at the sky. "Apparently some well-meaning Yankee spy got it into her head that my father's estate was being used for storing an arsenal."

Pippa froze, her heart in her mouth. "A woman?" she asked with swelling horror, but there was no accusation in Jared's eyes as he looked at her.

"I saw a woman that night, a woman I've seen before; one I know to be a spy. A message was recovered relaying the ridiculous information about my house being an artillery arsenal."

"Do you think she was responsible for burning your house?" asked Pippa in amazement. Her shock was fading, but she felt sick to think Jared blamed her for the destruction of his estate.

"She was responsible for a lot more than that," said Jared, and Pippa shuddered when she saw the hard set to his full jaw.

"What more?" she asked weakly.

"My mother and youngest sister were there at the time."

"I didn't know that."

"They had just arrived and afterwards, it seemed best to let it be forgotten."

"Were they injured?" asked Pippa.

Jared hesitated before answering. "The Yankees who raided the house were less than gentlemanly," he told her carefully. Jared sighed, and Pippa nearly quailed to see the distress in his fair face.

"My sister is a gentle, fragile girl," Jared said sadly. "Not unlike you, though her coloring is fair."

Pippa inwardly doubted she had much in common with Jared's delicate, blonde sister. Despite her ladylike appearance, Pippa had no lack of energy or vitality. She knew nothing would subdue her while she had the strength to fight.

"I'm sorry for your house and your family, Jared." She could think of nothing else to say.

She longed to tell him the spy he blamed had nothing to do with the burning of his house. Her mission that night had been otherwise, but of course, she could do nothing. Her small face was sorrowful as she gazed down at him.

"It's over now," he sighed. "Far worse happens in war, though I won't forgive them for what they did to my family. But, Philippa Reid, I thought that darkness would never lift."

As he spoke, Jared sat up and moved close to her. Pippa's arms went about his neck and she leaned against him, pressing her mouth against his face as she held him. Jared drew back to kiss her again. As his lips found hers, Pippa's desperation faded and she melted into his arms.

Pippa's honey-brown hair framed her face with a golden light, and Jared thought he had never seen a more beautiful sight. He ran his hand through the soft mass, freeing it to fall upon her shoulders and down her back.

"You look like a beautiful, woodland sprite," Jared said as he gazed in admiration at the long, wavy hair that framed Pippa's face.

"Yet something is missing."

Jared rose and Pippa watched him in wonder as he went around collecting flowers. He returned to again sit beside her and began to decorate her long hair with the little buds.

After a time, Jared sat back to survey his work. "Perfect," he told her with a smile, and then he pulled her close to kiss her again.

Pippa broke the kiss and got up. She wandered about gathering long leaves and flowers, then rejoined him with a bright smile lighting her face.

"I trust you are not intending to put those in my hair," Jared warned her, though his own eyes sparkled as Pippa carefully entwined the reeds and flowers together.

"What are you doing?" he asked as Pippa completed her task.

Pippa turned to him with pride. "Not in your hair, Jared. On it," she corrected. "It's a crown. See," she explained as she held up her creation. "Now stay still while I see if it fits."

Jared reluctantly complied and Pippa rose up on her knees to place the wreath upon his head. "Lay this laurel," she whispered. Her face glowed with pleasure when she saw how well-suited was his sensually angular face to the wreath, despite Jared's obvious misgivings.

"You look very handsome," she told him with feeling.

"I look very foolish," he replied, but he pulled her close and kissed her.

Pippa answered his kiss passionately, and when she felt his tongue slide across hers, wild shivers erupted throughout her body. Sweetly tasting him, she answered his seeking caress with a light touch of her own, and she felt Jared shudder as desire coursed through him.

Jared eased her back on the blanket, his crown falling beside them, but neither noticed. He cupped her face in his hands, tasting the sweetness of her lips with a light tease. He pressed soft kisses against her face and eyelids, and then along her delicate jawline and down the long column of her throat.

"Jared," she whispered. Pippa felt a storm rising within her that was frightening in its intensity.

He drew back to gaze into her eyes, and Pippa saw the heat of passion written across his face. "Are you frightened of me, Pippa, of this?" he asked.

Pippa couldn't answer, for too much was hidden beneath that truth.

"I wouldn't hurt you for the world," he whispered.

Pippa forced a small smile and she looked away as a trace of embarrassment flooded her cheeks.

"I don't think my aunt would be very pleased with my behavior," she said in a weak voice.

"Then we won't share it with her," said Jared, obviously disinterested in Charlotte Reid's opinion on the matter.

"Pippa, do you want to be here, with me?"

"Yes," she said without thinking.

"Do you trust me?"

"I do."

"Then you will forget whatever your aunt has taught you about what ladies may and may not do, and you will not fear your feelings, ever. Do you understand?"

"I want to be with you, Jared," she whispered, and his smile was all she needed to see.

Again he kissed her, and this time Pippa surrendered to the sensations his touch created. She abandoned her will beneath his, and reveled without fear in a cavalcade of feeling.

"It grows late." Jared spoke with regret, and as Pippa glanced over his shoulder, she saw the sun low on the horizon.

"Do we have to go?" she asked wistfully. "Perhaps you'll stay for dinner."

"That will be pleasant," said Jared. "Although I prefer enjoying your company in privacy."

"Yes," agreed Pippa.

"Then perhaps you'll agree to go riding with me tomorrow," Jared suggested. He paused. "Though I believe few Yankee girls ride. Can you?"

Pippa hesitated, suddenly remembering herself. "I can ride," she began slowly. "Although not as well as you do down here, of course."

"Then I'll find you a gentle mare, and by tomorrow afternoon, you'll be able to take your place amongst the wildest hunt."

"And beside Jeb Stuart himself, no doubt," laughed Pippa. "My expectations are somewhat more limited."

Jared kissed her, then helped her to her feet. "Then we must hurry back, I'm afraid. If I bring you in scandalously late, your aunt will deny me the pleasure of your company tomorrow, and all will be forfeited."

Pippa placed her small hands on his broad chest and gazed into his eyes. "A whole day before I see you again," she mourned. "It will be as a year."

Jared kissed her. "The hours will pass slowly," he agreed. "Come, we must go."

Charlotte did invite Jared for supper, an offer he graciously accepted, but Pippa felt deprived having to be on her best behavior in her aunt's company. She tried not to glance Jared's way too often, lest Charlotte guess how much had passed between them. Whenever their eyes met, Pippa was aware of a yearning too intense to be denied.

"I must see your mother before she leaves, Major," said Charlotte as Jared prepared to leave. "When is she returning to Richmond?"

"Tomorrow afternoon," he answered, though even as he spoke to Charlotte, Jared's eyes went to Pippa.

"Then I'll see her tomorrow morning," decided Charlotte.

Charlotte bid Jared good-night, and discreetly left him to say his farewells to Pippa. Pippa accompanied him out the door and together they stood in silence on the front porch. Jared turned to Pippa, and her heart leapt when she saw the expression on his face.

"Meet me tonight, Pippa," he said, and the intensity of emotion between them felt heavy in the evening air.

Pippa never wavered nor doubted her reply. "Where?" she asked. At her unquestioning response, Jared smiled.

"Would the carriage house yonder suit?" he suggested, and Pippa nodded.

"How soon can you safely escape unnoticed?" he asked.

"Ten-thirty, perhaps eleven o'clock," she replied without hesitation. Seeing Jared's look of surprise, Pippa caught her-

self. Too easily, she knew the time she could slip unseen
from her aunt's home.

"At least, that seems reasonable," she added quickly.

"Then I'll await you."

With that, he took her hand and kissed it, and Pippa stood
watching Jared drive away in the Carltons' carriage. Pippa's
heart was already racing with the excitement of an adventure
unlike any she had taken before.

A soft, yet heavy wash of rain fell against the window of
Pippa's bedroom and her heart sank. It seemed unlikely that
Jared would venture forth in such weather. Pippa had bathed
earlier in the evening, carefully washing her long hair. She
sat on the windowseat peering out into the oppressive gloom
of the night.

I can't sleep, Pippa thought, *and it will be good to be out
in the air, however damp.* She felt trapped, cornered, in her
small room. She was restless, almost desperate. Behind that
restlessness lurked an unease, a dark premonition.

The need to escape that fear became unbearable, and
Pippa hurriedly removed her nightclothes and put on a simple calico dress. The rain was falling heavily as Pippa
stepped outside, and she felt certain Jared wouldn't leave
the Carltons' warm estate on such a night. Yet it was often
on just such nights that messages arrived from the North.
That was enough to justify Pippa's adventure as she faced
the dark rain.

Pippa hurried across the wet lawn toward the carriage
house, and her slippers were soaked by the time she reached
the door. The building was more than a storage house for
buggies, for at one time it had housed several drivers. Char-

lotte only utilized the services of Emmaline's husband now, but he lived in the main house quarters.

Pippa tugged at the door and it popped open, surprising her. She slipped inside, then tugged the door closed behind her. She took a deep breath and closed her eyes, though the room was already black.

"I thought this night might keep you away, my love," came Jared's soft, low voice, and Pippa began to tremble.

Jared came across the long, wide room toward where Pippa stood shivering.

"I thought the same of you," she whispered as his tall form became visible against the faint light of the window.

"And yet, you came. As did I."

Pippa felt every part of her body go weak as he drew her into his arms. She knew he would kiss her, and he did. His firm, full mouth melded against hers with a tenderness and feeling that drove away her nameless fears. Pippa's arms went about his neck as her lips parted against his.

Jared's tongue brushed lightly across hers, a gentle awakening, but he deepened the kiss when he felt Pippa's shy response. Wild surges of need shot through Pippa, centering low and deep within her slender body. She squirmed restlessly against him, searching instinctively for an unknown answer that only Jared could provide.

Jared understood the reason for Pippa's restlessness, and he groaned as his own body's fires rose in primal force. All his good intentions threatened to abandon him, and he moved back from her, putting his hands firmly on her small shoulders.

In the faint light, Jared saw her upturned face, the wide eyes bright with feeling. He ached to give himself over to the natural progression between them. But even in the darkness, he saw her trust and, with effort, he turned away.

"Why did you stop?" she asked innocently. "Don't you like kissing me?"

Jared groaned. "I like kissing you too much, Pippa," he told her huskily.

"As do I," sighed Pippa. Jared turned back to her and pulled her gently against him, cradling her head to his wide chest.

"You're such a temptation, Pippa," he murmured. "Perhaps it was unwise for us to meet this way, after all."

Pippa could feel and hear the pounding of his strong heart as he held her close, and she knew his words didn't indicate his true desires. Again she thought of Lucy, and now she understood fully this blinding need to become part of her lover.

Pippa moved from him, raising her small hand to trace a line across his lips. She smiled slightly as he trembled at her touch. She knew what she wished from him, and Pippa stood on her toes to press a soft kiss against the corner of his mouth.

"Philippa," he began, but Jared's voice was hoarse and strained as he endured the onslaught of desire.

"I love you," she whispered close against his mouth. "I want to be with you, Jared."

Pippa heard her own vow, unfamiliar thus far in her life. There was a time when the only such powerful feeling in her heart had been hatred . . . a hatred that had surprised even a runaway slave as he told her tales of his captivity.

Pippa stared up at Jared, but for an instant she saw Byron before her. Byron, reading to her from Frederick Douglass's impassioned Boston speech. Pippa, at thirteen, listening as she seethed in fury . . . "I hate Southerners!" she had cried, her small face wild with the intensity of her feelings. "I hate them all!"

Jared was warm, close, as Pippa reached to touch his face. Her old hatred was forgotten, and her heart expanded when he smiled at her. "I love you," she whispered again. Once again the force of her feeling had gotten the better of her.

Before meeting Jared Knox, Pippa had scoffed at the smitten girls who pined for their absent soldiers. Yet here she stood, alone with a man who could move her heart to flight with the power of his smile. And that man was a Southerner.

Jared looked into Pippa's face, and though he didn't fully comprehend her emotion, he was moved by the size of her feeling. He saw no pretense, no deception—just the fiery glimpse of untamed passion. Jared wondered how he would ever resist the impulse to surrender to its force.

Pippa's bright eyes glittered, and again her soft mouth played against his. For a strained moment, Jared didn't move. He let her tease him into a response he was powerless to resist. But when he felt the delicate tip of her tongue against his lips, Jared's restraint was shattered. He pulled her forcefully against him, taking her mouth with a passion as yet untold.

Without a word, he swept her up into his arms and carried her into the darkness at the back of the building. Pippa's heart raced uncontrollably as Jared carried her into the old drivers' quarters. She fought to contain her spinning emotions as he gently lowered her to the bare bed.

It was dark, but a small window let in what there was of the night's faint glow. Pippa lay back on the bed, and watched mesmerized as Jared lowered himself above her.

"Do you know what we're doing here, angel?" he asked, and Pippa could see the smile she loved cross his face as he looked down at her.

Pippa smiled, too. "Not exactly," she confessed.

"Well," Jared began slowly, careful in the words he chose. "I'm going to show you how much I love you, and how much fire there is between us."

As he spoke, Jared lowered his mouth to hers, kissing her softly before drawing away to look at her again. Her long hair was loose and fell about her face and across the bed like waves of a dark, stormy sea. As Jared took in her strangely pagan beauty, Jared was reminded of something, someone, but he was too enraptured by desire and love to place the feeling.

The impression served to increase the size of his passion, for it was wildly tempting, irresistible. It was something he had to contain, at any risk. The image was vaguely at odds with the sweet Philippa he loved, for it was challenging and even dangerous. His Pippa had no such edge in her gentle character.

"I'm going to love you," he said again, fighting the violent strength of his need. "But we'll be careful that you're not left with a child when I'm gone," he told her as his eyes searched her trusting face.

"I don't think that would be so bad," Pippa said honestly, but Jared shook his head.

"Pippa, I must leave in two days. There's no time for us to marry, love. Not yet. I couldn't leave you knowing you might bear my child when there's a chance I won't return."

"Don't say that!"

Jared sighed. "How can I not, love? I've seen so many fall, arbitrarily and unexpectedly. Who is to say I won't join them? No, don't look away. It is truth, and you and I must face truth if we love."

Pippa paused. So much truth was unsaid between them. Slowly she realized the woman Jared loved wasn't really her at all. If he knew who she really was, however wrong he was in blaming her for what happened to his house, he would never understand what she had done since moving to Virginia.

If I told you, would you still love me? But Pippa remembered the anger in his eyes as he spoke of the Yankee spy, and her hope faltered.

I had to do something, she told him wordlessly. *I couldn't feel so strongly, care so much, and remain idle in the land of my enemy.*

Pippa closed her eyes, and she knew her feelings about abolition were mirrored by what she felt for Jared Knox. It wasn't enough to adore him from afar; she had to hold him, to make him a part of her.

"There are other ways, Jared," she said calmly. Pippa was matter-of-fact and cool, detached, and her voice held a hint of fatalism.

" 'Other ways'?" he asked in confusion, doubting she could possibly mean what she seemed to mean.

Pippa nodded, her bright eyes still meeting his, directly and with resignation. "Yes. Other things we might do, so I won't have a baby."

Jared stared at her in amazement. "There are, my love," he replied slowly, humor lacing his voice. "Yet I'm curious—how do you, little one, know of this?"

Pippa hesitated. She couldn't very well tell him that the supposedly simple Lucy had explained these variations to her. She couldn't even hint that women might speak graphically of such things.

"Well," she began slowly, this time casting her eyes to the side. "I've gathered as much from . . . bits of conversation I've . . . overheard. Of course, I'm not certain as to what precisely they refer."

That much was true, for Lucy hadn't been all that graphic.

Pippa peeked back at Jared to see his reaction, and her confidence grew when she saw the wide grin across his handsome face.

"Tonight you will learn firsthand, my love."

Pippa caught her breath as Jared spoke, but when he bent again to kiss her, all thoughts took flight. As his perfect lips trailed a line downward across her jaw to her throat, she gave herself over to whatever he might wish to do.

With skilled fingers, Jared unfastened the tiny row of buttons that lined the bodice of Pippa's simple dress. She lay motionless as he parted the thin fabric and bent to kiss the soft flesh above the line of her light corset.

Jared slid his hand up the slender line of her body, where it came to rest beneath the swell of her bosom. His hand brushed across the tingling mound. Pippa gasped as his seeking fingers centered their touch across the tautening peaks that pressed against the constraints of the thin material.

But Jared had only just begun. He felt Pippa's arousal. His own was a raging sea within him. Gently, with infinite tenderness and care, he ran his lips across the lightly concealed buds. Tidal waves of need crashed across him as Pippa twisted maddeningly beneath his skill. Jared's hands trembled as he pushed the corset back to expose her rounded breast to his touch.

Pippa felt the cool, damp air on her skin. Her breath came in quick, tiny gasps as Jared again took a rising peak in his mouth and laved it with his tongue. What was happening between them was so unlike anything in her life's experience that Pippa couldn't accurately gauge how far from propriety she had drifted. But as Jared teased her flesh to burning sensitivity, Pippa didn't care.

"You taste like the heavens," he whispered, his voice thick with passion.

Again Jared kissed her mouth, and Pippa answered with ripening passion. "No, angel, this is just a beginning," he told her. As he spoke, his hand traveled the slender length of her body to pull up her skirt.

Pippa tensed as he pushed aside her petticoats and slipped his hand beneath to lightly graze the sensitized flesh between her thighs. His fingers explored deeper, closer to the wellspring of her desire. Pippa found she couldn't deny the intimate pleasure of his touch, and she lay helpless to resist the oncoming tide of swirling sensations.

Pippa moaned softly as his fingers centered around the tiny bud that ached for unknown release. As he witnessed the intensity of her need, Pippa met Jared's warm kiss with an urgency that fired his desire, met perfectly with her own.

Over and over, he teased her throbbing flesh until every breath came as soft gasps of need. Pippa struggled beside him, twisting against him as he kissed her. Her fingers grasped his soft hair as Jared brought her again and again to the edge of a precipice she couldn't imagine. He held her there, wavering on the brink of a total surrender, delaying his complete control over her, while Pippa wantonly reveled in his artistry.

"Now then, my love, you will belong to me forever," Jared whispered as he drew away to look into Pippa's wide, passion-filled eyes.

As he spoke, his fingers dipped into her honeyed depths and she gasped. Her back arched to meet him and Jared groaned at the instinctive invitation. The intensity of his touch increased, and Pippa's breath caught as the sudden, shattering force of pleasure took hold of her.

Wild, pagan shocks coursed through her quivering form. Every thought, every feeling took flight as Pippa surrendered to Jared's perfect mastery of her body. The soaring spiral upward ceased, and eased back gently to her, Pippa opened her eyes to see him looking down at her.

Her breath came ragged and deep, but she saw on Jared's sensual face a feeling she now recognized intimately. His eyes were blazing, his face seemed swollen with desire. Pippa felt a new pleasure knowing she was the cause. With gentle curiosity, she reached to touch his mouth. When Jared's eyes closed with the effort of restraint, Pippa smiled.

"Now, my love," she said in a low, seductive voice. "What satisfaction can I bring to you?"

There was vulnerability as well as surprise in Jared's eyes, but he saw that she understood his condition. "Do you know what you're offering, angel?" he asked, but his face was lit with a barely concealed smile.

"No," she admitted. "But I thought you would teach me."

"If you wish," he said lightly.

"I do."

His eyes upon her, Jared sat up. Pippa drew together her corset and tied the strings loosely together, though she didn't bother with refastening the buttons of her disheveled bodice.

"What do I do?" she asked.

Jared saw both her innocence and curiosity plainly written across her face as she looked at him. Touched, he drew her close again and kissed her. It seemed impossible that in the midst of the darkest years of his life, he had found a woman so lovely and open in her feelings. Yet here beside him sat Philippa Reid, eyes blazing with love, face flushed with passion, waiting eagerly to do his bidding.

"You're a perfect woman, Pippa," he said. "I almost fear you're a dream."

Pippa smiled, but she was troubled by his words. Pippa knew that she was far from perfect. If he knew her . . .

Pippa forced the discordant thought away, shoving it reck-lessly to the back of her mind.

"You haven't answered me, Jared. Although some things I might guess."

To Jared's great joy, as Pippa spoke her small hand wound its way across his chest and taut stomach to slip beneath the waistband of his uniform.

"I'd say you're heading in the right direction," he mur-mured hoarsely.

"Indeed," she replied, and her deft fingers undid the but-tons that fastened his trousers.

Jared watched her with untamed desire, but when her long, slender fingers brushed against the fiery heat of his skin, he groaned and kissed her forehead. Pippa's touch met with the hardened length of him. As she allowed her fingers to explore its unexpected size, a new and powerful desire took hold of her.

To make him feel as he had made her, to learn of him this way—these things brought a strength to Pippa she hadn't imagined. There was an eagerness in her touch that Jared found irresistible. Her fingers wrapped about his heated staff, and she felt its rapid throb as she held him. "What do I do?" she asked again, but she saw that thus far her actions had exceeded Jared's expectations.

Without a word, for his throat was constricted with desire, Jared put his hand over hers and demonstrated briefly the motion of lovemaking. Pippa learned quickly. With adora-tion, she did the same, delighting in the size of Jared's re-sponse, reveling in the power she had over him.

He grew even larger with her touch, hotter, and Pippa knew she was pleasing him. To see his face when he met with that perfect moment he had shown to her, that was what she wanted. To lead him where he led her, and be with him when the perfect warmth enveloped him afterwards.

To that end, Pippa gave herself over to his pleasure, seeing nothing but him, feeling nothing but what she gave to him. It was a world totally of their own, and she believed nothing could disrupt its perfect ecstasy.

"Philippa, wait, stop." Jared's sudden, abrupt voice, thick and raw with passion, cut into Pippa's joy, and brought her around to reality with a crash.

"What?" she whispered, but she heard what had distracted Jared.

From the carriage room beyond, movement could be heard. Footsteps. Pippa's heart thundered with dawning awareness.

"Someone's out there," he told her in a harsh whisper. "Hush." Jared swung from the bed, fastening his trousers, and he went stealthily to the door.

Pippa was frozen with terror. She guessed who was in the other room, and why. Forced into sudden, desperate activity, she flung together her dress, buttoning the top as she too slipped from the bed and went to Jared's side.

Soundlessly, Jared opened the door. As Pippa peeked out behind him, she saw a familiar figure silhouetted against the early morning light. There was nothing to be done but the obvious.

She glanced wildly around until she saw a tiny glint of metal of a carriage rack. Closing her eyes, she pushed it with her foot. The rack tipped and crashed to the floor, and the intruder, startled, bolted for the door.

Jared leapt after the intruder, but as Pippa heard the footsteps racing away, she knew Jared was too late. In moments, he returned and Pippa met him at the doorway. Pippa shuddered to think he had learned of her subterfuge. Yet she hadn't counted on the depth of affection Jared bore her.

"I'm sorry, Jared," she began. "I bumped into something, you see," she continued unnecessarily, but Jared merely took her in his arms.

"It's all right, Pippa," he said against her hair as he held her. "It's not your fault."

Jared paused to brush her wayward hair from her small, worried face. The morning light was growing steadily, and his handsome features brought a painful ache to Pippa's heart. Too clearly, the futility of her love had been revealed.

"Who do you think it was?" she ventured, but she mourned the necessity of such a professional inquiry.

Jared shook his head. "I don't know for certain, but I could hazard a guess."

"What?" questioned Pippa with mounting dread.

Jared paused, but answered her interest. "I suppose this is one of the meeting places used by Yankee agents," he told her, and Pippa held her breath as he continued.

"Tonight, at least, there will be no meeting, nor are they likely to use this place again in the near future," he told her with small satisfaction. "Though I doubt very much it will make any impact on the eventual outcome."

"What is that?" Pippa asked in a small voice.

"If we have our say, their end will come at the gallows," Jared said flatly, but Pippa winced at his sudden cruelty.

"Not just prison?" she asked weakly.

"For what they've done? I think not," replied Jared.

Tears started in Pippa's eyes, and she looked away, but Jared saw her grief.

"What is it, love?" he asked. "Does your tender woman's heart feel for a miserable lot of spies, or is it something else?"

Pippa gulped, but she couldn't look at Jared. "It's just that it's morning already, and you'll have to go. And we haven't, we haven't . . ." she fumbled as she remembered their thwarted paradise.

"There's no need to tell me what we haven't done, beloved," Jared reminded her, and he kissed her warmly on the forehead.

"But we'll see each other again. Does that appease you, angel? Go back to your room, and sleep all morning. I'll come back this afternoon with a gentle mare. You and I will find a place where we can be alone, and . . ."

Jared stopped when he saw Pippa's face brighten visibly at his suggestion. He kissed her cheek and took her hands in his, kissing them also.

"You must go now, angel, lest your aunt discover our nighttime rendezvous and forbid me from ever seeing you again."

Jared's smile was kind and tender and Pippa ached with her hopeless love for him.

"You don't want that, do you?" he asked gently.

"No," she whispered, but tears again threatened in her eyes and she turned quickly away.

Turning back again, Pippa kissed Jared's face and then slipped past him out the door. Without looking back, she hurried up the path to the house.

Three

"Are you feeling well, Jared?"

Caroline Knox looked intently across the dining room table at her son as he idly examined the newspaper.

"I'm perfectly fine, Mother," he reassured her. "Why do you ask?"

"You rose late," she explained. "That's not like you. Though I see you're enjoying a hearty breakfast."

Caroline smiled. "Perhaps I worry too much. Forgive me, but I can't seem to help myself. After, after you were . . . gone for so long." Her voice trailed and Jared took her hand across the table.

"I'm fine, Mother. Please don't concern yourself."

His warm smile comforted Caroline and she sighed. Jared did look well, strong and healthy. He wasn't as thin as many other soldiers, nowhere near as emaciated as the men she tended in Richmond's hospitals. Caroline shuddered at the unwelcome memory.

They had taken breakfast together, later than had the Carltons, but Caroline noted Jared had dressed for riding.

"Are you planning to go out?" she asked. She noticed the distracted expression on Jared's face as he glanced out the window at the warm, spring morning.

"As a matter of fact, I intend to take Miss Reid riding this afternoon," he told her.

"You're going to see her again, so soon?" asked Caroline with concern evident in her modulated voice. "Are you certain that's . . . wise?"

Jared laughed. "Wise? I don't know. But certainly enjoyable."

Caroline smiled despite herself. It was good to see her son finding pleasure in life after so long in darkness, but she was not at all certain his method would bear out that happiness.

"Mother," began Jared more seriously. "I can't believe you would think ill of Philippa. Surely not because she's a Yankee."

Caroline shook her head. "I don't think ill of her, Jared," she told him. When she continued, her voice was softer, wavering. "But there's something . . . something about her I can't explain. Yes, she's a sweet-mannered girl, and lovely. And yet . . ."

Caroline's voice faded and Jared waited with the trace of impatience in his expression. " 'And yet'? What is it that bothers you about her, Mother?"

Caroline sighed, struggling for the correct words to describe her vague feeling. "It's hard for me to describe," she began. "I don't find her objectionable, Jared, don't mistake me. It's just that there's something . . . not quite real about Philippa. She's so remote, even cold."

"Pippa is in no way 'cold,' " corrected Jared. "I can assure you of that."

But Caroline was unimpressed. "Oh, I see she isn't cold with you. I've never seen her so animated. But, Jared, and I pray you hear me, it's not her usual way. Normally, she watches us as if from a distance. How can I explain? Something isn't right."

Jared sighed. "It couldn't be your image of New Englanders as cold and calculating intellectuals, could it?" he suggested.

Caroline looked at him with sudden intensity as she shook her fair head. "No, Jared, they are not cold! It's the fire of abolition that they fling at us, without remorse, with single-minded violence. They are not cold!"

Jared sat back, surprised by his mother's emotion. "But you've just called Philippa cold."

"No, I say she seems that way, that's all." As she spoke, Caroline's impressions became clearer, and she looked her son directly in the eye.

"That's what frightens me, Jared. If I believed she was as cool and detached as she seems, I might not fear for you. But I saw her eyes as she looked at you at the ball. There was a fire, visible even across the room."

"I don't understand, Mother," began Jared, but Caroline interrupted him.

"Don't you? She has fire, Jared. I assume you know that as well as anyone. Yet she conceals it beneath a veneer of ice. Why? Doesn't that thought intrigue you?"

Jared shook his head. "No, Mother, it doesn't. Pippa feels things very deeply. It's only natural she'd hide this side of herself. Society disapproves of passion in women. Pippa probably learned very young to disguise the size of her feeling," he finished with a ring of sympathy.

Caroline looked at her son with deep misgivings. "Then why was she willing to reveal this portion of her *feeling* to you, whom she's barely met?"

Jared started to speak, but Caroline stopped him. "No, Jared, I'd like to believe what you say. Maybe there's a chance you're right. Philippa Reid loves you—and this I can believe—and it's impossible for her to disguise that fact.

"But, Jared, such . . . passion doesn't come, shall we say,

from an empty well. Such a woman would go to great lengths for what she believes, desires. Lengths that might surprise you. I don't see in Philippa Reid any real concern for society's requirements."

Caroline paused and looked intently at Jared. "Do you?"

Jared didn't answer. Pippa had shown no hesitation at meeting him the night before, nor had he seen any real effort at convention in the presence of her aunt. Unbidden into his mind came the image of Pippa stopping to help the simple-minded Lucy with her fallen tray. Jared frowned, though he wasn't certain why the simple gracious act should be troubling to him.

Jared stood up. "I must go, Mother," he said somewhat abruptly. "I'll see you in Richmond, though not for long. The general has asked me to speak with President Davis."

Caroline sighed and nodded. "That is well. Your sisters are eager to see you."

Jared kissed her cheek, but when he walked to the door, he turned back. "I intend to marry Philippa Reid, Mother. As soon as she'll have me," he told her. "I hope we'll have your blessing, and Father's, for your opinion carries much weight with him."

Caroline took a deep breath. "I'll treasure any girl you marry, Jared. You know that." She forced a smile to her troubled face and stood to bid her son farewell. "You go now, and enjoy yourself. Charlotte Reid is coming over for lunch. I must see that things are ready in the dining room."

Jared left, but Caroline stood watching him ride away with a heavy heart. The warm Virginia sun had risen high overhead, and Jared's golden hair glinted like a god's. But to Caroline's eyes, there was darkness riding close behind him.

Jogging beside the great, long strides of Jared's black war horse was Elspeth Carlton's gray mare, already saddled.

Caroline wondered why it was necessary to provide such a gentle palfrey for a girl as capable as Philippa Reid.

"Parson Frederick was in the carriage house last night," Pippa told Lucy as she surveyed her reflection in the looking-glass.

"What did he want?" asked Lucy as she handed Pippa her riding habit.

Pippa looked at Lucy with a shade of embarrassment. "I don't know." She paused, then offered her confession. "I was with Jared. I didn't get the message."

"What?" exclaimed Lucy in horror. "Dear Lord, what happened? Did Jared see him?"

"Yes, but I . . . warned the parson by knocking something over. He got away. Jared had no idea who it was, of course."

"That's lucky," replied Lucy. "The parson risks much by his activities. He's a good man."

Pippa sighed and nodded. Parson Frederick had, in utmost secret, educated countless slaves. Lucy was among the most gifted, and her gratitude to the man who had recognized this was deep and strong.

"I expect he was a day too soon. Perhaps he believed Burke had returned from Richmond last night," speculated Pippa.

"Poor, unsuspecting Mr. Mallory will be back today, I understand," said Lucy with grim humor, though Pippa glanced at her reproachfully.

Having disclosed the details of her near disaster, Pippa dressed. When she heard Jared outside, the barely avoided catastrophe was forgotten. Smiling brightly, she turned to Lucy.

"He's here," she breathed. Lucy watched Pippa spin on

her heels and hurry downstairs with a heavy heart. Too much could go wrong. If it did, Lucy feared it wouldn't go well for the girl who looked nightly to the northern star.

"Are you ready?" asked Jared as he took in the sight of Pippa's charmingly attired body.

Pippa nodded shyly, and he led her out to where the horses were waiting. Pippa smiled when she saw the small, fat mare Jared had chosen for her, but her eyes gleamed when she looked at his own magnificent steed.

"That's . . . a fine horse," she said in admiration as the big horse stamped restlessly. "What's his name?"

"Boreas," he told her.

"The God of the North Wind?" asked Pippa. "That's not exactly appropriate, Jared."

"He was a gift from Garrett at the start of the war. He has an enormous horse farm in Maryland, and he gave me the finest animal he had. Perhaps there was a message in the name, but he didn't expound upon it," Jared explained.

"It was very good of him."

"This is Mrs. Carlton's mare. She's called, strangely enough, Pippa's Song," Jared told her.

"Like the Brownings," Pippa whispered romantically. "She must be an especially intelligent mare."

"She's pretty and gentle," said Jared. For an instant, it surprised him that the quality Pippa valued most about herself was her intelligence.

Jared helped Pippa into Mrs. Carlton's fine leather side saddle, and Pippa adjusted herself as he mounted his own tall horse. Pippa sighed as she looked at him, for horse and rider made a noble picture. Despite Jared's Confederate uniform, he was breathtakingly beautiful.

They rode across the meadows side by side, Jared reining in his mount to a slow walk. Pippa wasn't used to riding sidesaddle, but a horse's pace was familiar to her, and one with such a smooth gait proved no trouble.

"You're a very graceful equestrienne, Pippa," Jared told her, but Pippa shook her head.

"At the walk, I imagine I'm immensely accomplished."

Just as she spoke, a deer leapt from a dense thatch of bushes, and Pippa's Song startled and bounded away. Boreas snorted, but he had endured battles beyond count. No mere woodland creature could shake his hardened nerves. Jared spurred on the great horse in pursuit of Pippa, fearing an accident lest the runaway animal, often used in fox hunts, might leap the nearby fence before he could catch her.

He needn't have worried. Indeed, Pippa's Song did jump the fence before Pippa had gained control of the frightened mare. As Jared caught up to her, he saw the mare guided gracefully over the high fence and come to a quiet stop on the far side. Even more surprising was the sound of Pippa's calm voice as she spoke reassuringly to the little mare.

"Easy, my little namesake. It's hardly necessary to flee in the face of a silly deer. It meant you no harm."

Pippa looked over to see Jared staring at her in amazement, and she smiled. The sweetness of her face drove away the inconsistencies of what had just happened, but there was confusion on Jared's face when she called to him.

"Aren't you coming? I didn't think to have to wait for you, Jared."

Boreas jumped the fence, to him only a small obstacle, and Jared rode to Pippa's side.

"You have more skill than you led me to believe, little Pippa," he said in a soft voice. Pippa looked quickly at Jared, but she saw that he was smiling and she smiled, too.

"Well," she began slowly with downcast eyes. "I thought you'd be more inclined to stay near me if I was a bit helpless."

"I'm inclined to stay near you no matter what," he told her. He urged his big horse into a sudden canter. This time, Pippa felt no hesitation about following him.

The two horses grazed side by side as Jared and Pippa sat down to rest. As on the previous afternoon, Jared lay on his side, propped up on one elbow, but now he motioned for Pippa to join him. Curiously compelled, Pippa did so, lying on her back to look up at him. The blue Virginia sky crowned his beautiful head with white clouds floating high above. When he bent to kiss her, Pippa knew she had found heaven.

Jared took her lips in a slow, seductive kiss, tenderly savoring the sweet taste of her mouth as her arms went about his shoulders to hold him closer. He drew back to gaze into her eyes, and the sight of his gentle smile pierced Pippa's heart. Jared stroked the soft skin of her cheek and she leaned her face against his hand, pressing her lips against his palm.

"How can any one thing be as perfect as you, Philippa Reid?" he murmured, but he saw the sadness rise to the surface in her eyes.

"What brings you sorrow, Pippa?" he asked.

"You will leave," she answered. As she spoke, hot tears welled in her eyes, though she didn't look away from him.

"Don't cry, my love," he said tenderly. "I wouldn't cause you pain."

Through her tears, Pippa smiled. "I don't want to lose you, Jared. I'm so afraid I'll never see you again."

"Of course you're afraid, love," he said. "But you'll never lose me, Pippa. That is a promise." Jared softened her hair as light wisps blew across her brow.

"It's only natural you should fear another loss in your life." Jared paused and gazed lovingly into her sorrowful green eyes.

"How did your father die?" he asked gently, but Pippa hesitated. The circumstances of her father's death weren't widely known in Virginia, yet when she looked into Jared's kind face, she found it impossible to lie.

"He died in camp, of diphtheria, in the first months of the war," she replied. When she saw Jared's expression change, her breath held as she waited for his response to her revelation.

"He was a soldier?" asked Jared. "I understood he was a college professor."

Pippa swallowed hard, but forced a casualness to her voice that she didn't come close to feeling. "He was, and perhaps he should have remained so. Father wasn't particularly well suited to the army, I'm afraid."

"Then why did he join?" asked Jared, the very question Pippa dreaded.

"I imagine he felt it was his duty," she answered quietly.

"He can't have been a young man," pressed Jared. "Such duties are more usually thrust upon the young."

"Your father is in the army," she reminded him.

"Ah, but on his own soil. That is another matter."

Pippa felt cornered, but she forced herself to speak evenly. "Apparently Father thought differently. He was inspired by another professor at Bowdoin College—Joshua Chamberlain. Father joined shortly after he left."

"So your father never saw battle?"

"No, he died before the regiment went south. Perhaps that was for the best," she added softly.

Pippa feared the continuation of their conversation, but she was powerless to change its direction. Yet even as she looked away from the nearness of Jared's face, she heard approaching hoofbeats, and Boreas whinnied as the rider approached.

Jared got up to greet the rider, and Pippa rose as well. As she stood, a uniformed, officer dismounted and came hurriedly to greet Jared. He was a broad, strong man with a heavy beard, but Pippa had never seen him before.

"What is it, Webster?" asked Jared. Pippa came to stand behind him.

"I might have guessed you'd be entertaining a young lady, and what a charming one at that!" the big man exclaimed.

The officer bowed to Pippa, and Jared drew a patient breath. "This is Miss Reid." The other man seemed to expect the formality of introductions despite his obviously pressing purpose. "And here is Captain Judah Webster." Pippa smiled weakly at the burly man.

"Now, why are you here?" Jared asked. Pippa got the distinct impression he had expected the captain.

"It's good news, Major, and you'll be glad to hear it. He's back, and we've got him!"

"Who is?" put in Pippa, forgetting her place, but Jared's face was grave.

"I'm sorry, Philippa," he said carefully. "I'd hoped this wouldn't involve you."

"What's going on, Jared?" Fear soared in Pippa's heart.

Jared paused, considering how best to handle the situation. "Burke Mallory is a spy, Pippa."

"No," she began. Jared stopped her.

"I'm sorry to break it to you this way, Pippa. It will be hard for Charlotte as well, yet you must be strong."

"Burke isn't a spy," she maintained.

"He is, Pippa. He's been often between here and Richmond, and we've long suspected him of running messages for the Yankees."

"He was just brazen enough to get away with it, too," added Captain Webster. "Had the letter strapped above the carriage wheel, barely hidden. We had no trouble finding it."

"Then you're holding him already?" asked Jared, and Pippa's eyes widened in horror.

The captain nodded. "At Mrs. Reid's. It's fortunate the lady herself is out. Putting up quite a fuss, he is," Webster told them with relish. "But there's more."

"What more?" asked Jared.

"I think we may have the girl you're after as well, Major," Webster told him calmly. "Doesn't exactly fit your description, and it's hard to imagine she'd have the brains to do it, but I'll let you be the judge."

Pippa's heart quailed at the captain's words, for she could guess to whom he referred. Jared looked doubtful. The woman he remembered would never be noted for lack of intelligence.

"We'll see, then," he agreed, and he turned to Pippa. "I'm afraid our ride will have to be cut short, Pippa," he told her as the other man went to mount his restless horse.

Jared took Pippa's hands. "I am sorry, though. There was something I intended to ask you."

He smiled, and Pippa's heart quaked within her breast when she saw the light in his blue eyes. "Perhaps later tonight," he suggested. Though Pippa nodded, she knew this opportunity would never come.

* * *

They rode back to Charlotte Reid's elegant home, and as they dismounted, Pippa saw that two other horses were already standing outside. From inside, Pippa could hear raised voices, and one she plainly recognized as that of Burke Mallory. Pippa followed Jared up the stairs. As she passed beneath the threshold of the door, she felt as if she had stepped through a portal of doom.

"I knew nothing about that damned letter!" shouted Burke, his voice raised in both anger and fear.

As the others entered the dining room where Burke was being held, Pippa saw Lucy seated at the far end, and their eyes met. Burke turned to Jared and fury was evident in his flushed face.

"You! You're responsible for this, Jared Knox," he shouted angrily.

"Your activities in my country are your own design, Mallory," replied Jared as he glanced at the contents of the crumpled note. "Your capture, though timely, is not my doing."

"Like hell! You want me out of here, and it's plain enough why," accused Burke with a knowing glance at Pippa.

"You've arranged all this, and you'll live to regret it, I promise you."

"Who gave you this message?" demanded Jared as his patience wore thin.

"Damn it! I have no idea who put the thing in my carriage." Burke looked toward Lucy. "But this girl was snooping around for it. Why don't you ask her?"

Jared looked at Lucy doubtfully, but Lucy didn't meet his gaze and seemed to be in a state of simpering terror. Pippa felt her heart beat so weakly that she wondered if she might faint.

"Come, sit at the table, Lucy," said Jared.

Lucy didn't move, and one of the soldiers went to her, roughly jerking her from her seat. Pippa closed her eyes tightly, but she knew better than anyone the courage of the woman who faced her enemy.

"What were you doing with the note, Lucy?" asked Jared calmly. As Jared spoke, Captain Webster drew forth his saber and held it out for Lucy to see.

"Don't know nothing 'bout no note," replied Lucy obstinately.

"Then what were you doing with it, damn you?" put in Webster.

"Don't know," said Lucy.

"You'll talk if I have to make you scream," said Webster savagely.

Pippa's heart leapt to her throat as he grabbed Lucy's wrist, stretching her arm out across the table. He held the saber as if to cut off her hand. Pippa had heard of such monstrosities committed on slaves, and her face blanched.

"Now, who involved you in . . ." began the captain, but as he raised his saber, Jared stepped forward.

At the same time, Pippa gasped, "No!" and the others turned in surprise.

Lucy's eyes commanded her silence, but Pippa couldn't obey and forfeit her friend's life.

"I did," she said in a low, trembling voice. "I told her to take the letter."

Pippa was aware of Jared's face as he turned toward her, but she couldn't look at him. "Lucy was simply doing as I asked her," she went on with effort. "She's no spy."

Pippa paused, but her lie was convincing to the others.

"She can't read, of course," she told them, and not a man in the room disbelieved her.

Jared stared at her with incomprehension, yet his heart throbbed with a pain he had never before endured. There beside him she stood, this woman who had brought to his heart a happiness he never dreamed possible. Jared knew her now, as he should always have known her had his senses not been clouded by desire.

The other soldiers looked to Jared, doubtful of how to handle the young lady's declaration. Jared looked away from Pippa, but she saw the hard set of his jaw.

"Let the girl go," he said, gesturing to Lucy, and she got up to leave.

Before she left, Lucy looked to Pippa. Pippa felt her compassion as Lucy finally left the room.

"Take Mallory," ordered Jared, and the soldiers went to bind the Yankee.

Burke struggled briefly, but Judah Webster struck him in the abdomen savagely, and Burke surrendered to the inevitable. Pippa winced at the violence, but she forced herself to remain calm.

"Burke had nothing to do with it," she said in a low, controlled voice, but even without looking, she could feel Jared's disgust.

"It's noble of you to protest his innocence," Jared said quietly. Pippa flinched as if struck by the cold hatred in his voice.

"But despite evidence to the contrary, I'm not a complete fool, Philippa," he continued.

Jared turned to the three soldiers. "Leave us, and you may start for Richmond."

"What about the lady?" asked Webster, looking at Pippa.

"I will deal with . . . the lady," said Jared in a low voice.

"If you lay a hand on her, Knox, you'll live to regret it," vowed Burke Mallory, but Jared ignored him.

Jared waited until they had led Mallory from the house, and then turned to Pippa.

"Sit," commanded Jared, and Pippa took the seat at the table that Lucy had used.

She didn't look at Jared, but the wait for his first words was agony. She felt his hurt and his anger, and his anger was greater.

"You and I have met before," Jared stated in a deep voice, threatening in its intensity. "But you've known that all along, haven't you, Philippa?"

He paused, awaiting her reply, but his voice trembled with anger when he pressed her. "Answer me!"

Pippa didn't look at him, but nodded. "I knew your voice," she said in a tight whisper. "I thought you had come for me."

Jared's face was hard, and the curve of a smile upon his lips nowhere reached his eyes. "As indeed I had."

Pippa's eyes shot briefly to his face, but seeing the inflexibility there, she quickly looked away.

"Which makes me even more the fool, I suppose," he said, but then Jared fell silent as he stared at Pippa's bowed head.

The moments of silence dragged interminably for Pippa, but she dared not speak as she waited for him to continue.

"Where was the message to go?" he asked, and Pippa's teeth sunk hard into her lower lip before answering.

"A Union agent," she replied in a small voice, but Jared's laugh was cold and cutting.

He leaned forward, bracing his powerful arms on the table before her. He slammed his fist upon the tabletop, demanding her response. "Who involved you in this, Philippa? I will know who leads this ring of spies."

Pippa felt Jared's anger as if the force of it could reach out itself and strangle her. With barely restrained power, Jared took Pippa's chin in his large hand and forced her head up, by his will, forcing her to meet his eyes.

Pippa rose her eyes slowly to meet Jared's frigid glare. She didn't answer, but she lifted a shaking hand and stretched it before her on the table, mimicking in accusation what Captain Webster had done to Lucy earlier. Her fingers outstretched and tense, Pippa's eyes burned with a fire that would not be quenched.

"I will never give you the answer you require, Major," she said clearly. "I will die rather than betray the Union I serve."

"Why, Philippa?" He ground her name and Pippa looked numbly into his pain-racked eyes. "Why did you do this? What are you that you could do this?"

Jared's voice was tortured with pain, soaked with his anger, but Pippa faced him directly and her eyes were free of deception. Pippa leaned towards Jared, and her voice was laden with the size of her feeling when she spoke.

"I am the daughter of a New England abolitionist, and the servant of a Higher Purpose."

Jared's throat constricted with his own emotion, but the force of his own passion was equal to hers. "Then your days of service to that purpose have ended, my lady," he growled, and Pippa looked away from him.

"What are you going to do with me?" she asked, her voice now small and young and defeated.

"Like Mallory, you'll be taken to Richmond and tried as a spy," Jared began brutally. He paused before continuing. The ruthlessness he revealed was in bitter opposition to the perfect love he had known only an hour before.

"Then, by rights, you will both be hanged as Union agents."

Pippa froze, her eyes squeezed shut, but her words were strangely selfless considering Jared's threat. "Burke is innocent, Jared. If you hang him, it will be murder."

Pippa's defense of the Yankee was more than Jared Knox could take and he stepped back from the table lest he be tempted to do her harm.

"Be that as it may, you're going to Richmond tonight."

"Tonight?" she asked. The journey to the Confederate capital was long. Surely Jared didn't mean to send her off into the night with three burly soldiers.

"You're going to send me off with those men, tonight?" she questioned in horror. Jared grimaced, loathing the violence in his heart and his soul.

"While they might enjoy the sport of such an adventure, it would be better if you reached your destination . . . intact, shall we say. I won't have it said you were mistreated, my lady . . . however lacking in innocence you may be."

What blood remaining in Pippa's now pale face drained as she stared at Jared in disbelief. She had known he would be angry if he learned of her subterfuge, but Pippa had believed he could be made to understand, that his love for her would rise above their differences.

Never had she imagined in her darkest dreams that he could turn on her this way.

"I'm taking you myself," he told her. This frightened Pippa more than anything else.

As being with Jared was heaven when he loved her, it would be hell likewise enduring his hatred. Still, she didn't dare argue the point. In that moment, it seemed to Pippa that her heart died. As she looked up at him, she felt nothing, merely numb.

"Get your things," he ordered.

"My things?" asked Pippa without understanding.

"A small bag. We'll be riding, so don't bring anything you don't need." Jared's face was cold and hard when he looked at her. "Your requirements in Richmond will be severely limited, I'm afraid."

Without a word, Pippa darted from the room and ran upstairs, but when she went inside, she stood, her face blank and white. No tears came, and the numbness permeated her entire being. The door opened behind her, and Lucy entered. Pippa looked at her, eyes wide with shock, but she couldn't speak.

"Pippa, I'm sorry," she breathed. Lucy didn't surrender easily, and even now she was desperately searching for a way to save her cohort.

"If you're quick, you might escape here, Pippa, and go north."

Pippa shook her head. "He would follow me," she said. "He would never let me escape him."

The barriers of Pippa's feeling broke down. With a strangled sob, she fell upon the bed. Lucy came to Pippa's side and wrapped her arms about the quaking girl. Pippa buried her head against her friend's shoulder.

"He hates me, Lucy. He wants me to die!" she sobbed.

Lucy hesitated, for words of comfort were hard to come by. "He's angry, betrayed, but perhaps when he has time . . ."

"No," broke in Pippa. "He'll never forgive me."

With that, Pippa's tears flowed in torrents down her cheek as Lucy stroked her hair like a child's. Pippa cried until there were no more tears. When she sat up, her eyes were dry. Again, she allowed the numbness to creep across her heart; it was buried as if in a shallow grave.

Dreamlike, now turned to a nightmare, Pippa rose from

the bed and found a bag suitable for such travel as Jared had described. She put in underthings, her mother's hairbrush, a daguerreotype of her father, and her toothbrush and mint flakes. She would need nothing more on the journey she was about to take.

Lucy watched her, helpless to offer comfort, but her heart ached to see the emptiness in Pippa's green eyes. There came on the door a sharp rapping, and Jared called to Pippa, his voice strained with impatience.

"Come, Philippa," he commanded. "I want to be out of here before your aunt returns."

"Aunt Charlotte! Dear God, what will she think?" groaned Pippa.

"You might have considered that before you began using her home as a refuge for Yankee spies," said Jared as he pushed open the door. "You need not concern yourself with informing her of your fate—I'll handle that in due course."

Jared explained this no further, and Pippa was too weak to press him. It didn't matter, she knew. Charlotte would be far more devastated because of Burke's loss than her own. That troubled Pippa as well. Though she herself was indeed guilty, Burke was not, and she was the one responsible for his condemnation.

"You'll need your mantle," Jared told her harshly. "You won't be in Richmond before tomorrow night. Nights in Virginia can be . . . cold."

Pippa didn't move, and Jared gestured to Lucy. "Fetch Miss Reid's mantle, Lucy," he said, as his ice blue eyes burned into Pippa.

Lucy obeyed and went to Pippa's wardrobe. She drew out the deep blue embroidered cloak that Charlotte had provided for her niece. Looking at it, Pippa lifted her chin proudly.

"No. Not that one please, Lucy. The other. I will have my own."

Lucy hesitated, but Pippa nodded firmly. "It's in the back . . . hidden," she added with a defiant glance toward Jared.

Lucy fumbled through Pippa's outerwear, then drew forth a well-worn gray cape. Jared recognized the garment from their first meeting, and his eyes narrowed.

Pippa seized the cape, and glared back at Jared. "I'm ready," she said, but Jared's smile was mocking and cruel when he held the door for her to pass.

"Poor little thing," murmured Emmaline as she stood beside Lucy watching Pippa ride off behind Jared.

Lucy sighed, but didn't reply to the old woman's comment.

"Anywhere else, and they'd be riding off into the sunset," continued Emmaline wistfully. She paused, then her heavy brow furrowed.

"Strange though, isn't it? What he told me I should tell the missus?"

Lucy looked at Emmaline in confusion. "What did he tell you to say?"

Jared didn't speak as they rode along, but Pippa felt the tension emanating from his taut body. It grew more and more unbearable, until she had to say something.

"Do you intend to simply steal Mrs. Carlton's mare?" she called as Pippa's Song jigged along behind Boreas.

Jared abruptly brought Boreas to a halt and waited until

Pippa came up alongside him. Jared's gaze was cold, but Pippa's was equally challenging and she met his eyes boldly.

"Elspeth Carlton has gone to Richmond with her son," explained Jared glacially. "I'll see that the mare is returned here when you no longer have need of her."

"Her service to the noble Confederacy is untold," commented Pippa, undaunted. "If only she was faster," she muttered as Jared urged Boreas forward. Immediately he halted the big horse and turned in the saddle to face Pippa.

"Don't even think it, woman," he said with force, and Pippa's green eyes widened.

"And, please remember, I am armed."

With that, Jared again started off, but Pippa held the little mare back. "Oh, dear. I hope you don't shoot me," she called. "I wouldn't want to miss my hanging."

A flare of anger surged in Pippa's breast. With a sudden ferocity, she tore off her riding bonnet and coat, and flung them to the ground. Pippa's Song stamped to follow the other horse, but Pippa held the reins fast. Drawing forth her gray cape, she swung it over her shoulders, and then freed her long, wavy hair from the neat chignon.

Jared's face changed when he glanced to see what was delaying her. "The Yankee witch has returned, I see," he commented with a curve of his sensual mouth.

"She has never been away," returned Pippa as her eyes flashed in the afternoon sun.

The sun was setting behind the rolling hills to the west as Jared and Pippa mounted the crest of a low rise. A loud clap of musket-fire broke the stillness of dusk. Pippa startled in perfect unison with her mare, but Jared galloped farther ahead, in the direction of the noises.

Answering fire was heavy, and Pippa got the clear impression that one force far outnumbered the other. As quickly as it had begun, the gunfire stopped, and Pippa moved her nervous mare to join Jared.

"What was that?" she asked as she drew near to where Jared stood, shading his eyes against the setting sun.

"Fighting," he answered unnecessarily. Pippa frowned.

"That much I guessed," she replied.

Jared's brow furrowed. He whirled Boreas around, and grabbing the reins of Pippa's mare, he hauled her along down the long hill.

"What are you doing?" shouted Pippa, but Jared didn't answer.

They were galloping recklessly toward the far woods to the south. Pippa had no control of her mare, so she was left to cling to her seat. She had no idea what possessed Jared to this sudden, violent activity. Pippa's Song's sides were heaving convulsively when they reached the shelter of the trees. Keeping up with Boreas's great stride had taken its toll.

Jared leapt from the black horse's back and led both into the woods. He stopped and critically surveyed the gasping mare that Pippa still rode.

"Get off, Philippa," he commanded. Pippa slid from the mare's back without argument.

As Pippa watched in confusion, Jared rapidly removed the mare's saddle and bridle, then set her free with a slap to her hind quarters. Pleased to escape the demanding ride, Pippa's Song tossed her delicate head and hurried away as fast as her strained legs could carry her.

Pippa watched in amazement as the little gray mare disappeared across the pasture, and then turned to Jared. "What did you do that for?"

"She's more of a hindrance than a help," said Jared flatly. "She'd be no use on the paths I intend to take."

"What paths? I thought we were taking the road," questioned Pippa.

"Not anymore," Jared informed her without further explanation.

He started off, heading into the thick forest, but Pippa refused to move. "Where are we going? What happened back there, Jared? What did you see?" she demanded. Jared took a deep breath before responding.

"As I've told you, we're going to Richmond," he explained patiently. Pippa frowned at the inadequacy of his response.

"As for what I saw, well, I'd think a woman of your experience might guess. Yankee raiders, I assume, have met with rebels, and there has been a fight. It's my judgment that your side as always outnumbered ours, and this time it has come out on top—which is less usual. If I'm right, they'll pass this way. I don't intend to lose my prisoner."

Pippa was still somewhat confused, but she wondered if she had possibly acquiesced too easily when a rescue might have been imminent.

"We'll be forced to take a longer, more roundabout route," Jared continued idly. "But I know this land as well as anywhere on earth. You needn't fear being lost."

"That would be a tragedy," retorted Pippa with vigor.

"And one best avoided," said Jared without hesitation. Both glared at the other with undisguised resentment.

Jared set Pippa atop Boreas's broad back, and she was obliged to pull her skirts high to sit astride. Her bare legs dangled against the horse's powerful sides, but since Jared Knox had already seen much of her body, Pippa reasoned propriety's standards had already been shattered beyond recall.

Jared himself walked as he led the horse through the trees, always within sight of the long, green fields. Pippa often ducked to escape low-hanging branches. As she passed beneath one, her long, thick hair was caught by the grasping fingers of an ancient evergreen.

"Ooh, Jared!" she called. "Wait!"

Jared stopped the horse and looked back at Pippa as she struggled to disentangle herself. When freed, she slapped the offending branch away with vigor, as if in its Virginian heritage the tree had deliberately attacked her.

"There!" she exclaimed. Jared repressed a grin as he led the horse forward.

The rage he had experienced at her confession and subsequent defiance was slowly dissipating. It was being replaced by an emotion that might prove even more difficult to contain.

Why do I still want you? he thought painfully. *Why does that little face still have the power to move my heart? How could you be false, when you gave love so perfectly?*

Jared's mind wore on in anguish, but if his heart ached at the loss of his new love, his body burned with desire. At every turn, destiny seemed determined to thwart his intent.

They went on until well past nightfall, but as Boreas picked his way through fallen branches and bracken, suddenly Jared stopped, listening. Just as Pippa discerned what he had heard, he pulled her roughly from the saddle. To her great annoyance, Jared flung her to the ground beneath him.

"Stand!" he commanded the horse. To Pippa's wonder,

the great animal stood motionless despite the nearing sounds of many horsemen.

Jared clapped his hand tightly over Pippa's mouth as the riders approached, but she had no clear thoughts of escape. At least, not until she knew who passed by, and for what purpose.

"It's too dark now, sir," said a man, his accent ringing clearly of the North, and Pippa's heart leapt at the sound.

"He must have gone this way," replied another, sounding older to Pippa's ears. "But you're right, Corporal—there's no point pursuing him tonight. We'll never find them in the darkness."

But Pippa started at the next who spoke. Without question, it was Burke Mallory.

"Good God, Sergeant!" exclaimed Burke. "That crazy rebel has taken my cousin, and you intend to give up the search already?"

"Now calm down, there, sir," replied the sergeant, and with strained patience for the distraught New Yorker.

"There's nothing we can do tonight. But the lady will be all right."

"How can you say that?" gasped Burke, his voice raised in disbelief. "Who knows what atrocities he'll commit upon her, now that she's without the protection of her aunt and myself?"

"From what I know of young Jared Knox, that hardly seems likely," responded the sergeant calmly, disregarding Burke's fears.

"A proper gentleman, I believe," he added thoughtfully. "As a matter of fact, I served beneath a cousin of his with the Maryland Cavalry. A finer man there never was than . . ."

"Oh, for God's sake!" shouted Burke. "I don't give a

damn about his cousin, Sergeant! I know Jared Knox, and he'll stop at nothing to get what he wants."

Burke groaned. "Poor little Pippa. She has no idea what might befall her. Oh, my poor darling!"

Pippa felt Jared's hold on her intensify but Burke's comments confused her. He had never shown more than a passing interest in her, and she believed he was in love with someone else, though she had never known who it was. To hear him speak this way took her by surprise.

"Set your mind at ease, Mr. Mallory," reassured the sergeant. "There's nothing you can do for the girl now. Her fate is with that young rebel."

"A rebel betrayed," argued Burke grimly. "A rebel who believes Philippa a spy. You know the fate of spies in Virginia."

But the sergeant sighed. "I do, but you needn't fear for this one. The Rebs may send the Coloreds swinging if they're caught spying, and the likes of yourself as well. But a lady . . . hell, no.

"You take my word for it, Mr. Mallory, that girl will be treated like a princess. This is the land of chivalry, after all. She'll be fine. But you'd be best to get yourself out of Virginia, and go back where you came from."

Pippa listened to this revelation hopefully, while Jared sighed. But Burke Mallory was not swayed by the sergeant's logic.

"No, Sergeant. I intend to remain close by. There are worse fates to befall a lady than hanging," insisted Burke, but Pippa was uncertain what Burke feared if not her death.

"If anything dishonorable befalls my Philippa, Jared Knox will pay with his life."

Pippa listened in confusion, but the voices faded beyond

her ability to discern them. They finally disappeared, but it was long before Jared released her from his hold.

"Well, it seems your lover has his precious freedom," remarked Jared. "Pity the same will not be said of his mistress."

Pippa frowned. "Jared," she began with the intention of correcting his erroneous impression, but Jared cut her off ruthlessly.

"Don't," he ordered ferociously. "Don't say a word, Philippa. My restraint is wearing very thin with you this night."

Pippa followed Jared back to the edge of the pasture, and she despondently watched him prepare a place upon the grass to sleep. But then he took the reins from Pippa's Song's bridle and, to Pippa's horror, proceeded to bind her wrists.

She said nothing as he checked the tie, but tears welled in her eyes at this final indignity. "I don't know where you think I'm going to go," she murmured, but her throat was tight with misery.

"I don't intend to watch over you all night," said Jared.

He fastened the other end to a tree, then lay back on the grass, but though his eyes were closed, Pippa knew he wasn't asleep. The hot tears fell silently down her cheeks. As the night darkened about them, Pippa knew he couldn't see her mood. For this, at least, she was grateful.

"Jared." Though he didn't respond, Pippa knew he was listening. "There's something I must tell you, about your house."

"Don't say something you'll regret, Philippa," he growled. "Nor is there any need to protest your innocence. I've abandoned taking you at your word."

Pippa swallowed hard, but forced herself to go on. "You

needn't believe me, of course," she agreed. "But I'll have it said all the same. Once we're in Richmond, I'll never see you again," she continued with effort. Once again the tears threatened in her eyes.

"I've been a spy, or more accurately, a message-bearer, but I swear to you I had nothing to do with what happened to your house, or your family."

"I saw you that night, Philippa," said Jared, pain unwittingly revealing itself in his soft voice.

The long road from Gettysburg . . . His heart soared at her image, the glorious silhouette against the moonlit sky. He had wanted to run to her then, not as her enemy, but as a man spellbound by an enchantress. Only to find his home in ruins at her hand, and worse . . .

Pippa sighed miserably. Jared would never accept her innocence in this, but she made the attempt anyway. "That may well be, for I'd been . . . north that night, and I recall that I stopped to watch the glow in the sky. But I had no idea what it was, Jared," she told him earnestly.

"More than that, no one I know had any idea why your house was ravaged. I promise," she maintained, but then her voice faltered. "Of course, there's no reason you should believe me," she added sorrowfully.

"No one you know? Burke Mallory was there, not hours after I myself arrived," said Jared. "Quite a gentleman is your Mr. Mallory. He even offered to take the property 'off my hands.' All to the good of Virginia, of course."

"That doesn't sound like Burke," said Pippa doubtfully. "Burke isn't normally so . . . tactless. He thinks of business first," she added, more in an effort to understand the Yankee's actions herself than to explain them to Jared.

"Again you defend him," commented Jared.

"I know no ill of Burke," she said. But then Pippa herself

laughed. "Except that he isn't particularly loyal to the country you accused him of serving. That, I've always felt, is a failing."

Jared gazed over at Pippa, but he saw no more than her outline as she leaned against the tree to which he had bound her.

"As an actress, you are unmatched, little witch."

"Do you really think I could love Burke and . . . do what I did with you?"

"I have no idea what you could do, Philippa. Your cohort prevented me from learning fully what lengths you were prepared to reach in the service of your precious Union."

"What did you expect from me?" she cried with frustration. "You said yourself that you had come for me. And I guessed as much. What was I to do?"

Jared's voice was agony when he replied to her passionate entreaty. "Do you think had you come to me and told me the truth, can you believe I would cause you any harm?"

"Yet you're taking me to Richmond now," Pippa reminded him.

"You made your choice, Philippa. For God and country, for abolition, for whatever it is that moves your heart. Your fate is of your own design."

With that, Jared rolled over, but Pippa surrendered to silent tears, for she knew his words held truth. But she had loved him, despite all that stood between them. It was bitterly clear what he thought of her now, and she chastened herself for wishing it could be different. Yet well into the night, long after Jared's breath came even and slow, Philippa Reid lay awake beside the tree that was her prison, and longed to be safe in his arms.

Part Two

The Wilderness

Go from me. Yet I feel that I shall stand
Henceforward in thy shadow . . .
            —Elizabeth Barrett Browning

Four

"Take it off," commanded Jared.

Pippa shook her head and backed away from him until she bumped against a tree, but Jared was in no mood that morning for needless delays. As he stepped towards her, Pippa understood the threatening light in his glittering blue eyes.

"We don't have time for this, Philippa," he said as he approached her. "Take it off. Now."

Again Pippa shook her head, and she wrapped her arms tightly around her waist. "I will not!"

"There's no need for a corset nor extra petticoats on the road we'll take. They'll only slow you down."

"I wasn't slow yesterday," she argued, but Jared was unconvinced.

"You were riding yesterday, Philippa," he said. "But the woods are thick where I'll lead you today. There will be little opportunity for riding. It will be hot today, and you'll need all your strength. You can't bear the extra weight of a woman's trappings."

Jared stood directly in front of Pippa, and her white teeth cut into her lower lip. "Take it off."

Pippa raised her chin. "Very well, but you must turn around," she told him as calmly as she was able.

Jared's eyes rolled heavenward and he took a deep breath.

"I would think our previous . . . intimacy would negate such a necessity." Jared felt satisfaction when the color rose to Pippa's cheeks.

"But, as you wish," he finished, and dutifully Jared turned his back to Pippa.

She hurriedly stripped off her cumbersome petticoats save only her undergarments, and then she unfastened the long row of buttons to remove her corset. As she untied its strings, Pippa couldn't deny its absence was a relief.

Pippa dropped the corset unceremoniously to the earth and began to button her bodice. Jared, feeling she'd had time enough, turned around. His eyes were drawn against his will to the pink, bare flesh revealed between Pippa's lightly covered breasts.

Jared's breath intook sharply and Pippa looked up. She recognized the raw flash of desire across his sensual face, and her own body tingled in response. Her reaction was so far beyond her control that she began to tremble, and for a moment Pippa couldn't force her fingers to finish their task.

Seeing her dilemma, Jared stepped towards her, but he felt as a man enchanted. Without a word, he reached to the half-bound bodice and began to do the buttons for her. Pippa's arms dropped to her sides, but she could barely breathe as his hands worked close to her throbbing heart. She lifted her chin, eyes averted from Jared's as he buttoned her lace collar, but he didn't move away when he was done.

Pippa held her breath, wondering if he would kiss her. He leaned toward her, and she closed her eyes. But Jared regained control of himself and backed away from her. Pippa opened her eyes and looked at him in wonder, but her heart sank when she saw the anger in his expression.

"You're not going to do this to me again, girl," he said

in a voice low and thick and husky with the desire he was suppressing.

"I've done nothing," she began hotly. Jared laughed and turned away from her to fetch the grazing Boreas.

"Like hell," he replied over his shoulder. Pippa felt her own anger rise and replace her momentary loss of dignity.

Jared saddled his horse and mounted as Pippa watched him, wondering if it would be her fate to walk at his side in disgrace. His anger seemed to have no bounds, and at this point, it didn't seem unlikely.

"Front or back?" said Jared enigmatically. Pippa's brow furrowed in confusion.

"What do you mean?" she asked suspiciously.

"Do you want to ride in front of me, or in back?" he asked more clearly, but Pippa was uncertain how to respond. His words had a hidden meaning she didn't immediately comprehend.

"No preference?" he mocked. "Very well, then I will choose."

Before Pippa could consider this, Jared leaned from the saddle and swept her off her feet and into his arms. Pippa's green eyes widened, but she had promised herself she wouldn't allow him to intimidate her in any way. She looked away from him, and settled herself comfortably in his lap.

"I'd be better behind," she commented casually.

"That is a matter of opinion," replied Jared.

As soon as they started off, Jared realized his error. He had considered it more of a possible temptation to have Pippa seated bare-legged behind him, arms about his waist. But the horse's jarring gait jostled them together relentlessly and Jared found himself in a state of virtual agony.

Pippa was unaware of Jared's aroused condition, but that became an even greater provocation to him. She leaned against his chest, dreamily watching the big horse's shoulders rise and fall as they rode along the edge of the long field.

"He's so fast, yet his stride is effortless," she mused as they went along. She stretched out her small hand to stroke the horse's muscled neck.

"Unlike that heavy old plow horse you used to gallivant about on," replied Jared.

"That's true," Pippa responded, but as she peered up at him, a small, teasing smile crossed her face.

Jared groaned inwardly at her charm but Pippa wasn't finished. "Yet even on that old carriage horse, I had no trouble evading you, Major Knox. Of course, that perhaps had more to do with our relative intelligence than the skill of our respective mounts," she added with sparkling eyes.

Pippa's rounded mouth curved into a beguiling smile, and Jared had to force himself to look away over her head, so strong was his desire to abandon all reason and kiss her. She looked agonizingly kissable as she waited for his response. But Jared's voice was grim when he answered her.

"Your cleverness is unquestioned, Philippa," he said coldly. "And it was no difficult task for you to make me the fool. But I warn you, girl, it won't happen again. My illusions about you are thoroughly shattered, so you need no longer cast your lovely shadow my way."

Pippa's eyes traveled from his eyes to his full mouth and down across his strong chin. She knew that though his words were hard, they were a guise for another, more powerful emotion. The thought affected her strangely. For a wild moment, Pippa longed to kiss his face despite his bitter words. She longed to press her lips against the corner of his and run her tongue along them until he could no longer resist the passion between them.

The desire was so overwhelmingly powerful that she felt herself lean toward him despite herself, and she wet her lips unconsciously as the thought took hold of her. Jared saw the change in Pippa's face, and his body washed with wild heat when he recognized the powerful sensuality in her gaze.

Yet he was saved from her certain seduction by the pasture's end. It was with an audible sigh of relief, or yet, regret, that Jared swung off the horse's back and lowered Pippa to the ground beside him. Pippa shook her head as if to drive the vision from her mind, and she too breathed deeply at the respite to their passion.

"Now what?" she asked weakly as Jared loosened the girth of his saddle to allow Boreas his comfort.

"Now we walk," he told her, and he started off into the forest.

Hours passed and the day wore on, yet Pippa couldn't see they had made much progress in any particular direction. Jared had barely spoken to her since they had entered the cover of the trees. He seemed to be concentrating upon the path ahead.

Despite the shade of the forest canopy, the heat was sweltering. Worse was the condition of her feet. First sore, now Pippa was certain they were bruised and torn. Her riding boots weren't designed for walking, certainly not through bramble and over rough ground. She stopped briefly to ease their pain, but Jared called to her impatiently.

"Hurry up, girl. What's keeping you?"

"My feet hurt," she told him, but Jared frowned.

"There are worse fates," he said. Pippa's pride forced her to walk onward despite her discomfort.

"I know that, Jared," she said coldly. "It's my neck I should be worried about, not my feet."

Jared ignored her reference to hanging, but he looked on with irritation as she shouldered the heavy length of her felt cape after it dropped to the ground, not for the first time.

"What are you bothering with that cape for? It'll be hot tonight, Philippa," he informed her needlessly. "You might better discard it rather than hauling it along with you."

Pippa was indignant. "Never!" she said fiercely, and Jared's brow rose.

"This is mine," she explained, though he had no comprehension of her attachment. "For your information, Jared Knox, if I have to face death, I want this around me, so that I remember what I died for."

Jared sighed. "I think you'll face a lesser punishment than hanging," he admitted with a faint smile. "As you heard from the good Yankee sergeant who rescued Mallory."

"You won't hang me?"

"No." Jared paused, and his short laugh mocked the fervor of his own anger. "At worst, you'll be imprisoned, but even that is unlikely. You'll probably be sent safely north, with the strict instructions never to tread upon Virginia's sacred soil again."

Pippa wasn't at all relieved by Jared's reassurance. "You're going to send me away?" she asked, her voice a clear indication that she considered this a fate equivalent to hanging.

Jared hesitated, and for a moment he wondered if Pippa wanted to remain with him. Spying seemed to have a greater hold on her heart, and his jaw hardened.

"Perhaps you would prefer it if I left you here or back in Fredericksburg where you can best serve your precious Union," he mocked with irritation, but Pippa frowned.

"You don't understand, Jared," she countered. "It means everything to me, seeing a country free for all people. I couldn't be here, live here in the South, and do nothing. I couldn't feel so strongly and watch the days go by without adding to the outcome."

Pippa's voice was filled with emotion, her green eyes blazed with the depth of her feeling, but Jared looked away as they walked on. *Such passion doesn't come from an empty well,* he remembered. Jared was forced to acknowledge his mother's judgment in this aspect of Pippa's character.

He had adored that passion, but now it turned against him, burned him as would a blazing fire. He glanced at Pippa as she trudged along beside the big, black horse, and she fingered her cape wistfully.

"I don't understand what's so special about that worn-out old thing," he ventured as he eyed her dreamy expression. "Although I have to admit, wearing it you have a certain pagan allure."

"Someone I love gave it to me," she said with pride.

"Your mother?" he speculated.

"I never knew my mother," she told him with a lingering trace of sadness. "But yes, it was hers. She was Scottish, and such things would be useful there. It was hidden in our attic, until a man found it and gave it to me."

"Not your father, I gather," remarked Jared as he held a branch away for Pippa to pass beneath.

Pippa paused. "No, not my father. But he means as much to me."

Pippa sighed as she thought of one who was far away, and when Jared saw her expression, he felt a stab of pain. So much was in Philippa Reid's heart that he didn't know. So much she was that he had never guessed.

"He was a man who came to live with us, when I was a

young girl," she told Jared wistfully. "He had been a slave, and he had run away. Father wanted to help, so he opened our house in Maine to those seeking refuge. Byron was special, and he stayed with us for many years."

Jared stopped and stared at her in shock. "Byron?" he asked in a low voice. "That's an unusual name for a slave."

"Byron is an unusual man," said Pippa. "Full of excitement, and despite his former life, I've never known anyone with such capacity for happiness." As she looked toward Jared, Pippa stopped.

"Except in you," she added wistfully before realizing the awful opening for retort she had given him.

Jared didn't avail himself of the opportunity to remind her what she had done to that happiness. "Where was he from?" pressed Jared, seeming not to notice the inequity of Pippa's statement.

"Virginia," she told him, but now she wondered at his interest. "Why?"

Jared's blue eyes were veiled to her, and he just shook his head.

"No reason. So my little abolitionist sheltered contraband slaves," he said.

"We did," she replied with pride. "Most went on, to Canada, or other places. But Byron and another younger man, Jefferson Davis, stayed with us."

"Davis? Are you making that up, woman?"

"No, I'm not. That's his name, and I'm sure he's more a credit to it than your miserable president."

Jared frowned. "You underestimate our leader, Philippa. As do many," he added with a sigh. "President Davis is a good man, though his task is daunting. He's leading a country at war. That has never been easy."

Pippa rolled her eyes. "He's leading a band of traitors,"

she retorted. "Although more guilt lies with Lee . . ." she continued, but Jared was aghast.

"Guilt! How can you speak thus of the finest man—"

"He's a traitor," Pippa cut in, but Jared was incensed at this slight to his great commander.

"You should be so lucky to have such a man in command of your armies."

"Had he been a loyal American, he would be," Pippa asserted willfully.

"And turn against his own people? It's a shame you're not more open-minded, Philippa," said Jared. "You might enjoy Richmond, and the gentleness of her people."

"Gentleness! Ha! People of color flee north for a reason, Jared Knox. Gentle, indeed. I've never heard such foolishness."

Jared drew a patient breath. "I can't answer for every misdeed of my people, Philippa, nor have I any intention of defending slavery to you. I strive to remind you it's not what we're fighting for. I, for one, believe that if left to our own devices, slavery will be eliminated in its own course, without the hatred and rancor your New England idealism will inevitably produce."

"How many will live and die in bondage, in shame, before your noble Virginians decide that day has come?" asked Pippa fiercely.

"There's no shame in having been a slave," Jared responded. "I'd wager some of our own ancestors spent time in bondage."

"No, the shame is with those who made them slaves," flared Pippa. "How many like Byron and Jefferson will be beaten into submission when their spirits are at least the match of yours? You should hear Jefferson when he plays the piano, Jared. Few are as gifted as he, yet who would come to listen if a colored man played? Byron has the clearest mind and the bravest heart. Even now he fights with a Colored Regiment . . ." she continued, but again Jared stopped to listen more carefully.

"He's in the army?"

"Yes, they both are. Jefferson was allowed to fight with a Massachusetts company. Byron joined the U.S. Colored troops almost two years ago."

"Have you heard from him? Is he well?" asked Jared.

"Why do you care?" asked Pippa, but Jared's shrug was careless.

"It is . . . interesting to me, that's all."

"Well, then. Yes, Byron is well. I've heard of him, though there have been no letters since his regiment moved south."

Pippa beamed with pride. "But he's distinguished himself in battle, and they've given him a higher command. He's now the highest ranking noncommissioned officer in his regiment."

Jared said no more on the matter, but Pippa got the distinct impression that he was pleased.

The day wore on, and Pippa's feet no longer bore signs of mere discomfort. Every step was agony, and she no longer concerned herself with disguising that fact from Jared. Her pride was failing with every inch she covered, and tears were welling in her eyes from the pain.

They crossed a shallow stream, but the water only served to irritate her sores further. At the far bank, Pippa stumbled and fell to her knees. Jared looked back, and gave in to his surge of pity. He walked back to where she knelt and took her arm, but angered by the emotions she provoked, he pulled her roughly to her feet. Pippa gasped in pain, and Jared scrutinized her face suspiciously.

"What's the matter with you, woman?"

"I told you," Pippa said as she fought tears, her head turned away from him. "My feet hurt."

"Your feet?" asked Jared. He glanced down, and realized her light boots were lacking in practicality.

"Here, sit," he ordered.

Pippa nearly fell to the ground with relief. She eased herself upon a rotting log, her long fingers digging into the soft bark to keep herself from crying out when he knelt to unbutton her riding boots.

Jared removed first the left, but as he pulled it off, Pippa let out a strangled cry of pain. Her thin stockings were shredded, and the skin of her small, elegant foot was bloody and torn. Pippa winced with pain at the slightest touch.

"Dear God, Pippa, why didn't you tell me?"

The tears in Pippa's eyes fell to her cheeks, and Jared's pity filled his heart. "You told me to hurry, that it didn't matter because of . . . what's going to happen to me," she explained in a small, choked voice.

Jared couldn't speak, but he carefully removed her other boot, finding her right foot in even worse condition. He removed his white cravat and tore it, gently binding each foot. Without a word, he lifted her into his arms, and Pippa was stunned to see his eyes glistening with unshed tears.

He bore her to the waiting horse, and set her upon the saddle. "We'll have to go a way further, but as it happens we're near the far edge of my own estate. There's a place there where we can pass the night."

"But your estate is burned, Jared. You said there was nothing left," Pippa reminded him.

"There's something, as you'll see, at the far south border.

The acreage is many miles long, and far from the sight of my old home, though I spent much time in this quarter as a child."

Jared said no more about his destination, but Pippa believed his heart had softened unfathomably toward her.

"You'll have to stay low, Pippa," he told her. "The woods are thick and low, and the going will be rough. Take care," he advised, but Pippa was barely listening.

For the first time since he had discovered her duplicity the day before, Jared had used her pet name, a clear sign of gentleness. Her heart leapt into life again, and suddenly Pippa realized what she wanted.

If she was to be sent away, never to see the man she loved again, to have one last night with Jared Knox was all that mattered in the world.

Another hour passed as they went through the darkening forest. By the time Jared had brought them from beneath the shadow of the trees, the first stars were appearing in the east. Jared led the horse along the edge of the pasture, then started inward once again.

"Here we stop, my lady," he said pleasantly, and he reached to help Pippa down.

"Sit," he commanded. Pippa did what she was told without argument. With the condition of her feet, she had little choice. Jared removed the horse's tack, and as Pippa watched in wonder, he let the animal go. Boreas wandered off in search of grass and Jared turned away without concern.

"What makes you think he'll be here in the morning?" asked Pippa as the tall, black horse moved farther away.

"He'll be here," Jared told her indignantly, but Pippa plainly held misgivings.

Jared held out his hand and Pippa took it, rising painfully to her feet. Before her weight lowered, Jared again lifted her into his arms. He carried her along a barely discernible path leading deeper into the woods.

"What are you looking for?" she asked as he stopped to gauge his position.

"Ah!" said Jared, and without explaining further, he bent low beneath an overhanging branch and carried Pippa from the path.

As they passed beneath, it seemed to Pippa that the branch had formed a mystical portal. Carrying her through its threshold, Jared led her into another world.

"Here we are," said Jared.

Pippa stared in amazement as he directed her attention to a small clearing. Pippa gasped, her eyes lit with wonder. At the back of the clearing was nestled a tiny house, a perfect miniature of a far greater dwelling.

"What is this place?" she asked, looking to Jared in disbelief.

"It's a house," said Jared.

"For dwarves?"

"For children," he explained with a smile.

Jared pulled open the perfect, arched door and carried Pippa inside. As Jared set her down upon the bed, she saw that the inner adornments were as thoughtfully crafted as was the outside. Jared found and lit an old oil lamp. As it flickered to dim life, Pippa took in her incredible surroundings.

Two old, but comfortable, chairs made a sitting area complete with a coffee table. Various neatly crafted cabinets lined one end of the little room, ostensibly a kitchen. The bed on which Pippa was seated was large and covered with a fine old quilt. It wasn't exactly spacious, but Pippa marveled at the time someone must have put into the creation of this tiny house.

"For children?" she asked. "Who made it?"

"As a matter of fact, Miss Reid, you're looking at the architect now. Do you like it?"

"Yes," Pippa replied. "What possessed you?"

Jared shrugged. "I wanted a place to be alone, that was mine only."

"I built this place, on the farthest border of my father's estate, and my mother allowed me some of her older furniture," he continued. "It was quite a haven when I was a boy. Though as I got older, I spent less time here. At least, until I discovered it was a clever spot to bring innocent young ladies."

Pippa frowned slightly at his intimation, but redirected their conversation. "Did you do this all alone?" she asked.

"No," he admitted. "Another helped me."

Jared himself now wanted the subject changed. "Are you hungry, Pippa?"

Pippa gasped. "Good heavens, Jared! We haven't eaten since yesterday's lunch! How could I forget such a thing?"

"It's been a strained time, Pippa," he said. "But I have food in my haversack. It's not fresh, I'm afraid, but at this point you probably won't care."

"Quite so," she replied, and her eyes blazed with hunger when Jared began laying out dried meat and hardtack.

Jared left Pippa to devour her meal in privacy, then returned carrying a bucket of water. Pippa noted that Jared's blond hair was damp, and he had washed, a promising thought.

"Where have you been?" she asked rather thickly as she finished the last of her sparse meal.

"There's a spring not far from here. You can bathe there if you'd like."

Pippa's face brightened visibly at the suggestion, and she nodded vigorously. Pippa grabbed her small bag, which contained soap flakes, and Jared directed her toward the spring. The ground was covered by a thick layer of soft moss and Pippa had no trouble walking by herself.

"This is lucky," she called as her sore feet sank comfortingly into the receptive growth.

"Lucky indeed!" responded Jared as he tossed her a towel. "It took us weeks to get this growing."

He turned and went back to his little dwelling, but as Pippa went down the narrow moss path, she wondered just who Jared had meant by *us*.

The spring water was cold, but it felt good, numbing, to Pippa's anguished feet. She removed her dusty dress and undergarments. Taking a deep breath, she stepped into the water. Pippa squealed at the chill, but forced herself into the icy depths.

With utmost happiness, Pippa washed herself, even taking the time to soak her long hair. There was a great deal of gasping and shivering as she did so. The past days seemed as a dream, a nightmare to which she'd surrendered, and the war that raged beyond had never seemed farther away.

Jared sat on the moss waiting for Pippa to return. Strangely, he knew she wouldn't try to escape, though the condition of her feet would serve to dissuade any such impulses. He could hear her splashes and her spirited reaction to the cold water. As he imagined the scene beyond his sight, Jared's body burned with desire.

Pippa got out of the water and put her dress back on, though she wished she could wash that, too. She toweled her hair, and let it fall damp about her shoulders to dry.

Pippa straightened her dress as best she could, and proceeded back up the path to where Jared waited.

Jared stood up when Pippa approached and opened the door for her. The whole evening seemed unreal to Pippa, but she was powerless to change its course. Inside, the lamp glowed warm, and the darkness of night seemed to fall on cue as the door closed behind them.

Pippa sat on the bed, dangling her feet from the edge. Jared sat back in an old, comfortable armchair opposite her. In the warm light of the lamp, Pippa thought he looked frighteningly handsome, and the new growth of his beard only served to heighten his masculinity. Distracted, Pippa looked away, and peered with seeming fascination at her surroundings. "Did you learn all this in . . . architect school?" she asked.

"No, but I suppose this fired my interest. Though I have to admit, studying architecture was more of a pastime during my stay in France."

"What were you doing then?" asked Pippa suspiciously.

Jared's eyes gleamed, and his smile widened before answering. Pippa's brow furrowed as she awaited his reply.

"As a matter of fact, one might say I studied the romantic arts for a time."

Pippa's frown deepened and Jared laughed. "It's somewhat easier to explore the subject in full when an ocean separates you from the watchful eyes of your family."

"Wasn't your cousin there to restrain you?" Pippa inquired in obvious disapproval.

"Garrett? He's only four years my senior, Pippa. At twenty-three, he was as interested as I in the pursuit of the fairer sex. No, I'm afraid neither of us did much to discourage the amorous adventures of the other. Quite the contrary, actually."

Pippa grimaced and looked away from Jared as a surge of unwelcome jealousy coursed through her. She had no wish to hear any further of Jared's love affairs, and the thought he had delightedly indulged wounded her.

"But Garrett left France before I did," Jared recalled, seemingly oblivious to Pippa's distress. "And I returned to England. My . . . interests there diminished a year or so later, and I too returned, but to find my country in turmoil."

"And he stayed with the Union, while you . . ." speculated Pippa.

"I was with Garrett in Maryland when Lincoln was elected, and we both knew war was coming," Jared told her. "That was when he gave me Boreas."

"Weren't you afraid you'd meet in battle?"

"Oh, we were certain we would," replied Jared with a self-mocking laugh. "But in gallant splendor, sabers bared. We would salute each other, behave honorably, and do proud our common name."

Jared fell silent, but then he sighed deeply. "War doesn't go as one expects," he commented wearily. "Like love, it seems."

Pippa's heart labored at his words, but Jared didn't go on with his thought. "We stepped forward for Virginia without fear, and of those who joined with me, fewer than half remain. No, it isn't what we expected at all."

Yet as Jared spoke, his eyes brightened, and Pippa discerned an undefinable pride in his bearing. "But we haven't faltered, despite the army massed against us. We've learned more of ourselves and our courage, and yes, honor, than even the knights of old could have known."

Jared's eyes were gleaming now, and despite her abhorrence for his cause, Pippa felt the chill of admiration surge in her heart.

"We don't go because we're ordered, as the knights did. No rebel soldier does anything just because he's ordered," he asserted proudly.

"Then why do you continue to fight?" interrupted Pippa, voicing the common wonder of her Northern countrymen.

Jared paused, reflecting well his answer. "For the right to decide our own fate. And for love, I suppose. For the love of Virginia, and the man who leads us."

"General Lee?" asked Pippa doubtfully.

"You haven't seen him, Pippa, so you couldn't understand. Men will go where he asks them without thought of their lives, just to do his bidding."

"Would you?"

"I have," said Jared quietly.

As Pippa sat listening to Jared, the night outside turned cold, a chill air replacing the stifling heat of the day. Pippa's hair and dress were still damp and she shivered as she sat dangling her feet from the bed.

"Maybe you should get undressed," suggested Jared wryly, but Pippa shook her head.

"I'm perfectly fine," she lied.

"As you wish," Jared replied calmly, but immediately he got up to place a blanket about Pippa's slender shoulders.

"Thank you," she said politely, through chattering teeth.

Jared lay back on the bed beside her, and the tension between them built until Pippa felt compelled to break the silence.

"Why have you never married, Jared?" she asked. "You're quite old, after all."

Jared put his hands casually behind his head and took a thoughtful breath. "I came fairly close to wedded bliss once," he began lightly. "My mother was intent on my marriage to a young lady who lived next door to our Richmond home."

"Why didn't you?"

"I suppose I would have," he told her slowly. "But it was at that time that my father decided I should return to Europe to stay with Garrett. Thus, my mother's hopes for an engagement were put aside."

"What did you want?" asked Pippa, surprised by his nonchalant attitude toward such a topic.

"I was fairly agreeable to marriage, though I was only eighteen at the time. But as well, the idea of returning to Europe was particularly appealing. I couldn't resist sampling a bit of life."

Pippa frowned as she speculated what this might mean. "Did you meet a lady there?" she asked with restrained dread.

Jared recognized her tone, and grinned. "Several, actually."

"So why didn't you marry one of them?" questioned Pippa in what she hoped appeared an unconcerned fashion.

"Well, the lady who most caught my fancy, as they say, was a countess. Marriage wasn't considered, needless to say."

"Do you mean she was married?" cried Pippa in abject horror.

"Yes. To a count, of course."

"Jared!" gasped Pippa in dismay.

"Oh, for God's sake, Pippa. She was in an arranged marriage to a Frenchman thirty years her senior. He had mistresses all over Europe, so our affair seemed relatively harmless. Most enjoyable, really."

Pippa felt sick, but she forced herself to behave as he did. "She was English, then?"

"She was."

"Why didn't she divorce her husband?" asked Pippa.

"He was one of the wealthiest men in Europe," replied Jared.

"I don't see why that should matter if she loved you," said Pippa earnestly.

Jared shrugged. "I never asked her to marry me."

"What happened to the first girl?" asked Pippa, though suddenly she wished she hadn't asked.

"Christina married a boyhood friend of mine."

"Have you seen her since?" asked Pippa hesitantly.

"Yes. She's a friend of my youngest sister, Kimberlite," he replied. "As well, my mother still holds her dear."

Jared's manner indicated clearly he had no wish to discuss the subject further. He smiled when he saw Pippa's furrowed brow and the tight frown upon her rounded lips.

"Now tell me, Miss Reid, you are of marriageable age. How have you escaped taking a husband?"

Pippa knew Jared was deliberately changing the subject, but that suited her well enough. She didn't want to hear about Jared's romances, and she hated the jealousy that twisted through her. Her small mouth curved upward thoughtfully and she hesitated a time before answering.

"We in the North don't generally marry as young as is done here," she began. "Nor have we elevated courting to such a fine art as have you."

"Then how do you find a husband? Surely your marriages aren't arranged."

"Of course not!" Pippa replied indignantly. "But perhaps our marriages don't come about in such a fanciful way as yours."

"Then where do your young lovers meet?" Jared asked with amused interest.

"At readings and lectures, concerts and such," she answered carefully. "Or at church, I suppose."

"How scintillating!" remarked Jared. Pippa looked at him reproachfully.

"It's the best way to find someone with a like mind," she began sincerely.

"Which is infinitely important in love," interrupted Jared, his lips curved in an amused smile.

"It is, it is!" insisted Pippa.

"So you would meet your future husband at a meeting of abolitionists, or at a lecture of your favorite Transcendentalist?" questioned Jared with growing mirth. "No doubt you'd catch the eye of a young Emerson, Pippa. That is, if he could see you through the thickness of his spectacles. But such a man might prefer a plain wife, so that she wouldn't distract him from his studies, my dear. Where would your inherent passion be then?"

Pippa fumed. "You would never understand the passion of intellect, Jared," she said through clenched teeth.

"Perhaps not," agreed Jared, when he had contained his mirth.

As he spoke, Jared sat up from the bed and reached out his hand to Pippa. Clearly, he expected her to come to him. As if she wasn't his prisoner, but his lover. As if they were to stay forever in this tiny, magical house, and he wasn't in fact bearing her to Richmond and the end of her life.

Pippa couldn't resist the magnetic force of his attraction, and slowly she lifted her hand and gave it to him. His strong fingers were warm on hers as he drew her near, and Pippa's heart throbbed relentlessly in her breast.

"But it isn't 'passion of the intellect' that bonds us, is it, little witch?" he asked in a voice low and husky, irresistible as he bent to kiss her.

His lips brushed hers, but then he drew back to gaze into her eyes. Jared saw clearly her pain and confusion. He knew he had hurt her, perhaps even more than she had hurt him. Yet his heart was on fire as he looked at her, his blood raced at the softness of her kiss. *You own me,* he thought with resignation. As he gazed into Pippa's tilted green eyes, Jared knew her own passion was unabated by their differences.

The damp cloth of her dress clung against her small, rounded breasts, and Jared's desire coursed into every angle of his body. Pippa's rounded mouth was opened slightly, her eyes wide with confusion and desire. Jared knew he had never wanted a woman so powerfully in his life.

"I need you so, Pippa," he murmured. "But I cannot bridge the distance you've put between us." Pippa's eyes squeezed shut as he spoke, yet all the same, her heart spoke clearly.

"I'd rather be in hell with you, Jared," she began quietly, "than in heaven without you."

With a gentleness that pierced Pippa's aching heart, Jared took her face in his hands and kissed her. His lips merely grazed hers at first, but when he felt her soft gasp, he ventured further. Pippa's hands went to the firm expanse of Jared's well-muscled rib cage. As she pressed closer against him, she felt the fine cloth of his white shirt against her breasts. Pippa sighed, and Jared's hands left her face to travel down her back.

"Pippa, you are unimaginably sweet," he said, as she closed her eyes. But Jared lifted her chin, entreating her to meet his gaze.

"Look at me, Pippa," he commanded gently, and Pippa opened her eyes with hesitant fear. "I promised you once that I would never hurt you. I failed of that promise, and I'm sorry," he continued with effort. Hot tears stung Pippa's eyes as they fell to her cheek.

"I would give you anything, Jared," she whispered. "But there's no need to ask my forgiveness when you were the one deceived."

Pippa touched Jared's mouth, and she sighed sorrowfully. "You first came to my aunt's house to find a spy, didn't you?"

"I did," Jared replied.

"Then why didn't you accuse me then?"

A self-mocking smile crossed Jared's sensual face, and he stroked her soft cheek before answering. "I didn't accuse you, angel, because it was impossible to imagine you as my enemy."

"I didn't wish to deceive you," whispered Pippa. "I know I shouldn't have danced with you, nor been your friend, nor ever gone to you as your lover. I knew that then, but I couldn't help it, Jared."

"You're saying you shouldn't have let me love you, Pippa," replied Jared. "Yet in this you had no choice, for I loved you from the first moment I saw you. Maybe I didn't ask your loyalties because in my heart I already knew."

Pippa met Jared's eyes in amazement as she considered this. "Had you asked, could I have lied? I think not, but I feared to lose your affection if you learned of my true heart. If I couldn't have you forever, it seemed better to love you as I could rather than not at all."

Pippa knew that this had never changed, and she knew what she wanted to give him. She smiled, her green eyes sparkling like an enchantress's. "But now I'm your captive, my friend, and yours to do with as you please," she suggested meaningfully.

Jared drew her close and kissed her forehead. "No, my little Pippa, I am the prisoner. Yet the future is uncertain," he added raggedly. "What can I give you when the distance between us is so wide?"

But Pippa touched his face, her fingers grazing the new growth of his beard, and she kissed his mouth tenderly.

"Then give me now," she whispered, and it was all Jared needed to hear.

He returned her kiss with a surge of passion, and he knew it was the passion of a long-fought surrender. With well-skilled hands Jared undressed Pippa, and though she was trembling, she made no effort at resistance. Any such gesture would be false. She watched him spellbound as he stripped off his own clothes. A tingling heat washed across her skin as her eyes met the sight of his magnificent arousal.

They lay back together on the bed, and Jared's eyes were warm with desire as he looked at her. The curve of her rounded breasts beckoned beyond resistance and the soft, pink glow of her skin demanded his touch. He ran his hand down her slender arm, then ran a finger along the inviting swell of her breast.

With infinite gentleness, he lightly brushed his palm across the firm mound. Pippa gasped as he encircled her fullness, tighter and tighter spirals closing inward until his finger grazed the taut peaks at the proud summit.

"Jared," she whispered in a trembling voice, but Jared chuckled as she arched beneath the skill of his touch.

A soft moan came from low in her throat when the moistness of his lips and tongue replaced the caressing fingers. Back and forth across the swollen buds, Jared ran his tongue, tasting her sweetness even as he was driven mad by the urgency of her response.

As he teased her beyond the control of her ravaged senses,

his hands slid along her taut stomach and down the length of her long thigh, back to the very center of the raging storm of her desire. Jared's fingers met the dampened invitation of her flesh, and he groaned when Pippa wiggled against his touch.

"You're the most unbearable torture, little angel," he murmured as she turned her face to receive his kiss.

"Yes, my love, but it is sweet torment," she replied in a gravelly voice.

Jared's lips met hers, light and teasing, but as he kissed her, his fingers stroked the tingling flesh at the apex of her thighs. His touch centered around the tiny bud crowning her glorious warmth, and he teased her until Pippa was senseless with her desire. Jared delved into her moistened depths, his searching fingers meeting there the fine enclosure of her innocence. As Pippa writhed beneath his skill, Jared sought to widen the primal entrance, but Pippa was unaware of any pain. She was lost on surging waves of pleasure.

Need pulsated through her body, and Pippa called to Jared as if from a great distance. "Jared, please," she murmured.

"You must," she moaned, her voice fading as a rise of hot pleasure spilled into her, centering with abandon about the site of Jared's touch.

Jared chuckled at the sound of her small voice. "Yes, I must," he replied with pleasure. "I must indeed."

Jared rose above her, and with an instinctive understanding of what would now occur, Pippa pressed her hips against his. As she did, she felt the heat of his turgid staff between her legs and she gasped at the knowledge of what she desperately craved.

Jared understood, and as he felt her soft, moist warmth welcome his maleness inward, he moved against her. Pippa arched as she clasped her arms about his back, and he could no longer resist. Mad with desire, Jared drove himself within her, and Pippa gasped as she felt the power of his entrance. The brief tear of her virgin flesh was replaced instantly by a sudden heat of pleasure so strong she arched again to contain it.

"Oh, Pippa, you are heaven," he groaned as he felt her passionate heat enveloping him, urging him to a completion he couldn't begin to avoid.

"You are mine, angel," he murmured as he began to move within her.

With the urgency of Pippa's response, Jared thrust harder and deeper until he was mindless to anything but their mutual pleasure. Tentatively at first, then with the shock of rising ecstasy, Pippa moved against Jared, her hips rising to meet his ever more penetrating thrusts, withdrawing to rise again.

Closer and closer, they brought each other to the ultimate crest of their need and desire. Jared felt Pippa tense beneath him, her warm breath coming rapid and shallow as he surged within her. As he plunged deep into her, Pippa felt the spirals of her pleasure tighten and soar, rising to shatter suddenly into wild, surging stabs of ecstasy that shook her very soul heavenward.

Jared buried himself deep within her and at last gave himself over to the power of his own release. Pippa clung to him as they crashed together against a heavenly shore neither had ever approached before.

They lay still in each other's arms, ragged breath intermingling as their hearts together slowed the thunderous pace. Jared kissed Pippa's forehead tenderly as she settled against his shoulder.

"Tell me this wasn't preferable to intellectual passion,"

he teased. Pippa wrapped her arm tightly across his chest and squeezed him lovingly.

"I suppose there wouldn't be much comparison," she agreed sleepily.

Jared chuckled and kissed her soft hair. As he held her, feeling the gentle pounding of her slowing heartbeat, Jared was stunned to see that Pippa had already fallen asleep. No words had been spoken about her fate in Richmond, no questions as to how this night might change that fate.

But Jared Knox knew that what Pippa was expecting and what he had planned were two different things entirely. He sighed as he held her, remembering the force of his anger when he learned she had only loved him to save herself.

Tell Mrs. Reid that her niece and I have eloped, he had said to Emmaline when they left. As he recalled his words, Jared knew his intention had never really changed.

"Wake up, angel."

Jared's voice came low and soft in Pippa's ears, and as she stirred in his arms, she brushed against the hardened evidence of his arousal. Pippa murmured sensually and pressed closer to him in response. Jared found her lips, their taste all the sweeter for what they had already shared. Pippa felt the magnificent heat of his strong body against hers, enveloping her, and she slipped a long leg over his to draw him closer to the heart of her newly awakened need.

"You learn quickly, my love," he breathed hoarsely against her neck. Pippa's soft moan when his hardened length brushed against her moist heat brought his words to a close.

Pippa clasped the hard muscles of his back, and cried out with delirious pleasure when Jared thrust deeply inside her.

Her body arched and twisted beneath his, striving for completion. They kissed as their bodies joined again in the mystical dance, and Pippa allowed her eyes to meet Jared's as he watched her face. This was more intimate than anything they had yet shared. Jared was spellbound by the wild, voluptuous beauty now revealed in Pippa's delicate face as she was transformed by her pleasure.

Their eyes locked, and they became as two bright colors melding into a radiant white. They shattered together into tiny shards of the light they had created. But when Jared withdrew from her, Pippa was aghast to think she could have been so brazen.

"Oh, how could I?" she murmured, hot embarrassment flooding to her cheeks as her passion cooled and the full force of her rising indecency took hold of her.

Jared guessed the direction of her thoughts. "You aren't regretting this, are you, angel?"

"I seem to have no . . . self-control where you are concerned," she whispered, but she dared not look at him.

"Oh, Philippa," he said, and he took her face in his hands, forcing her to meet his eyes.

"You and I are passionately connected. How could we resist, despite everything that lies between us, when such a fire burns? Dear girl, I've wanted you since I first beheld your beguiling form across that mist-shrouded ravine. And, God help me, I want you now."

Pippa's eyes widened, glimmering in the dim flickering lamplight, but Jared didn't allow her the opportunity to question him about his declaration. His eyes holding hers, Jared entered her slowly, and with rising force, he began to move inside her.

A fiery wash of desire again flooded Pippa's senses. Together, they soared to the lofty heights of passion, driving

each other to a blissful ecstasy. Long after they had fallen
asleep wrapped in each other's arms, the blue-white stars
glittered above the little house in the wood.

"Pippa! Wake up, quickly!"

Pippa startled at the sudden hiss of Jared's voice, but she
opened her bleary eyes and struggled to sit up. Jared had
already risen. In the early morning light, she could see
something was agitating him greatly.

"What's the matter?" she asked groggily.

"Riders, in the field. Soldiers," he explained hastily. "I
saw them when I went out to find Boreas. I'm afraid they
found him first. Get dressed."

Pippa did as Jared asked, but she had no idea what to
expect from him next. Just as Pippa had buttoned the bodice
of her worn dress, she heard the sounds of men outside the
little house.

Jared drew out a revolver. "Pippa, you must hide behind
the bed," he ordered hoarsely, but Pippa shook her head,
adamantly refusing.

"Do it! Now!" he commanded, but Pippa didn't move.

"I can't leave you," she insisted, but Jared was furious.

"Damn you, girl, do as I say!"

Pippa reluctantly complied, and huddled behind the bed
as he ordered. Hot tears welled in her eyes. She had no time
to consider how she might save him. The door was kicked
open and a tall, lanky rebel stepped inside, weapon bared.
Pippa's heart stopped, but to Pippa's astonishment, the two
men embraced.

"Major Knox! I wondered if I'd find you here, sir," said
the rebel. "Saw your horse, we did, but you was nowhere

about. Wondered if them Yanks got ahold of you, but I'm as pleased as anything to see you in one piece."

Hesitantly Pippa peeked out from behind the bed, eyes wide with wonder as she looked at the bearded man.

"It's all right, boys," called the rebel, and three other men entered the tiny room.

"Billy here remembered you had this place. We thought we'd check it out. Right good that we did, too . . ."

As the man spoke, his eyes were caught by Pippa's crouched form, and his grin broadened when he saw her small, lovely face peering nervously between himself and Jared.

"I might have known you'd not be alone," he laughed loudly. Considering the night's activities, Pippa blushed furiously.

Jared grinned and glanced toward Pippa. "You need have no fear, Miss Reid," he told her. "We're safe. This is John Wilkeson, one of Mosby's famed Raiders," he continued, and John beamed with pride.

Pippa stood and looked shyly at the man. "I'm pleased to meet you, sir," she said. When John Wilkeson heard her voice, his mouth dropped and he looked in amazement at Jared.

"Well, now, Major. Looks to me like you've been doing some raiding on your own. Bringing Yankee girls over the border! Nope, you can't keep a rebel down. She's right pretty though," he said with a critical eye cast Pippa's way.

"Maybe we've been looking in the wrong places," he added with a grin.

"This is Miss Philippa Reid," said Jared, and after a pause, he added, "my fiancée."

Both Pippa and the rebel looked at Jared in surprise, but

Wilkeson bowed to Pippa and smiled. "A lovelier wife you couldn't have found anywhere, sir, North or South."

"Wilkeson, you'd better tell him now," broke in a younger rebel who stood holding open the small door.

"Oh, yes. Well, as a matter of fact, we was on the lookout for you. Heard you'd already left Carltons' estate."

"Why? What's going on?" asked Jared.

"Yankees swarming all over the place," John Wilkeson explained with disgust.

"Word has it they're fixing to cross the Rapidan. Looks like any day now. That fellow, Grant, seems dead set on a meeting. Not that it'll do him any more good than it has the rest, but there you have it. Lee's marching out to take on the new fellow, and he wants every man ready"

Jared nodded, his eyes burning with a fire Pippa couldn't begin to understand. "I will come."

"I thought you were taking me to Richmond!" exclaimed Pippa.

John Wilkeson smiled indulgently. "Isn't that like a woman? Wanting that wedding ring right now, eh, little miss?" he asked pleasantly, but Pippa frowned at his assumption.

Jared turned to Pippa. "That will have to wait, Philippa," he said patiently. "I must go where I'm needed most."

Pippa was aghast. "What are you going to do with me?"

"Take you with me, of course," Jared replied calmly. "What else?"

Five

The Army of Northern Virginia was camped around Orange Court House. As Jared rode through its midst, men nodded, greeting the young officer in a friendly manner. Pippa received no more than polite glances. She guessed that the sight of a bare-legged woman riding behind Jared garnered great speculation when they moved onward.

Jared rode to a randomly assorted group of tents and was met by a small officer. The boy's sleeves were rolled up casually, and Pippa noticed a toothbrush propped through the buttonhole of his dusty jacket. He was younger than she, and Pippa wondered how he attained such a high ranking.

Jared stopped, and the captain addressed Jared easily, without the abrupt formality expected in the North. "Good to see you back, Major," he said cheerfully. Clearly his voice was still in the process of deepening.

The captain gave an individualistic interpretation of a salute, which Jared returned with a similar lack of concern. "How are you, Nicks?" asked Jared casually. "You were out of sorts when I left, as I recall."

"Better, sir. Can't complain," replied Nicks. "Just got some new socks from my ma," he added conversationally, and Jared nodded. "Forgot my drawers, though. The pair

I've got's full of holes, sorry to say. Damn near rotting off my body." Nicks sighed and shook his head. "Don't get much chance for washing," he added regretfully.

"That's unfortunate," agreed Jared as Pippa listened to the boy nonchalantly discussing his innermost wardrobe with his commander. "Where's the colonel?"

"You're to report directly to the general," said Nicks as he reached out to pat Boreas's nose.

"Why?" asked Jared. "Where's the colonel?"

"Dead, sir," replied Nicks unemotionally. "Hit by a damned sharpshooter day before yesterday."

"He's not been replaced?" asked Jared.

"Not yet, sir."

"Aren't you his commander?" asked Pippa as Jared urged the horse forward.

"You're on the rebel side now, my dear," replied Jared. "We do things differently here. When we give an order, we'd better have a damned good explanation for it, and we'd better not forget to ask about a soldier's family first."

Pippa wasn't certain whether to believe him or not. Surely the Confederate Army hadn't run circles around the Yankees with such a casual attitude.

They rode to a tent only slightly more spacious than those Pippa had already observed. Only the presence of a number of aides indicated the importance of the tent's occupant. Jared dismounted and helped Pippa down, though as had been the case since they left the little cabin, he seemed distracted and paid her very little attention. A valet took Boreas, and Jared went into the tent.

Pippa's feet were carefully bound, her riding boots unlaced and loose, and not knowing where else to go, she

gingerly followed Jared. Inside, she saw a surprisingly ordered room, well-fitted and very neat. Behind a large desk
sat a handsome general with a dark mustache. The general
rose as Jared entered, and the two men saluted each other
formally. The general dismissed his aides, who brushed past
Pippa, each doffing their caps respectfully, but otherwise
she was ignored.

"Major Knox," began the general. Pippa looked up at the
sound of his voice, for it bore the same trace of English
inflection as did Jared's. "You've heard that your colonel
was killed?"

"Yes, General. Captain Nicks told me when I arrived."

"I want the men to choose his replacement," the general
went on, and Pippa listened intently. She knew the rebels
chose their own officers, at least those of lower ranks, but
she hadn't heard this applied to colonels.

"Major Hallett has arranged the vote for this afternoon,"
continued the general, pausing to check his pocket watch.
"In approximately forty minutes. You will be there, of
course."

"Yes, sir," replied Jared.

This matter handled, the general looked to Pippa. A faint
blush touched her cheeks beneath the penetrating gaze of
his dark eyes. She wished acutely that she had remained
outside, and she fidgeted, backing toward the door. A tiny
smile appeared on the general's lips as he watched her, and
shaken by his scrutiny, Pippa darted from the tent. The general looked back to Jared, his expression a half-amused in-
quisition.

"Miss Philippa Reid," said Jared, now also smiling.

"Miss? I had heard otherwise. So that's the little Yankee
girl?" he asked with amusement, but then his face darkened.

"Grant will cross the Rapidan tomorrow, possibly tonight,

Major. He wishes to fight us in the open, where his greater numbers may serve his own ends. But Lee has our ends in mind, and so we'll meet him beyond its banks, on our own terms."

"Yes, sir, that seems wise," concurred Jared.

The general paused, and nodded briefly towards the opening through which Pippa had fled. "See to it, Major," said the older man, and though his words were cryptic, Jared understood.

"I will, General."

The commander saluted, then returned to his desk. Jared went out to find Pippa. She wasn't where he had expected, but an aide pointed to a path leading up one of the surrounding hilltops. Jared followed in the direction Pippa had taken. The path wound sharply uphill, and on an offshoot, he saw Pippa's figure as she stood gazing over the vast landscape.

Jared came up behind her, and he saw what held her attention. Here was the lowest observation position, though higher in the mountain far more panoramic views were provided. To the north, across the Rapidan River, were the white tents of the Army of the Potomac, clear in the afternoon sun. Pippa sighed and turned, but startled when she saw Jared standing close behind her.

"As always, to the north," he said quietly, but Pippa looked back to the vast city in the distance.

"There are so many," she murmured. She had considered Lee's army vast when first entering the rebel campsite.

"There are indeed," Jared agreed. "Always, there are more. Always replacements."

Pippa didn't reply. Faced with the vastness of the war's fighting force, she felt small and helpless. Yet despite the ravaging Virginia endured, spring brought great beauty. White dogwood blossoms gleamed against the rich green background, and the air, apart from the camp, was fragrant and sweet.

"Who was that man?" asked Pippa.

"Do you mean the general?" replied Jared, bemused by Pippa's mood.

"Yes. He's . . . imposing, isn't he? I wish I hadn't followed you in there."

"Then he would request an audience with you. And, yes, he can be imposing." Jared paused, and his smile was faintly sad. "That was General Knox, as a matter of fact," he told her, but seeing Pippa's look of surprise, his smile grew. "Yes. My father."

"Your father!" gasped Pippa. "You didn't address each other as father and son," she added before thinking better of her comment.

"Not in a military setting," replied Jared. "Of course not."

Pippa was bewildered by the rebel army. Captain Nicks discussed his missing undergarments with his commander, but Jared spoke to his father in tones of regal formality. Jared guessed the nature of Pippa's confusion, but his relationship with his father was not something easily explained.

"Now we must attend to your future," Jared told her as he took her hand. Though Pippa gazed at him suspiciously, his only explanation was a slight smile.

Jared led Pippa to the far end of his regiment, and held the door of a small tent open. Seeing a cross by the door, she stopped and looked at him aghast.

"You're not going to put me in a convent, are you?" she asked in horror.

Jared grimaced, his face lit with a teasing smile. "After our night's activities, I hardly think that would be appropriate," he whispered close to her ear. Pippa's face flushed crimson.

A short, pudgy man greeted them inside, and Pippa gazed in wonder as he hurried forward to take her hand. "Major Knox!" he said in a buoyant, lively voice, much belying his rounded shape.

"How good to see you! This is such a happy occasion," he continued breathlessly. "Your father has alerted me to your needs, and all is nearly ready. If you wouldn't mind waiting a moment, there's just one more thing."

The little fat man darted from the tent. Pippa turned to Jared, who to her mind was smiling somewhat guiltily. "What on earth is going on, Jared?" she asked. "What was that little man talking about?"

Jared took her hands in his, and for the briefest moment, Pippa imagined he was shy. "Perhaps I should have warned you, Philippa," he began. "But I was frankly afraid you wouldn't come, and there isn't time for that."

Pippa's brow furrowed at the inadequacy of his response, so Jared rather reluctantly went on. "We're here for a wedding."

"Really? Whose?"

"Ours, of course."

Pippa gasped, her eyes wide with amazement. Her lips parted to speak, but Jared stopped her. "No, Pippa, you must listen. Tomorrow, or even tonight, I'll go to fight. I may not return. Hush," he said when she again made an effort to speak.

"After our . . . intimacy, you might well bear my child. I can't leave you, or our child, unprotected by my name, at the least. I must know you'll be cared for, and my name will guarantee that."

Pippa stared blankly at Jared. Not once did he mention

love, nor his own desire to marry her. That was what she wanted to hear. His arguments were logical, they were honorable, and she was hardly in a position to refuse, even if she had the courage. Their night together seemed like a dream, though every time their eyes met, her heart jumped, and her face flushed with the memory. Now Jared was logically telling her that passion must lead to marriage lest she bear his child in disgrace.

Pippa wasn't afforded an opportunity to answer him, for the little minister returned. With him came two middle-aged women to serve as witnesses. Both were smiling, pleasant-faced, and oblivious to Pippa's distress.

"Dear girl," began the minister. "What a lovely child you are! Oh, that this day should be unmarred by these evil times! But in this hour, let nothing intrude on your happiness."

Pippa said nothing, and the minister proceeded to recite the sparsest of marital vows for Jared and Pippa to repeat. Pippa spoke numbly, her voice small in comparison to Jared's clear, deep tones. She heard herself say, "I do," and she knew he had given her himself as well.

"Have you a ring?" asked the minister doubtfully, but Jared promptly drew forth a gold band and slipped it on Pippa's finger. He gently kissed her, and then Pippa was warmly embraced by the minister and the two women.

Jared led her from the tent, but Pippa heard one of the women speak to the minister. "A pretty girl, isn't she? But I could've sworn she sounded like a Yankee!"

As they emerged from the tent, Pippa began to giggle. Jared's brow furrowed in concern as he glanced at his new wife, but his disconcertment only served to fire Pippa's peculiar amusement. Tears started in her eyes, and though she took great breaths of air to calm herself, her wild giggling refused to cease.

Jared sat her down on the edge of an artillery wagon, but her reaction to their wedding wasn't at all what he expected. Pippa bit her lip, but when Jared asked in a hushed voice, "Are you all right, dear?" she burst forth with renewed laughter.

"Perfectly fine, thank you," she managed to utter before new convulsions of laughter overtook her. "It's nothing, really," she gasped, but it was long before she was able to contain herself.

Jared waited beside her, not certain what had provoked such an odd reaction. But at least Pippa was not in tears, and that was a relief. Ever since they had left his cabin, Jared had fought the need to stare at her, to study her face, to relive the night they had spent together.

It wasn't the wedding he had imagined when he first knew he loved Philippa Reid, but then, Pippa wasn't quite the woman he had imagined either. As Pippa regained her shattered composure, Jared wondered how much there was to learn of his wife, and then he wondered if he'd ever get the chance.

"Now what?" she asked, green eyes still shining with the force of her outburst, but Jared was content to let the moment pass.

"It's time I learn who our new colonel will be."

"Oh," replied Pippa, as he helped her to her feet. "Will the old one be hard to replace?"

Jared hesitated, not liking to speak ill of his former commander. "Well, I hope this time our colonel will be a man with cooler wits than was our last."

"Didn't you like him?" pressed Pippa as they walked along.

"As a gentleman, he excelled," replied Jared evasively "As a leader, he was . . . less than resolute."

Pippa followed Jared to a circle of mulling soldiers. The men were talking and laughing casually among themselves, a far cry from the ordered discipline of New England regiments. Yet though Pippa had seen nothing firsthand of battle, she guessed these men were well-seasoned and brave. There was a certain confidence exuded from the group as a whole that she suspected was lacking in the battered Army of the Potomac.

Rather than taking an ordered vote, the men simply discussed their choice for a new colonel. Having come to a quick, unanimous decision, they waited only for the brief formality of a show of hands before presenting their choice.

General Knox came from his tent to watch the proceedings, and Pippa stood beside Jared as they waited. Jared sat on the rail of a fence, and another major came to join him. He had a full, red beard, and Jared introduced him as Major Hallett.

"I don't envy the man they put up," remarked the major casually.

"No," agreed Jared with a nod. "I just hope they choose someone we can follow."

"Someone with battle sense," added Major Hallett.

The presiding captain struggled to regain control of the proceedings. On the whole, he was ignored by the enlisted men, who placed less value on his input than did the captain himself.

"Have you made your decision, gentlemen?" he shouted, striving to be heard above the din. Beside Pippa, Jared laughed.

"We have, sir," replied an old sergeant.

"Who then will lead you, Sergeant?" asked the captain

importantly. The major beside Jared drew an irritated breath. "Get on with it, Davie," he murmured. "I've work to do."

The sergeant looked past the captain, and gestured in the direction of those by the fence. Major Hallett looked toward Jared, whose own face was fairly blank.

"Knox," called the sergeant, and for a moment, Jared didn't move. Seeing this, the sergeant repeated himself, louder. "Jared Knox will be our colonel."

The captain looked brightly to Jared, and Major Hallett grabbed Jared's hand and shook it vigorously. "Well, well, Colonel," he said. "A wife and a regiment in one afternoon! Let me be the first to congratulate you!"

Jared nodded, said a subdued, "thank you," and jumped down from the fence. Pippa felt a swell of pride when he walked over to receive his new command from his father. Yet he had never seemed more distant from her.

Standing among the men he now commanded, Pippa realized as if for the first time how very tall he was. His uniform was unbuttoned and dusty, yet Jared appeared commanding and stronger than she had ever seen him. She knew he didn't desire this command, but now that it was thrust upon him, he accepted it resolutely. Every face that turned toward him bore the conviction he would lead them skillfully.

The soldiers were dismissed to do their various tasks, and Jared returned to Pippa. Their eyes met, but a familiar voice called and both turned to see Edward Carlton's beaming face as he approached them.

"Congratulations, Colonel!" he said, as he shook Jared's hand. "I'm glad I made it in time to see you take command."

"Edward! What are you doing here?" asked Jared, and Pippa was certain he wasn't pleased with Edward's presence.

"Transferred from Richmond," replied Edward. "Into your father's command. It's Major Carlton now, and I await your orders," he continued cheerfully, but as he spoke his eyes went to Pippa.

"Well, well! I heard you'd brought your wife," he continued happily. Pippa wondered how on earth all these people knew about a marriage that had taken place less than a half hour previously.

"But wouldn't she be better off in Richmond with your mother, Jared?" Edward asked with a knowing smile.

"This was unavoidable," explained Jared.

"No doubt," laughed Edward. He took Pippa's hand and kissed it. "I had a feeling about you two," he told her. "I, too, am in need of your good wishes."

"Why is that, Edward?" asked Pippa.

"I've asked Miss Fanny Woods to be my wife, and she has graciously accepted."

"That's wonderful!" Fanny was a gentle person, and their marriage seemed destined for happiness. Pippa's own fate was less certain.

But Jared seemed less pleased with Edward's announcement. "In that case, Edward, do you think it wise to transfer from Richmond? Fanny could accompany you there," he began, but Edward stopped him.

"No, Jared. I've dallied in Richmond long enough. I want to be where the fighting is. That will be here, if what I hear is true."

"But you'll be needed in Richmond if it's overrun," argued Jared.

"That day won't come if we hold the Yanks here. Another battle like Chancellorsville, and they'll retreat. If old Abe is ousted next fall, the war will be over. I want to be a part of our victory, not hiding out in Richmond. This Grant doesn't want cities. Said so himself. He wants Lee's army."

Jared frowned, but his argument was lost. "Then I'm

proud to have you, Edward," he said, but Pippa was certain he was sorry that Edward had left his former post.

Edward left to join the other officers, and Jared turned to Pippa with a sigh.

"What's the matter, Jared?" she asked. "Don't you want Edward here?"

"It's done," he replied with resignation. "But it might have been better if he had remained where he was."

"Why?"

"Edward is . . . not cut out for fighting. Especially not where this battle is likely to lead us."

"Where is that?" asked Pippa.

Jared pointed north and west, and Pippa saw the gray-green haze of a thick forest. "We'll meet them there," he speculated. "In the Wilderness, where the numbers of our respective armies matter less. Many Southerners have lived in such woods. Most Yankees know only the streets and buildings of your giant cities."

"You've never been in Maine, have you?" Pippa observed. "Not all Yankees come from New York or Philadelphia or Boston, Jared," she reminded him. Her mind went to her father's friend, Joshua Chamberlain. Pippa doubted he would be troubled by the shadows of trees.

"Be that as it may," Jared went on, "we'll have the advantage, though a slim one at best." As he spoke, Jared took Pippa's hands, and his eyes searched her with a need she couldn't guess. "In another time, my little wife, this week for us might be spent with great festivity. It will be otherwise, I'm afraid."

But the cloud of foreboding left Jared's fair face. "Tonight, at least, we'll dine on rations reserved for the few. My father has requested our presence at dinner tonight."

Pippa was far from relieved. "Does he know we're married?" she asked fearfully. Jared's father could hardly be expected to welcome a Yankee daughter-in-law, especially not one arrested for spying.

"What will he do when he learns of my . . . my guilt?" she asked in a hushed voice.

Jared took a deep breath. "Webster and his men were killed when Mallory was freed," he told her. "Thus, your secret is with me alone, and as your husband, I'm unlikely to turn you in. Does that reassure you?"

"You're not going to put me in prison?"

"Of course not. Pippa, I was going to ask you to marry me when Webster interrupted us. Things may not be the same between us," he admitted, and Pippa's eyes cast downward to her sore feet, "but no one need suspect that. Emmaline will tell your aunt we've eloped, and my mother will guess as much. Even Edward has heard, apparently. Let us leave it that way, shall we?"

Pippa nodded, but her eyes welled with tears. An irresistible passion had bound them together, but not once had he told her he wanted her.

"What would you have said, Philippa?" Jared asked her quietly. "Had I asked you to run away with me, would you have come?"

Pippa swallowed hard, but she had no idea how to answer. "I don't know," she whispered. "I hadn't expected you to ask."

"No, I can see that," replied Jared, and Pippa saw the distance plainly written between them. How could it be, she thought miserably, when they had surrendered everything in each others' arms?

"I'm not what you thought I was, I know," she said with effort. "But I didn't mean to hurt you. Had I been stronger,

I wouldn't have seen you after our first meeting. I tried, Jared, I did."

"But I wouldn't let you alone," he finished for her. "Had I been less . . . smitten, I might have seen your true heart, but I was blind."

Pippa said no more. Her throat was constricted with misery, but despite what Jared believed, Pippa knew her heart no longer rested with the North. It was as divided as her country.

Waiting in the colonel's tent was a small tub of steaming water. Draped across the bed was a dress of light green cotton. "Virginians think of everything," said Jared.

Pippa's eyes gleamed as she gazed at the tub. At least she wouldn't have to dine with her new father-in-law unwashed and in a dirty dress.

"After you, my lady," said Jared. Though a blush rose in Pippa's cheeks, she allowed him to unbutton her dress.

"I shouldn't have left my corset," she said ruefully.

"You don't need one, Pippa," Jared replied.

His eyes were glinting as Pippa's dress slid to the floor, but she flushed crimson and quickly stepped into the little tub. The water covered very little, and she wondered painfully if Jared intended to stand there watching the entire procedure.

Sensing her discomfort at his presence, Jared offered her a respite. "Well, my dear, I think I'll allow you to bathe in privacy." His grin widened, but he moved to the doorway. "Because if I stay, it's very likely that you and I will be late for dinner. That wouldn't please the general at all."

Pippa bathed in private, and then she tried on the dress loaned to her by the unknown benefactor. It fit perfectly, well-shaped to her slender form even without a corset. It was hardly suited to an evening with the general, but in the midst of an army camp, it would have to do.

Jared returned, and Pippa averted her eyes when he stripped off his uniform and began to bathe as well. Seeing her diffidence, Jared grinned. "I'd think as my wife, you might be inclined to make yourself useful at such a moment."

"What do you want me to do?" asked Pippa in a rather shrill voice.

"Wash my back, if you please," he said casually. "I would naturally have done the same for you, but I think the . . . temptation of such a moment might have led me astray."

Pippa bit her lip, but went to Jared and knelt beside the tub. She soaped his broad, smooth back, running her hands along the hard muscles with care. Jared sighed, but as Pippa continued, her heart pounded more and more fiercely, and a growing heat flushed throughout her body.

Naked, Jared was a glorious sight, and though she knew the pleasures of his lovemaking now intimately, Pippa had never studied him in the light of day. Try as she might, Pippa couldn't restrain her gaze from traveling the length of his lean body. Her eyes settled on that mysterious part of him that evidenced clearly the extent of his desire, but Jared seemed oblivious to his obviously aroused condition. Pippa's hands slowed their task, and she felt enchanted by the power of his masculine allure.

Seeing this, Jared chuckled with satisfaction, but rather than giving in to a hurried intimacy, he got out of the tub and toweled himself off. "I would ask you to do my front as well," he teased, "but it appears you've done enough already."

Pippa got up quickly, and occupied herself by arranging her hair while Jared dressed, but the curious flash of heat refused to abate. Memories of their passionate night together danced across her mind. When she saw Jared studying her face, Pippa was certain he knew what she was thinking.

Jared led Pippa to his father's quarters, but Pippa stopped him before they went in. "Jared! What will he think when he learns we've known each other barely a week?" she agonized. Considering this further, Pippa groaned. "No lady would have done what I . . ."

"True," agreed Jared none too helpfully. "Nor would a fine gentleman have taken advantage of your wilder nature as did I. That makes us well-matched."

Pippa clasped her hand to her forehead. "I should have been more . . . restrained," she moaned, but Jared laughed.

"Now, at the entrance to the lion's den, you consider this. I don't recall the thought troubling you before this point."

"You aren't being particularly helpful, Jared," Pippa chastised miserably.

"Well, if it's our short acquaintanceship that worries you—because my father needn't learn where your pagan tendencies have borne us—then consider this—you and I have, in fact, known each other for two years. That seems respectable enough to me."

Pippa frowned. "Two years? One could hardly call that a courtship, Jared."

"Well, we met, we spoke," Jared reasoned thoughtfully. "I must admit to a certain fascination with your image. You remembered my voice, at least. That should count for something."

To Pippa, this seemed a far stretch of logic. But standing outside the tent of the formidable General Knox, it would have to serve.

"Very well," she agreed. "Then I've known you for two years."

They continued toward the tent, but again Pippa stopped Jared. "You were fascinated with me?"

Jared took her arm and moved her forcefully to the entrance. "I was, and am. Later tonight I'll show you the results of that fascination."

Pippa gasped and, to her acute mortification, her cheeks were hot and flushed when she entered the tent to greet the general. David Knox was standing by his desk, and a small table had been elaborately set for dinner. The pleasant smells of roast chicken met her awareness instantly and drove away her embarrassment.

The general went to Pippa without addressing his son, and surveyed her carefully. "I've waited for some years for my son to choose a wife," he said slowly. "It gives me great pleasure to see he has chosen so well. I may yet see grandchildren that bear my name."

Pippa had no idea what to say to this, but shyness in a lady was fortunately acceptable, and taken now as proof of her delicacy.

"I'm pleased to meet you, General," she said in a tiny voice. The general clasped her hands and kissed her cheek.

"You will call me 'Father,' as do my own daughters," he told her, and the gentleness of his voice reminded Pippa of her own father.

She looked up and into his eyes, and despite her fears, found she liked David Knox very much. His eyes were dark brown and green. His expression reminded her of someone, though it was not his son. Both father and son were unusually handsome, but there was in Jared a gentle mockery, of himself, of her, and perhaps of life. In David Knox, there was a hint of battered innocence that Pippa had known somewhere before. But try as she might, she couldn't place the connection she felt.

"You haven't eaten?" questioned General Knox carefully, but seeing the barely concealed gleam in Pippa's gray-green eyes, Jared laughed.

"My wife isn't yet used to army rations," he explained as Pippa squirmed with embarrassment.

"She need not become so accustomed tonight," reassured the general, directing Pippa to her seat.

They were attended by an elegant black servant. The general was unusually polite to the man, and Pippa decided this kind gentleman shouldn't bear needless guilt over his country's practices.

"So you're Charlotte's niece?" questioned the general.

He had graciously allowed Pippa to eat without much interruption as he spoke with his son, but as Pippa's attention began to waver from her meal, the general apparently considered her open for conversation.

Pippa nodded. "Her husband and my father were brothers," she told him.

"William Reid was Scottish, as I recall. Was your father born there also?"

"Actually, my father was much younger than my uncle. He was born in Maine," she said, feeling more and more comfortable in her father-in-law's presence. "But he went to Scotland as a boy, and there he met my mother."

"Then perhaps we share a kinship from afar," suggested the general. "My own great-grandsire was born also in Scotland."

It pleased Pippa to think there might be a connection to

Jared in the depths of their pasts, but glancing at her husband, she saw he looked doubtful.

"My grandfather, Damian Knox, was an Englishman. He came to this country with the British forces during the Revolution," continued David Knox with pleasure. "But here he met my grandmother and found it impossible to leave at the war's end."

Pippa sighed sentimentally at the hint of romance, but Jared wondered if loving one's enemy ran in his family. If so, then perhaps surrender would follow for him as well. Into his mind came the gray-blue calm of northern waters, but the image was fleeting and vanished when his father spoke again.

"You and I share another similarity, both having been born Yankees."

This surprised Pippa more than the Scottish link. "Of course, there's perhaps a wider difference between Maryland and Maine than between Maryland and Virginia."

"I should think so," put in Jared.

"At least, there was before the war," finished the general. "Now, who knows?"

"Why did you come to Virginia?" asked Pippa, not liking the direction of the conversation.

Almost imperceptibly, David Knox's face clouded, and he paused before answering. "I suppose I came to seek my fortune. My older brother had built our father's farm to great splendor, and the lines of horseflesh he bred are still in great demand."

The general sighed as he remembered his brother, then continued. "But I was interested in the future of cotton, which was fortuitous. I met Jared's mother in Richmond and, after we married, was given the management of her father's plantation. I was adequate in this capacity, and my father-in-law made me his heir when he died."

Pippa guessed David Knox was being modest. She had heard of his success from Charlotte Reid, who had often used his example of a gentleman in business to Burke Mallory. This line of conversation seemed to disturb Jared in turn, and he also made an effort to change the subject.

"Have you spoken to General Lee?" he asked, and David Knox turned to him, sufficiently distracted from his reminiscences.

"He took several of his officers to Clark's Mountain earlier in the day. He believes Grant intends to cross at Germanna Ford, possibly tonight. There was an unusual amount of activity across the river today."

"Then we won't attempt to prevent that crossing?" asked Jared, though he guessed the answer.

"No, no indeed," replied the general. "Lee has something different in mind. In a short time, that swaggering Grant will be sent the way of Joe Hooker. With a Yankee election in the wings, that should be that."

Pippa frowned inwardly. Privately, she had great faith in the Union's new commander. She had heard splendid things about his valor and fortitude in the West. At least, she couldn't believe his performance would be as disappointing as the ineffectual Hooker's.

Pippa and Jared departed the general's quarters, and despite Pippa's earlier reservations, it was Jared who was more eager to leave. They walked in silence back to his own tent, and Pippa noticed that the other rebels in camp seemed particularly restrained that night. Nervousness surfaced in

Pippa as she wondered how this might affect Jared and his kind father.

"Did you enjoy yourself?" asked Jared as they stepped into his quarters.

"Yes, very much," said Pippa. "I like your father immensely, Jared."

"I saw that," he replied. "He was obviously taken with you. But then, that shouldn't surprise either of us, should it? You have a way with men."

Pippa ignored Jared's intimation. "Do you think he liked me?" she asked. "I was relieved he didn't ask how we met."

"That was surprising," agreed Jared. "But of course he liked you, Pippa. Even to the extent of likening your Yankee roots. Ha! That's a far stretch for the imagination."

Pippa frowned. "He wouldn't know how deep those roots are in me," she replied defiantly. "But he was born in Maryland, after all. Your cousin is a good Yankee, Jared."

"Make no mistake, Philippa," said Jared firmly. "David Knox is everything you despise in us. A truer rebel there never was."

"I can't believe that!" replied Pippa indignantly. "He seemed terribly polite to his manservant," she began as proof, but Jared stopped her.

"You can be very young at times, Pippa," he said, but after a pause, Pippa saw a smile grow on his face.

"But I'm glad you enjoyed yourself this evening," he added, and his voice was a sweet caress to Pippa's ears. "I'm pleased you won't be distracted tonight for want of food."

"What will happen tomorrow, Jared? Will you go?"

Jared sighed, but he touched her face. "I can't see the future, angel. I'll go when I'm called. You need not worry for yourself, however. You'll be safe with the other wives.

"It may surprise you to find how many accompany their

husbands to the edge of battle. When it's possible, I'll ar-
range your passage to Richmond."

Pippa's heart thudded heavily in her breast, and fear
closed in from all sides. Jared understood this, and he drew
her into his arms, holding her tightly against him. Words
seemed useless now, for nothing she could say would change
his leaving. She had no idea what he wanted to hear from
her. But for the moment she was holding him, and she was
safe in his arms.

Pippa turned her face into his strong neck and pressed a
soft kiss against his throat. Instantly, Jared's pulse quickened, and Pippa felt the sudden tension in the arms that held
her. She longed to wrap herself around him and keep him
protected while it was in her power to do so.

Jared felt Pippa's mood change, felt her rising need like
fire in his own veins, and he bent his head to kiss her. "Tonight is ours, angel," he whispered against her mouth.

Pippa returned Jared's kiss with an urgency that spoke far
more clearly than could words. Pippa felt as one on the edge
of a cliff unfathomably high, and her only hope was to cling
to him while she had the chance. In silent understanding,
they parted to undress, and Pippa lay upon the bed to await
him.

Jared lowered the lamplight and then joined her, their bodies close upon the little cot. "Tonight I'll make you glad
you are my wife," he said huskily, and Pippa shivered with
expectation.

Little more could she imagine than he had done already.
Yet even in the dim light, she could see his eyes glittering
with promise and desire. Pippa was aware of camp noise
outside, yet as Jared brushed her hair from her face, all was
forgotten.

With infinite tenderness, his lips grazed hers, but Jared

didn't further the kiss. Instead, he kissed the fine line of her jaw, then her throat, moving lower across her collarbone until he reached the rising slope of her breast. Pippa bit her lip to restrain the moan that threatened as Jared took a rosy nipple in his mouth. Her breath came shallow and quick, and all that separated their two hearts fell away. But knowing such paradise wouldn't last only served to fire Pippa's need to grasp whatever the moment yielded.

"Jared," she began. Though he understood the nature of her plea, Jared had barely begun to take command of Pippa's body.

"No, angel," he whispered hoarsely, his bearded face still close to her sensitized skin. "Not yet. There's much more I have yet to sample of you."

Jared's lips trailed a line downwards across the delicate flesh of her torso and stomach, but Pippa gasped and squirmed in alarm when his kisses moved lower. Jared held her still, large hands cupping her slender hips, and he tasted the quivering flesh of her inner thighs.

Pippa had no choice but to yield to his skill, and even as her thoughts cried out their protest against such foreign intimacy, they were lost in a whirling spiral of sensations. With agonizing leisure, Jared's kiss moved inward until meeting with the very core of Pippa's unleashed femininity.

Pippa's hands clenched convulsively, but she was powerless to resist the flaming tide of desire that Jared's skillful teasing released. She was lost on a raging sea of wanton, reckless pleasure. Though briefly she struggled against such a final surrender of self-control, with each throbbing beat of her heart, Pippa gave herself over to Jared's mastery.

Jared felt her surrender, and a wild thrill of surging need coursed through him. As Pippa moaned and twisted beneath

his artistry, Jared marveled that he had restrained himself
from taking all the sweetness her body offered.

"Jared, please," Pippa murmured deliriously. "Please, I
want you so."

Her inner core was on fire, filled to its extremes with the
tension Jared had wrought. Pippa's body began to quake with
abandon, and Jared rose to fulfill that quivering need. He
plunged deep within her aching softness, groaning with the
madness of his own desire as he felt the moist heat close
snugly around his size. Pippa arched beneath him, deepening
his entrance. With primitive knowledge, her hips drew away
to rise again, meeting each powerful thrust with equal urgency.

Jared's mouth sought hers, and they kissed passionately
as their bodies fused together. Wild, shocking heat, currents
of fiery force, swept through Pippa. Her sensations were
mirrored perfectly in Jared, and together they gave themselves over to the force that bound them.

When he moved away from her, Pippa lay weak and
breathless beside him, stunned that he possessed her this
completely. Jared eased Pippa into his arms, half on top of
him upon the narrow cot, his fingers playing in the thick
mass of her hair.

Pippa was lulled by Jared's strong heartbeat as she lay
against his chest, yet sleep didn't overtake her as it had their
first night. She belonged to him utterly, but Pippa guessed
Jared had no idea how much he meant to her. Pippa wriggled
from her comfortable position to gaze down into Jared's
sleepy eyes.

"Jared, I . . ." she began hesitantly. Despite their passionate bonding moments earlier, Pippa felt suddenly shy and
unsure.

"What is it, angel?" he asked drowsily, but when Pippa
saw the soft curve of his smile, her courage grew.

"I love you," she whispered. As the words escaped her lips, her breath caught in fearful expectation.

"So you've said before," replied Jared quietly. "I believed you then."

He paused, and Pippa's heart began to labor. These were not the words she longed to hear. *Tell me it doesn't matter,* she wished, and her eyes closed with the force of her prayer. *Please, tell me you still love me, too.*

"I trust you aren't confusing . . . passion—though some might even call it lust—for a deeper emotion," he continued.

Pippa's eyes opened, and her pain was clearly revealed.

"You are very young, Pippa," he added. "I wonder if you truly know what you feel."

Jared sighed deeply, and the gentle, self-mocking smile returned to his face.

"But I love you, Philippa," he told her in a gentle voice. "That is what you want to hear, isn't it? And I can't deny it. I've loved you since I first saw you, when every bit of reason told me not to trust you."

Pippa's heart lightened instantly upon his words, but as their meaning became clearer, she frowned. "Don't you trust me?"

"Should I? If your heart is with me, and when you lie in my arms, this I cannot disbelieve. Still, given the opportunity, you'd do whatever you were able to aid your cause."

"Would you betray the South for me?"

"No. But I wasn't living in New England luring hearts as you've done here," replied Jared.

"I was not . . ." she began hotly.

"Oh, no? I beg to disagree, my love. Women have used their . . . charms, shall we say, to separate men from their own better judgments since the dawn of time," Jared told

Pippa bluntly, but Pippa was thoroughly shocked by his insinuation.

"Do you think I deliberately seduced you?" she gasped in horror, but Jared's brow rose.

"I think you're a woman with unique power over a man's need, and I can't believe that fact has eluded you while every man in Virginia falls at your feet."

Pippa's face puckered angrily and her green eyes blazed as she glared down into his calm face. "Indeed? I might say the same about your gifts with women," she retorted hotly, but Jared grinned.

"True enough," he agreed. "I say again that you and I are well-matched. Neither of us is above using the power of passion to meet our own ends."

"Falling in love with you had nothing to do with my . . . service to the North," Pippa maintained.

"I see. It was incidental," mused Jared. "The fact I once came close to capturing you in no way made it necessary for you to dissuade my purpose, by whatever means available."

"Jared!" Pippa broke in.

"Oh, I freely admit to handing you the perfect solution. 'Take his heart, and he'll never harm you.' Well, you've done so. But I warn you, angel, my love will protect you only so far. I've given you my name, and I expect you to honor it. I will tolerate no further betrayals from you. You need not love Virginia, but you will not aid in her destruction either."

Pippa was furious. "Some might say the preservation of a country is more important," she maintained fiercely.

"I won't argue the politics of this war with you, Philippa," Jared stated firmly. "You and I will never agree on this, so there's no point. I only tell you that as my wife, you must have a care for your behavior now. I've given you the protection of my family. You must not dishonor them."

"What of my own father's memory?" replied Pippa, unrelenting on the subject. "What about Byron, and Jefferson, not to mention simply what I hold as truth."

Jared drew a patient breath before continuing. "I'm not asking you to uphold the Confederacy, Pippa," he told her patiently. "Merely to realize your place has changed."

Pippa argued the point no further. As much as she loved Jared, her loyalties to the Union remained strong, a part of herself. It was something she didn't intend to lose.

"Very well, Jared. You have my word. I won't act on behalf of the Union again, but neither will I do anything to hurt them. I'll be a good wife, I promise."

"You've proven that tonight," remarked Jared, and he pulled her close to kiss her forehead. "I do love you, Pippa. Never forget that."

Pippa forgot her momentary anger, and she leaned against him to kiss his mouth. Immediately, he grew hard and stiff beneath the pressure of her body. All their thoughts centered now upon furthering an arousal that would carry them deep into the night.

Six

"Good morning, Colonel!"

The cheerful voice of Captain Nicks startled Pippa from sleep, but Jared was already dressed. The captain peeked through the opened flap of Jared's tent, and Jared returned the boy's exuberant salute as he tied his golden sash.

"What is it, Nicks?" he asked.

"General Knox sent me to fetch you," the boy began breathlessly. "Grant's crossed the Rapidan, just as Marse Robert said he would! We're moving out shortly, sir."

"Major Hallett is already assembling the men," Jared told the captain. Nicks appeared only momentarily crestfallen to learn his new colonel was aware of the situation.

"Very good, sir," said Captain Nicks, and he nodded excitedly before withdrawing.

Pippa sat upright in bed, her tousled hair falling about her shoulders, and Jared's smile bore a trace of sorrow as he gazed at her. "If you're quick, my love, we may yet have breakfast together." Jared spoke idly, as if he had no more awaiting him than a ride into the city.

Pippa leapt from the cot and dressed rapidly as Jared adjusted his frock coat and loaded his Colt revolver. Pippa noted that his uniform bore the markings of a colonel. The gold star upon his collar was neatly affixed, and she wondered who had taken the time to perform this task on the eve of a major battle.

"You look very handsome," she said shyly as she hurriedly combed out her hair and tucked it away in a simple knot.

Jared smiled at her, and gave her his arm as they left his tent. They dined with the general at what seemed to Pippa a remarkably leisurely pace, considering the circumstances. She was too nervous to eat much, but the men were almost casual. Neither seemed surprised by Grant's nighttime maneuver.

"He crossed at Germanna Ford, just as Lee said he would," said the general as he finished the thick bacon and took a sip of the rebel's makeshift coffee.

"Then he'll be heading through the Wilderness," Jared said with a shake of his fair head. "Some never learn."

General Knox nodded. "It seems to be our job to repeat the lesson taught to Hooker. Yankee bones clutter the forest where they march, yet they would add to that grim collection."

Pippa grimaced, and the general glanced deferentially in her direction. "I beg your pardon, daughter," he said gently. "These are grim days, but I forget myself. Major Hallett's wife has been with us for several months, and you'll stay with her and their children."

"Children?" asked Pippa in disbelief. It hardly seemed possible a man might bring his wife, let alone his children, to such a place. Perhaps even grandparents accompanied their loved ones to battle in this strange army.

"There are many families who visit from time to time. General Gordon's family has been with him from the start of the war," the general told her.

"You won't be lonely, Philippa," Jared reassured her, but that wasn't Pippa's concern.

"When are you going?" she asked weakly, but even as she spoke, the two men rose.

"The march, in fours, has begun already," answered the general casually.

Pippa followed Jared and his father from the general's tent. She saw a long column already moving out, away from the campsite. Mounted officers cantered up and down the lines, and Pippa's heart twisted when she saw a valet leading Boreas toward Jared. She looked desperately at the big horse and back to Jared, but he seemed purposefully to avoid her eyes. She swallowed hard, but never had she felt so close to panic in her life.

Jared took the horse, saluted his father and then looked to Pippa. "Take care of yourself while I'm gone, little one," he told her, but he saw her white face and he held out his hand to her.

"Don't worry now, angel," he said softly, and Pippa brushed at her tears.

Jared drew her into his arms and held her, but Pippa wrapped her arms about his neck as if she would never let him go.

"Please come back," she whispered, and Jared kissed her brow.

"That is always my intention." He kissed her softly on the mouth, then turned without another look to mount the great black horse. Pippa stood by Boreas's massive shoulder, placing a small hand upon his glistening coat. Her misty green eyes appealed to Jared in a way words could never match.

"Good-bye, angel," he said quietly. Pippa's heart was ripped from her breast as he moved the horse through the mustering men, taking his place alongside the endless column of gray and butternut-clad infantrymen.

"Good-bye," she whispered.

Just behind Jared rode Edward Carlton, and as he waved to Pippa, it seemed to her that only he looked confident of a quick rebel victory.

As the veil of silvery tears descended across her vision, Pippa felt a strong but gentle hand upon her shoulder, and she turned to see David Knox standing tall beside her. Now that Jared was gone, David's own face revealed guarded emotion, and Pippa realized his love for Jared neared her own.

"He will return," he said. But Pippa knew he spoke from hope and not premonition. The general had seen too many other brave men fall who should not have fallen, had courage been a truer measure.

Pippa watched the column pass by, and Jared had long disappeared into the gray-green distance before she was able to look away. Soldiers marched along the narrow roadways for hours. Pippa imagined there was no end, yet all knew the Army of the Potomac had three times as many marching to meet them.

The general's handsome chestnut mount was brought to him, and Pippa realized with shock that he, too, would be going to battle. As he adjusted his slouch hat and took the horse from his valet, a small, red-haired woman approached. She smiled brightly when she saw Pippa.

"Ah, Mrs. Hallett," called the general, doffing his hat. "Allow me to introduce Mrs. Knox, my daughter-in-law. If you'll be so good as to see she's well," he began, but Mrs. Hallett had already taken Pippa's arm.

"She'll be just fine with us, General," said the little woman.

The general mounted and rode away with his group of aides, and Major Hallett's wife led Pippa from the roadside. "You just call me Sally," she said.

"I'm Pippa." Sally squeezed Pippa's hand. It was a warm, firm grip, and Pippa felt a flood of relief. Sally Hallett was obviously a strong woman, and it would be comforting to be in her presence while waiting for Jared's return.

"You stay right with me, and they'll be back in no time. Don't you be worrying about a thing."

"I'm grateful to meet you," replied Pippa. "To have somewhere to go while . . . while . . ." she faltered and her throat constricted, preventing further speech.

Sally Hallett understood Pippa's emotion. "I know, Pippa. Hallett has gone into more battles than I can count, and every time I get so sick I can barely move. Every time I pray it will be the last. But don't you worry. Jared Knox is a clever man. It'll take more than a few Yankees to finish him!"

This wasn't entirely encouraging to Pippa, since she guessed there were more than a "few" Yankees preparing to meet the rebels. Not for nothing had he been chosen to lead his men. She had to trust in Jared's strength and skill to protect him in that dark forest. With nothing else, Pippa clung desperately to that fragile hope.

The Army of the Potomac slowly marched south through the woods. Bottled up on the narrow roads of the Wilderness, they struggled to reach the open territory, but Robert E. Lee had his own ideas. The Army of Northern Virginia was always the more mobile, and while the morning was still young, the first shots were fired.

Pippa sat on an overloaded wagon, hearing the intensifying musket-fire in the distance. For a time, it seemed her heart would quail with the terror. The morning wore on. As noon approached, word came back from the fighting lines of a hideous battle.

"Can't see ten feet in front," a young infantryman told the waiting crowds. "We're getting the best of it, they say, but I can't see how they'd know anything back there. There's no front, no flanks. It's a hellish mess in those thickets."

His own arm was soaked in blood and hung limply at his side, yet Pippa marveled at his calm. More and more of the rebel wounded poured to the rear, all bearing such tales, and there were many others who were unable to retreat.

Ambulances were passing by at an ever-increasing rate, and beside Pippa, Sally Hallett shook her head. "Looks to be more than they can handle," she judged and her face was set and determined. "They'll be needing nurses," she added, and without further discussion Pippa nodded.

Both women got off the stalled wagon, and headed in the direction the ambulances were taking. Pippa had no idea what use she might be, but sitting idle while the terrifying sounds of battle reached her ears was more than she could stand.

For an hour, Pippa and Sally Hallett trudged forward towards the Wilderness, pausing often to allow the racing ambulances by. As they went on, Pippa saw that many other women, aides, and even colored servants were moving forward with the same intention of service.

Clouds of smoke spiraled randomly through the thicket, turning the high noon sun to a dusty red, and each step Pippa took towards the horrendous lines of battle it grew more heavy.

"What do we do?" she asked Sally. Rounding a corner, she saw what was necessary.

Spread all over the area were wounded men, awaiting ambulances, stumbling through the trees to the relative clearing. Pippa froze as she looked around. There were screams of unbearable pain, yet worse were the low moans of those able to exact control. If she found Jared there . . . with all her force, Pippa pushed the fear to the back of her mind.

"You there, ladies!" A beleaguered doctor called to them, waving frantically as Pippa and Sally drew near. "Start binding wounds, if they're not too big. Stop the bleeding first," he ordered. "Give 'em water if you've got some. Just keep 'em going 'til there's an ambulance available."

The doctor went back to his grisly work, and Pippa found a great stack of cloth to do as he said. Sally did the same, and the two parted to begin their task. Wounded were strewn all around, gaping injuries open to the earth. Pippa's knees went weak as sickness and revulsion swept over her.

An old sergeant lay closest to her, his face calm despite the gruesome tear in his thick leg. Pippa knelt beside the man and he smiled at her.

"Well, pretty lady, they say sometimes it's worth getting yourself shot," he drawled pleasantly, though from his pallor Pippa knew his pain must be brutally intense.

"Here, Sergeant," she said gently. "I'd like to bind your injury, if I may."

At her voice, the sergeant's eyes widened, and Pippa realized her Northern accent might be disturbing.

"You're a little Yankee!" the sergeant exclaimed as Pippa tore a portion of the cloth. "You'd better be telling me I came back to the right side now! In these woods, it's hard to tell which side's which."

"You're safe here, Sergeant, I promise you. My husband is a Virginian, you see," Pippa explained.

The sergeant winced as she peeled back the torn fabric

of his trousers, but his effort to ignore the wound was remarkable.

"Is he now? Who's your husband?"

Pippa took a quick breath as a surge of fear rose within. "Colonel Jared Knox," she replied as she carefully bound the sergeant's injured calf.

"Well, what'dya know!" he said with pleasure. "That's a fine man you've got there," he went on, but Pippa stopped her task to look at him.

"Do you know him? Have you seen him?" she asked desperately.

"We're in the same brigade," the sergeant explained. "But no, ma'am, I haven't seen your husband today. Hell, that don't mean nothing though. Haven't seen anyone not within arm's reach. Been shooting at Yankees all morning, and haven't actually laid eyes on a one of 'em."

Pippa nodded, finishing the bandage with a quick knot, and she rose to attend another. "The doctor says an ambulance will be here shortly, Sergeant," she told him. "I think you'll be fine."

Her next cases were less promising. The man she went to next murmured incoherently, and since his injury was in his chest, there was little Pippa could do but staunch the blood. It came in short spurts, a bad sign she thought, but she did what she was able.

Worse still was the officer she attended next. He was already missing an arm, and now a shell had gone completely through the bone in his leg. Only flesh connected it to the lower extremities, and there was no way it could be saved. Pippa made an effort at binding the limb, but the man stopped her.

"There's no need, miss," he told her calmly. "It's as good as gone. I've been through this before," he explained as he glanced toward his missing arm. "You go on to someone you can help."

Pippa gulped and nodded. She offered him water from her canteen, and went on to the man beside him. Blood seeped from beneath his once white shirt, its dark red dying the soft gray of his coat beyond recognition.

Pippa opened the coat and drew back in horror when she saw the bloody hole in the man's mid-section. Blood poured freely from the wound, disguising the torn flesh, yet despite the extent of his injury, the man was fairly alert. Pippa bit her lip hard and proceeded to pack the wound, but it was a useless task.

"Don't know why they bothered to drag me back here," he said in a weak voice. "Except the woods are burning, catching the fallen with them. Most you can't reach. I tried, I tried," he murmured. His soft gray eyes clouded over as he spoke.

"Would you like some water?" she offered helplessly, but he shook his head.

For a moment, Pippa couldn't move, couldn't bring herself to leave him. His blond hair was matted with blood, blond like Jared's, his face young and handsome, and still she couldn't move.

Again he looked up at her. "Who would have thought the angels would be Yankees?" he whispered. Even near death he seemed amused by the thought.

His eyes closed, and his face went blank, his chest no longer rose and fell with labored breaths. Slowly, Pippa stood up and backed away from the dead soldier. It seemed to her that all around spirits rose from battered bodies, taking flight, and leaving behind only shells.

Pippa, a lost Yankee girl, was moving about the prostrate forms, trying to keep them from leaving. She had no idea how, for it seemed an insurmountable task. Pippa shook her head, her loosely bound hair escaping to brush across her face. With a determination she didn't know she possessed, she went to the next that lay beyond.

Evening came, but with the falling darkness, the rate of musket-fire decreased and finally halted altogether. The two armies moved back through the trees to wait out the night. But for Pippa and Sally, work continued well past midnight.

"Will it be like this again tomorrow?" Pippa asked Sally as the two women found a place to sit and rest together.

"Oh, honey, I'm afraid it'll be worse. The Yankees aren't backing off, and there's no way Bobby Lee will budge. No, it'll get worse before it gets better. The second day of a battle is always worse."

Both women fell into silence, trapped in their own thoughts and visions of each individual misery they had seen. Worse than the day's continuous musket-fire was the far-off odor of burning woods. All that day, they had heard gruesome tales of wounded men burning alive, but neither Pippa nor Sally could bring themselves to mention this horror.

Faint to Pippa's ears came the shrieks of entrapped men, or perhaps it was only her blackened imagination that carried the sounds far beyond their reach. She had heard nothing of Jared, though that was unlikely, nor had Sally heard of Major Hallett.

Sally fell asleep, but Pippa stared out into the darkness of the forest. Sleep crept over her, bringing with it nightmares that mirrored her day. As she surrendered to their dark paths, she sighed and whispered soundlessly, "Jared."

* * *

Pippa woke with a start at five o'clock the next morning. Both the Union and Confederate army commanders had ordered their attacks for that hour. They struck each other simultaneously all along their twisted line. Not an hour had passed before Pippa realized how truly Sally had spoken. The carnage she had seen the day before was met and surpassed, and early information indicated that the Yankees were pushing forward.

All morning, Pippa and Sally aided wounded men. Pippa was learning better and better ways of binding the worst injuries. She recognized instinctively which wounds were most devastating, and bound them accordingly. Seeing her newly learned skill, a doctor approached her and checked her accomplishment.

"Well done, Mrs. Knox," he said with a brief nod. Pippa was heartened to see he was pleased with her work.

News of the battle looked darker for the rebels as the morning wore on. As noon approached, General Longstreet and his corps arrived from their winter quarters. They moved rapidly through the wounded, and Pippa was forced to press against a tree as they passed by.

"That should send the damned Yankees back where they came from," remarked Sally when the corps disappeared into the thicket.

The firing became deafening from beyond the shadow of the trees. By noon, the rebels had pushed forward again. Word from the front lines was encouraging, and Pippa was stunned to realize her own heart lifted upon hearing of the Confederate success.

"Old Pete was magnificent," boasted an injured Georgian. "We'll drive them back to Maryland in a day at this rate."

So excited was he that both Pippa and Sally had to forcibly restrain him from returning to battle, though a shell had deeply grazed his scalp. Pippa wondered if it had rattled his brain. But as the afternoon progressed, Old Pete himself was carried back through the lines.

Grievously wounded, the general had been hit by a wayward volley from his own troops. Pippa watched the large, burly man as he was borne away from the thicket battle. She felt an admiration she hadn't expected. General Longstreet looked calm, even dignified, despite the blood from his mouth and the whiteness of his face.

The mishap devastated the rebels in the rear. Barely a year ago, they had lost their great Stonewall Jackson in nearby Chancellorsville in just this fashion. To them, it seemed a troubling omen.

The sun was lowering over the trees when a wounded officer reported that General Gordon was taking on the Union's right flank.

"Going on right now, from what I've heard," he told Pippa as she tended him, but her face paled as he spoke.

Jared served beneath John Gordon, and even now he might be advancing on the Yankees. In her heart, she was certain he was, almost as if some part of her was truly with him. She knew he had never faced greater danger than he was enduring now.

Night came, and though Gordon's attack hadn't entirely succeeded, most felt with the horrendous losses the Yankees had endured, they would retreat. The musket-fire had ceased, but flames burned like distant lanterns throughout the forest. The odor emanating from the ghastly fires reached Pippa as she sat huddled by herself. Unable to resist further, she wept silently until sleep overtook her with its merciful peace.

Morning came, and Pippa woke to hear that Grant's army had moved from its Wilderness positions. The rebels were certain that Grant, like Hooker, was in retreat, and word from prisoners and scouts bore this out.

"Where are we going?" Pippa asked Sally. She had lost all sense of direction over the past two days.

"Going? They're already gone."

"What do you mean?" asked Pippa in confusion. "Who has gone?"

"Our boys, of course. Apparently Bobby Lee doesn't believe Grant intends to retreat at all. He's rushed the army off toward Spotsylvania to put up entrenchments and wait for the Yanks."

"Where do we go now?" asked Pippa.

"To Spotsylvania, of course," replied Sally nonchalantly.

Two days of mind-numbingly slow travel followed, and by the morning of May seventh, Pippa found herself once again at the Confederate rear. A day's preparation made caring for the wounded a less daunting task, but neither she nor Sally had heard any word of their husbands' fates.

Worse still, David Knox came seeking Pippa to see if she had heard from Jared.

"No," she replied miserably. "Then you haven't seen him either?"

General Knox shook his head. He had aged since she last saw him, only a few days previously, and her heart thudded heavily to see how desperately worried he was.

"I haven't seen him since we left camp," the general told her. "Nor any of his men, which perhaps is encouraging.

Yet I know they were in some of the heaviest fighting.
Where the fires were burning," he finished in a toneless
voice.

Pippa's heart stopped, then slowly resumed its labored
pace, but there was nothing she could say to alleviate the
gruesome fear.

"I haven't had the chance to look for him at length here,"
the general added. "We're in desperate preparation to meet
Grant, and when I heard you were back here, daughter, I
hoped. I hoped . . ."

His mournful words trailed, and he sighed.

"Then General Grant hasn't retreated, as I've heard?"
asked Pippa.

"It appears not. Our early reports were misleading. This
Grant, he's not a retreating man, though I believe his losses
must be far greater than the other Union commanders'."

"What happens now?" asked Pippa.

"We're building entrenchments and breastworks. Here, in
this tiny crossroads village, the two armies will meet again.
Already Jeb Stuart's cavalry has gone forward to meet the
Union column, and behind them our infantry waits."

Even as General Knox spoke, Pippa heard the distant fire.
The noise level carried farther, louder in the open spaces
around Spotsylvania. Artillery was in use, crashing violently
through the shattered trees, rending the air in fiery destruction.

"It has begun," the general said grimly, but Pippa saw
the strange light of battle in his eyes. "I must go, daughter.
If you see my son . . ."

Pippa understood, and she nodded. Her heart was heavier
than it had ever been as she watched Jared's father mount
his chestnut horse and ride back to war.

The battle beyond her sight had intensified beyond her

imagining. Pippa was kept from hysteria by caring for the
multitude of wounded that flowed back from the battle lines.
No longer was there time to speak to those prepared for the
racing ambulances. By early afternoon, Pippa's dress was
stained with dark blood. She stopped bothering to wipe her
hands clean.

For three more days, Pippa dressed and bound wounds
she couldn't begin to heal. *I've wandered into a nightmare,*
she thought blearily. *Soon I will wake, soon I will wake.*

"Any word?" she asked Sally. Sally merely shook her
head as she passed by.

The question was oft repeated, always with the same reply,
but Pippa kept asking. The evening of May eleventh brought
torrents of heavy rain, adding to the torments of the
wounded and those who fought on both sides. Pippa no
longer spoke, but went numbly about her business. A doctor
approached her and patted her slumped shoulders.

"Take some time, Mrs. Knox," he said, but Pippa looked
at him blankly. "It's night now," he reminded her. "There
won't be many more tonight."

"But tomorrow," said Pippa in a small voice.

She turned and walked away, unsure where she was going.
Gradually she realized that far from finding a spot to rest, she
was now headed in the direction of the fighting. Stumbling
as she walked, Pippa made her way towards the entrenchments. The rain and the encroaching darkness prevented her
from seeing very far. Men moved to and fro along the narrow
road, and often she barely avoided being trampled by passing
horsemen.

Pippa stopped. There was nowhere to go. She stood facing
the direction of the entrenchments, and tears poured down

her cheeks. She had barely eaten for days, yet she felt no hunger, and her dress hung loosely about her waist. The rain beat upon her small face, mixing with her tears, soaking through the blood-stained dress. She wondered vaguely where she had put her cape, but that was surely lost by now.

"Can I help you, child?"

Pippa heard the kind voice, but it was long before she realized the man was speaking to her. She turned around and saw a gray horse halted beside her. As her eyes lifted to see who had spoken to her, she took in the animal's black mane, its noble head carriage, but it was the face of the rider that astonished her.

Never in her life had she seen eyes of such compassion, such inner strength. Even as she tearfully met the old man's gaze, her heart was strengthened by his presence. His gray beard was streaked with white, yet he looked strong and vibrant despite his age. He seemed familiar, but then, Pippa had seen many faces over the last few days.

"What is troubling you, dear girl?" he asked again, and now Pippa was able to respond.

"My husband," she answered in a broken voice. "I don't know where he is." The old man smiled, and again Pippa was touched by his unearthly compassion.

"Who is your husband, child?" he asked gently.

"Jared Knox," Pippa responded with a sniff. "He's a colonel, serving beneath General Gordon, and his father, General Knox."

The old man nodded thoughtfully. As Pippa's shattered senses began to clear, she saw that he wore the mark of a general himself.

"Colonel Knox," mused the general. "I have seen him, yes. That was the second day of the Wilderness."

The general paused, studying Pippa's upturned face, and

he easily read her strain and heartache. For all he had seen
over the years of war, her grief still touched him, for he was
a man of deep feeling.

"You have been caring for our wounded?" he asked, and
Pippa nodded. "Then go back there where you'll be safe. I
will learn your husband's whereabouts, and have word sent
to you. Does that ease your heart?"

Pippa's eyes widened and her heart leapt at his words.
Life seemed to flow back through her tormented soul, and
her face lit in a bright smile.

"Yes, sir. Oh, thank you for your kindness," she said
breathlessly, though the response seemed inadequate.
"Thank you!"

The general doffed his slouch hat politely before urging
the gray war horse forward toward the entrenchments. Pippa
watched him go, and her heart soared with overwhelming
gratitude. Again her tears flowed, but this time in response
to the unexpected kindness of the old man who had seen
one lonely Yankee girl weeping in the evening rain.

That night, Pippa found her cape among Sally's things
and wrapped it tightly around her shoulders. She slept more
soundly that night than she had since Jared had gone to
battle, but at dawn she was once again startled from sleep
by the deafening thunder of a Union artillery strike.

The battle raged through the soft rain and again Pippa
was kept from dwelling too much on its outcome by the
influx of wounded men. From them, she learned what had
taken place.

"They took the Mule Shoe," a small soldier from North
Carolina told Pippa. Seeing her confusion, he added, "A
salient, at the center of our line."

Pippa nodded as she wrapped his bleeding forehead in a neat bandage, though she understood very little.

"Lee himself tried to lead Gordon's men in a charge, but Gordon stopped him. Good God, it was something to see, little miss!" he exclaimed excitedly.

"Gordon said, 'These men have never failed you on any field. They will not fail you here.' Every man there shouted he would not fail Marse Robert. They blocked Traveller, and finally Lee turned and left."

The Carolinian soldier wept as he spoke, and to Pippa's own astonishment, her own eyes filled with tears at his story. Gordon's men—if Jared was alive, he was with them.

"What happened?" she asked.

"We pushed the Yanks back all right, and that's where I got hit. Just bind me up and I'll get back. All the blood was blocking my sight. It's a hell of a fight still, though," the little soldier told her passionately. "Bayonets, bodies everywhere. I've never seen anything like it, and I've seen all there is to see."

Pippa shuddered at the description, but she secured the soldier's bandage and watched as he hurried back to the front. All that day such stories were brought back to her, yet there was no word from the old general. Perhaps the violence of the battle had put her individual grief from his mind, but Pippa waited.

The wounded came back and were jostled away in overcrowded ambulances bound for Richmond, and still the battle showed no signs of slacking. Men climbed over the bodies of the fallen to shoot and fall themselves, fighting with muskets, sabers, bayonets and then using their muskets as clubs. The scene of this most intense fighting had already been given a name, a gruesome name: the Bloody Angle.

* * *

They fought continuously through the rainy night, and Pippa and Sally worked side by side tending the fallen. Pippa lost the hope the old general gave her, but her energy didn't falter despite her weariness. Sally, heavier and stronger, collapsed for a brief rest, but Pippa sat with a very young infantryman who had no hope of survival.

Shot near his heart, he slowly bled to death, but though he couldn't speak, his eyes reached Pippa with a plea not to leave him. She didn't. She sat with his head on her lap while his life ebbed away, and gently stroked his hair until his breath no longer filled his chest. His eyes went blank, empty, his body went limp.

Pippa just sat, tears flowing freely down her cheeks. Laying his head to the muddy earth, she rose. She stood looking down at the boy's face for a long time, but then she sighed. There would be another, and then another. There was no end to the fallen, the dead and the dying. Pippa wiped her tears from her face and looked to the next who needed her.

A battered-looking soldier stood watching her, blood-stained himself, but at least he didn't appear on death's door. An unkempt beard shaded his face, and his hair was stained with mud. He looked strong and powerful to Pippa, a welcome sight after so much destruction.

The man smiled at her, a slow smile. A smile she knew. Seeing her widening eyes, he came to her. Pippa stood immobile as he approached. Her hands shook, her heart crashed violently in her chest, but still she couldn't move.

"Don't you know your own husband?" he asked. He ran his hand along the side of his face. "But then, perhaps I do look the worse for wear."

Pippa's breath came in sudden, quick gasps. She jumped

into his arms, wrapping her own tightly about his neck and he lifted her from the ground as he hugged her.

"Jared!"

"You've missed me then?" he asked.

"Missed you?" she repeated in disbelief. Wildly, she kissed his bearded face as an answer.

Jared was forced to let her go when an ambulance sped past them. He looked tired, far older than she remembered.

"Are you all right?" Pippa asked, patting him as if to reassure herself he was really there, this wasn't a dream.

"I'm fine," he reassured her. "Tired," he admitted, but then he took her hands in his. "I'm sorry for bringing you here, Pippa," he said in a strained voice. "I had no idea it would be this terrible. Like too many of us, I suppose I underestimated this Grant. God forgive me for leaving you in the midst of this."

"No, Jared, I want to be where you are. Even here. I've been helpful," she added proudly.

"I see that," he said. "He told me you were caring for the injured. He seemed to like you."

Pippa's brow furrowed. "Who did? Do you mean the old man I spoke to yesterday?" she asked in confusion.

"Old man?" cried Jared. "My dear wife, that 'old man' was Robert E. Lee himself!"

"What?" gasped Pippa in disbelief. "I think you're mistaken, Jared. Such a man wouldn't . . ."

"Oh, yes, he would," Jared told her. "And he did. He told me so himself. He said I was to report to the rear and reassure my wife of my safety, that she could continue to perform the very good aid she gave our wounded."

Pippa's mouth dropped in complete astonishment, but as she considered this, she realized why Lee's men spoke his name with love. He was a man others would follow into hell itself and back. A man even she would follow.

"Have you seen your father? He was here, looking for you and he seemed terribly afraid, Jared."

"I received a message from him last night, which I returned," Jared told her, and Pippa sighed with relief. "He's on the farthest flank now, so I haven't seen him."

Pippa saw Sally across the field of wounded, and she took Jared's hand. "Is Major Hallett . . . well?"

"He's fine," replied Jared slowly. "But, Pippa, Edward is gone."

"Gone? Jared, no," she breathed. "What happened?"

"In the Wilderness," Jared began. The memory was bitterly painful to him, and Pippa took his hand, holding it tightly in her own. They stood together, hand in hand, drawing strength from their nearness.

At last, Jared drew her fingers to her lips. "I'm sorry, angel, but I must leave you."

"Where are you going?" Pippa asked in rising panic.

"I have to go back," he began, but Pippa cut him off with a shrill cry.

"No, you don't!"

"Pippa, my love, please don't make this harder. But know that my heart is lighter for seeing you well, for holding you again. It's better than food or drink to see your beautiful—if dirty—face. Please, love, kiss me and say good-bye."

Pippa felt faint, but she couldn't resist Jared's gentle plea. Hot tears stung her eyes and fell to her cheeks, but she stood up on tiptoes and kissed his mouth tenderly.

"I love you so," she whispered, and Jared kissed her again.

"Good-bye, Pippa," he answered. But then, like a dream

passing beyond recall, he turned and left. Pippa watched him go, fighting the desire to run after him, stop him any way she could. He disappeared from her sight, and she gathered herself together to tell Sally that Major Hallett was alive.

Two days passed before Pippa saw Jared again, but this time it was Sally who brought her to his side.

"Pippa," she called gently. Seeing Sally's face, Pippa's own went white. "Come with me," said Sally, and she took Pippa's arm.

In a daze of fear, Pippa went with Sally across the field. It was strewn with bodies, many untended as they waited for an ambulance, others for death alone. Pippa saw Major Hallett kneeling beside one, and she swayed when she recognized Jared.

Sally caught and braced her, and Pippa forced herself to go to him, though her fear made it impossible for her even to breathe. The major rose and stood aside, but Pippa fell to her knees at Jared's side. He lay motionless, his handsome face was still. Pippa believed he was dead.

"He lives," the major reassured her, and apart from a bloody wound on Jared's brow, Pippa saw no injury.

David Knox himself arrived as Pippa sat with Jared, and his face was white with fear as he bent over his son. "What happened to him?" he asked in a voice that shook with emotion.

"Our line was threatened," Major Hallett told him in a low, restrained voice. "We were faltering. Dead on our feet. Your son led us back, took the position from the Yankees and we held it."

David Knox nodded, and there was pride in his face, despite his anguish, as Major Hallett went on. "Outnumbered five to one, we were. But Jared shouted, 'Charge!' and we charged. Took the Yanks by surprise, we did, but it was close fighting. Jared was at the head of it. The Yanks moved back, but one big fellow swung around and caught the colonel on the side of the head with a rifle butt."

Major Hallett sighed. "He fell, and he was as you see him now."

The general nodded, but his next words came with effort. "I must go back to my men," he told them with resignation. He looked to Pippa. "You'll stay with him, daughter?" he asked, his voice a plea to do for his son what he could not.

Pippa nodded tearfully, and David Knox knelt beside his son. He touched Jared's head, then bent to kiss his brow. Without another word, he rose and went to his horse. He didn't look back, but Pippa knew the incredible strength of will it took to ride away from his son.

Major Hallett went back to the front with the general, and Sally left Pippa alone with Jared. Her alarm at his condition grew as a deathly pale crept over him; it was a warm day, but he looked cold. Without thinking what use it might be, Pippa took her cape from the bag she carried and put it over him.

She didn't think Jared was cold, but she believed her cape might protect him as it had her. She carefully bound the bloody wound on his forehead, and sat beside him to await an ambulance wagon. How she would get to Richmond remained to be seen, but Pippa knew she would find a way.

A way presented itself. When three ambulances arrived at the sight simultaneously, more physicians were arriving from Richmond than were ready to leave. The driver saw Pippa beside Jared and invited her to accompany him.

"Take care of him," called Sally, as Pippa climbed up

beside the driver, and Pippa nodded as the wagon pulled away.

"Don't worry, ma'am," drawled the aged driver when he saw Pippa nervously glance back at the jostled men. "Been over this road now four times, and believe me, I know every rise and fall. They'll get a smooth ride, missy. I promise you."

All the same, the ride to Richmond was a prolonged nightmare of endurance for Pippa. Occasionally, they stopped to allow the injured water, but Jared lay motionless, pale beneath the protection of Pippa's gray cape. She touched his brow and kissed him, but the cart started off again.

Into the night and over countless hours they went on, and in Pippa's acute fatigue, she had no idea how many miles they covered, nor had she any notion where they were. Leaning against the lurching wagon rail, Pippa fell into a merciful sleep. She woke with a start, then fell asleep again as they traveled a road now deeply furrowed with the passage of heavily loaded wagons.

They arrived in Richmond late at night, and Jared was taken to the Chimborazo Hospital. Pippa was allowed to accompany him. She sat by the tiny, metal bed, her head on his shoulder, and there she slept until morning.

Jared woke to feel a labored sensation in his chest as air filled his lungs and departed. For a long while, he could bring his mind nowhere else. He gradually became aware of a strange pressure against his shoulder. It wasn't unpleasant, it was even comforting.

His head throbbed with unrelenting pain, and his vision blurred, but he gathered he was in a hospital. No sounds of battle met his ears, just the low, methodical noises of an overcrowded ward. Even to move his eyes caused pain, but as Jared strained his sight, he saw the mass of thick dark hair close to his face. His heart gained strength as he realized the source of the endearing pressure.

Power flowed from Pippa's sleeping form and into his ragged muscles, and Jared lifted his hand to touch her soft hair. Pippa didn't move, but the nurse walking by saw his tender gesture.

"Waking up finally, are you, Colonel?" she asked as she went to his bedside.

Jared tried to speak, but he was still too weak. He glanced toward Pippa, and the nurse understood his concern.

"Yes, I know. Poor little thing. Arrived with you last night," she told him. "We tried to get her to sleep on one of the empty beds—there aren't many, to be sure—but she wouldn't hear of it. Stubborn, your wife."

The nurse paused. "She's a Yankee, isn't she?" she said in a hushed, commiserating tone. Jared smiled faintly, and the nurse nodded. "That would explain it. Yankees can be that way."

Jared's eyes wandered to an empty cot beside his own.

"Poor fellow didn't make it, I'm afraid," the nurse said sadly. Her voice indicated this wasn't unexpected for many in the great hospital.

"I see what you're thinking, Colonel, and I'll get right on it. It'd be a shame to wake her up, wouldn't it? I'll get one of the orderlies to pick her up. Why, I could almost do it myself, she's so thin. I'm afraid she's not going to fatten up much in this city, though. There's just not a lot to be had anymore," the nurse finished with a sigh.

Despite her words, Jared thought she looked fairly hefty herself, and guessed some nourishment was available somewhere. A black orderly came by shortly and lifted Pippa from her crumpled position at Jared's bedside. He placed her carefully onto the cot, and Jared was able to watch his exhausted wife for the next several hours.

Pippa woke, and her first thought was that it was unseasonably warm for coastal Maine. She had been dreaming of her childhood home, of her father's summer cottage by the sea. All through her dreams, she walked the shore searching for someone. Jared appeared, only to vanish again when she reached him. It was disconcerting to her, and disturbed the pleasant peace of her memory.

Pippa opened her eyes and stared at the high ceiling. A soft, low voice spoke her name, and she looked over to see Jared's smiling face.

"You're alive!" she exclaimed as she struggled to cast off her body's sleepiness and sit up.

"Of course I am. Though I was beginning to wonder about you. I had no idea you were such a late sleeper," he teased. "But then, we have much to learn about each other."

Pippa wriggled from her bed and went over to where Jared lay propped up on one elbow, and she studied his smiling face intently.

"You look much better," she said seriously. "You were so pale. I thought . . ." She stopped, and her eyes were wide with the force of her emotion.

"I know what you thought, angel," he replied quietly. "But I'm much recovered. So much so that I think you and I will leave this place today. I'll take the rest of my recuperation at my own house. How does that sound to you?"

"That will be . . . good," answered Pippa, but a vague worry crept across her heart.

Staying at Jared's Richmond home meant living with his mother and sisters, and Pippa wasn't sure they would welcome her as warmly as had his father. But she couldn't let Jared see her doubt, so she said nothing about the matter.

"I've sent word to my mother, and I expect she'll send a coach."

"Did you tell her about me?" Pippa asked hesitantly.

"It was a short message, Pippa," replied Jared. "It didn't seem the place to explain our love affair at length."

Jared said nothing about his own misgivings, but he remembered his mother's warnings about Pippa. Such things were best handled delicately. He, too, felt fairly certain that Caroline Knox's response to her new daughter-in-law would be less enthusiastic than her husband's.

There was also the matter of his youngest sister, whose hatred for Yankees was both justified and powerful. Jared couldn't imagine she would show Pippa much affection. But he didn't want to alarm his exhausted, brave wife with this likelihood until she was better suited to contend with the intricacies of feminine interaction.

"I can't believe we're out of that horrible place," said Pippa as she reached to brush the hair from Jared's bandaged brow. "You're safe," she sighed. "It doesn't seem possible. Like waking from a hideous dream."

Jared nodded. "Though sometimes I fear this is the dream, and war my reality."

"No, Jared," Pippa said sternly. "The war is over for you now."

"For a little while," he sighed, but he closed his eyes, and Pippa determined not to press the issue.

The thought of Jared returning to battle was impossible to consider. Her only hope was that the war would end before he was sufficiently recovered to go back. After seeing

Grant's tenacity and determination through the Wilderness and at Spotsylvania, well matched by Lee's courageous force, this seemed a very forlorn hope.

Part Three

The Crater

Men could not part us with their worldly jars,
Nor the seas change us, nor the tempests bend;
—Elizabeth Barrett Browning

Seven

Jared's mother lost no time sending a coach for her son. The coachman hurried off for Chimborazo Hospital, and Caroline Knox flew around her elegant Franklin Street home preparing for her injured son's arrival.

"Mother, he won't care if all the vases have flowers or not," teased Caroline's youngest daughter.

Kim followed her mother down the hall and shook her fair head as Caroline rearranged another bouquet.

"He's been at war, Kimber," Caroline explained needlessly. "Jared needs something to brighten his return."

Kim knew how desperately her mother had feared for Jared while news of the battle trickled back to the Richmond papers. No word had come of either Jared or David Knox since the Yankees had crossed the Rapidan. Jared's brief but reassuring note had released a flurry of excited emotion in their household.

"How long do you think he'll stay?" asked Kim as they proceeded upstairs for a final check on Jared's bedroom.

Caroline sighed. "Not long enough, I'm afraid. He says his injury isn't severe. But it means he'll feel obligated to return to his post as soon as he's able."

Kim patted her mother's shoulder comfortingly. "Then we'll see that he's well cared for while he's here." Kim paused. "Should we tell Christina?"

Caroline considered this. "Well, I know she's anxious to hear of him."

"If I tell her, she'll come," Kim reasoned.

Caroline nodded. "I don't think that would be unseemly. Christina is in mourning, but as your friend and our neighbor . . . Yes, you may tell her."

"She was Jared's 'friend,' too, Mother," teased Kim.

"That was a long time ago, dear," chastised Caroline, but she smiled faintly at the prospect.

With her mother's agreement, Kim hurried away to visit her friend. Caroline sighed and shook her head. If the rumors she had heard were correct, it might be too late. But perhaps in this matter, if nothing else, General U.S. Grant had served some purpose with his attack on Confederate positions. Thus occupied, her son might be spared the results of a hasty deed Caroline was certain he would long regret. Still, she knew it might have been wiser to wait before consenting to Kim's suggestion. Rash actions were often disastrous.

Despite his eagerness to leave the hospital, Jared found getting up from his cot unexpectedly difficult. Rising, his head swam and Pippa grabbed his arm to offer what support she was able.

"Maybe you should stay here another night," she suggested, but Jared was adamant about leaving.

"No, Pippa. This bed should be used by someone who needs it."

Pippa relented with a deep sigh. "Very well. But I'm going to fetch an orderly to help you," she insisted. Caroline's aged coachman stepped forward to offer assistance, but Jared refused.

"There's no need," he told them firmly, but Pippa winced when he slowly stood up again.

His face was strained, but Jared was able to walk unaided. In silent agreement, Pippa and the old coachman stayed close at his side, but Jared didn't sway as both obviously expected. As they passed the long line of beds, a familiar voice called to Jared, and he turned to see the young Captain Nicks.

"Nicks!" he said. Despite his own weakness, Jared went to the boy's bedside. "What happened to you?"

"Don't know exactly," admitted Nicks with a shake of his head. "Didn't even feel it at first, but it sure does hurt now."

Jared nodded. "I know exactly what you mean," he told the boy, and Pippa gazed lovingly at her husband.

She could see the fear on the captain's face, and she knew that Jared's understanding would reassure the boy it didn't speak ill of his manhood.

Jared took Nicks's hand. "You listen to the doctors, Captain," he ordered. "Your company has need of you."

Pippa saw the young face brighten. "Yes, sir," replied Nicks with pride. "I believe they do."

Jared left the hospital without assistance, but once settled in the coach, Pippa knew the effort had severely drained his strength. He looked pale again, and her heart ached to see his strong body affected this way. Pippa sat close to him, wrapping her arms about him, and Jared accepted her determined support without argument. He rested his aching head against hers, and Pippa closed her eyes in bliss.

From the hospital to Franklin Street, they held each other in this way. When the coach came to a halt, Pippa was loath to have the connection broken. The old coachman helped

Jared down the step, but Pippa jumped down unaided. Used to the natural delicacy of women, the old man looked at her reproachfully, but Pippa was far too concerned with Jared to notice.

"Well, this is it," Jared told her. Pippa gasped when she saw the elegant Federal home before her. "You may be interested to know that Robert E. Lee himself has a house down the street," he added with pride.

Pippa looked up at the house as if it might suddenly close its shutters and bar her entrance. It was much larger than she had expected, and breathtakingly beautiful. The brick siding was rose-colored, and great flowering bushes lined its expanse. Pippa had expected Virginian city homes to be less grand than the plantation mansions she had seen. Looking down the quiet street, she saw this wasn't the case.

None were as splendid as the one before her, but all surpassed Pippa's expectations. Pippa looked down at her dress, and saw to her horror that its original shade of green was all but unrecognizable beneath the grime accumulated over the past week.

"Jared, I can't go in there!"

Jared turned to her quizzically and noticed the stricken look on her face. "Why not?" he asked.

"It's so big, so . . . grand! And I'm . . . not," she fumbled.

"Pippa, are you feeling well? You're not making sense, my dear."

Pippa shook her head impatiently. "Look at me, Jared. I'm a mess." As she spoke, she lifted her hands and groaned when she saw the stains of blood and dirt that were imprinted upon her once fair skin.

"In many ways, angel, you've never looked more beau-

iful. But we aren't going to a party, Pippa. This is my home,
nd yours. You need not concern yourself about dress."

With that, Jared took Pippa's arm, and they walked up
he wide, marble steps to the front door. Pippa wasn't con-
inced by Jared's reassurance, but she didn't want to strain
im with her fears. She swallowed hard when he rang the
ell, but never had Pippa felt more unprepared for anything
n her life.

The large, white paneled door opened, and Caroline Knox
ppeared beneath the threshold. At first, she didn't notice
ippa standing behind Jared, and Pippa wished she was in-
isible.

"Jared!" cried Caroline tearfully as she embraced her son.
She pulled him in the door, and Pippa followed, though
very tiny portion of her being commanded she stay right
vhere she was. Behind Caroline stood several women; Pippa
guessed these to be Jared's sisters. Two were fair-haired, and
he youngest closely resembled Jared's mother. The other
blonde woman was dressed in mourning, but Pippa saw that
he was beautiful despite being clothed in black. No one
aw Pippa behind Jared, and when the coachman entered,
he was further hidden from their line of vision.

"Darling, your sisters are all here to welcome you home,"
aid Caroline, and the other women crowded around Jared,
hugging him and weeping. The lady in mourning, however,
tood back reticently, but Jared's youngest sister turned to
her.

"Christina came by this morning, too."

Jared noticed the woman in black for the first time, and
Pippa sensed his shock when he saw her. "Christina!" With
a shy smile, the blonde woman went to him and he took her
hand.

"You're in mourning," he observed quietly, and Christina looked away.

"Charles has died," said Caroline in a solemn voice. "He contracted the typhoid over the winter. It took him when we were visiting the Carltons. Christina has been very brave," Caroline added squeezing the girl's hand.

Pippa knew she would never be this composed had Jared died. It occurred to her that Christina wouldn't either.

"I'm sorry for your loss, Christina," said Jared in a careful voice. "I hadn't seen Charles since before Gettysburg," he added, but then he stopped.

"Will you be needing me for anything else, Missus Knox?" asked the coachman. He lowered Pippa's small bag to the gray marbled floor of the foyer. Caroline turned to dismiss the old man, but gasped in astonishment when he moved back to the opened door, revealing Pippa.

"No, thank you, Wilson," said Caroline in a forcibly calmed voice.

She waited for his departure before turning her eyes again to Pippa. Pippa felt every grain of dirt that she was certain covered her face and clothing. She chewed her lip in distress as she realized how long it had been since she had considered her hair.

Jared realized the strain of the situation, but he turned and held out his hand for his wife. With painful reluctance, Pippa stepped forward and took his hand, but she felt acutely the astonished stares of the other women.

"Mother, I would like you to meet Philippa," he began. "My wife."

Pippa pressed her lips together hard, and held her breath when she heard the collective gasp of the women present.

"Your wife?" asked Jared's youngest sister in dismay, and Christina looked at Pippa with undisguised shock.

"But you've been at war!" exclaimed a tall, darker woman. Though surprised, she sounded more amused than horrified by Jared's announcement.

Jared smiled. "So I have, Katy," he agreed. "Philippa has been with me, tending the wounded, as perhaps you can see. I intended to bring her here, of course," he went on easily. "But General Grant had other plans, and I was diverted from my original intention."

"You poor thing," said Katy, as she stepped up to take Pippa's arm. "I've been working at the hospital since the war began, but I can't imagine actually serving during a battle. It must have been horrible for you," she said sympathetically.

Pippa looked to her gratefully. "Less horrible for me than for those fighting."

At the sound of her voice, the women in the room again reacted with shock. Kim in particular was horrified.

"Jared! She's a Yankee!" she gasped as if there could be nothing worse in all the world.

Katy recovered quicker than the others. "Now she's a Virginian," she said firmly.

Kim was plainly not convinced, but Katy didn't allow her to speak further. "Where are your things, Philippa?" she asked. "You'll want to change your dress, and . . . bathe, I'd imagine," she said, as delicately as possible.

"I'd like that very much, thank you," replied Pippa gratefully, but then she glanced at Jared doubtfully. "But my things . . ." she began hesitantly.

"I'm afraid Philippa's bag was . . . lost," he told them. Pippa saw Caroline's eyes narrow, and she guessed Jared's mother could tell better than anyone when her son wasn't being completely honest.

"We'll send for her things right away," said Caroline. She

was less shocked than the others by Pippa's presence, but i had taken her awhile to accept the reality of the situation.

"Philippa," she began as she took Pippa's hand. "Let m welcome you to our family."

"Thank you," said Pippa, but as Jared's youngest siste glared at her, she knew her welcome was doubtful.

"I know this is a poor time to give you bad news, bu you must learn sooner or later, I'm afraid."

Pippa's brow furrowed as she looked at Caroline. "Wha news?" she asked in wonder. How much worse could thing get?

Caroline took her hand in sympathy. "Your Aunt Char lotte," she began carefully. "She suffered a seizure whil having lunch with Elspeth Carlton and myself. On the da you and Jared . . . left."

"Aunt Charlotte is dead?" gasped Pippa.

"I'm sorry to bear such news," commiserated Caroline "Let it ease your loss to know it was quick and withou warning. She can have felt no pain."

"Then she never knew . . ." began Pippa weakly, but per haps Charlotte's death was merciful considering what he reaction to Burke's arrest would have been.

Misunderstanding, Caroline shook her head sadly. "No she had no idea that you had left. Although she did expres to me the hope you might marry."

"We should let Philippa go to her room. She'll need t rest," said Katy.

Katy reminded Pippa of David Knox strongly, and Pipp hoped at least this sister would like her. Jared's two othe sisters were more reserved, especially Kim, and Pippa kne they would be much harder to please. Jared was unusuall quiet, and she looked up at him with concern. His face ha grown pale, but before she could address the situation, Caroline Knox took her son's arm.

"You don't look well, Jared," she commented. "Come into the sitting room and rest. I'll have food and drink brought around, and then you must go to your room."

The dark sister who hadn't spoken brushed passed Pippa to take Jared's other arm. "Yes, darling," she said, as they led him away. "All of us have been nursing at the hospital. You won't lack for care!"

"I imagine I'll never have a moment's peace," teased Jared, but Pippa saw him sway as he left the room.

She wanted to go to him, but already Kim and Christina were following him. Only Katy stayed with Pippa, and her face was kind when she patted Pippa's shoulder.

"I'm afraid you're a shock to them," she said, and Pippa nodded. "But don't worry, Philippa," Katy added. "They'll get used to you. It's hard at first, but it will get easier, I promise. As a matter of fact, I married a man whose family had set its hopes on another girl. They were already engaged when we met," she confided, and Pippa was bolstered by this confidence.

"Have they . . . accepted you now?" asked Pippa, but Katy shrugged.

"More or less," she admitted. "They're at least polite. But Robert and I are very happy. That's what matters."

Katy took Pippa to Jared's room, and showed her the bathroom upstairs. "You and I are about the same height," observed Katy thoughtfully. "You bathe now, Philippa, and I'll go home and fetch you some things to wear. I'm afraid my dresses may be a bit loose on you, but I'll find something that's easy to adjust."

"That's very kind of you," said Pippa.

Katy smiled at Pippa, and Pippa thought of Byron. As an only child, Pippa had been terribly lonely, and as well, painfully shy. Byron entered her life and befriended her, and Pippa had never forgotten his kindness. Now Katy had done the same, and Pippa was intensely grateful.

"Please, do call me Pippa," she suggested shyly.

" 'Pippa'? That's a charming name. Is that what Jared calls you?" asked Katy.

"Sometimes," replied Pippa. Her face clouded briefly as she recalled the change in Jared's voice when he had called her 'Philippa' in frosty anger.

"Well then, Pippa. You bathe now, and rest. I'll return later this afternoon with a wardrobe that should do until Mother can have your own things sent."

Katy paused, assessing Pippa's tattered, stained dress. "You'll need petticoats, won't you? And a hoop skirt. I have several corsets and such that I've outgrown since having children. Those should do well for you."

"Have you children?" asked Pippa with pleasure.

"Three," replied Katy happily. "Two boys and a baby girl. They're the joy of my life."

"And your husband?" asked Pippa. "Is he at war?"

"No, thank heavens, he's not a soldier. Robert is an aide to President Davis!" Katy told Pippa with pride.

Pippa's eyes widened. "That must be . . . interesting for you," she said. Another she knew of, one she had never met, also served close to Jefferson Davis. But this person's service was to the Union.

Katy left, and Pippa bathed thoroughly. By the time Pippa returned to Jared's room, Katy had already sent several dresses and a collection of undergarments for Pippa's use. Pippa tried on the lightest corset Katy had sent, and it fit perfectly. The dress she tried, a light cotton fabric with a tiny floral print, was loose around her waist, but it easily cinched to her shape.

Pippa left her long hair loose about her shoulders. Though she was now more properly attired, she had no courage to descend those stairs. Without Katy, the rooms below seemed threatening, and she decided to await Jared right where she was.

Pippa went to the large window by Jared's huge bed and held back the light drapery to see the street beyond. The trees hung low with leaves, flowers blossomed everywhere, and Pippa thought she had never seen a place more beautiful.

"I see you've found my sister's gifts," said Jared from behind her, but Pippa startled when he walked in.

"Weren't you expecting me?" he asked with amusement.

Jared had bathed and shaved, though such a task must have been done only with effort. He was wearing a new shirt as well, white and opened at the neck, and Pippa thought he looked very handsome despite his condition.

"I just didn't hear the door, that's all," Pippa explained, but suddenly she felt shy with her husband.

"It's very pretty here," she said as she glanced back out the window.

Jared nodded and came to stand beside her. "You belong here, Pippa," he said, and his arm went about her shoulders, but Pippa looked at him doubtfully.

"I think you'd be hard pressed to convince your mother and sisters of that," she ventured.

"Katy liked you," he told her. "Of course, she's been the one on the outside herself."

"Yes, she told me that," said Pippa. "I liked her very much. She reminds me of Byron."

"Byron?"

"Yes. Oh, they're a different sex, and a different color, of course. But they're both kind. It's hard to explain exactly," she went on, striving to define the similarity she felt between the two. "Perhaps it's just that Byron was kind to me when I was alone, as was your sister today."

"Perhaps," agreed Jared, but his expression was strange when he looked into Pippa's eyes. "I'm sorry about your aunt, Pippa."

Pippa sighed. "At least she won't have to learn about Burke," she said. "She loved him very much, like a son."

A divergent thought flashed into Pippa's mind. "Jared! What will happen to Charlotte's servants? Emmaline and her husband . . . and Lucy?"

"Emmaline and her husband are old," reflected Jared. "I'd imagine Charlotte has provided for their situation. Lucy will probably go to another household."

Pippa's mind raced in fear for Lucy's fate. "But Lucy . . . Lucy might not do well with other people," she said, fumbling for a solution.

"No," agreed Jared. "I'm surprised she was ever chosen as a household servant. Apparently she was evaluated only by her appearance."

Pippa swallowed to keep herself from correcting Jared's erroneous assumption, but she knew Lucy's safety was in her hands.

"Would you like me to bring her here?" suggested Jared.

"Jared, would you? She'd be happy with me, I know. Oh, thank you!" Without fully understanding, Jared had come to her aid, and Pippa beamed at him gratefully. "Perhaps she can bring my own clothes," she suggested.

"It will be good for you to have someone familiar here. Though I'd think you'd prefer someone with more to say."

"Lucy will like it here," she said reflectively. "Aunt Charlotte's home could be tedious at times. She disliked modern things; so the servants had to work very hard. Why, there's even running water here! How did you manage that, Jared?" she asked with admiration. "I've never seen such a luxurious bathroom, except in a hotel."

Jared shrugged, but he was pleased with Pippa's praise. "It's nothing that extravagant, really. There's a water tank hidden on the roof."

"Beneath the little widow's walk?" asked Pippa with interest, thinking of the captains' homes on the coast of Maine.

"Is that what you call it?" he asked. "Yes, it's there. I liked the facilities in Europe, and I spent the year before the war renovating this house."

Jared sighed. "It will probably prove a wasted effort, though. If the Yankees should overrun Richmond . . ."

"They won't destroy people's homes, Jared," replied Pippa assuredly.

"No? I've seen otherwise. But you've never seen such a city after shelling, Pippa. Little remains standing and undamaged."

Pippa sighed. "Shouldn't you be sleeping?" she asked. Jared looked weary to her eyes, though she had to admit that his color had improved with his mother's care.

"I should, at that. It's with those orders that I'm here," he replied. "But you might prefer to have lunch downstairs."

"I'm not hungry," Pippa lied quickly. Going downstairs alone was something she couldn't imagine, no matter how hungry she was.

"As you wish, angel," said Jared, and he went to lie down on his bed.

He didn't bother to undress, and he fell asleep within minutes. For a long time, Pippa sat in an armchair watching him. Though she would have liked a nap, the gnawing hunger in her stomach prevented it.

When Jared woke, it was already dark outside, but Pippa had turned up the crystal gasolier and the room was lit pleasantly. She was reading, still in the armchair, and Jared smiled when he saw her.

"Haven't you slept, Pippa?" he asked as he got up.

"Reading is restful," Pippa explained, fighting an urge to yawn. She put the book away and stood up. "You look better," she told him.

"I'm recovered, thank you," said Jared as he went to his closet.

"Not recovered," Pippa stated firmly, but Jared smiled.

"You needn't worry, angel," he said gently. "I'm not ready to head back to the front lines yet."

"Good," said Pippa. "Because even when you seem better, things inside take a long time to be completely healed."

"Quite a little physician you've become, haven't you?"

"As a matter of fact, several of the doctors remarked on my abilities," she replied happily.

"And they don't know the half of it, do they?" he teased, and Pippa blushed.

"What are you doing there?" she asked as Jared turned back to peruse his old wardrobe.

"Well, I've been wearing a uniform for so long, I've forgotten what should be worn to dinner. You look perfect," he said as he glanced back at Pippa.

Jared drew forth an elegant dinner jacket and in a short time he was dressed more formally than Pippa had ever seen him. He tied his cravat and then held out his arm to her. "Are you ready, my dear?" he said.

"My hair!" she exclaimed. It wouldn't do at all to enter Caroline Knox's dining room with her hair halfway down her back. Especially not when Jared looked like an English nobleman.

"I wish Emmaline was here," she moaned as she attempted to do up her own hair.

Jared sat back in the armchair himself now, and waited patiently as Pippa fumbled with her long, heavy hair. It took some time, but she didn't seem completely satisfied with her results. Her hair was decidedly wavy, and try as she might, Pippa couldn't make it lie flat against her head as did the other women.

"Oh dear," she said, as she peered into the looking-glass. "This will never do."

"You look beautiful, Pippa," said Jared as he watched the procedure. "When have you not? And stop squashing your hair down. I like it better as it is."

"Do you?" asked Pippa earnestly. "It doesn't look like it's supposed to at all, like the other ladies'."

"When have you wished to be like 'other ladies'?"

"Not often," Pippa admitted. "But tonight, at least, it would be a good thing."

"And an impossible thing, I believe," said Jared as he rose from his chair. "Your hair has a will of its own, my love. How could it be otherwise?"

With that, Jared took his wife firmly by the arm and led her toward the door. But another worry came to Pippa and she stopped. "Will that other girl, that Christina, be there, too?" she asked.

"Christina? No, I doubt it." Jared paused, and his brow furrowed slightly. "Why do you ask?"

Pippa hesitated, but she felt compelled to address the subject. "Well, I don't think she cared much for me. As your wife, I mean," she speculated nervously.

Pippa gathered her courage and looked up into Jared's blue eyes. "Was she the girl you almost married?"

Jared didn't answer immediately, and plainly he was taken aback by Pippa's question. A faint frown gathered at his lips. "As a matter of fact, she was. But that was many years ago."

Pippa felt a dull ache surface in her heart, but she dared not pursue the matter further. Something in Jared's expression told her this would be unwise, so she said nothing more. After all, Jared hadn't chosen to marry Christina when he was a young man. Yet Pippa had little doubt that his family would have preferred Christina to her.

Pippa gazed around in wonder as Jared led her toward the dining room. Great Persian carpets graced the floors of elegant sitting rooms, and impressive paintings hung at tasteful intervals. The dusty rose hue of damask-upholstered furniture picked up the rose of the carpets, yet all was carefully understated in tone.

It was altogether a beautiful home, with large windows allowing the golden Virginia sun to filter beguilingly through the rooms. The restrained elegance reflected Caroline Knox's taste perfectly, and when Pippa entered the large dining room, she felt small and out of place in the presence of Jared's serenely beautiful mother.

"Well, darling, you look much better," said Caroline as she took Jared's arm.

Her eyes were drawn to Pippa, and Pippa was acutely aware of Caroline's cool appraisal. "Philippa, how lovely you look. I hope you also were able to rest?"

"Yes, thank you," replied Pippa less than truthfully.

"Katy's dress fits you perfectly. How lucky you're of a similar height," added Caroline.

"It was very kind of her," agreed Pippa, but she wished Katy herself was in attendance. Jared's other two sisters were already seated at the long table, and neither looked pleased to see her.

Caroline directed Pippa and Jared to their seats, and took her place at the head of the table next to her son. David Knox's chair remained respectfully open, yet Pippa felt his presence in the room almost as if he sat beside her.

"I understand you've already met General Knox," said Caroline as elegantly attired servants entered the room.

Pippa was surprised by the formal title used by David's wife, but she nodded. "We dined with him before . . . before . . ." Pippa began, but remembering the Wilderness battle, she wavered.

"It was the last night in camp," explained Jared, and his eyes were kind as he glanced at his wife.

"I see," said Caroline. Her expression altered slightly as she looked at Pippa, and her voice betrayed a sadness when she continued. "He must have been pleased to meet you, Philippa," she guessed with unexpected accuracy. "He has expected Jared to marry for some time."

"I doubt Father expected him to marry a Yankee," said Kim, but a sharp glance from Caroline ended the girl's opinion.

Jared seemed unaffected by his little sister's disapproval, but Pippa wished she could simply disappear. Kim accepted her mother's silent reproach, but Pippa's endurance was further tested by the darker sister.

"You're from Massachusetts, Philippa?" she asked suspiciously.

"Pippa is from Maine, Mary," corrected Jared. If possible, this brought an even darker suspicion from his sisters.

"My father was a professor at Bowdoin College in Brunswick," Pippa added with resignation.

"Brunswick!" gasped Mary with horror. "Isn't that where that dreadful Stowe woman resides?"

Pippa cringed inwardly at the accusation Harriet Beecher Stowe's name could levy, but she met the other girl's eyes. "It is, yes. As a matter of fact, our winter home was on the same street as theirs."

"Where was your summer home?" asked Caroline in a tense voice.

"Father had a cottage by the sea," replied Pippa wistfully. "He liked to write and paint when he wasn't teaching."

"That sounds lovely," said Caroline without much feeling.

"It was," remembered Pippa with a sigh. "I much preferred it there, but winters are cold in Maine. It was best to live in town once the snow came."

"It sounds dreadful," put in Mary. "I loathe the cold."

Pippa wasn't particularly offended by Mary's observation. "No, winters are something I don't really miss," she agreed, and she was aware that Caroline sighed with relief at her reaction.

"We've sent Wilson for your things, Philippa," Caroline told her. "He'll bring Charlotte's maid back with him. I'm certain she'll prove useful. I've sent most of ours to work in the hospitals."

Pippa had noticed no lack of help when the dinner was served, but it lifted her spirits considerably to learn Lucy would be there.

"Perhaps when you've settled in here, you might consider nursing at one of the hospitals," suggested Caroline. "Jared says you served in the Wilderness."

"Yes, I'd like to do that," replied Pippa. If her reaction surprised Jared, she surprised herself even more.

"I don't think the wounded will appreciate being tended by a Yankee," said Kim derisively, and Pippa's heart sank.

It was plain neither sister liked her, and her willingness to help only annoyed them further. Yet she sensed a particular vengeance from Kim, though she had no idea why this should be. As the youngest and prettiest, Pippa guessed Kim might be spoiled, especially as she closely resembled her mother. But nothing adequately explained the veiled light of hatred she discerned in the girl's blue eyes.

"I'm certain our boys will be grateful for any attention they receive," said Caroline reproachfully, and Kim looked away with a frown.

"I don't recall any objections issued in the Wilderness," added Jared. "It pleased them to have a Yankee caring for them instead of shooting."

"They were very polite," said Pippa quietly, and her face clouded as she remembered the long line of injured men she had tended.

"I would like to help them very much," she added wistfully, and Jared squeezed her hand.

Pippa was more or less ignored for the rest of the meal, though she listened attentively to their conversation. She learned Jared had another sister who lived in South Carolina, and that Mary's husband was a cavalry officer with Fitzhugh Lee. But Pippa lost track of the many persons and goings-on discussed.

"While you're here, Jared, you must visit the President," said Caroline as the servants cleared the table.

"There's to be a lavish party soon," added Mary. "Dignitaries from England have come through the blockade, and everyone's making a great effort at entertaining them. Trying to show them how little the war has damaged the Confederacy."

"I hope they're kept inside then," remarked Jared.

Caroline frowned. "Robert says the Englishmen are being fed as if at court, and our soldiers are starving. I can't imagine what our Senators are thinking."

"I don't see any lack at our table tonight," observed Jared, but Caroline's face was serious when she turned to him.

"This isn't our usual fare, darling," she told him. "But I'm not without influence with our blockade runners. Tomorrow, you'll have to do with a lesser meal."

"Is that where you managed to get this coffee?" asked Jared appreciatively.

"It's good, isn't it?" said Caroline.

"It is indeed. It's the first time I've had real coffee since I met Garrett at Chancellorsville," recalled Jared.

"He gave you coffee?" asked Pippa.

"We had a polite exchange," replied Jared. "In the midst of a river, in the middle of the night. But this is better coffee."

"Actually this portion of your meal isn't courtesy of the blockade runners," Caroline told him. "Any coffee in the city is brought straight to those Englishman. No, as a matter of fact, Charlotte Reid gave this to me as a gift. Her nephew had brought it from New York."

"Burke Mallory?" asked Kim, and the others looked at her curiously.

"Yes," replied Caroline slowly. "I didn't realize you knew Charlotte's nephew, Kimber."

"I met him once," replied Kim. Although she said nothing

urther, Pippa sensed the mention of Burke's name made
Kim uncomfortable.

"Now that I remember," added Caroline, "Mr. Mallory
asked for you at Elspeth Carlton's party. He seemed disap-
pointed you had remained in Richmond."

Kim didn't reply, but Pippa was certain she detected a
flash of something that resembled fear in the other girl's
eyes.

"I don't believe I've asked you if you enjoyed the party,
Mother?" asked Mary. Pippa wondered if Mary was inten-
tionally changing the subject on behalf of her younger sister.

"It was pleasant, yes," replied Caroline slowly, glancing
at Pippa and Jared, who were smiling at each other. "It was
good to be back, though I must confess it was sad to be so
close to our old home."

Pippa's eyes widened and she grasped Jared's hand. "Why
don't you rebuild it, Jared?" she asked, and the eyes of the
other three women turned to him expectantly.

Jared was less enthusiastic. "With what?" he asked.
"Have you forgotten the blockade, my dear?"

Pippa's face fell, and Caroline sighed, but another idea
struck Pippa. "You could design it, Jared," she told him.
"You can build it when the war is over."

Again the others looked to him, but Jared contemplated
his suggestion with a frown. "When the war is over . . .
That's growing harder and harder to imagine."

"It will end," said Pippa with conviction. "It has to, and
the blockade will be withdrawn."

Pippa's excitement soared as she went on, considering the
possibilities. "When you're finished with that, you can design houses for other people," she said cheerfully. "Think
how many will need you!"

This seemed to please Caroline as well, and it was the

first thing Pippa had said that didn't bring a frown to Kim'
lips. But Jared himself wasn't convinced.

"I doubt very much I have the skill to restore Virginia to
what it once was," he said. "But I'm glad to see you have
such faith in me!"

Jared and Pippa retired early, and when they returned to
Jared's room, Pippa realized how much she had wanted to
be alone with him. Pippa immediately took off her shoes
for those Katy lent her were too large and they were uncomfortable. Jared removed his dinner jacket and sat in the
armchair, holding out his hand for Pippa.

"Come here," he commanded, and Pippa smiled shyly
when she placed her hand in his.

Jared drew her onto his lap and wrapped his arms about
her waist. "I hope you didn't find dinner too difficult, angel."

Pippa paused to consider the best way to answer this. "I
wasn't terrible," she said slowly. "But I was better prepared
for nursing in the Wilderness than for this evening."

"You handled it very well. Your willingness to work in
the hospital pleased my mother. Katy already likes you, and
though Mary can be rather difficult at times, she'll get used
to you. But I'm afraid Kim may take awhile to accept you
as a sister-in-law. She's very young, even younger than you
and she suffered at the hands of the Yankees that raided our
estate. Right now, she can't imagine there's anyone good
north of Virginia."

"What about your cousins?" asked Pippa.

"She hasn't mentioned that side of our family since. But
she never knew Garrett very well, and only met Adrian
briefly. I'm afraid they aren't enough to sway her opinion
of your kind."

"How does she know Burke?" asked Pippa curiously.

"Until tonight, I didn't realize they had ever met," replied Jared, and Pippa guessed he had sensed the same tension in Kim as had she.

Pippa's mind wandered from the subject. As she gazed into her husband's handsome face, desire surged within her. Pippa blushed as Jared's smile grew in recognition.

"Is your head sore?" she asked, glancing at his lightly bandaged forehead.

"I barely feel it," replied Jared, his smile deepening as he guessed the nature of Pippa's question.

"You must be tired, though," she ventured, still looking at his forehead.

"Not at all," he replied. His blue eyes were sparkling.

Pippa's heart began to pound so loudly she was certain Jared could hear, and she averted her eyes to her hands. Jared unbound her carefully netted hair, and freed it to fall sensually across her shoulders. His fingers played with a long waving tendril, and he stroked the petal softness of her cheek.

Pippa wanted desperately to look at him, to learn of him as openly as he had explored her. She wanted to taste his skin as he had tasted hers, to own his full desire, to please him as he pleased her. She wanted to learn what would bring him such pleasure, but she didn't dare to ask.

The long, hellish days and nights in the Wilderness without him, fearing desperately for his life, had been the worst in her life. Pippa wanted to draw Jared inside her, wrap around him and protect him with her life if she could. But she had no clear idea how to accomplish this, so she merely sat and waited.

Jared sensed that his wife had something on her mind

that she didn't dare to address, and he had a fair idea what that something was. "What do you want, Pippa?"

Pippa raised her eyes to Jared's, and she knew her feelings were safe with him. He had promised her that once, and she knew that this part of his feeling for her hadn't changed.

"I want to please you," she answered in a small but clear voice. "As you've done to me," she added mischievously.

Jared's heart thudded in response to her direct words, and his arms tightened about her waist. But then he released her. "Up," he ordered.

Pippa got up from his lap, but she had no idea what he wanted. Jared rose and took her hand, leading her to his bedside. He stripped off his clothes, but when Pippa started to do the same, he stopped her.

"Wait," he said, and Pippa watched him in confusion.

As Jared tossed his clothes to the chair, Pippa allowed her eyes to wander across his tall body and she felt a curious ache low in her own. His shoulders were broad, his back long and lean, tapering to well-muscled buttocks and powerful legs. Pippa thought him a beautiful sight.

Pippa longed to touch him, to hold him, and her hands were trembling when he turned back to her. She saw that he was already much aroused. When he lay back on the bed, she couldn't help but stare at him.

"Your turn, my love," he said in a low, deep voice. Seeing Pippa's incomprehension, Jared added, "Get undressed, Pippa. Slowly."

Pippa did as he asked, uncertain as to the purpose of such a thing. But when she saw his blue eyes darken as she undid the row of tiny, glass buttons on her bodice, she began to understand what he was asking of her.

A tiny smile crossed Pippa's flushed face as she slipped the dress from her shoulders and let it fall to the floor. A pile of petticoats was dropped to the floor, and then she slipped the thin straps of her silken chemise from each shoulder. It slithered to the floor, sending tiny shocks across her skin. Briefly allowing her eyes to meet Jared's, Pippa saw the sensual curve of his smile upon his lips and she knew he was pleased.

"The rest, if you please," he requested in a voice made husky with his arousal.

Pippa untied the strings of the gracefully embroidered corset and she heard Jared's intaken breath as she slid it and her silk stockings from her body.

"You are beautiful, little witch," he murmured, and Pippa saw how desire had changed his face, his wanting plainly revealed.

Her knees were weak, and Pippa crawled onto the bed beside Jared. "What do you want?" he asked again, his eyes burning with the fire she had started in him.

"I want to touch you," she responded in an unusually gravelly voice. Seeing Jared's smile, Pippa bent to kiss his lips.

"And I want to feel your touch, love," Jared told her with pleasure.

Pippa's trembling fingers went to Jared's face, running along his strong cheekbone and across his jaw to the angle of his chin. Her lips followed the touch of her fingers, and Jared closed his eyes as her soft mouth pressed against his skin.

His reaction pleased Pippa, and she found she enjoyed this command of him immensely. It fired her confidence, and she hungered to know more of him, to make him moan at her touch as she had reveled in his artistry.

"Oh, Jared," she whispered lovingly. "You are the most beautiful man."

"And you are sweeter than my wildest imaginings," replied Jared as he reached to brush the soft hair from Pippa's face.

Pippa kissed either side of his face, then trailed a line down his neck. The tiny tip of her tongue teased the surface of his skin with each soft kiss, and Pippa felt the heat of his body soar. She kissed his muscled shoulder and gently ran her hand across the expanse of his wide chest, then downward across his taut stomach.

Her lips brushed along the same path, and her hair softly teased Jared's sensitized flesh as her kisses moved ever lower. Pippa could hear the powerful beats of Jared's heart, feel the strong force of life that coursed through his aroused body, and it excited her wildly to be close to him.

"Does this please you?" she asked sweetly, pausing as she pressed a soft kiss against the taut skin below his navel.

Jared shuddered at her slow kiss, and his voice was raw with the flaming need Pippa inspired. "Yes, angel. You are pleasing me. Don't stop," he added, but he groaned as Pippa's tongue swept across his tingling flesh.

Her gradually descending kisses drove Jared wild with need, and his breath came forcefully as her hand met with his desire. Her fingers brushed the length of his hardened staff, and then closed about his thickness as the silken ends of her long hair teased his groin.

Pippa gazed with enchanted curiosity at his glorious arousal. Then, mesmerized by its power, she kissed the swollen tip. If Pippa harbored any doubts about whether this would please Jared, his harsh groan of pleasure drove them away.

"Pippa," he began hoarsely, and Pippa lifted her head to search his face.

"Do you like it?" she asked, but Jared let out a shuddering sigh.

"Yes," he moaned. "I like it."

She kissed him again, and her tongue darted from her lips to taste the slick surface. Jared's trembling hands clenched in her hair and Pippa took more of him in her mouth, lightly teasing the underside of his shaft with the tip of her tongue.

Jared's response was far more powerful than she imagined, and Pippa learned to mimic the motion of lovemaking. Jared's sharply intaken breaths and low groans told her she was bringing him along the same paths he had shown to her, and Pippa was consumed with his pleasure.

Jared's senses reeled as Pippa's warm mouth caressed him. When she drew back to tease his heated erection with little licks of her tongue, he knew he could bear no more of her sweet torment without fulfilling his raging desire.

"Pippa," he called, his voice thick and ragged with passion. "Pippa, come here."

Pippa brushed her lips across the engorged tip in a leisurely fashion. She cast her shaded green eyes to his face, a curved smile beckoning upon her lips.

"Pippa, now," he ordered heavily, and with a soft laugh, she rose to gaze into his blazing eyes.

Jared was wild with desire, his hunger for her raging uncontrollably. He lifted Pippa above him, then in one motion rolled her onto her back against his bed. Jared poised himself between her legs, teasing her in turn as he moved against the gentle swell of her sex.

Pippa writhed beneath Jared, her head tossed from side to side as she felt the hot pressure of him gliding back and forth against her.

"Jared, I need you," she moaned, but now it was Jared who delayed the final completion of their desire.

"How much, love?" he whispered against her ear, and he allowed his hardened tip to delve into the warm, slippery entrance of Pippa's body.

He didn't enter her fully, and Pippa was wild with need beneath him. "Oh, Jared, don't make me wait," she pleaded, and she arched beneath him. "Please love me, now," she murmured breathlessly.

"Whatever you desire, my love," he replied, and he took her mouth in a passionate entreaty as he drove within her.

At the force of his entry, Pippa's senses shattered. Her body took on a will of its own as it twisted mindlessly beneath him. Jared's powerful thrusts drove Pippa closer and closer to a complete surrender, and they surged together as their bodies thundered a passionate release.

Pippa's arms closed tightly around Jared's shoulders, and she held him against her, fearing ever to let him go. She kissed his hair, and he moved to kiss her mouth. The kiss was tender and sweet, slow now that they had loved.

"Pippa, you are heaven," he said. Meeting Jared's languid gaze, Pippa smiled.

"Had I known how good it is to be in your company, I would have let you catch me two years ago."

"But I've caught you now, my love. And now that you are mine, how will we spend the days?"

A sweet, teasing kiss was Jared's answer, and soon neither could remember a time they had been without the other.

Eight

Pippa lay drowsily in Jared's arms, her head resting comfortably on his shoulder as his fingers played in her hair. Through the window, she could see the half moon rising above the old elm trees, and she sighed.

"Was this always your room?" she asked as she pressed a fond kiss against the firm flesh of his shoulder.

"I have to admit it's been mine since I left the nursery," replied Jared guiltily. "My sisters shared a room, until Katy got older. So I was favored."

"Is Katy older than you?" asked Pippa.

"Two years, yes. She was the first."

"Are you the second?" Pippa wondered. Mary appeared closer in age to Jared, and she wasn't certain.

Jared hesitated before answering, though Pippa couldn't imagine why. "I was my mother's second child," he answered slowly. "Mary is twenty-five, and my other sister, Julia, is also married and lives in Charleston."

"It must be nice to have brothers and sisters," mused Pippa dreamily. As an only child, she was extremely rare, but Gordon Reid had never married again when his beloved Scottish wife died.

Pippa yawned. "Of course, I had Byron, and Jefferson. They were as good as brothers. Both had been slaves, but they weren't much alike. Such as when Roger Allen Pickney tried to kiss me . . ."

"Did he?" interrupted Jared. "The nerve."

"That's what I said. I was thirteen, and Roger said I needed a man."

"How old was he?" Jared considering hunting up this Roger Allen Pickney. Dueling still had its place.

"Twelve."

Jared laughed. "Then I guess I won't have to call him out."

"There's no need. Jefferson thrashed him quite thoroughly. But I think Roger preferred that to Byron's subsequent lecture."

"What did he say?"

"I don't remember, but it was long," said Pippa. "After that, he lectured Jefferson about controlling anger. I think Byron learned that in his own life, so it's important to him. He's very reasonable. About most things, anyway." Except about the man who fathered him. Byron's reason faltered there.

"I wish I knew where they are now. I miss them so." Pippa's voice faded, and her eyes closed sleepily. But Jared Knox lay awake, thinking of one he hadn't seen in many years. Pippa's words reminded him how deeply such ties could run.

Pippa woke the next morning to find Jared gazing down into her face, and her heart soared when she saw the tenderness in his eyes. He brushed a long strand of dark hair from her face, then kissed her forehead.

"Good morning, Mrs. Knox."

He looked well-rested, though they had woken together

in the early hours of morning to join again in passion. Pippa felt sated and she was aglow with her satisfaction.

"I trust you enjoyed your . . . rest," he added with a knowing grin.

Pippa smiled and stretched beside him. "I enjoyed the night very much," she agreed. "But what will we do during the days? We can't very well stay up here all day—that would be embarrassing at dinner time," she considered seriously. Jared laughed.

"Well, I, for one, am content. For the moment, at least. I believe we might venture forth from the bedroom. The idea of breakfast is particularly appealing," he said. Pippa sat upright with undisguised pleasure at his suggestion.

They dressed hurriedly, but when Jared stepped out into the hall, he heard his mother greeting a caller downstairs. He listened for a moment, then furtively slipped back into the bedroom.

"What's the matter?" she asked, half smiling and half in wonder.

"Mildred Smith has arrived," he told her, much in the same tone as if Abe Lincoln had popped by.

"Who's that?" asked Pippa, but she giggled when she saw the look on his face.

"Mildred is Christina's mother," he explained. "She and I don't care for each other."

"Because you didn't marry her daughter?" speculated Pippa, but Jared shook his fair head.

"Partly, but our antagonism goes back further than that. I imagine I was the very last boy she would've selected for her daughter, despite her affection for my mother."

"Why?" asked Pippa in amazement.

"As a boy, I was fairly troublesome," Jared admitted. "I raided her apple trees and picked her flowers to . . ."

"Put in girls' hair," guessed Pippa.

"My purposes were varied," laughed Jared. "But none pleased Mildred Smith. The situation with Christina only served to fan her already active dislike of me. I shudder to think why she's downstairs now."

Pippa giggled. "I can guess well enough," she said with pleasure.

Pippa's face clouded and she looked intently into Jared's eyes. "Did you love Christina, Jared?"

Jared shrugged. "At eighteen, who knows? I cared for her, but it wasn't a particularly passionate pairing. She was like a sister to me, and of course, my family liked her."

"Did your father want you to marry her, too?" asked Pippa a trifle jealously. She liked David Knox very much, and she hoped he wouldn't prefer Christina to her.

"My father's feelings on the matter were never expressed to me."

"But she loved you, didn't she?" asked Pippa, though she already knew the answer.

"I suppose so. Why does it matter now?"

"I think she still does," guessed Pippa daringly. "And I think you know it."

"She was married to my closest friend, Pippa," Jared told her.

"That's why it troubles you," replied Pippa, though inwardly she marveled at her courage to broach such a delicate subject.

Pippa's perceptions didn't seem to anger Jared, and he sighed. "Christina had known Charles all her life, as she had known me. He was gentle and kind, and he adored her. When I left, she turned to him and they married."

"Were they happy?"

"I believe so," he answered slowly. "Charles and I joined

the army together, and during those first days of the war, Richmond was wild with excitement. There were parties almost daily, dances, uniforms better called costumes complete with outdated weapons of chivalry."

Jared took a long breath and shook his head sadly. "Manassas showed us how unprepared we were for actual battle, but fortunately for the Confederacy, the Yankees were even less prepared. I found that my head remained fairly clear during the fight," he went on without special pride, but Pippa gazed at him admiringly all the same.

"It isn't that difficult to guess what an enemy is going to do, and out-think them. The land itself reveals the obvious," he explained as Pippa listened with interest. "Your Yankees rarely consider their attacks very well."

Jared stopped. "In fact, there's only one Yankee I encountered with the foresight to consider the uses of natural geography and use it to her advantage."

Pippa's face was blank at first, but then she smiled as Jared's meaning dawned on her. Jared kissed her, but then his face darkened. "After I led a small group from catastrophe at Manassas, they saw fit to make me a captain," he told her with a sigh.

"That in itself wasn't enough to come between a friendship such as I had with Charles, yet as the war continued, battle grew more bitter. The bravest of our officers led our charges, and all too often, were the first to fall. We learned our fates weren't determined by the size of our courage nor the depth of our honor."

Jared fell silent as he recalled the hard lesson learned. "At first, many refused to dig trenches, to fire from behind cover. It wasn't considered an . . . honorable way to fight. Those who refused to yield this chivalry fell. We learned that death in war is all too often arbitrary and without purpose. Charles took this grim reality of war hard."

Jared sighed before continuing. "As a result, he began to drink heavily. Drink affected him strangely—he became violent and belligerent. As often happens, the liquor released an anger that he vented at his wife."

Pippa's eyes widened. "Did he hit her?"

Jared nodded slowly, his face strained with the memory. "He did, and she came to me for help. I had no choice—I brought her here. Christina didn't wish Mildred to know what had happened. It was like the old bat to blame Christina for provoking her husband."

"What happened?" asked Pippa. "Did he stop drinking and come for her?"

"He did, but he couldn't forgive what he considered my interference."

"That doesn't sound completely fair."

"No, but by then there was a distance between them that little could mend."

"And with you coming to her rescue," murmured Pippa, but Jared looked at her quickly.

"That indeed led to a development I hadn't foreseen," Jared acknowledged quietly.

"She was still in love with you?" guessed Pippa hesitantly.

Jared drew a slow breath. "Yes. Charles had hurt her badly. Not just physically, but in spirit," he told Pippa raggedly.

"I'd been there for her, and I suppose she turned to me for that reason. But I realized I had unwittingly driven an even greater wedge between them. I convinced her to return to him. But Charles never forgave me," Jared said with a sigh. "Before Gettysburg, he accused me of trying to steal his wife. It was painful to see a boyhood friendship end in bitterness."

Jared sighed heavily, and Pippa squeezed his hand. "As a matter of fact, Mildred also accused me of disturbing her daughter's marriage. For this reason, and others, I'm not terribly pleased to see her today."

From the bottom of the staircase, Pippa and Jared heard Caroline calling, and Jared rolled his eyes heavenward before going to the door. He reluctantly appeared at the top of the stairs, and Pippa followed him.

"There you are, darling!" called Caroline, oblivious to all Jared had told Pippa.

"Mildred will be taking breakfast with us," she told him as they descended the stairs.

"Wonderful," replied Jared flatly. As he held out his hand to Pippa, their eyes met and she read everything that he couldn't say.

Mildred Smith was smaller than Caroline, blonde, but less attractive. She looked at Jared unsympathetically, and her eyes went to Pippa with undisguised scrutiny.

"Mildred, I'd like you to meet my daughter-in-law, Philippa," began Caroline nervously, but Pippa smiled brightly.

"I'm pleased to meet you, Mrs. Smith," she said, but Mildred Smith assessed her suspiciously.

"Indeed," the woman said coldly. "I understood you'd taken a wife rather abruptly, Jared. But I had no idea she was a Yankee!"

"A New England Yankee, as a matter of fact," Jared said with pleasure. Pippa and Caroline squirmed with discomfort.

"I'd have thought you might be more concerned with your family's good name," retorted Mildred.

Pippa realized Jared hadn't exaggerated the antagonism

between the two. She thought of Jared blood-stained and weary at Spotsylvania, leading a charge against a greater force, and her anger flared.

"Now you listen here," she began hotly. "I'd mind my own business if I were you," she said, as she faced the older woman fiercely.

Caroline gasped, but Mildred's lips formed a catlike smile. "Caroline, I am sorry. I had no idea your invitation for breakfast included a Yankee. You must excuse me," she said haughtily, and with a huff, Mildred Smith departed.

"Oh, I'm sorry," squeaked Pippa when the door banged shut behind the exiting Mildred.

"Never mind, Philippa," said Caroline calmly.

"I can't begin to count the times Mildred has left our house in this fashion. Most often, it had something to do with Jared. Quite frankly, I can remember worse incidents. Such as when Jared put a number of frogs in Mildred's sewing chest."

Pippa giggled, and again her heart was filled with happiness.

"I thought she might need them for her cauldron," Jared explained darkly. "But I can't imagine why you'd have invited that woman to breakfast, Mother."

"Invited, indeed. It was, as I recall, Mildred's suggestion. I believe she came over here with the intention of slamming the door."

"Well, I'm glad she slammed it with herself on the other side," said Jared as he turned to Pippa. "Shall we dine, my dear?"

The next days with Jared were the happiest in Pippa's life. When in the company of his family, their eyes met to exchange secret glances that burned with memories of passion. So completely enthralled with her husband's attention was she, Pippa rarely noticed his sisters' coolness toward her.

Caroline wasn't exactly warm to her new daughter-in-law, but since Pippa had spoken up to Mildred Smith, she seemed to accept Pippa's place as Jared's wife. But even had Caroline resented her, Pippa wouldn't have noticed. During those blissful days she saw nothing but Jared.

Nights were a pure, sultry heaven for both, and their nighttime activities saw them rising late the next morning. Often they skipped breakfast entirely to spend the morning alone in each other's company.

"We'll have an early lunch, angel," murmured Jared as he lifted her hair to brush soft kisses against the nape of her neck.

"I wasn't terribly hungry," Pippa agreed as he lifted her in his arms, and she let her nightdress fall to her feet.

A knock on the door interrupted the flare of passion between them, and Jared reluctantly let his wife replace her nightdress. Pippa went to the door, and to her delight, there stood Lucy. Her bright eyes were carefully shaded from Jared, but Pippa felt Lucy's joy at their reunion.

"Lucy!" exclaimed Pippa. "I'm so glad to see you."

"Yes, miss. I's pleased as anything to be here. I's brung your things, miss," Lucy said with a glance over her shoulder. Wilson stepped into the room bearing Pippa's smallest trunk.

"There's one or two more, miss," said Wilson breathlessly, and Jared understood the none-too-subtle hint.

"Let me help you with those, Wilson," he suggested wryly. "I know your back isn't what it used to be."

"No, sir, it sure enough isn't. Time was as I'd have carried all three of these here bags together. No more, though. No more."

Jared and Wilson departed to get the rest of Pippa's wardrobe. As the men descended the steps, Lucy hugged Pippa tightly. "It looks as though things have worked out better than you expected, Pippa," Lucy said.

"Oh, they have, Lucy!" gushed Pippa. "He still loves me," she told Lucy unnecessarily.

"I see that," replied Lucy.

"We're married," Pippa told her with joy. "I've never been so happy, Lucy. Sometimes I can't believe it's real, that it will last."

"I'd be curious to learn what softened his temper. Young Master Knox was in a fury when I last saw the two of you."

Pippa blushed, and Lucy laughed. "I see. Perhaps I shouldn't ask."

Pippa's smile widened, but she pressed her lips together to contain the impulse to giggle foolishly. "I believe Jared has come to see that our love is stronger and more important than any insignificant differences between us."

Lucy's brow rose at this, and her heart was troubled. Pippa's happiness seemed reckless to the girl who had seen so much hope fail of its promise. Lucy knew Pippa intended to be a faithful wife to her new husband. She also knew that those "insignificant differences" were likely to rise again between them before the war ended. Life offered many choices, and not all were easy ones.

"I'm glad you're happy, Pippa," she said. "And I'm grateful to you for bringing me here. Parson Frederick had promised to take me to his home, but this is better. There's so much to be done!"

Pippa wondered briefly why Lucy would prefer Richmond to living with the kindly parson, but at that moment Jared and Wilson returned. Wilson held the door open, and Jared walked in carrying the two heavy trunks by himself.

"It looks like you'll have plenty to wear," he commented as he set Pippa's baggage to the floor.

"I's put in your books, miss," said Lucy, and Jared groaned.

"That would explain it."

With Lucy in the house, Pippa felt more at ease. More and more, she began to consider it her home. News from the war was uneven, but she gathered a Yankee attack on Richmond wasn't imminent. Instead, their moves after the Confederate victory at Cold Harbor appeared to be a feint only, and the Yankees instead were headed for Petersburg.

So content was Pippa in Jared's company that she found she was actually looking forward to the party at the White House. It had been discussed every evening with great enthusiasm, and Pippa was as caught up in preparations as were his sisters.

"So why is it that my little Yankee wife is so excited about socializing with the President of the Confederacy?" asked Jared as they dressed for the occasion.

"Well, he'll be a part of history, one way or another," Pippa reflected thoughtfully as she began lacing her corset.

"Or do you just want to dance with me?" suggested Jared with a warm smile. He crossed the room to stand close behind Pippa, and she leaned back against him as his arms wrapped around her waist. Jared kissed the curve of her neck seductively, and Pippa sighed.

"That may be it, after all," she replied softly, and she turned in his arms to accept his seeking kiss.

But Jared drew away and took her hands in his. "Pippa,

my love," he began with effort. "There's something we must discuss, tonight, before the party."

He led her to the bed and they sat together, his head bowed as he gathered himself to tell her what he must. Pippa reached out to touch his golden hair. "What's wrong, Jared?"

Jared took her hands again and kissed them, then held them in his lap before he spoke. "My love, you know I wouldn't cause you pain for the world," he began, and Pippa's face paled as she wondered what such a statement could portend.

"What is it?" she asked fearfully, and Jared felt her hands go cold in his.

"It's time I went back to my duty," he said quietly.

"No, it isn't," she replied, but his eyes begged her understanding.

"How can I stay here with you while others are at war? Pippa, you must try to understand how duty might separate us, yet not threaten my love for you. I must go. My honor demands that. Do you understand?"

"Yes, Jared, I understand," she whispered, but her voice broke in sobs. "Oh, but I don't want you to go."

Jared pulled her close, kissing her desperately, wildly.

"Jared, please. Love me now," Pippa begged through her tears. "Hold me, please. Hold me."

Jared felt her desperate passion, and he pulled off her unlaced corset to kiss the bare, exposed flesh that shone before him. They fell together back upon the bed, and she tasted his own tears as their lips melted together.

Pippa wrapped her arms around him, and her legs entwined over his to draw him inside her. Jared buried himself deep within the warm, yielding flesh of his wife's love-soaked body, and her hips rose to meet him, to draw him deeper inside her.

They fused passionately together, desperate to hold on to each other when the world was determined to tear them apart. Their bodies rose together on the crest of their love and desire, crashing along a shore of violent ecstasy.

Lucy had packed an elaborately embroidered blue chintz and lace ball gown, one Pippa never had the occasion to don before. Tonight, however, she was delighted at the luxury. When she saw Jared's eyes widen with pleasure at the sight of her, she blessed Charlotte's good taste and generosity.

Lucy had learned much from Emmaline, and Pippa's hair was virtually a masterpiece. Escaping tendrils framed her small face, and delicate hair jewelry glistened artfully in the midst of the dark waves.

"You are lovely tonight, my dear," said Jared as he stepped forward to take his wife's arm.

Pippa's eyes blazed as she looked at him, for in full dress uniform, Jared had never looked more splendid. Kim and Mary joined them, and Kim in particular was beaming. Her gown was a rich golden chintz, and her fair hair shone, entwined about her beautiful head.

Having seen the success Lucy had with Pippa's wayward tresses, both girls requested her services that evening. Exhausted from her day's service, Lucy had subsequently disappeared before Caroline could choose to avail herself of the new maid's skill.

"Where is Mother?" asked Mary impatiently. Wilson had brought round the coach, and outside the horses stamped impatiently. Jared held the door open for the ladies, but no one noticed the tall figure that came up the walk towards the house.

"I'm coming, dear," replied Caroline, as she entered the room fidgeting with her crocheted purse.

Lucy raced into the hall from the kitchen and called to Pippa.

"What is it, Lucy?" asked Pippa in wonder. But Lucy was prevented from relaying her message to Pippa when a deep voice spoke from behind.

"Your mother always was late for an evening out."

All turned in astonishment to see David Knox standing in the threshold of his home.

"Papa!" cried Kim, and she raced to her father's arms.

He caught her and twirled her around, then set her down to embrace Mary. But Caroline stood still as stone, her face frozen with the force of emotion at seeing her husband.

Seeing her, Pippa felt strangely as if she was looking at herself from a great distance—herself looking at Jared after long apart. Loving him, yet not daring to run to him as she wished. Wished desperately. The impression troubled her, but she couldn't imagine a similarity between herself and Caroline Knox.

David was dressed in full military uniform, and Pippa guessed he had some idea of this evening's event. He caught sight of her and smiled. "I see you brought my son home in one piece, daughter," he said fondly, and Kim's face darkened temporarily at the warm tones her father used with Jared's wife.

"As ordered, sir," Pippa replied happily.

David turned to Jared. "I'm glad to see you well, son. Though I guessed with your little wife to wake up for, you'd be coming around soon enough. Thus assured, I've brought your horse."

This pleased Jared, and Pippa smiled fondly as he looked out the door.

"He's being stabled," David told his son indulgently.

"Where is Grant's army now?" asked Jared.

"It seemed at first he was headed here," David replied calmly, but Jared's sisters gasped. Kim's face went particularly white at the suggestion.

"But they're moving in on Petersburg instead," David added. "We'll entrench there first, as always, but I don't like what it portends."

"What are they trying to do?" asked Mary, but David sighed.

"Stretching the long gray line, my dear," he said with a shake of his head. "Stretching it until it breaks. It's with that concern I was sent here—to press our leaders for support, support that they aren't sending to General Lee's satisfaction."

Caroline stood watching her husband, her face impassive. But her blue eyes were shining with a love that Pippa recognized. She detected the quick rise and fall of Caroline's breast, and she felt the love almost as if it was her own. Again this troubled her, and Pippa looked to Jared for reassurance. Jared didn't seem aware of anything unnatural between his parents, and he stepped back to let the ladies pass.

"Are you coming to the party, Papa?" asked Kim excitedly.

"I would hate to send your mother without an escort," said David. "Especially when she looks as radiant as she does tonight."

The general held out his arm for his wife, and Caroline went to him. Pippa was touched to see the trace of shyness written now across Caroline's normally composed face. She looked beautiful—not young, but ageless.

Her maturity lent a grace and elegance that Pippa felt
surpassed the youthful bloom of herself and the other girls.
Pippa realized that despite Caroline's reservations about her,
she was growing fond of her mother-in-law.

They arrived at the Confederate White House amidst a
flurry of coaches, and Pippa walked beside Jared toward the
entrance. In the rush of arriving guests, Pippa was afforded
a brief opportunity to speak privately to Jared.

"Your father arrived at a perfect moment, didn't he?" she
said romantically. "How wonderful for your mother!"

Jared was quiet a moment, and Pippa glanced at him questioningly. "Yes," he said. "She loves him very much."

Jared himself sounded a little sorrowful when he spoke,
but his expression changed when he looked into Pippa's
face. "Well, what do you think, little Pip? Will you play the
Southern belle for me tonight?"

"Anything you want, my love," she answered, and the
glittering light in her eyes brought a warmth to Jared's body
he considered best neglected until later.

Jared led Pippa to a large room crowded with beautifully
attired guests. Pippa realized that though Richmonders suffered from dire shortages throughout the city, these favored
elite were not sharing that misery. Women might riot in the
street for bread, yet tonight, no expense was spared for the
English dignitaries. Now Pippa understood Caroline's irritation with the function.

"What can the English offer the Confederacy?" asked
Pippa. Across the room, she saw an exceptionally elegant
gentleman. As he was surrounded by a doting crowd of admirers, she guessed he was one of those in question.

"Perhaps our politicians still retain some hope of British

recognition," replied Jared nonchalantly. "Although I think that unlikely. While the English noblemen may favor the Confederacy, the poorer classes do not, and they're far more numerous."

"If it's unlikely, why all the fuss?" asked Pippa, shaking her head at the proffered wine.

"It may be these particular gentleman have something else to offer."

"What?" asked Pippa with growing interest.

"That, I don't know. Something to help the Cause, I trust. I hope it's something to benefit our army directly. Perhaps arms."

Pippa heard the music strike up, and she forgot the matter when she saw dancers take the floor. An older gentleman was leading Kim in a graceful dance. Despite Kim's antagonism towards her, Pippa was pleased to see her happy. Though Kim was beautiful, she also seemed tense and uneasy, and Pippa had often wondered about this since coming to Richmond.

"Has Kim a beau?" she asked, as Jared took her hand and led her among the other dancers.

"Not that I'm aware of, no," he replied. "Although many have favored her. She seems to prefer the company of older gentleman. Perhaps they're safer."

"Is she frightened of young men?" asked Pippa. "Because of those who raided your house?"

"I believe that's the cause, yes," answered Jared distantly. Pippa remembered that he had blamed her for the ugly event.

"Perhaps she'll meet someone who can make her forget her fears, and she'll no longer require those walls," considered Pippa. "Someone who makes her forget what she was and all the past, to live only for now," she added dreamily, but her eyes were shining when Jared looked down into her face.

"Is that what you've found, Pippa?" he asked, and there was hope revealed in his voice.

"It is," she answered, and Jared drew her closer into his arms.

"Who is that man?" asked Pippa. A tall, gaunt man entered the room with a statuesque, dark-haired woman. She stayed close by his side, gazing up at her husband lovingly. The music ceased when they entered, and many of the dancers stopped to look at the sad-faced gentleman.

"He looks a bit like Abe Lincoln," Pippa whispered excitedly.

Jared laughed and put his arm about her waist. "Pippa, my love, that is Jefferson Davis, not Abraham Lincoln."

"Is that him?" she asked in excitement. "Of course, I've never seen President Lincoln in person. Have you?"

"Once, yes," replied Jared.

"Did you like him?" Pippa admired the Union's President, especially since he had shown courage in issuing the Emancipation Proclamation. She hoped Jared wouldn't discount his genius as did other Southerners.

"Like him?" Jared mused thoughtfully. "I think I was a little frightened of him. He seemed a man of strong conviction, and to be on the other side of that conviction was disturbing. But I heard him speak, with Garrett as a matter of fact, and we were both moved by his words."

"I'd like to see him one day," said Pippa wistfully. As they spoke, a woman approached them, and when she spoke, Jared startled and turned to her in astonishment.

"Jared Knox, I believe," said a soft, melodic English

voice. Pippa saw an exceptionally lovely woman place her hand bewitchingly upon Jared's shoulder.

Jared was plainly stunned to see her, and Pippa's heart began to labor beneath a recognition her mind hadn't yet accepted. The woman's soft brown hair was lavishly coiffed, and her exquisite crimson gown seemed designed as if to accentuate to perfection the shapeliness of her body.

"Victoria!" Jared breathed, and his voice told Pippa all she needed to know about his familiarity with this woman.

"Then you haven't forgotten me, after all," the woman replied. The faint note of teasing irritated Pippa greatly.

Victoria's soft brown eyes turned to Pippa in careful scrutiny. Though Pippa was generally considered gracefully tall, beside the petite Englishwoman she felt large and clumsy.

"Who is this dear creature?" asked Victoria with a smile that Pippa felt certain was not heartfelt. "Some sweet Virginian flower?"

Despite the apparent flattery of Victoria's words, Pippa felt insulted. She guessed Victoria was about the same age as Jared, and the elegant woman exuded the international sophistication of one who took her place in the finest circles.

"Not exactly, no," replied Jared with a faint smile. "This is Philippa," he told Victoria simply, but then he paused. "My wife."

Only a tiny flash of Victoria's brown eyes indicated her surprise at this, but Pippa knew Jared's news didn't please the Englishwoman. Jared glanced at Pippa, and his face appeared unusually strained.

"Philippa, I would like you to meet Lady Victoria Beauchamp."

"How do you do?" said Pippa quickly, but at the sound of her voice, Victoria's eyes narrowed.

"You do not sound as the others do here," she observed. "Then you are not Virginian, Philippa?"

"I'm from Maine," Pippa told her, and she steeled herself for the inevitable response.

But Victoria looked rather blank. "Maine?" she asked in confusion.

"North of Massachusetts," Pippa explained reluctantly.

Massachusetts was a spot the Englishwoman recognized, and her brow rose speculatively. "Indeed! How awkward for you!"

"Not at all," lied Pippa, meeting the other woman's gaze evenly.

"I suppose, as Jared's wife, such minor details of origin would be of no consequence. He was always a man of strong will," continued Victoria. Pippa frowned at this hint of intimacy.

"It's good to see an old friend in this room of strangers," she added with a smile directed at Jared.

"What are you doing in Virginia, now of all times?" asked Jared, the very question Pippa herself would have liked to pose. "Are you accompanying your husband?"

"No. Andre passed away two years ago," Victoria replied without much feeling. Pippa noticed that Jared offered no sympathies.

"But kindly, he left me in control of his fortune, though of course I have advisers to manage things for me. I've spent more time in our English home since he died, and there became involved with a group interested in aiding the Confederacy."

Pippa's eyes narrowed, for though it was understandable for a Southerner to defend his own soil, she had no sympathy for those who would interfere with the natural course of her young country.

"Really? I thought such interests among the English ended ninety years ago," put in Pippa.

"I see you haven't completely abandoned the North, Philippa," said Victoria sweetly. Though Jared seemed decidedly uncomfortable beside her, Pippa refused to back down.

"No, I haven't," she agreed, and her gray-green eyes were blazing with the silent challenge. Her head was high, and a slow anger was burning within her.

"How courageous of you to live among the enemies of your people," said Victoria. "I wonder if you will allow Jared to dance with an . . . old friend? So that we may reminisce," added Victoria as she gazed up at Jared.

Jared plainly expected Pippa to object. Pippa wanted to object, but Victoria hadn't made that easy.

"Not at all," Pippa replied, careful not to meet Jared's eyes. "I'm rather breathless from the last dance. Please, enjoy yourselves."

"Are you sure?" asked Jared.

Pippa forced herself to look at him, and her face was open and sincere as she smiled. It took all her strength to muster such a deceitful response. But Jared was sufficiently convinced, and he went to dance with Victoria.

Pippa turned away, for she had no wish to see the beautiful woman in Jared's arms. She guessed this was the countess Jared had loved in Europe. Reluctantly, Pippa had to admit she could see why he might. Victoria was clever as well as beautiful, a formidable combination of qualities.

"Who is that woman with Jared?"

Pippa turned as Kim came up beside her, and she felt a little surprised at Kim's familiarity. After Victoria, Kim seemed a long lost friend to Pippa, and she welcomed her company with a rush of gratitude.

"That is Lady Victoria Something," replied Pippa. "Jared knew her in France."

Kim studied the woman dancing with Jared intently. "She's very pretty," said Kim after a practical assessment. "And her clothes are well-chosen."

"Yes," said Pippa with effort, but Kim patted her shoulder.

"I think you're prettier, though," said Kim, to Pippa's amazement. "I shouldn't worry if I were you, Pippa," she went on thoughtfully. "Jared seems very happy with you."

Tears started in Pippa's eyes at Kim's sudden kindness, and she realized how much she had wanted Jared's fragile sister to like her. She was prevented from telling Kim this by another unwelcome question.

"Who is that with Jared?" asked Katy, as she came to stand with Pippa and Kim.

"Some English Lady," said Kim importantly, and a little derisively. "Jared knew her in Europe."

"Ah," said Katy, and Pippa suspected that Katy knew more about Jared's romances than did Kim. "Is she with her husband?"

"She's a widow," Pippa explained.

"Is she? Then why is she here?" asked Kim.

"To offer something to the Confederacy, though I have no idea what," replied Pippa with a frown. Suspiciously, she had begun to doubt the nature of Victoria's purpose.

"I'll have to ask Robert," said Katy, and immediately she hurried off to find her husband.

Kim touchingly stayed at Pippa's side as the dance continued, but when a friendly-looking general came to request that Kim dance, Pippa encouraged her to go. Alone again, she turned to accept an offering of stuffed olives from a

maid. The woman tipped the tray forward, sending the contents of the tray spilling down Pippa's dress.

"I is sorry, miss!" exclaimed the maid, but Pippa detected
neither fear for retaliation, nor genuine distress at the unfortunate act.

"It's not your fault," said Pippa doubtfully. She started to
brush away the mess, but the servant stopped her.

"No, miss. Let me get that washed off for you. You come
to the washroom with me, and I'll clean you up good as
new."

Pippa glanced reluctantly toward the dancers, but when
she saw Jared and the lovely countess swirl across the floor,
she frowned and turned back to the maid.

"Very well. Thank you," she replied with a nod, and she
followed the maid from the room.

"I'll have no trouble with this," the maid said confidently.
"You slip this off for a moment, miss, and I'll take care of
it."

Pippa was obliged to set her small, crocheted purse on a
counter as the woman helped her from her gown, and she
sighed in exasperation. She didn't enjoy the thought of the
time Jared was spending with the countess, but the maid
took great pains to clean Pippa's dress.

When the task was complete, no trace of a stain could be
seen. Pippa glanced at the maid's face as she worked. Tall
and slender, her skin was truly black and her features were
handsomely sculpted. Pippa guessed her ancestry was much
the same as Lucy's. Neither showed any trace of the white
blood that lightened the skin of many slaves. Byron was
much fairer than Lucy or Jefferson, but this woman had a
regal beauty that elevated her far above her station.

The maid carefully rearranged Pippa's dress, then handed

Pippa's purse back to her. "Good as new, miss," she said cheerfully.

"Thank you," said Pippa, but her eyes wandered to the door. She hurried back to see if Jared had finished his dance with the countess.

The maid stayed a moment in the room Pippa had vacated, and she sighed. "Poor little thing," she murmured, but then she nodded. "Yet in war, they say, all is fair . . ."

"Pippa?" Jared came to Pippa as she entered the large room.

"Are you rested enough to join me in another dance, angel?" he asked, his eyes teasing her with the desire she felt for him. "We must leave soon, and I wish to hold you once more."

Pippa nodded and Jared drew her close into his arms. Pippa saw the countess watching them, but she didn't care. He belonged to her now, as she did to him, and no old flame would come between them. For the moment, Lady Victoria's arrival in Virginia seemed too trivial to mention.

The music stopped, and Jared drew away from Pippa regretfully. "It's time to go home," he told her, but he saw the twinkle in her eyes.

"Oh, love, you can't imagine how sorry I am to say this, but I'm afraid I won't be accompanying you in the coach."

"Why not?" asked Pippa with unveiled disappointment ringing in her voice.

Jared touched her cheek, and the love in his eyes eased her regret.

"My father has said he wants me to remain here. There's something he needs to discuss with me, though I have no idea what can be done at this late hour. But the President himself requested it, so I must allow you to leave without me. Katy will be spending the night at our house, as Robert also is remaining behind."

"When will you come home?"

"I'm not certain, angel. It may be late, I'm afraid." Jared's lips curved in his sensual, slow smile, and Pippa's fingers tingled as his warm eyes met hers.

"But I'll wake you, love. Then I'll show you how very much I've enjoyed dancing with you tonight."

Jared remained behind at the White House, but the women returned to the house on Franklin Street. All were too excited to go to sleep, and they decided to meet in the parlor for cups of hot chocolate after changing from their ball gowns.

Pippa hurried to her room, but Lucy was waiting for her, and she was greatly agitated by something.

"Why are you here, Lucy? You didn't have to wait for me."

Lucy sighed with resignation. "I did. I'm sorry, Pippa," she said. "I tried to warn you."

Pippa's eyes widened. "Warn me? About what?"

"May I have your purse?" asked Lucy, but she didn't meet Pippa's puzzled eyes.

"My purse? What for?" asked Pippa, but she handed it to Lucy.

Lucy opened the little crocheted bag, and to Pippa's amazement and growing horror, she drew out a small, folded note.

"What is that?" asked Pippa, her voice lowered with dread.

Lucy met her eyes squarely, and her exquisitely molded

face was held high and with pride. "It's a message, Pippa. A message that must be passed on tonight."

Pippa was aghast. "A message? Who put that in my bag, Lucy?" she asked indignantly. "It was that maid wasn't it, the pretty one! Did you tell her to do that, Lucy? Oh, how could you!"

Lucy didn't waver. "It was the only way, Pippa. We knew you could be trusted."

"What makes you think so?" said Pippa furiously. "Jared . . ."

"Jared need never know," said Lucy calmly. "If the Confederates are able to convince the English to recognize their government, even now, this war may be lengthened for countless years. Lincoln must know what the Confederates are willing to agree to so that he can put pressure on them by his own words. It's a delicate balance. Need I explain it to you now?"

"No. I understand," said Pippa miserably. "He'll say what the Confederates wish to say, and the English will be caught a step behind. That must be, I know. I know," she said again, but her voice cracked.

Pippa grabbed Lucy's arm. "I'll cover for you tonight, Lucy. But you must never do this to me again. Please," she begged, but Lucy's response was noncommittal.

"I'll go in the hour before dawn and meet the agent by the river—you needn't think of it again." Lucy stopped, but her eyes were kind when she looked at Pippa's glowering face.

"But the war goes on, Pippa. Even though your husband loves you, and for you there's no other world. The fate of my people hangs in the balance. No, I can't rest."

Pippa watched Lucy go, and she drew a deep, shuddering breath. She knew she had no right to stop Lucy. That wasn't her place, but she hated being part of something that Jared would be forced to consider a betrayal. From downstairs, Pippa heard Kim and Katy calling to her, and she pushed the grim thought from her mind as she went to join them.

"That countess fairly glowered at you, Pippa!" said Kim with pleasure.

"I don't think she expected Jared to have a wife," agreed Pippa.

Katy glanced at Pippa quickly, and seeing Jared's wife seemed to have some idea of his past associations, she relaxed.

"No, I'd imagine you were a nasty shock for Lady Victoria," said Katy with relish.

"You've met her before?" asked Pippa, and Katy nodded.

"When Robert and I traveled to France to visit Jared and Garrett, yes."

Katy paused. "I must say, I didn't care for her then. She can be . . . insincere," she added delicately. Pippa guessed Jared's gentle sister would have no tolerance for a woman whose main interest in a husband had been his title.

"I can't imagine what she's doing in our country now," added Caroline. "I hardly think it was necessary for her to come here. It is not . . . appropriate."

"I can imagine well enough, Mother," said Kim. "She's a widow now, isn't she? Ha! Such women are infuriating— she's so sure of herself."

Whatever happened to Kim when her house was raided had obviously shaken her, and Pippa wondered what it would take to give her back her confidence.

"Why did Papa and Jared stay behind?" asked Kim.

Katy leaned forward, and her voice was lowered in conspiratorial tones. "Well, I'm not certain exactly, but Robert told me it has something to do with a spy!"

"A spy?" gasped Pippa, and her heart froze in her breast.

"How exciting!" squealed Kim with shining eyes. "What are they doing?"

"Well," began Katy, delighted at being the owner of such information. Even Caroline leaned forward to listen.

"It seems someone in the President's household has been passing secret information, and much has been damaging. Now, with these English, he's certain the Yankees will want to know what they're offering."

"So?" asked Kim.

"Robert told me that a Yankee agent was caught yesterday, and has been replaced with one of our own. Someone, who was at the party tonight perhaps, will take a message to this person, thinking he's one of their own! Then they'll catch him, and we'll learn who in the President's household is false."

Katy sat back with pleasure. "Father, Jared, and Robert are to be there themselves. As a matter of fact, the whole thing was Father's idea!"

"How exciting!" exclaimed Kim, but Pippa was weak with shock. Lucy had already slipped from the house. There was only one person in the world who could save her. But it sickened Pippa to know who that person was.

Pippa waited until she was certain the others were sleeping, then she slipped on a simple, dark blue dress that would, she hoped, hide her in the waning night. She found her gray cape and wrapped it around her shoulders, then soundlessly crept down the stairs.

She went out the servants' door along the back street, her

cape wrapped around her tightly, and she pulled up its hood to shadow her face. The night outside was blackened by clouds, and a thick mist lay over the earth. But Pippa judged her position by the shrouded lamplights, and she knew where she was going. Her heart pounded so loudly she could barely hear, but finally she saw what she was looking for.

Lucy sat huddled in an alcove of a great abandoned warehouse on Cary Street. Pippa hurried to her, her light footsteps muffled in the thick fog.

"Lucy," she whispered in a low hiss, and Lucy startled at the sound of her voice.

"Pippa! What are you doing here?" asked Lucy as she stood up.

"Lucy, you must get out of here, now!"

"Why? What's the matter? Pippa, you shouldn't be here."

"Pay attention, Lucy!" ordered Pippa in frustration. "They know, they know about the message. Though, thank God, they don't know who passed it on. But they know about this meeting! They've replaced our agent . . . Oh, Lucy, you must hurry. We have to get back to the house, quickly!"

Lucy shook her head. "I must tell her, before she risks herself further."

"Do you mean the woman at the party?"

"Yes," said Lucy in a strained voice.

"For God's sake, Lucy. Don't bother with her. She got us into this . . ." Pippa said angrily, but Lucy shook her head.

"No, Pippa. You don't understand. I must go."

Lucy took a deep breath and Pippa saw the tears in her eyes. "That woman is my mother."

Lucy swallowed hard, but she met Pippa's astonished gaze proudly. "There are others at risk. Miss Elizabeth Van Lew placed my mother in the President's house. The divine spark of equality must not be extinguished now. Many fight this war, Pippa. Many who don't take up arms in the field."

Pippa was forced to remember the gravity of their cause, but she felt torn by the hands of two warring gods.

"Then go," she said. "But hurry, Lucy. There isn't much time. Give me the note. You can't risk being found with it."

Lucy agreed, and gave the little paper to Pippa. She hurried away, and Pippa watched to see her shape vanishing in the gray mist. She breathed a sigh of relief, but behind her appearing as if by magic, came the clatter of hoofbeats. Pippa was frozen with terror, but even had she attempted to escape, there would have been no time. The horse came to a stop barely a foot from where she stood.

"Don't move," came the harsh order.

At the sound of the rider's voice, Pippa swayed. She would have fallen to the earth if he hadn't leapt from the horse's back to catch her. The hands that braced her were not gentle, but Pippa felt no pain as she was slowly turned around to face her captor.

Jared saw her face, he knew her, but he couldn't make himself believe it was his wife that he held. He felt the hot, sick tide of recognition, of understanding what had transpired as he was lost in a sweet dream of love.

"Jared," she began, but even before he stopped her, Pippa knew it was no use.

She saw everything in his eyes. Every portion of the betrayal he imagined was etched plainly across his handsome face.

"Don't," he ground out, his agony raw in his low voice. "Don't say a thing."

Pippa felt dizzy, but she shook her head to rally her

thoughts. "No," she whispered. "This is not as it seems," she breathed desperately. "I am not—"

Jared cut her off with a harsh laugh. "Not what? Tell me, my sweet, faithful wife. What are you doing here, of all places, at such an hour? What explanation can you devise that will lull me into believing everything you say is true, that you are what you seem?"

Pippa didn't know what to say, but Jared didn't give her the chance. "They said a Yankee spy would be here, but dear God, I never dreamed it would be you."

"No! I'm not a spy!" she cried.

"Then why are you here?" he asked, plainly believing nothing of her denial. "A midnight stroll? But then, it's well past midnight."

Pippa gathered herself together and faced him. "I came to warn . . . someone. I couldn't let you take . . ." Pippa stopped.

She couldn't tell Jared it was Lucy she warned. There was no choice but to let Jared think it was she who knowingly bore the message and intended to pass it on at this waterfront meeting. He would easily guess it was Lucy otherwise, and the rebels were not merciful to colored spies. But neither could Pippa admit to a betrayal.

She cast her eyes from him, and her voice was small when she spoke. "Think what you will, Jared. But I didn't betray you, I swear."

For a moment, Jared hesitated and wavered. Pippa's sweet face was earnest, and Jared desperately longed to believe in her innocence. This was a mistake, her presence at the waterfront wasn't as condemning as it seemed. She wouldn't have used his love as a cloak while she betrayed his people.

Pippa saw Jared's tenderness, she read his doubt, but when she reached for him, the note Lucy had given her fell to the ground. Jared's face froze and he bent to retrieve it. A quick glance at the contents told him all he needed to know. He shuddered to think how willing he had been to believe his wife, to trust her in the face of overwhelming evidence.

Jared's grip on her arms tightened until she winced with pain. "How do you explain this?" he asked in a low voice.

Pippa started to speak, but Jared stopped her. "No, Philippa, say nothing. I might be fool enough to believe you. No, I will hear no more lies from you."

Pippa mouthed his name, but no sound came. The fog that surrounded them seemed to become a part of her, and Pippa's senses reeled. There was no escape. She had died, she believed, and her body went weak and crumpled in his arms.

She would never wake again, she would become a part of the fog and be nothing, forever. But Jared wouldn't allow her the escape, and when she fainted, he shook her and slapped her face to bring her around.

"No," she whispered when she came to her senses and again felt his anger. No, it was worse, it was hatred. Hatred now devoid of love.

"No, no," she whispered again, but he shook her harder.

"This is what you wanted all along, wasn't it? To be in Richmond," he growled hoarsely. "Tell me, Philippa. Were you bored running errands for others at your aunt's home? Was it not sufficiently . . . satisfying to you? Damn you," he said, and Pippa winced at the harshness of his voice.

"Damn you, how could a woman be this heartless? But I brought you here, didn't I? Right where you could do the most damage. Right where you wanted to be. And I've given you the protection of my name to do as you will. Damn you," he groaned, and Pippa felt the hot acid of her stomach rising to her throat.

"Jared, you don't understand," she began, but her voice was barely audible.

Roughly, he pulled her to her feet, his laugh cutting through the early morning air like a knife.

"Don't I? I can see where you might have formed that impression, my dear. I've given you every reason to believe I'm the greatest fool the world has ever seen."

"No, no," she sobbed, but his grip on her arm was unyielding.

"My father will find no spy tonight," he said dangerously. "But she will not evade her captivity this time."

"What do you mean?" she asked weakly. "What are you going to do to me?" Her words were empty. Pippa didn't care. Nothing mattered anymore.

"To you? What can I do to you, Philippa? You have sunk your teeth into my father's heart, and what of Katy? God, even Kim has called you her sister tonight. Damn you," he said with a fury that vibrated through Pippa, and again she swayed beneath the force of Jared's hatred.

"You have destroyed my love, you have destroyed me. But hear me now, I will not let you hurt them. No, I won't leave you to use them as your cover while you strive to destroy what's left of their world.

"No, my precious wife, you will go where I go, and it will be your prison as truly as any cell, I promise you. I will take you with me to Petersburg, and there you will endure the very worst the Yankees can devise. And God help me, I will enjoy knowing your fate is in their hands."

Nine

The next morning passed in a dark fog for Pippa. Rather than leaving unannounced, as they had before, Jared brought Pippa home and made a great ceremony of his decision to bring her with him to Petersburg. Jared's entire family was deeply moved at this evidence of the young couple's devotion. Even Kim could barely pass through a room without giving Pippa a quick, fond hug.

Now Pippa sat in a coach beside Jared, having no idea how long they had traveled on their journey from Richmond to Petersburg. She was as she had been before they left Franklin Street, alone in Jared's room staring down at the unmade bed. The tangled sheets left evidence of the last time they had loved, and Pippa had no resistance to the tears that coursed down her pale cheeks.

Jared said nothing to her now, and both stared out their windows at the last light of evening. Pippa's head rested on the hard wall of the coach. Through her window, she could see Boreas trotting along, again brought to war with his master. She fell into a bitter sleep, her dark dreams repeating the shock of losing the man she loved. Pippa felt her heart beating its furious denial when she woke, but her first thoughts were cruel.

"It was a dream," she whispered thankfully. "It was only a dream."

She would wake fully, open her eyes, and Jared would be lying in bed beside her. She would reach to touch him, and he would roll over and take her in his arms, he would kiss her, and love her. She would be safe, his, as she was meant to be.

But the coach lurched, and Pippa was jolted into full wakefulness. Jared slept beside her, but as she looked to him, she knew he would never take her in his arms again. It was dark outside, and she fell again into a dreamless sleep where nothing and no one entered her darkness.

"Get your things, Philippa. We're in Petersburg."

Jared's voice was cold and abrupt in the chill morning light, and Pippa dragged herself from a dreamless abyss. Even before she left the coach, Pippa heard the long whoosh and crash of artillery fire. As she stepped down to see Petersburg, it seemed she had descended into an endless, bitter dream of death, war and suffering.

It was the seventeenth of June, and the Federal troops were meeting the rebel defenses in force. They had succeeded in taking the outermost lines, but the Confederates had withdrawn to shorter and stronger positions, lining trenches and breastworks much easier to defend. Taking Petersburg wouldn't be an easy task, and even Pippa wondered why the Yankees were bothering after Grant's success with the siege of Vicksburg.

Jared left Pippa to rejoin his men, and Pippa found Sally Hallett hard at work tending the wounded. Pippa joined her, and she began binding the wounds. The natural ability Pippa had discovered in the Wilderness developed into a genuine skill at healing.

A heavy, bearded doctor, Captain Farraday, recognized

this and put Pippa to better use. "Come along, Mrs. Knox," he drawled pleasantly. "It's time you learned a little more about fixing up these boys."

Pippa followed him along the breastworks to a man who had been hit by a flying fragment of shell. "See here, Mrs. Knox," said Captain Farraday as he showed Pippa the nature of the boy's wound.

Pippa had long since gotten over a tendency to wince when she first saw the gaping, bloody flesh. Her brow knit thoughtfully as the doctor showed her the proper manner of stitching such wounds.

"Can you handle that?" asked Captain Farraday.

"I can."

Pippa spent the rest of the day and the next morning perfecting what the doctor had shown her. Her only alteration was to carefully cleanse the wound before stitching and binding it. The doctors felt this was a waste of time, but Pippa liked the neatness of it, if only because it allowed her to better see what she was doing.

Gradually, the ache in her heart for the loss of her husband's love moved aside, allowing for something new—a sense of purpose Pippa had lost when the cause of abolition was no longer within her reach. The work was difficult, and often there was little Pippa could do to help, especially when the injury involved a shattered arm or leg. Too often this meant amputation, and though Pippa felt the doctors ought to spend more time trying to save the broken limbs, they rarely chose this option.

"Leave it too long, and gangrene sets in," Captain Farraday told her when she had dared to question his decision to amputate a sergeant's leg.

"The break's too bad. Hell, most of the bone is missing. No, Mrs. Knox, this is the best we can do."

Pippa acquiesced, but it broke her heart to see the terror in the boy's eyes as he was taken to the surgeon's tent. Like most, he refused to cry out or show that terror, yet Pippa felt it as acutely as if it was her own.

Occasionally, Pippa's work brought her dangerously close to the forward lines of battle, yet that gave her the chance to see more of what was going on from the Yankee standpoint. Jared's men were fighting from trenches, and Pippa was sent there to care for a fallen soldier. She tended him dutifully, but as she was leaving, Jared saw her and she knew he wasn't pleased.

"Philippa, what are you doing here? I can't believe Farraday wants you this far forward."

Pippa frowned, but as she opened her mouth to answer him, a Yankee shell whizzed by her head. Pippa barely noticed and merely paused for enough quiet to speak.

"I am . . . necessary here, Jared," she said proudly.

Though Jared was well-prepared to retort, Pippa's eyes were caught by a Yankee advance across the rough ground of the field. A Maine flag flew, and though it wasn't the 20th he led, Pippa recognized her father's friend, Joshua Chamberlain. He was riding at the head of a brigade, and to Pippa's great wonder, the soft-spoken, reticent professor she remembered from Brunswick was now daringly advancing amongst heavy fire from his enemy.

Jared saw the shock on Pippa's face, he saw her lean forward against the breastwork, but he had no idea what she had seen. "What is it?" he asked roughly, but Pippa couldn't answer.

"Maine," she whispered. "Home . . . The colonel, Chamberlain, from my father's regiment, from Bowdoin College."

Jared turned to watch the advancing Yankees, and even as they approached a forward trench, a canister fell and blasted among them. Chamberlain's horse was hit to fall bloodily, but the colonel simply got up and kept going, his men following him as they will follow only a great leader.

The Yankees took the trench, settling in to withstand the fire that poured over the captured crest. They fired back at the rebels, and Pippa watched frozen with admiration and fear as her own land displayed its valor. Her eyes misted at the sight of the Maine flag, but it was obvious there was more to come.

"Oh, no," breathed Jared. In a virtual act of suicide, the Yankee brigade rose again from the trench they had taken and moved forward. It was painfully clear that the hopeless action was forced by orders from the rear, yet Joshua Chamberlain led his men against impossible odds.

"Go back," Jared ordered his wife, but Pippa didn't hear him. Jared took her arm. Despite his anger, he couldn't bear for her to see what would surely follow.

It was too late. The rebels pummeled the Yankee brigade with musket-fire. As the Maine colonel turned to order his men forward, a shell struck him, dashing violently through his pelvis.

Pippa screamed, but Joshua Chamberlain did not fall. He simply balanced himself on the point of his saber and waved his infantry forward. They passed in a great rush, but Pippa sobbed as he allowed himself to fall. She saw him carried off the field. After such an injury, its severity apparent even from the rebel lines, what man could survive?

* * *

The Yankee attack failed, and they were driven back to hold a position facing the impenetrable rebel line. The Yankee shelling of the besieged city was inconsistent, and some days passed with almost no barrage of substance. Yet every day, men fell—men who were not replaced. Robert E. Lee's thin gray line was stretching, and the line that faced him had the farther reach.

Summer grew hot and heavy, but nothing in Jared's manner toward Pippa had softened since he had discovered her at the waterfront. They shared a tent, sleeping at opposite ends, and when David Knox returned from Richmond, they dined together. But Jared rarely spoke to Pippa, he never touched her. And nothing allowed her to hope he ever would.

Jared was stationed with his men southeast of Petersburg. There were places here where Yankee and rebel trenches were separated by mere yards, and the threat from Yankee sharpshooters was great in this part of the Confederate line.

"You take care walking by here, Mrs. Knox," a young lieutenant told her. "There's Yankee sharpshooters not more than two hundred feet away in some spots. Though I don't think even a Yankee would shoot a lady, they might not notice until it's too late."

"I'll be careful, Lieutenant McCabe. I promise."

Yet Pippa didn't really care. Shells crashed and exploded near her every day, but Pippa didn't flinch. She barely noticed. As Pippa wandered back to her tent, she realized that it was her birthday. She was twenty years old. Pippa considered telling Jared, but then thought better of it. There was no need to open herself to unnecessary disappointments.

Pippa approached her husband, but she realized her usual dread at seeing him had dissipated. He could hate her, deny her his comfort and his love, yet she still lived. She still affected the world around her. She was still . . . necessary.

Jared sat sketching outside the tent. It was hot in July, but sweltering inside the tents. There was a light breeze and most had chosen shaded spots to find what enjoyment they could in the twilight hours. Pippa glanced over his shoulder as she passed, but she caught her breath at what she saw. On the stained paper he held was the most beautiful house she had ever seen, and Pippa stopped to admire it.

"I didn't know you could draw," she said, but Jared didn't look at her.

"What do you think architects do, Philippa?" he asked coldly. Pippa's heart sank. At the sound of her name, she turned away and went to sit gazing over the rows and rows of entrenchments that faced the Yankee position.

They sat together, silent and apart as the red sun set amidst an orange and purple horizon. Every time Jared's dislike of her was revealed, Pippa's heart ached and twisted in pain. Never once did the tears forget to well in her gray-green eyes.

Now the teary mists again drifted across her vision, obscuring the beauty of the sunset before her eyes. Sometimes, like a ghost, she imagined Jared coming up behind her, softly kissing her neck, his hands upon her shoulders. But Pippa never saw the faintest trace of affection upon his face now. Over and over, Pippa was forced to say, *he doesn't love me, he doesn't love me anymore.*

"That's a fine house, Colonel."

A vaguely familiar voice reached Pippa's humming ears. At the sound, the ache in her heart eased. As she turned, the tiniest spark of hope entered her, unbidden by her own will.

"I'm glad to see you are considering Virginia's future. Too many think only of her past," said the old man who looked down over Jared's shoulder.

Robert E. Lee stood tall and straight behind Jared, his

white hair touched with the golden sunset, and again Pippa felt her heart moved by the general's presence.

Jared started to rise in salute, but the general waved him down. "As you were, Colonel," he said. "So you're designing a new home for your estate?"

"It's little more than an attempt to while away the hours, I'm afraid, General," Jared replied, the sorrow unwittingly revealing itself in his voice.

But the general shook his head vigorously. "No, Colonel. You must plan for Virginia's future. She will have one, one way or another. Either way, it will be yours to see that it is a bright future."

Pippa knew Jared was moved by the vigor in General Lee's soft-spoken voice. There stood a man who would never be defeated, not entirely, for he would never give up. Pippa admired him, and that admiration was very close to love.

"Yes, sir," said Jared quietly. "I will do that."

The general patted his shoulder, but then his bright eyes turned to Pippa. "Well, then, little Mrs. Knox, it is you I have come to see."

"Me?" asked Pippa with a surge of warm pride.

"Indeed. The very great service you are performing has come to my attention. Captain Farraday has told me the wounded soldiers you've tended have a remarkable rate of success. Such an accomplishment is worthy of praise, wouldn't you say?"

Pippa's sad face lit with a smile, but tears welled in her eyes. "Thank you, General Lee," she said, but her voice was small and broken with her emotion.

The general smiled and nodded. In the depths of his kind eyes, Pippa found a well of encouragement that had long now given men courage to take their strength beyond its limits, to do the impossible. As he walked away, Pippa came to believe she could do the same.

"Where are you going?" asked Jared harshly, but Pippa turned back to him with a frown.

"I'm going up to the artillery position on Elliot's Salient," she told him defiantly. "There's no need to haul those men down here. They'll bleed too much," she explained with irritation.

Jared had forbade her from going to the forward entrenchments, but she felt she was needed there most, even if it was dangerously within the reach of Yankee sharpshooters.

"You are not to go there, Philippa. I've told you . . ." he began with rising anger, but Pippa's face was lit with fury also.

"Why not, Jared? What does it matter?" she cried raggedly. Why did he care if she was felled unawares by some bored Yankee marksman?

"You said you'd leave my fate to the Yankees," she ground out. "Well, now is your chance."

Jared's face was hard, but his eyes were blazing. Nowhere did Pippa do as he expected. He expected fear at the shelling, yet she showed none. He expected defiance, then remorse, yet he had seen neither. Like her Yankee countrymen, Pippa doggedly resisted defeat, and final victory still eluded Jared's grasp.

"It would be demoralizing to the men if you were shot down in their midst," he said, but Pippa frowned.

"It will be more demoralizing to slowly bleed to death without help. There has been shooting all day, and shells hit there twice. The doctors are busy."

With that, Pippa swung on her heels to depart, but Jared

caught her arm. Her efforts seemed thwarted until the sound
of a soft, melodic voice called to Jared. Jared turned in disbelief, but Pippa's heart hardened. Victoria Beauchamp
came along the narrow path from the direction of the city,
and to Pippa's annoyance, she was dressed as if for a stroll
along the Champs Elysées rather than for a visit to a bat-
tlefield.

"Victoria! What on earth are you doing here?" asked
Jared as the delicate woman came to him.

"I can't imagine," said Pippa icily.

As she spoke, a shell whirred over their heads and crashed
well behind them. Neither Pippa nor Jared flinched, but Victoria grabbed Jared's arm in terror so acute that Pippa could
almost feel sorry for her.

"Come, let me take you from here," said Jared kindly.
Pippa's teeth bit into her lip when she heard the gentleness
in his voice.

"This dreadful shelling!" gasped Victoria. "Does it happen often?"

"All the time," answered Pippa flatly.

A small smile tilted the corners of her mouth when Victoria glanced disparagingly her way. If Pippa had looked her
best at the party in Richmond, now in Petersburg she was
dirty and blood-stained. Her hair was loosely bound behind
her head, and most of its soft brown length was falling down
her back.

To Pippa's amazement, her smile grew. At the short
laugh—her own—Pippa wondered how one knew if one was
going mad.

"But don't worry, Lady Victoria. You don't hear the ones
that get you. It will just land . . . Smack! Right on your
head. You'll never know what hit you."

Victoria gasped in horror, but Pippa chuckled. Her brow

rose rather dangerously—as she imagined it—and with a toss of her unkempt head, Pippa turned and headed proudly towards the forward breastworks of her enemy.

It was a long day for Pippa. The Yankee sharpshooters had been particularly active near the redoubt. The whooshing and pop of musket-fire sounded around Pippa's head, but she was better prepared to handle the injuries she found. Pippa welcomed the diversion—it kept her from dwelling on what Jared was doing with the beautiful countess.

"Well, thank you, Mrs. Knox," said a gaunt Georgian as she sat back from bandaging his shoulder. "I was as glad to see you coming as anything," he went on. "You did up my brother last week, and he's back here today."

"Maybe he should've stayed in the rear," said Pippa. "It's not exactly pleasant up here."

"No, but it can be entertaining," laughed the Georgian. "Heard the Yanks tapping away this morning. Rumor has it they're digging under us," he said with appreciative humor. "Like a bunch of rabbits."

The infantryman next to him nodded. "If they can't go over us, they'll go under us—is that it?"

Pippa herself giggled, but as she walked back to her tent that night, she began to wonder what was going on over on the other side.

When she returned to her tent, Pippa stopped, half afraid to enter lest she find Victoria there with Jared. She didn't think it beyond him to keep the woman there as his mistress to torment her. Into her mind came the image of Jared lying in a tangled web of passion with Victoria. A wave of nausea crashed through Pippa and she raced inside to vomit.

Jared wasn't there, but she fell to her knees with a pot before her. Her stomach was empty and heaved itself in vain. Gasping for air, Pippa regained herself. She found a jug of water and dampened her face.

Night deepened, and still Jared didn't return. Her sickness passed, but the tears flowed freely into Pippa's makeshift pillow as she lay listening to the occasional whoosh of artillery fire in the distance.

Jared finally entered the tent, but Pippa squeezed her eyes shut lest he know she had been waiting for him. But Jared saw the telltale stiffness of his wife's body as she lay, the soundless, short breaths she drew, and he laughed.

"Sleeping already, Philippa?" he said knowingly, and Pippa opened her eyes in exasperation.

She didn't answer him, but when she saw him set a tall bottle upon their little table, her brow knit in wonder.

"What's that?" she asked curiously. Such things hadn't commonly been available among the fighting men.

Jared again lifted the bottle and squinted as he looked at it. Pippa realized that he had been drinking fairly heavily, and it surprised her as she had never seen him intoxicated before.

"Bourbon, I believe," he told her as he sat down at the table. "Would you care to join me for a drink, Mrs. Knox?" he asked mockingly, but Pippa sat up and her face was thoughtful as she considered this.

"Spirits?" she asked doubtfully, but Jared's face flinched with sudden anguish at her innocence.

"Yes," he replied. "Spirits."

"They make you numb, don't they?"

"They do."

"Very well, then. Thank you. I believe I will," said Pippa with resignation.

Pippa struggled to her feet and went to sit across from him. Seeing her willingness to partake, Jared set two short glasses upon the table. He poured the amber liquid into each, and passed one to Pippa. She lifted it suspiciously and sniffed. Jared watched her with a curious quandary of emotions on his face, but Pippa didn't notice. She took a small sip, and then coughed wildly.

"It doesn't taste very good!" she exclaimed, when she was able to speak.

"That isn't really the point of . . . spirits, Philippa," he told her.

Pippa looked at him with dire misgivings, but she took another taste and shuddered. Jared drank half his glass in one gulp as Pippa watched in amazement. She waited for a moment, then shook her head in disgust.

"I don't feel any different, Jared," she said, plainly having decided that the effects of liquor were greatly exaggerated.

"It takes more than two tiny sips, my dear."

"Does it?" asked Pippa, and again she lifted the glass to her lips. She tried a somewhat larger mouthful, but she coughed and sputtered in horror.

"Ooh, it's awful!" she exclaimed. "Worse than medicine," she added.

Pippa set the glass firmly on the table and went back to her little mattress. Jared poured the remainder of Pippa's glass into his and drank it, but then Pippa felt his eyes upon her as she lay back on her bed.

"Do you know, you are most remarkably beautiful, Philippa," Jared said rather thickly. At his words, Pippa began to tremble and her chest felt heavy as she fought to breathe.

Jared leaned forward across the table, and his eyes were fire as he looked to where she lay, her long hair spread out around her face.

"I look at you, study your face trying to see something, anything that isn't perfect. Any flaw to which I can turn my eyes and forget. I look at your body, but there isn't one curve that does not beckon a man to your bed."

Jared's voice was raw and husky, and Pippa's heart was thundering in her breast, but she dared not look at him. Jared rose and came to kneel before her, taking her shoulders firmly in his hands as she sat abruptly upright on her bed.

"Tell me, Philippa. What do you do when that perfect little body of yours starts to ache?"

Pippa felt weak, a steamy heat prickled her skin, but still she looked away from him. She wet her lips nervously, but Jared saw and his eyes darkened with desire.

"You do remember, don't you? Tell me, do you think of it? Hmmn? How it was between us, before you killed my love?"

Pippa winced now, and closed her eyes tight.

"But this isn't love we feel, is it?" Jared went on brutally. "I wonder how it would be, to take you now when it isn't serving your secret purposes. Yes, for lust's sake alone."

Jared's hands on Pippa's shoulders were trembling, but her eyes shot to him. "Haven't you had enough of that with your countess?"

Jared released her. "Ah! Victoria. Yes, that's what she wanted. God, how I wish I could tell you I accepted her gracious offer to become my mistress!"

Pippa swallowed to contain the hot acid that boiled in her stomach, but Jared didn't stop. "And so help me, I brought her to this room with that intent. To lose myself in her," he continued savagely, and Pippa swayed as she sat. "To bury myself in her and forget you, Philippa."

Jared ground out the words, but then he paused to draw a long breath. "But she kissed me, and nothing happened. She told me she loved me, had waited for her husband to die so she could come to me, and it meant nothing to me. She ran her hands over my body, and I felt nothing."

Jared took Pippa's shoulders in his strong grip. "Nothing, Philippa. Yet I can't even be in the same room with you without, without . . ."

He stopped and took Pippa's hand roughly in his, then pressed it against the hardened bulge beneath his trousers. Pippa gasped, but her own body was a sea of raging desire.

"Yes, my glorious wife, you do this to me. Every time I look at you. Do you know what a torment you are?"

Pippa was shaking now, but she had no idea what to say.

"Do you feel this way, Philippa?" he asked, his voice raw and hoarse with desire. "Are you slippery and wet for me, do you ache for me?"

Pippa didn't answer, but she leaned to him, and Jared pulled her hard against him with passionate force. They fell back across her little bed, and Jared pushed her skirt up above her waist. He tore off her light undergarments as if they were nothing, then freed himself to enter her.

Pippa knew she was crying, she knew her body arched when she felt the stiffened heat of him against her thigh, probing upward with primitive force. She heard herself cry out when he entered her with a primal groan of need. Yet it all seemed to be happening as if she watched from a distance.

Their two bodies crashed together like two great waves meeting upon a violent sea, melding and dissolving into one.

Pippa's body quivered and shook as she received him, and then Jared lay silent, buried within her, his face turned into her neck.

Pippa's arms encircled him, her legs held him against her, and still her tears flowed in rivers from her eyes to disappear in her mass of dark, tangled hair. Jared knew she cried, he knew, but when he moved away from her, he didn't reach to hold her.

Instead, he lay upon his back staring at the fold of the tent. His body still throbbed with the power of a long-denied release; even now, he felt the tiny echoes of his ecstasy still flashing through him. But now that it was over, Jared Knox had no idea what to say.

Beside him, Pippa wept softly, but Jared couldn't move to comfort her. His own eyes squeezed shut as he faced the slow realization of what he had done to her. If the liquor had deadened his senses, destroyed his better judgment, it had done nothing to cool the long torment of his desire.

Day after day, Jared fought his need for his wife, fighting himself as he waited for her to crumble beneath the stress of the siege. Perhaps he was waiting for her to crawl back to him, beg his forgiveness, but Pippa refused. She just went on with her duties, gently tending her enemy. Sinking her perfect teeth into the hearts of every rebel she touched.

Even General Lee has succumbed to your charm, Jared thought ironically, and the faintest of smiles touched his face. *I stand in good company, at least.*

Jared wanted to turn to her, to hold her. He heard her muffled sniffs, he felt the tiny motions of her sobs beside him, and his heart quailed. He had forced himself upon her, without tenderness or words of love. He had taken her to satisfy his own raging lust; he had convinced himself she felt the same.

Now Pippa lay weeping beside him. *What have I done to you?* he thought, but the bourbon took its final hold and Jared fell into a merciful, dark sleep.

Pippa lay awake at Jared's side, listening to his deep breaths as he slept. She pulled her covers over him, moving closer, but she didn't dare touch him. *Why don't you hold me?* she wondered miserably, but the answer seemed obvious enough.

Jared had been confused by drink, he had surrendered to lust. When it was over, he was disgusted by their intimacy. Their passion had been rain upon a desert. Pippa longed desperately to believe it held the embers of love.

Pippa woke very early the next day. Jared was sleeping with his back toward her, and only the faintest light through the gap in their tent told Pippa it was near morning. Jared's broad, bare back was barely inches from her, and she longed to touch him as she once would have done. She would touch him, run her hand along the firm muscles of his back, and kiss his shoulder. He would turn to her, he would smile the slow, sensual smile Pippa adored . . .

No, no, I can't do this to myself, she moaned inwardly. She was tortured by those sweet memories, by the love she remembered in his blue eyes where now there was no love at all. She had seen passion the previous night, she had seen desire, but she had seen no evidence through the long weeks that he would ever love her again.

Pippa sighed, and it seemed a good idea to be gone when Jared woke. She got up from her mattress on the floor and eased quietly past Jared to dress. It was hot already, just past four-thirty in the morning of July thirtieth.

Pippa decided she would question a picket she knew

about breakfast. "Lieutenant McCabe," she called softly when she found a familiar face.

He turned and smiled brightly when he recognized Pippa. "Mrs. Knox!" he exclaimed. "What are you doing about at such an early hour?"

"I woke early—it's so hot," she explained, and paused.

"I thought you might be heading up to Elliot's Salient," said the lieutenant with a sigh. "Heard some fellows were shot during the night."

"Oh?" asked Pippa with concern. She forgot about breakfast and looked to the bluff. Here was something she could do. A place she might be needed, be useful. She would worry about Jared later.

"Then I'll go on up there," determined Pippa.

"Well, have a care up there, ma'am," he said.

Pippa sighed. "I will."

Jared woke with a start. A tremendous explosion shook the earth beneath his tent, and a deafening roar split the calm of morning. Jared leapt from the bed and raced from the tent, but Pippa was nowhere in sight.

He started down the path, but he saw Lieutenant McCabe racing toward him, his face white with terror. A great column of smoke rose from the bluff, and debris fell all around to where Jared stood.

"Colonel," cried the lieutenant wildly. "She's up there! Your wife, sir," he gasped. "She went up there, just before it. Oh, God, it's all my fault."

Jared froze, but his eyes went to the sight of the explosion, his mind reeling as the lieutenant went on.

"Lord, I told her some men were down, and she went up . . ."

Jared sprang away up toward the salient, joined in force by his own men. Major Hallett was with him, and Jared sent him back for orders from the general as he ran up the crowded paths to the scene of the disaster.

Thundering in his mind were his own words: "And God help me, I will enjoy knowing your fate is in their hands."

A tremendous barrage of mortar-fire opened on the miles of trenches near the salient as the first Federal troops poured from their trenches. They came across open ground and down into the steep pit created by the underground explosion.

Jared arrived with the other rebels who raced to the sight, but the scene was chaotic and Jared saw no sign of Pippa. Federal troops formed battle lines in the pits. All were now tangled in the hole after driving off the small force of South Carolinians who were trying to hold them off.

Jared's brigade was joined by others as Confederate reinforcements converged around the crater. The crater pit itself was crowded with Federal troops. A great battle erupted, and Jared was forced to abandon his search for Pippa as he led his men in a desperate fight for control of the rebel lines.

It had been four hours since the mine exploded. Though things looked promising in the beginning, it became clear the Yankees had no idea how to take advantage of the surprise attack. Jared's men withdrew, and a larger brigade was handling the situation without much trouble.

"Colonel, they've found her," called Major Hallett, and Jared left him in command while he went to Pippa.

He stopped when he saw her, unable to move for the force

of his relief. There she sat, looking a bit dazed and dusty, but otherwise unharmed. She turned to see him, a faint look of surprise crossing her face as her head tilted to one side. Jared thought the light from her eyes would break his heart.

Lieutenant McCabe was hovering about her, patting her shoulder protectively. Jared heard her speak to the boy, and he was amazed to hear her calm voice, though she sounded a little dazed to his ears.

"It's not your fault, Lieutenant. No, thank you, I've had enough water, truly. How would you know the ground would explode?"

Jared went to her, but he couldn't speak. Pippa herself didn't seem particularly emotional. "Jared, did you see it, all the fire in the sky? I thought the world really was ending after all!"

Pippa's tone gave every indication she had for some time considered this a likely occurrence, and Jared smiled. "I'm afraid I missed that part of it."

Pippa's brow knit as she looked at him. "Have you been fighting?" she asked. It hadn't occurred to her that Jared would be in danger.

"We're out of it now," he told her, and his tone was reassuring.

"I should help," said Pippa doggedly, and she got up.

The lieutenant shook his head vigorously, and Jared took Pippa's arm to stop her. There was a light in his eyes she didn't completely understand, but she guessed his fear had been intense.

"Are you coming?" she asked with a faint smile. Jared, seeing she was well, had no clear idea how to prevent her from doing a task that had occupied her attention daily.

"Very well, I'll come with you," he agreed, and together they hurried back to the scene of the battle.

* * *

When Pippa looked across the entrenchments to the gaping hole in the earth, a new and hideous development had taken place. The rebels were clearly in command of the situation, and the Federal troops were now trapped in the crater they had made themselves. They were surrounded, and were surrendering in droves. A vast number were colored troops, and these men weren't allowed to surrender. The rebels were taking prisoners, but shooting men of color as they gave up their arms. Pippa heard the loud cries from all around her.

"Take the white man, kill the . . ."

"No!" Pippa's wild, plaintive voice drowned out the hideous command as she ran to Jared. But Jared saw the furious carnage. He called his men, but Pippa grabbed his arm.

"Pippa, get back!" he yelled, but Pippa didn't hear him.

"Byron! Jared, Byron is there. They'll kill him. Oh, help, help!"

Pippa was past hysteria, and she began to run for the deadly pit, but Jared caught her. "Pippa, stop. Stay there," he ordered. He gathered a small force of his men and raced along the edge of the precipice.

Pippa nearly swooned, but she crept forward unnoticed between the soldiers and watched as Jared took command of a rebel force. He began taking prisoners, and most of them were black. Pippa saw Jared meet Byron amidst the battle, and to her lasting wonder, she saw that Byron knew his captor. Without a word, Byron lay down his weapon and surrendered to Jared.

Pippa raced to meet them, but she shouted when a furious rebel turned his musket toward Byron. Jared turned and aimed his revolver at the man's head.

"Do it, and you die," he threatened raggedly.

Pippa ran past the rebel and called to Byron. Byron stopped and looked to her in amazement. His face showed the strain of the ill-planned battle, but even so, his slow smile warmed her heart.

"Miss Pip. What brings you here?"

"Mrs. Pip," Jared corrected him.

"Indeed? Well, I warned her," said Byron, but he seemed pleased by Pippa's marriage.

Jared led his small group of prisoners along the breastworks and, to Pippa's confusion, away from where the others were taken. Pippa followed, but Jared led them down into an abandoned rebel trench.

The two young men faced each other silently, and Jared looked up and back at the lines behind him. No one noticed where he took them, and now they were hidden from view. But he was a colonel and few questioned what he did, however unorthodox it might seem.

Jared took a breath, and looked back to Byron. "Go," he said, but Byron didn't immediately depart.

"For the second time, my friend," he said cryptically. But then he turned to Pippa. "Until we meet again, little one. Farewell."

With that, Byron bounded over the breastworks, followed by the others Jared had taken. Jared didn't move as they ran away, and though Pippa heard shots fired, no one would guess how the small group had escaped.

Pippa stood behind Jared and touched his shoulder. "Thank you," she whispered.

"I didn't do it for you, Philippa," he told her distantly.

Jared stared in the direction of the Yankee lines and sighed. "He's my brother."

Pippa's eyes widened, but Jared turned around to go back to his men. "Your brother?" she gasped in disbelief.

Jared shrugged. "Half-brother. It shouldn't take much imagination for you to guess how I came to have a brother but five months my senior."

Pippa was stunned. Jared walked away, but she couldn't move. David Knox was Byron's father! The man he hated, upon whom he vowed revenge. It didn't seem possible. Such things were done by vicious men, not kind gentlemen. Not the father-in-law she had come to love.

Pippa didn't see Jared that night, for he was busy restoring the shattered rebel lines. Worse were the burial details. When Pippa rose the next morning, troops from both North and South were busy on the battle site removing their dead.

Pippa went in search of Jared, but when she reached the area near the crater, she stopped. Men with handkerchiefs tied over their faces moved slowly about the field, men in both blue and gray. The dead had swollen in the heat, bloated and purple, and Pippa felt sick as she watched the soldiers lifting the stiff forms to carry them away.

As they removed their dead, the solemn task took a strange turn. A band played upon the rebel breastworks honoring their dead, and then in turn the Union musicians played their airs. It was sweet and respectful, and Pippa's eyes misted with tears as she listened, transported by the haunting music.

Men from both North and South mingled together, exchanging friendly words as they toiled. Upon the breastworks, both Yankees and rebels sat across from each other without fear. It didn't seem possible that those who had fought brutally the day before could be so easy today in each other's presence.

"Pippa, you shouldn't be here," said Jared as he went to

his wife. Her face was pale as she surveyed the ghastly sight, yet he saw her eyes were serene when she turned to him.

Pippa's glance caught the familiar face of a man sitting on the Yankee line. Jared saw her shock and turned in the direction she looked. The music from the two opposing bands had ceased, and now came the gentle sounds of a single guitar. A low voice rose in a sorrowful melody.

Pippa stared in wonder towards the Yankees, and Jared saw a ragged man with a guitar. Beside him sat a tall, slender black man, and in his long hands he held an accordion. From that simple instrument came the most beautiful music Jared had ever heard.

Pippa was trembling. Without warning, she ran towards the Yankee musicians. Jared darted after her, stunned by his wife's agility as she sprang like a deer over the breastworks and trenches.

"Jefferson!" she cried.

The young man stopped to stare at her in disbelief. He set the accordion aside as he stood up, but the ragged man with the guitar continued playing, watching Pippa with a smile. Jared caught Pippa as she reached the Yankee lines. Had they wished, the two musicians could have nabbed Jared with ease. But neither bore such impulses.

Jefferson's face brightened as Pippa came to embrace him. If such foreign intimacy startled the toiling rebels, Jared's presence kept them from any marked reaction.

"Miss Pip," said Jefferson with a smile. "I heard you were here, though I could hardly believe it was true."

"Then you've seen Byron?" asked Pippa eagerly.

Jefferson nodded. "Came back behind the lines last night. Funny thing, that," he added with a glance at Jared. "I've seen him often since we set in here. He wanted me to join the U.S. Coloreds, but I'm happy enough where I am. Hell, after yesterday, I can say I'm glad I turned him down!"

"What happened?" asked Jared with military curiosity. All along the rebel lines, there had been great speculation as to how such a clever Yankee plot had blundered so badly.

"Well, it was a good enough idea," mused Jefferson thoughtfully, but then he shook his head. "The U.S. Coloreds under Ferrero were trained to go in after the mine went off. But when the time came, some idiot decided sending blacks in first would look bad in Washington. Can't have that!"

"Who was in command?" asked Jared. Such reticence didn't sound like U.S. Grant.

"Burnside," said the guitar-playing Yankee, and Jared laughed.

"That would explain it."

"The best intentions . . ." began Jefferson with a shake of his head. But then he turned to Pippa again. "It's Mrs. Pip now, I understand."

Pippa nodded shyly and glanced at Jared. "This is my husband, Jared Knox," she said to Jefferson, but Jefferson gazed at Jared in wonder.

"You, I've seen before," said Jefferson.

"Where?" asked Jared in surprise.

"Chancellorsville," replied Jefferson.

The guitar player looked up. "Don't remember me, do you?" he asked in a deep, rumbling voice that matched his guitar very well.

"No," admitted Jared.

"Got me and my mates into a rebel ball, you did," said the scraggly Yankee. "Had a fine night of dancing thanks to you."

Pippa eyed Jared doubtfully. "You got Yankee soldiers into a rebel ball?"

"That was earlier in the war," said Jared. "Before Gettysburg." Before he learned the woman he admired from afar had destroyed his home, his family. Before he met Pippa Reid.

"Them was gentler days." The Yankee sighed. "Didn't seem gentle then. But them was the good times, for sure. Had the Major with us then, young Watkins . . . All gone now." The Yankee turned back to his guitar, and the music was sad.

"You're not in Garrett's company anymore?"

"We are," said Jefferson. "But after Gettysburg, the Major went back to the cavalry. Made a good name for himself there, but we miss him. Never had another half as good in the field."

"Is Garrett here now?"

Jefferson shook his head sadly, and Pippa's heart leapt to her throat when she saw his expression. "He went down at Cold Harbor."

"Where is he now?" Jared's voice was strained with fear.

"He was sent to Washington. I believe he lives, but it was a bad wound."

"He'll live." The ragged man beside Jefferson still strummed his guitar, but he looked to Jared with utmost confidence. "He's got a woman worth living for. He'll hold on to life beyond other men, just to see that face again."

"Woman? Has Garrett a woman?" asked Jared in surprise. Garrett Knox had no shortage of lovers, but as far as Jared knew, he'd never met a woman he couldn't forget.

The Yankee just smiled and looked back to his guitar, his song turning to a flower on a field of war.

"You can ask him when you see him next, Colonel," said Jefferson. "But then, war brings together the unlikeliest of couples. Wouldn't you agree, Mrs. Pip?" Pippa blushed.

"Not quite the same girl I first saw scampering across the lawn with a satchel full of toads, are you?" observed Jefferson.

"Toads?" asked Jared doubtfully.

"The first time I saw her—she'd have been about twelve then, I suppose—little Miss Pip was gathering up tiny, spring toads. I couldn't guess what such a demure little thing was up to, so I followed her."

"Jefferson," warned Pippa uncomfortably, but Jefferson was not to be stopped.

"I followed her down the street—at a safe distance, of course—and she slipped into a neighbor lady's house. I watched her through the window while she put all those hop toads into the lady's pantry."

Jefferson shook his head in mock disapproval before he continued. "Never have I seen such a devilish look as that on your face, Mrs. Pip, when you hid behind the rose bushes to hear old Mrs. Goth screaming."

Jared turned to his wife, his brow raised. Pippa squirmed with embarrassment when she felt his gaze.

"Mrs. Goth spanked me for . . . something trivial," she explained with reddening cheeks. Jefferson laughed.

"Trivial indeed! You stole her rhubarb pie, young lady. Her prize-winning entry for the fair! Honestly," chastised Jefferson in the perfect imitation of Pippa's old nemesis.

"I intended to present it to you, Mr. Davis, as a welcoming gift. If nothing else, Mrs. Goth was a very good cook. How was I to know the old crow entered her pie in the fair? She probably invented the story to gain Father's sympathies. She was always blaming me for something."

"Probably because you were always doing something," remarked Jared, but his smile was wide when she glanced reproachfully to him. "Come, Pippa. We must go back now."

Pippa's eyes glistened as she looked back into Jefferson's handsome face. He seemed older than when she last saw him, though he was barely twenty-one now. Yet he was no longer fighting for the right to live, and possibly die, as a man.

Pippa saw that he felt accepted, he won his place among other men, regardless of color. She saw his pride, his assurance, and she knew nothing that could happen to this lesser-known Jefferson Davis would break his spirit now.

"Good-bye, Jefferson. You can't know what it means to see you again."

"Where neither of us ever thought to meet. Take care, Mrs. Pip." Jefferson turned to Jared. "If I see the major, I'll tell him we met. That will please him."

"Is that still his commission?" asked Jared. "Then tell him I now outrank him. That should rouse him from his bed!"

"I will do that. And have an eye on young Mrs. Pip. I see there's still much devilment in her eyes."

Pippa glanced nervously at Jared, but he was smiling. "That, I've seen for myself."

Pippa looked to the man with the guitar and he nodded at her, a slow smile growing on his bearded face. She smiled in return, but he didn't speak. Yet as she walked away beside Jared, she heard the deep power of the Yankee's voice. The words of his song spoke of a time when sunshine followed rain, and love washed away all pain.

"Your Jefferson," began Jared as they walked back along the breastworks. "He seems a remarkable man. I begin to understand your loyalty, Pippa," he continued thoughtfully, and Pippa's eyes were filled with hope. "There are few, white or black, his equal."

"The same might be said of Byron," Pippa ventured hesitantly.

"That's true," answered Jared with a trace of pride. Pippa wondered if he was even aware of the sentiment.

They stopped to take a portion of a flavorless cornmeal gruel, then sat together to eat. Pippa dipped her stale bread into the mush, but its lack of taste allowed her concentration to waver.

"How do you know Byron is your brother, Jared?" she asked in a carefully lowered voice, certain they wouldn't be overheard. "Did . . . did your father tell you?"

Jared looked to her with knit brows and shook his head. "No. My father and I have never discussed the subject." Jared paused and drew a breath, but since Pippa now knew his connection to her friend, he could see no point in avoiding her question.

"As a matter of fact, Byron told me himself."

"Did he?" asked Pippa. "And you believed him?"

"I didn't at first," replied Jared as the old memory resurfaced in his mind. "We were thirteen or so at the time, and as you've heard, I was a less than exemplary boy myself."

Jared's eyes glinted briefly on her face, and Pippa's cheeks flushed. "Which makes us two of a kind, it would seem," added Jared with a knowing smile.

"Among my other faults was a tendency to be rather impertinent—bossy, one might say. I took it upon myself to direct Byron in his activities. As I recall, I felt he wasn't working hard enough on my father's behalf."

"Oh, dear," said Pippa shaking her head. "Byron wouldn't like that at all. He's very independent."

"Indeed, as was I. We were bound to clash. But it was at this juncture that he told me in no uncertain terms what an arrogant and willful monster I was. It might have been no more than a fight between boys had he not likened my deviant qualities to those of my father."

Jared sighed, and his face was sad as he went on. "Though I myself was less than ideal, I considered my father beyond reproach, as did all those I knew. I believed he was a great man, without weakness or any vice. Yet there stood this arrogant slave calling my father every derogatory name he'd ever heard.

"I said, 'How dare you speak of my father?', or something similar, and Byron glared at me. 'He's my father also,' he told me."

"What did you do?" she asked in dread.

"Hit him, of course. We fought like tigers, neither of us giving an inch. We were the same height, the same build. The same . . ." Jared's voice drifted and he took a long breath. "As we held each other off, hate filling our hearts, I looked into his eyes, and I saw my father."

"Yes," agreed Pippa. "I've seen that, too."

Jared glanced at her, but then he continued. "I knew then he hadn't lied, and Byron saw that I knew. We stopped fighting and stared at each other. Then I ran off as if hell itself was behind me."

"Did you see him again?" asked Pippa. Thus far, she didn't like the way Jared's story had gone.

"Not for a long while, no. Yet perhaps I became more withdrawn—it was at this time I began building the cabin in the woods. One day when I was working on it, Byron came and started helping me."

"He helped you build our . . . your little house?" cried Pippa, deeply moved as she envisioned the scene between the two reluctant brothers.

"He did, and without ever mentioning our connection

again, we became friends. The moss path to the spring was his idea, actually."

As Jared spoke, Pippa remembered wondering who Jared had meant when he said *us*. She sighed as the answer was revealed to her at last.

"Were you close?" asked Pippa with rising sentiment, but Jared shrugged.

"We understood each other. I had always wished for a brother. But after the house was complete, my father sent me to school in England. I came home for the summers, and I would see Byron then. I was home when he left."

"Do you mean when he ran away?" asked Pippa.

Jared nodded slowly. "I had returned from my fourth year in England just the night before, and I went to the cabin early the next morning. It was still gray out, but I saw Byron coming from the path in the woods."

Jared sighed, but as he continued, his voice was rich with emotion. "He saw me, but he didn't run. His eyes defied me to stop him, but that was never my intention. We didn't speak, not a word, but he knew I wouldn't betray my own brother"

Jared's eyes cast briefly to Pippa, and she flinched at his mention of betrayal.

"And so he ran, all the way to you," sighed Jared. "Life takes strange turns!"

"It does indeed," came a deep voice from behind them, and Jared turned to see his father standing behind him.

David Knox was smiling, but Pippa dared not meet his eyes after all she had learned. Even now, standing there tall and proud, his handsome face like Jared's, she found it almost impossible to believe he would violate a slave woman and betray his devoted wife. Pippa wondered what David

Knox would feel if he knew his son now faced him across the Yankee lines.

"I wonder if you might lead a party for me, Colonel," requested David. Pippa knew that the military title portended like action.

"What are we doing?" asked Jared. As he spoke, Pippa saw Boreas being led their way, and he was already saddled.

"General Gordon needs a small party to ride scout around an area of the left flank. I suggested you be sent." The general glanced over at Pippa. "Of course, it will tear you away from your young lady for a few days, but I'll see she's cared for."

Jared looked to Pippa and she saw the faintest shading of regret in his eyes. It was a regret she shared intently. Alone together, she had hoped they might find occasion to work out their differences.

She couldn't endanger Lucy by including her in any explanation, but she was certain she'd find a way to convince him she had in no way betrayed his love.

"Are you interested in the detail?"

"Yes, sir," said Jared, and his spirits rose with the task at hand.

"Take Nicks with you," suggested David. "He just got back from the hospital today, and he could use the activity."

"A good idea," agreed Jared. Nicks waved happily as he rode up on his own little horse.

Jared rode off with Captain Nicks, and Pippa was obliged to accompany her father-in-law around the camp. They took an early evening meal together, but Pippa was spared the awkwardness of conversation by several other officers who joined them at dinner.

Pippa barely heard a word they said, though she issued the correct, if perfunctory, responses. So much of Byron was evident in his father, and shared as well by Jared. Yet she didn't feel the loathing for the man that she expected to feel. She hated what he had done. Even so, she couldn't hate the man.

Part Four

Surrender

"Guess now who holds thee?" —"Death," I said. But, there,
silver answer rang,— "Not Death, but Love."
                                   —Elizabeth Barrett Browning

Ten

Jared was gone for two nights, and though David Knox saw that Pippa was entertained, she missed her husband terribly. Even though their nights together had been distant, save for the night before the Battle of the Crater, Pippa had taken comfort in Jared's presence.

"Well, daughter," said David after they had finished dinner. "It's a lovely evening. Shall we walk along the breastworks and greet your husband? Jared should be returning from his errand tonight."

Pippa longed to see Jared. She was desperate to learn if his feelings for her had softened. That would be very clear once they retired to his quarters.

"There!" The general pointed south, and Pippa turned to see Jared riding with a small party along a low ravine. Pippa's heart warmed at the sight of him, but another group of men charged from the woods east of Jared's position.

Shots rang out, and Pippa's cry pierced the heavy evening air. General Knox yelled for reinforcements, but already the rebels along the line were returning the Yankee fire. Pippa raced to a higher breastwork position, but she leaned helplessly against it. Her fingernails dug into the soft wood as Jared leapt from his horse and directed the small group in defense of the forward line.

The Yankees moved forward into abandoned trenches and

formed a new line. The hiss and pop of muskets roared briefly as they tried to overwhelm Jared's line. Pippa's breath stopped, held interminably as she watched Jared leading his men forward to meet them.

She had never actually seen him in battle; she had no real idea why his men had him to lead them. But now she knew. Jared was magnificent. Even from her distant position, she saw he had no fear, or, at least, fear had no mastery over him.

His actions were considered and calm, and he moved among his undersized company with clear-thought intent. The rebels fired, now reinforced by the men in the trenches behind. Jared again moved his men forward, but Pippa's heart was in her throat as she saw that he himself was at their lead, his saber wielded in his right hand, a revolver firing from his left.

The Yankees began pulling back, but as Jared leapt upon the trench, a blue-clad soldier spun around and fired. He in turn was felled for his daring, but Jared lurched forward, catching himself with the saber. Again the Yankees fired, and Jared fell to the ground.

"No! Jared, no!" Pippa's high voice rang out as she started to climb over the breastwork to go to him.

David Knox held her back, yet his own voice was shaking as he spoke. "They'll bring him here, daughter. They'll bring him here. There's nothing you can do. Wait," he commanded, but he started down the path to meet his son.

Pippa followed, but she barely saw the ground beneath her feet. Nothing seemed real, it was impossible. *It can't be,* she cried out to herself. As her mind chorused its denial, the Yankees withdrew. The brief skirmish ended, and Captain Nicks carried Jared back to the rear of the Confederate lines.

Pippa and General Knox met them along the path. Nicks

was sobbing as he laid Jared on the ground. As they approached, Jared moved, and Pippa's heart leapt into furious activity.

"Jared, Jared," she cried, and she crumpled to her knees beside him as Captain Nicks raced away for a stretcher.

Pippa fought the dizziness that threatened to overwhelm her and she forced herself to assess his wounds. He had been shot twice, in the shoulder and through his leg. The injury to Jared's thigh was most frightening to Pippa. Clearly, his leg had been broken by the impact of the musket shell. She knew such wounds most often meant amputation, but she pushed the ghastly premonition from her mind.

Jared's face was white, but he opened his eyes and smiled when he saw her. "Pippa," he whispered. When she took his hand, his grip told her his pain was almost unbearable.

Though hot tears flooded across her cheeks, she smiled in return, lest her terror move to him.

"Captain Nicks has gone for a stretcher," she told him as calmly as she could. Her hand shook as she reached to push the hair from his handsome face.

"I'm going to pack your leg, then your shoulder," she told him. As David Knox watched in amazement, Pippa proceeded to peel away Jared's torn trouser leg and examine the gaping wound.

It was soaked in blood, caked with dirt from where Nicks had laid him, and Pippa frowned in frustration. "Could you fetch me some water, sir?" she asked the general without looking up. David Knox looked around, mystified by her request.

"Captain Nicks should have a canteen among his things there, she told him, gesturing to Nicks's pack. David's hands as he passed it to Pippa were trembling and white.

Pippa ground her teeth together, and tearing her petticoat

for cloth, she began to clean the wound. Jared winced, but made no utterance. And all at once, Pippa knew he trusted her after all.

The injury was severe; the shot had torn through the outside of Jared's thigh, cracking the bone as it passed. Yet though the bone was obviously broken, Pippa didn't see the telltale bits of fragment that indicated a limb shattered beyond help. But as Captain Nicks came toward them followed by stretcher-bearers and the surgeon, Pippa knew they would call for amputation.

Captain Farraday arrived, and Pippa waited impatiently as he examined Jared's shoulder first, then his leg. It was plain enough to her that the shoulder required less attention, but Jared's thigh was soaked again with blood before the doctor turned his attention to that.

"It's bad, I'm afraid, Colonel," he said shaking his weary head. "Bone's broken all right. Right through."

Pippa saw Jared's jaw set, and she knew he was resigning himself to the gruesome ordeal of amputation. She thought of the hideous stack of blue-white limbs outside the surgeon's tent. She knew there was no one to protect her husband. No one but herself.

"It didn't go through the bone," Pippa argued.

"It's a bad wound, Mrs. Knox," said Captain Farraday reasonably.

"I see that," she replied. "The bone is broken, yes. But I do not see that it's shattered."

The doctor frowned, but David Knox listened to Jared's wife with interest. "What difference would that make, Captain?" he asked.

"Not a hell of a lot in this case," replied the doctor, but Pippa's anger swelled. "It might be a clean break, who can tell right now? But it's broken in at least two places, and

the flesh is torn right through. Too much danger of gangrene,
I'm afraid. No, we'll have to take the leg."

"Oh, no you won't!" said Pippa fiercely. "You can set it
and stitch it. But so help me God, you are not cutting off
his leg when there's no need!"

"Pippa," whispered Jared. "It's all right."

Tears rolled down her face, but Pippa refused to budge.
"No, it's not."

But Pippa had no further argument, no way to sway the
surgeon used to quick amputations and doubtful recoveries.
In her heart, Pippa believed Jared could be healed, that he
could keep his leg and not endure a grisly amputation that
itself killed many.

Pippa looked desperately to her father-in-law, though she
had no idea how he could help. But now he was her father,
and if anyone could prevail upon the captain to spare Jared,
it was David Knox. David understood, and he turned again
to the captain.

"Is it the risk of gangrene you fear, Farraday?" he asked
slowly.

"It is, General, and it's a substantial risk at that."

"But could you set the bone, stitch the wound?"

"I could set it," replied the doctor. "But Mrs. Knox here
can stitch up a tear better than anyone. Not many doctors
are seamstresses."

Pippa saw her hope and her chance, and she grabbed it.
"If you did so, you might still . . . take his leg at the first
sign of gangrene," she suggested, and the doctor relented.

"Yes, I could do that. But the colonel will need constant
care, my dear. More than he'll be getting in a hospital."

"Then he will not go to a hospital," said David Knox
firmly. "He'll be sent to Richmond, and he'll have the finest
group of nurses I know."

* * *

Jared was taken to the surgeon's tent, and there Captain Farraday set his broken leg.

"The orderlies will keep it still now, Mrs. Knox," he said to her. "You stitch him up, and I'll be back to put on a brace. No cast I'm afraid. A wound like that will have to be dressed daily. Now you get busy—I've got to go to work on the other boys they're bringing in," said Captain Farraday wearily.

Pippa nodded, but though Jared had been remarkably restrained during the agonizing setting of his leg, Pippa was loath to cause him more pain.

"No morphine?" she asked as the surgeon turned to leave, though she knew no such medicine had been available in Petersburg for several weeks.

"I'm sorry," said Captain Farraday compassionately. "There's no morphine now even in Richmond since the blockade tightened with this damned siege."

"Don't worry, Pippa." Jared's voice was weak, his face pale, but he smiled as her agonized face turned towards him.

An idea flashed across Pippa's mind. "Wait right there!" she said excitedly. Jared watched as his wife darted from the tent.

"Wait here?" he mused to Captain Nicks. "What choice do I have?"

Pippa returned breathlessly, but Jared smiled grimly when he saw the tall amber bottle she carried.

"Will this do, do you think?" she asked. Had Jared the strength, he might have laughed when she produced a neat little glass for his use.

"Very thoughtful," he replied, and Pippa poured a full portion for him to drink.

Captain Nicks helped Jared up to swallow the fiery liquid,

and he turned to Pippa with admiration. "Now there's a wife a man should have!" he exclaimed. "Why my ma wouldn't bring my old man liquor if he'd lost both his legs!"

Pippa smiled weakly, then checked Jared's face to see if he appeared sufficiently numbed. He looked unaltered and she frowned. "Perhaps you should take a bit more, Jared."

"This will be fine," he replied. "Now, if you please . . ."

Pippa's brow knit tightly and she glanced at the glass Jared had returned to Captain Nicks. To the great surprise of Captain Nicks, Pippa calmly relieved him of the glass again and took a large mouthful of the bourbon. It burned her throat and Pippa sputtered and coughed. She shook her head and turned her attention to the job at hand.

"Most reassuring," commented Jared as she set the glass aside.

But Pippa saw the faint trace of a smile across his beautiful face. It gave her courage to use every ounce of the skill she had acquired since the day he dragged her to Petersburg as his prisoner.

General Knox provided for a separate coach to take his son to Richmond. Unlike the hideous journey from the Wilderness, Pippa was able to remain at Jared's side along the way. Captain Farraday put a brace on Jared's thigh, and taught Pippa the proper manner of adjusting it so that his dressing might be changed.

"But don't go changing the bandages too often," the captain told her. "Leave it as it is. There's no good poking around in there. If it's going to get better, it'll do most of the healing on its own."

Something about this advice struck Pippa as wayward,

but she was determined to do what was necessary to save Jared's leg. He was to be examined in a week by a Richmond physician, and if all was progressing well at that time, then he would be periodically checked afterwards.

To Pippa, and to Jared as well, it looked to be a long, painful time before he would be certain his leg would remain. Jared slept most of the way to Richmond, but he woke once to see Pippa beside him. She took his hand, and as he gazed up into her eyes, he whispered, "Thank you," before falling back to sleep.

Pippa believed they might find a way back to each other after all. Once in Richmond, she determined to do every thing she could to win back his approval.

Jared was brought to his own house on Franklin Street, and there he received the finest, most attentive care in Richmond. But it was Pippa who took charge of his welfare, and it was she who changed his bandages and re-braced his leg afterwards.

"Do you really think it's necessary to change his dressing twice a day, Pippa?" asked Mary. "At the hospital, we do it only once, and then only if it's bleeding heavily."

Pippa was adamant on this point. "If it isn't changed, it will tear when it's removed. I'm sure it's better to keep it clean, or the blood cakes up and sticks to the bandage."

Mary wasn't convinced, but Caroline approved of the neatness of Jared's wound. "It's coming along well," she said to Mary. "Pippa must be doing something right."

Kim was less suited to nursing, but she spent long hours at Jared's bedside reading English novels. When she lost interest in those, she started on dime novels written by

American ladies. Kim became tearful relaying the sentimental passages, but Jared was distinctly bored.

His leg was swollen to nearly triple its natural size, and he was in a great deal of pain. He flinched when Pippa changed his bandages, and ground his teeth together to keep from worrying her with his agony.

"I hope this is worth it," he told her when she readjusted the brace.

"Of course it is," Pippa replied assuredly, but privately she began to wonder.

Jared had been home for nearly a week, and if anything, his pain had intensified rather than abated. If Pippa had known the agony he would be forced to endure, she might have quailed before demanding the surgeon leave his leg.

If when the physician arrived the next morning they were told the leg would have to go, Pippa knew she would never forgive herself.

"It looks . . . promising," said Dr. Wachtel after examining Jared's thigh extensively.

The women in the room issued a collective sigh of relief.

"Then we should continue as we've done?" asked Caroline, but the doctor sighed.

"Yes," he replied. "But I'll be back to check on the Colonel in a week."

He turned to Jared and patted his arm. "There's still a long way to go, son," he admitted. "I can't lie to you, it's going to be damned painful for some time yet."

Dr. Wachtel left, but Pippa saw the strain in Jared's face when they were left alone. "Do you wish I'd kept my mouth shut about this, Jared?" she asked, but she dreaded to hear his answer.

Jared took her hand and with effort, he smiled. "Pippa, if this works, and I believe it will, then you've saved my leg. Have you any idea what that means to me, to know my leg won't end up on that grisly pile? It's painful, I admit. But I can't imagine amputation would be less so."

"But it would be over," reasoned Pippa tearfully.

"I can cope with this," Jared reassured her. Inwardly, he wondered how much longer he could endure the agony that intensified daily.

Pippa sat alone with Lucy in the kitchen, drumming her fingers restlessly on the broad oak counter. "Morphine," she murmured. "If only I could get him some morphine. Just to get him through the worst of it."

Lucy thought a moment, then nodded. "There might be a way," she began, but Pippa shook her head.

"There's no morphine in Richmond, at least none we can get our hands on, Lucy."

"Not in Richmond, no," replied Lucy slowly. "But in Washington . . ."

Pippa's eyes widened, and her heart leapt. "What do you mean, Lucy? How would we get that, especially for a rebel officer?"

"We might not be able to get much," cautioned Lucy. "But even a little bit would help."

"It would," said Pippa excitedly. "How do we get it?"

"There are ways. Yes. I may be able to find someone," said Lucy with growing confidence. "Leave it to me, and I'll see what I can do."

Pippa left the matter in Lucy's capable hands, and the next night Lucy caught her attention after dinner.

"What is it, Lucy?" asked Pippa.

"I've found someone who might help us. A wandering merchant of sorts," replied Lucy.

"What do we do?" asked Pippa gleefully.

"I'm afraid he'll deal only with you," Lucy told her reluctantly. "He doesn't seem to trust a colored woman to pay him adequately."

"Payment!" groaned Pippa. "I hadn't thought of that. Of course, he'll want money. And I have none."

"No, I doubt he'll accept Confederate currency," agreed Lucy. "That could be a problem. People of his kind care for nothing else," she added with disgust.

"Never mind," said Pippa. "I know what to offer. When do I meet this man?"

"Tonight, at midnight. He'll come to the lamppost down the street from here. That should be safe enough."

Pippa nodded. "Very well, I'll meet him."

"He won't have the drug tonight," Lucy reminded her. "He just wants to see what you're offering, and then he'll make the necessary arrangements."

Pippa grimaced, but sighed. "I hope it doesn't take too long. Jared is in so much pain."

At midnight, Pippa donned her cape and slipped silently from the room. But Jared's pain kept him from a deep sleep, and he saw her go. For a moment, the pain in Jared's thigh was nothing as his heart throbbed in his chest.

He struggled to sit up, and from the window at his bedside, Jared saw Pippa appear upon the street below. She glanced furtively left and right, then hurried away. As he stared out the window, Jared's blue eyes filled with tears and his hands clenched as Pippa disappeared around the corner.

* * *

Pippa went to the designated lamppost and waited for the mysterious merchant. A swarthy little man approached her, but though Pippa had expected to be afraid of him, he appeared pleasant.

"You want drug?" asked the man in hesitant English.

"Are you Arabic?" she asked.

The dark man frowned. "I American," he told her proudly. Pippa was suitably chastened.

"I'm sorry," she said.

"Not Arabic before. Persian," he added, but Pippa was uncertain of the difference.

"Called Darius. You want drug, lady?"

Pippa remembered her purpose. "Yes, Mr. Darius. I need morphine very badly."

"Not good, too much," said Darius with a shake of his head. "Once start, no stop. No, lady. You go home."

Pippa sighed in exasperation. "No, Mr. Darius, you don't understand . . ."

"I do. Seen it before. And not called 'Mr. Darius,' " he added petulantly. "Darius first name. You not say last," he added with a chuckle.

"I beg your pardon," replied Pippa. "Darius, then. I don't want the morphine for myself," she explained carefully. "It's for my husband. He was shot, in the war," she added, as if Darius might not know a war was in progress.

"Hurt bad?" asked Darius kindly.

Pippa nodded, and tears started in her eyes. She wondered if the Persian would be swayed by a woman's tears, but looking at his intelligent eyes, she decided not.

"Very badly, yes. He might lose his leg if I don't care for it well enough. He's in terrible pain. It's my fault, I wouldn't let them cut his leg off, and now he hurts. Please, Darius, can you get me morphine for him?"

"I can. Maybe not much. Is hard to get now."

"I know that."

"What you give for it?" he asked in a more businesslike tone.

Pippa drew a breath, then drew out a stack of papers which she handed to Darius. "I have no money, except Confederate."

"No want rebel money," said Darius clearly, then he looked at the papers. "What this?"

"That's the title, the deed, and all the papers to my late father's home in Maine . . . North of Massachusetts," she explained. "I'll give it to you, for morphine. Houses in the north still hold value, I believe. You can sell it for a good price."

Darius looked at Pippa with misgivings. Pippa knew she had no choice but to trust the little Persian. "Take the papers with you, and you may check what I've told you. The house is mine to do with as I please, and I please to give it to you."

Darius nodded. "Yes. Good. Will return," he assured her.

Curiously, when the little Persian merchant disappeared into the darkness, Pippa had no doubt she would see him again. Jared was apparently sleeping when she slipped into bed beside him, and Pippa sighed happily when she thought of her accomplishment. She would come to his aid in a most unexpected way, and then he couldn't help but see how much she loved him.

Part of Pippa longed to wake him and tell him all about it, but she reasoned it would be best to wait on the off chance Darius wouldn't be able to get the morphine. Still, she fell asleep with more happiness filling her heart than she had known since Jared had fallen. Her dreams that night were of peace.

* * *

Pippa woke early to tell Lucy the good news, though Lucy plainly had misgivings about Pippa's decision to leave her papers with Darius.

"I can trust Darius," said Pippa indignantly. "Don't worry so, Lucy. You can be so skeptical at times!"

Lucy shook her head, but she smiled as Pippa went to bring Jared his breakfast.

"How are you feeling?"

Pippa carried the tray to Jared, and she was stunned to see the anger snapping in his blue eyes. "What's the matter? Are you ill?"

Pippa's hands began to shake, and the saucer on her tray rattled against the cup. "What have I done?" she asked in a shrill voice.

Jared was cold and hard when he answered. "Nothing, Philippa," he replied mockingly. "You're the perfect, attentive wife."

Pippa's anger flared. " 'Philippa'? You must really be angry with me. Perhaps you would be good enough to tell me what I've done to provoke you."

Jared looked away. "There is no point."

"I see that," replied Pippa, but her eyes were brimming with hot tears. "I need to check your leg," she added, but he didn't speak as she pulled the covers away to clean and re-bandage his wound.

It was still painfully swollen, and Pippa wondered if Jared's anger came from his pain. Her mood softened, and she looked to him sympathetically.

"Is it terribly painful?" she asked, but Jared's eyes shot to her with ripe annoyance.

"What do you think, my dear? But you've managed to confine me in bed for God knows how long. There isn't much I can do about . . . anything, is there? But please, go about your business. Whatever that is."

Pippa was shocked. It was unlike Jared to lash out at her for nothing, but she had never considered that he might rightly blame her for his condition. It was true that if his leg had been amputated, he would be recovering by now—if he lived. He would at least be able to move about in a chair, and that gave Pippa an idea.

The tears were hot upon her cheeks, and Pippa turned quickly away to leave the room. But Jared called her back.

"Philippa," he commanded in a low, dangerous voice.

Reluctantly, she turned to him, dreading to hear his words.

"It might be better if you removed your things to the room at the end of the hall," he told her calmly, but Pippa's face blanched at the request.

"If you wish," she replied in a tiny voice.

"I do."

The next days for Pippa were agonizing. It was plain Jared was furious with her, but she had no idea why. She saw him twice daily to tend his injury, but if he spoke to her at all, it was cold and biting.

More annoying still, Christina came by to visit Jared, and he seemed both happy to see her and comfortable in her presence. She spent the better part of an afternoon reading to him, and it was all Pippa could do not to order the other woman away.

Pippa suggested to Caroline that Jared might make good

use of a wheelchair, and Mary brought one from the hospital, but it improved Jared's temper very little. Pippa was bowed with the weight of his anger, and even his mother and sisters were aware of the strain between the couple.

"He's in a great deal of pain," Caroline said comfortingly to Pippa. "It's a strange fact, but at such times, men often turn on their wives. Give him time, Pippa."

Pippa said nothing, and she was sure there was more to Jared's anger than that. But if his pain was a factor, only Darius could help her now. That night, Darius came to Pippa's aid at last.

Pippa woke to find Lucy shaking her. "Pippa. Pippa, wake up!" she whispered. "He's back."

"Who's back, Lucy?" Pippa wondered groggily.

"Mr. Darius."

"Darius," corrected Pippa dreamily. "Darius is his first name. You couldn't pronounce his last . . . Has he the morphine?" she asked as she woke more fully and came to her senses.

"He does, and he'll be waiting to meet you tonight. Now, in fact. You must hurry. Unfortunately, Mrs. Knox was up until late, and I had to wait for her to go to sleep before waking you."

Pippa leapt from her bed and dressed in a flash. "Is he at the lamppost?" she asked as she headed for the door.

"He is. Now hurry!" commanded Lucy, but Pippa was already scurrying down the hall.

"Darius!" she called as she approached the lamppost. Darius was heading down the street again, and Pippa realized just how close she had come to missing him.

"You late."

"I know, I'm sorry. Have you the morphine? Did you find out about my house in Maine?"

Darius hesitated and shook his head, and Pippa's heart crashed in her breast. "No?" she asked miserably.

"I got drug. Yes. But not big. Little drug."

"Are you willing to trade?" pressed Pippa.

"Now, lady, I check on these," he said, waving Pippa's deed and title.

"Aren't they in order?" asked Pippa with a wave of horror. Her father hadn't been a very practical man, and it occurred to her that something might well be amiss.

"They all good," reassured Darius. "Try to tell you. You sell house, get much money. Yankee money. Is good house, I learn."

"Then what's the matter?" asked Pippa impatiently. "Don't you want the house? If it's not enough, I also have a little cottage by the ocean. It's not worth as much money, though. No one wants to live down by the water."

"No, no. Only want one house," said Darius, but then he drew out a vial of morphine. "But this all I got. Good for a week, little more. Not worth house."

Pippa breathed a vast sigh of relief. "That's fine, Darius. Please, the house is yours. But my husband needs this medicine."

Darius shook his dark head, but a light in his eyes revealed admiration. "Your husband blessed. That sure."

"I wish he thought so," whispered Pippa, but Darius took her hand and kissed it. He pressed the vial into her palm and then turned to leave.

"Thank you, Darius," she called happily, and he raised his hand to bid her farewell.

* * *

Pippa clutched the vial tightly in her hand and ran back to Jared's house. Lucy met her at the door, and Pippa held up the vial triumphantly. Lucy stepped back, and Pippa raced up the stairs to Jared's room.

Jared was waiting for her at the top of the stairs. Even in the low light of the evening gasoliers, she saw his fury. Her heart caught in her throat as he moved his chair back towards the open door of his room.

"Come," he said, and his voice was ice. Pippa followed him into the room and shut the door, knowing without question he intended to speak to her where no one else would hear.

"What's wrong?" she asked weakly, but Jared turned up his lamp before answering.

"I want you out of here," ordered Jared in a low, trembling voice.

Pippa was stunned. "What?"

"I want you out of my house, out of Virginia." He ground out the words as Pippa stared at him in disbelief.

"What have I done?" she whispered plaintively. "I thought you might forgive me," she said in a broken voice, as the tears fell to her cheeks. "If I was a good wife . . ."

Jared laughed bitterly, and all hope in Pippa's heart died. "Where am I to go?"

"I'll see that you're sent safely back to your precious North," he replied, his voice now blank and empty. "You can go back to Maine. That's what you've always wanted, isn't it? You have your father's house there."

"Not anymore," murmured Pippa. "Though I have the cottage by the sea. I can go there," she said tonelessly. It didn't matter now. Inside, she was already dead.

"What happened to your father's house?" asked Jared suspiciously.

"I gave it away," Pippa told him tearfully. "For this."

Pippa held out the little vial of morphine and Jared took it, staring at it in wonder.

"What is it?" he asked slowly.

Pippa sniffed and drew her sleeve across her wet cheek. "Morphine," she explained brokenly.

In a tortured flash, Jared understood, and his heart twisted. His breath came shallow as a hot wave of sickness heralded the extent of his error.

"You traded your house for a vial of morphine?" he asked. Tears started in his own eyes as he looked at Pippa in utter disbelief.

Pippa nodded. "You hurt," she whispered.

"Oh, God," Jared groaned. "Pippa, is that where you were going?"

Pippa's teary face revealed puzzlement, but Jared reeled in anguish. "I saw you leave, several nights ago. And again tonight," he admitted. "I thought . . ."

All became clear to Pippa, but rather than relief she felt anger. "You thought what? That I had taken this marvelous opportunity to betray you? Is that it?"

Jared couldn't meet her eyes. "Yes."

Pippa's breath came in furious gasps. "How could you think that?" she sputtered. "Do you think I've spent every day at your side so that at night I might sneak away?"

Pippa was wild with fury, her thoughts a mad jumble, but she couldn't conceive of the distrust he bore her. That she might purposely have kept him bedridden and in agony to meet her own ends—he must really think her a monster.

"You will take this," she said in the fiercest voice Jared had ever heard her use.

Pippa administered the drug quickly, then backed away from him, her eyes blazing with a green fire.

"Pippa," he began, but Pippa whirled around to face him.

"How could you think those things? I would die for you, Jared Knox!"

Pippa burst into broken sobs and darted from the room, banging the door shut behind her. Jared just stared at the door, his agonized body already feeling the effects of the morphine. But nowhere did its relief touch his heart, and softly he whispered his wife's name.

"Pippa. Pippa, what have I done?"

For the first time in the long years of war, the tears in Jared's eyes fell to his strong, beautiful face and glistened there in the fading light of the gasolier.

Pippa dutifully went to Jared's room the next morning, but she was careful to bring Kim with her so that they wouldn't be left alone together. Jared was obliged to endure a long morning of dime novels, and he was afforded no further chance to speak to his wife in private until the evening.

This time, Pippa brought Mary along, but Jared wasn't willing to allow her this escape from his company. "Would you mind leaving us alone, Mary?" he asked. "I would like to talk to my wife in private."

Mary looked to Pippa hopefully, and quickly exited the room. Pippa chewed the inside of her lip in agitation, but she didn't wait for Jared to speak.

"Are you angry because I'm still here?" she asked with a quick frown, but she stopped when she saw the stab of pain her words brought to Jared's face.

"Pippa, please listen. I am sorry. You've been good to me, kind and thoughtful, and I repaid you with cruelty. Please forgive me. This is your home. There's no need to leave."

Pippa allowed herself to meet his eyes, and she knew he meant what he said. He was a good man, and realizing his error, he was sorry. But that didn't mean he loved her or wanted her. It certainly didn't mean he trusted her.

Pippa nodded. "As you wish," she whispered. Tears were threatening again in her eyes, and she hurried from the room.

Jared watched her go and he sighed heavily. He saw her pain, he knew he had caused it. So much stood between them, so much that wasn't easily resolved. Jared Knox could see the future he wanted, as all rebels could, but he had no idea how to surmount the obstacles that stood in his way.

Jared and Pippa fell into an uneasy truce, neither saying anything that could upset the other, yet neither dared say what was closest to their hearts. Pippa tended Jared still twice a day, and she felt a great relief as the swelling in his leg reduced. Dr. Wachtel pronounced Jared well on his way to recovery, and though the vial wasn't entirely empty, Jared insisted he had no further use for it.

"Take it, Doctor, and use it where it's needed most," he said, and Dr. Wachtel accepted the morphine gratefully.

The weeks passed and since his wound had healed, a cast had replaced the brace. Jared was able to move about the house with a cane. More and more, his eyes followed Pippa as she went to and fro, but he wasn't certain how to approach her.

Something had changed since he had ordered her from his house, but Jared wasn't certain what it was. Pippa had never been this distant; there were no longer peaks to her mood, she was neither high nor low. She seemed to avoid him, yet she was polite and pleasant when in his company.

But Jared couldn't seem to reach her, and as summer gave its full way to autumn, he saw no sign that she wanted him to. Pippa had begun working in Chimborazo Hospital, and Jared saw even less of her. When she came home at night, she was tired and often went straight to her little room without supper.

Pippa's long days at the hospital were draining her more than anyone guessed. Granted none of the freedom of decision she had known on the battlefields, she felt her medical creativity wasted. There was little to do but follow orders, and Pippa said as much to Caroline at dinner. Though Caroline was understanding, she didn't offer much hope of change.

"There are so many, Pippa. And we have so little medicine."

Pippa had no argument for this, but the rate of amputations still bothered her. But without sufficient quantities of morphine, she couldn't imagine many choosing the hell Jared endured. Few had his strength, and even fewer had a group of women who could tend him daily.

Lucy witnessed the estrangement between Pippa and Jared with regret and a certain amount of unaccustomed remorse. Her own mother was safe, but Pippa suffered. More than once Lucy had passed her door to hear her friend crying softly.

Yet Pippa never discussed her husband now with Lucy, and Lucy knew without encouragement, neither would know how to find their way back to the other. Lucy saw Jared watching Pippa, she knew he stood by the window in the parlor to watch for her return from the hospital. But Lucy watched with regret as he hurried to seat himself carelessly when Pippa came in the door.

Lucy saw Pippa glance at her husband, a faint look of hope, of expectation in her eyes when she first entered the room. It grieved Lucy to see the disappointment that followed when Pippa saw him engrossed in a newspaper or a book, but Pippa refused to listen when Lucy suggested he might care more than it seemed.

"Please, don't," Pippa said raggedly when Lucy ventured to broach the subject. "I can't talk about that now. Please."

Lucy acquiesced, but as autumn grew nearer to winter, she wondered if she might take a hand in the matter. It was late in October, and despite Jared's objections, Caroline had planned as extravagant a birthday party as could be devised under the circumstances.

In fact, there was little food but many guests. As Lucy served the small crackers and cheese, she saw that though Jared seemed to enjoy himself, Pippa was very quiet. Christina was in attendance, and hovered at Jared's side throughout the afternoon. Lucy guessed that Christina was aware of the friction between Jared and his Yankee wife, and intended to make the most of it for her own purposes. What those were, Lucy could guess all too well.

Caroline's guests left before nightfall, and Lucy watched regretfully as both Jared and Pippa went alone to their respective rooms. A light rain started outside, and as Lucy went about the house closing windows, an idea came to her.

"That's not necessary, Lucy," said Jared, as she struggled to pull shut his window. "The rain is coming from the other direction," he explained patiently.

Lucy abandoned her task and nodded. "True enough. Right into Miz Pippa's room." Lucy clucked her tongue and shook her head regretfully.

"Poor little thing," she went on. "It's such a cold, damp room. Not at all like this. Why, it's as warm as toast in here! With all the coughing she's been doing . . ."

That was enough for Jared. "Pippa has been coughing? I hadn't noticed that," he said with concern, but Lucy repressed a grin when she saw his furrowed brow.

"Yes, sir, she sure enough has. I don't like it one bit, and her being such a fragile little thing."

Jared had seen enough of Pippa's fortitude to know she could hardly be called 'fragile,' but he was deeply moved to think of her in distress.

Jared considered this a moment while Lucy watched him from the corner of her eye. "Would you mind telling my wife I'd like to speak to her, Lucy?" he said. Though Lucy's eyes were wide and innocent, her smile was triumphant when she left Jared's room.

Lucy hurried to Pippa's room and knocked on the door. "Pippa?" she called when she heard no answer.

Lucy opened the door and saw Pippa struggling with her window. Unlike the others in the house, Pippa was trying to open hers.

"Pippa?" she called, and Pippa jumped at the sound of her voice.

"Lucy!" she exclaimed. "I didn't hear you come in."

"What are you doing?"

"This window is stuck again," said Pippa in irritation, as she tried again to raise the heavy glass.

"What on earth are you trying to open it for?" asked Lucy in wonder, glancing to see the rain beating hard on the windowpane with which Pippa struggled.

"It's hot in here," she explained. "A little rain won't hurt." Pippa gave up her feeble attempt and turned to Lucy. "What did you want, Lucy?"

"Your husband would like to speak with you," said Lucy
evenly.

"Jared? What does he want?" asked Pippa. "Is he all
right?"

Lucy started to reassure her, but then reconsidered. "I'm
not certain. He seems a bit . . . feverish, I thought."

Pippa's eyes widened and, without a word, she darted
from her room and down the hall. Lucy sat down on Pippa's
neatly made bed and then lay back comfortably.

"I believe a nap might be in order," she said to herself
with satisfaction. "It's been a long day." Lucy drifted into
sleep. As always, her dreams were filled with the perfect,
golden-brown face of the man she had lost many long years
before.

Pippa peeked into Jared's room and saw that he was waiting for her. Jared noticed her, but his face was serious when
he called her in.

Pippa glanced at his open window, then turned to him
with concern. "Are you hot?" she asked, her face knit in a
worried expression.

"No," replied Jared in confusion.

He paused, looking puzzled, and then continued. "Pippa,"
he began, and Pippa thought he sounded almost shy.
"There's something I'd like to discuss with you."

Jared paused again and his eyes searched his wife's young
face. "I've been thinking . . . Your room is perhaps the least
comfortable in our house. I wondered if you had tired of
it," he suggested.

Pippa was puzzled as she waited for Jared to finish his
point. "Well, that's true," she answered slowly, uncertain
where this was leading.

"The climate isn't very pleasant, I believe," added Jared

"Yes," she sighed. "So hot and stuffy. Not airy and coo, as it is here."

Jared stared at her, caught off balance by her unexpected reply. He glanced toward the door, his brow knit in confusion as he recalled what Lucy had told him. *Perhaps she is dim,* he thought.

"Really?" he asked. "I understood it was cold."

But either way, Jared's decision was made, and there was no reason not to go on. "Be that as it may, I've been thinking that you might want to move back in here."

Pippa looked at Jared doubtfully and a tiny frown tugged at her lips. "With you?" she asked rather suspiciously. It didn't seem unlikely that Jared intended to go somewhere else in light of his offer.

Jared hesitated. "Yes, with me," he replied, holding his breath as he awaited Pippa's response.

Hope resurrected so fast and so powerfully in Pippa's heart that for a moment she could neither breathe nor speak. Jared wondered if he had cornered her with his offer.

"I wouldn't be . . . in your way?" she asked hesitantly.

"No. You'd be more comfortable here," he told her, but Pippa felt a shade of disappointment that Jared didn't say he wanted her back. Maybe he felt it was improper that they sleep apart, but at that point, Pippa didn't care.

"Well. Then, yes. I will," she replied, but she didn't meet his eyes.

"Tonight?" asked Jared, trying not to seem too eager, but Pippa nodded.

"I'll get my things," she said.

The hope caused her heart to pound, and Pippa hurried back to her room to retrieve her belongings. Lucy was sleeping, and Pippa was careful not to disturb her. But she wondered how Jared ever got the idea her stuffy little room was cold.

Pippa returned with her little bags and replaced them on their former shelves and in cabinets that had been left empty since she had left Jared's room. Jared watched her, helping a little here and there, but they didn't speak as Pippa was re-ensconced in the bedroom.

"How is your leg?" Pippa asked as Jared lowered himself to the bed.

Jared started to tell her that it was fine, but then thought better of it. "Oh, it's coming along well enough," he told her slowly, looking out the window despondently.

Pippa gazed at him with concern. "Are you sure?"

Jared nodded and looked back at her innocently. "I imagine I'm just . . . bored," he told her sadly. "Tired of the procedure it takes just to climb the stairs," he added gloomily. Seeing Pippa moved by his admission of distress, Jared's eyes brightened.

"Perhaps you wouldn't mind entertaining me," he suggested casually.

Pippa looked around the room doubtfully. "What do you want me to do?" she asked. In light of the strain that had been between them, Pippa's duties had been solely to tend his wounds. His entertainment had fallen to others, mainly Kim and an assortment of visitors.

Jared considered her question, but decided his most honest request might be better restrained. "You could read to me," he suggested.

Pippa glanced at the book Kim had left on his bedstand. "Oh God, please, not that!" groaned Jared.

"What's wrong with it?"

"It's the most unbearably awful book," he told her. "Christina gave it to Kim, and she likes it. A noble, perfect heroine suffers for endless pages at the hands of a succession of evil men—the latest being a fiancé who has taken to drink and has departed for Mexico with a woman of questionable repute."

"Really? That sounds rather interesting, Jared," said Pippa as she picked up the book, but Jared groaned.

"Put that down, woman," he ordered. "If I have to hear one more word about that dreadful, self-righteous Emily . . ."

Pippa giggled. "Perhaps she takes up with the gardener in the end, and lives a life of sin," she suggested with a bright smile.

Their eyes met and Jared grinned. "Not a chance, my dear. She'll eventually die of consumption, pontificating and issuing judgments on mankind until the last. Spare me."

"Well, what would you like me to read then?" asked Pippa.

"Kim has been through every novel in the house," admitted Jared, fearing his chance would be lost. "What about poetry?"

Pippa went to fetch her small bag of treasured books and dug around in it looking for something suitable. Her first volume was questionable.

"Emerson?" she asked, and Jared rose a brow at the mention of the Massachusetts abolitionist. "That's mainly essays. I suppose not."

She pulled out another book by a lesser known author and considered it. "I got this at a reading in Concord with my father. *Leaves of Grass* by Mr. Walt Whitman."

"I've never heard of him," said Jared.

Pippa remembered the forceful passion revealed in Mr. Whitman's works and hesitated. "Perhaps not," she decided.

Pippa put the two works of Yankee authors back into her bag and drew out another slender volume with a sigh. "Well, Mrs. Browning it is, then," she said. "That should be safe."

"Very good." Jared leaned back on his pillows and Pippa opened the little book, choosing a sonnet at random.

" 'Go from me,' " Pippa began, but her voice wavered. She gathered her courage and tried again, but as she read further, her fingers went cold and she began to tremble.

" 'Go from me. Yet I feel that I shall stand henceforward in thy shadow.' "

Pippa's voice faltered and her heart labored. "Perhaps we could do this another time. I . . . I forgot something downstairs," she said quickly. Before Jared could say a word, Pippa darted from the room and disappeared.

Eleven

Jared waited for Pippa's return anxiously, for although he wasn't certain what disturbed her, he feared she might change her mind and remain in the other room. Pippa did come back, and Jared was relieved to see that she wore her nightdress. Pippa found Jared waiting for her, and she knew he would expect an explanation for her behavior. Pippa drew a quick breath before speaking, but then forced her eyes to meet his.

"I'm sorry, Jared," she said. "I don't know what came over me."

She swallowed and waited for his response, but Jared was willing to let the matter pass. "I understand, Pippa," he told her gently. "You've been spending long days at the hospital. That's hardly an easy way to spend one's time. It's no wonder you'd be . . . emotional. Don't think of it again."

Pippa glanced at him doubtfully. She couldn't imagine he didn't know he was the source of her outburst. But Jared had simplified her explanation, and she was content to leave it alone.

Pippa went hesitantly to their bed, and she slid beneath the covers, far to the side. Jared watched her with eyes of regret, then sighed and undressed. He lowered himself into the bed beside Pippa, laboriously positioning his leg where it was most comfortable. Jared glanced over at Pippa and smiled ruefully.

"It's rather awkward still," he told her apologetically.

"It won't be long now, Jared," Pippa assured him. "Dr. Wachtel says the cast will be removed soon."

It occurred to Pippa that Jared would return to his army in the sieged city of Petersburg as soon as he was able. She attributed his growing restlessness to this, but Pippa felt she must stop him at any cost.

"Of course, it will be a long time before you can . . . do much," she added hurriedly, but Jared looked to Pippa with unveiled disappointment.

"I suppose that's true," he said sorrowfully, but Pippa let out a breath of relief. It appeared Jared accepted his limits.

For a moment longer, Jared searched Pippa's face, but seeing her reaction, he sighed. "Well, good-night then," he said, and he closed his eyes.

Pippa peeked at him. His beautiful face was composed, resigned, as he lay on his back beside her. It felt good to be close to him again, to inhale his warm, masculine scent, to feel the warmth of his strong body beside her. Pippa longed to touch him, to run her hands across his smooth skin and feel his heartbeat race beneath her touch.

But calling her back to his side was enough for the present; there was a long road yet. With that in mind, Pippa counted herself fortunate and fell into a sleep that offered more rest than any she had known since she had lost Jared's love.

Jared lay quietly beside Pippa, but he was totally unable to sleep. If Pippa was given peace by his nearness, Jared found the yearnings that had been growing daily in him near a state of bare control. Pippa's long, soft hair brushed against his shoulder, her leg touched his when she rolled over on her side.

Jared reached over to touch the mass of dark waves that faced him now, and his fingers tingled at the sensual feel. Despite the cumbersome cast, Jared wanted Pippa. He wanted her with all the passion that had built over the long months without her. With painful clarity, he remembered each detail of the last time they had loved.

It might be long before Pippa regained her comfort in his presence. Knowing this, Jared forced himself to look away from her sleeping form. When sleep found him, it brought vibrant images of passion and need. Jared found that even sleep rendered him an agony of its own.

"What is the matter with Jared?"

Kim sniffed tearfully as she entered the sitting room where the others had gathered to sew. Lucy was dusting, and outside a cold wind rattled the windows of the house. Katy's three children had come to spend the day with their grandmother, and Pippa sat holding the baby in her lap. The little girl was especially fond of Pippa, and Pippa reveled in unfamiliar bliss.

Caroline looked up at Kim with concern. "Why, dear? What's wrong?"

"Jared is being just beastly, Mother," said Kim, and tears were still fresh on her cheeks.

"What did he do?" asked Pippa sympathetically.

Jared had been difficult to live with lately, though he always apologized quickly if he was short with her. Pippa didn't understand it, because he was wearing only a light cast, and his strength was improving daily. Pippa was relieved to hear he was the same with the others.

"He swore at me!" said Kim in a shaking voice. "He told me he didn't care a fig—and those were not the words he chose—what happened to Miss Emily Honeycastle!"

Kim was indignant at her brother's lack of sentimentality, but Pippa repressed a smile.

"Oh, dear," said Caroline doubtfully.

"Who's Miss Honeycastle?" asked Katy's son, Bobby.

"Miss Honeycastle is the heroine in the book I'm reading to Jared," explained Kim earnestly. "She's as sweet and pure and without rancor as one could imagine. Her life has been so hard, yet she is always good, she's never . . . afraid."

Pippa listened to Kim with compassion. If Kim was comparing herself to the perfect-tempered Emily, no wonder she felt insecure about her own reactions to the terror of war.

"Anyway, Jared told me he didn't want to hear another word," said Kim, as tears again started in her eyes. "And then . . . and then he told me to leave, that he couldn't stand it anymore!"

Kim began to cry and Caroline rose to comfort her. "There, there, Kimber. Really, I don't know what's gotten into him."

Mary nodded. "Jared has been impossible for any of us to get along with. He was down here this morning, criticizing the way I stitch socks, if you can believe it."

Lucy stopped her dusting and nodded vehemently as Mary spoke. "And this here's why I'm cleaning now instead of this morning as I was 'posed to. Said I was dusting too loudly!" she said indignantly.

Pippa laughed. "I believe it. Last night he became quite incensed at the way I brush my hair. He felt I was doing it too slowly. 'Removing luster rather than improving it,' were his words. He even left the room!"

"Really, Mother," said Mary after hearing this. "What's to be done with Jared? He's driving us all crazy!"

Caroline sighed. "We must be patient. I'm afraid Jared's temper is more than the healing arts can remedy."

Katy arrived to fetch her children, and the others rose to greet her. But Lucy bent close to Pippa and whispered low, "His mood might be improved by use of the harem arts."

Pippa was aghast, but Lucy laughed and left the room. Pippa handed the sleeping baby back into Katy's arms, but her heart ached to feel her arms empty again.

"She loves you, Pippa," said Katy. "You're the only one she'll allow to hold her." Pippa beamed at the praise.

"I love her, too," Pippa replied softly.

"You'll have a baby of your own," said Katy confidently. "Then you'll know—it's as if a whole new wing to a house is opened," she went on as Pippa listened enviously. "A whole new wing of love."

Pippa sighed as she watched Katy and her children depart. She wanted children of her own very much, but her passion with Jared had yielded no pregnancy. As things were going now, her chances of motherhood didn't look too promising.

Pippa accompanied Jared to their bedroom after dinner, but she didn't dare broach the subject at first. His full, beautiful mouth had been curved in a tight frown throughout dinner, and Pippa guessed this mood was not one best approached.

"Didn't you like the roast duck, Jared?" she asked, hoping to improve his temper by reminding him of the delicious meal they had enjoyed, thanks to Wilson's having spotted a flock of northbound fowl.

"It was cold," replied Jared, and Pippa sighed.

"Only because you waited so long to try it," she replied.

Jared looked at her in irritation. "Perhaps if someone had told me that dinner was going to be early, I might have made it downstairs soon enough to eat. I'm not exactly mobile, or had you all forgotten?"

Pippa groaned. "How could we forget?" she said, but then she smiled. "Perhaps the cook will reheat some for you to-morrow."

Jared grimaced. "That doesn't sound very appetizing."

"Have it your way, then," Pippa relented, seeing that Jared was bound and determined to find fault with whatever crossed his path. It seemed sensible to wait until he was in a better temper, so she simply undressed and went to their bed in silence.

Jared watched Pippa slip from her dress, her back turned toward him. At the sight of her briefly bared bottom, he caught his breath. She was so perfectly curved, so painfully enticing, and despite it all, she was totally unaware of what she did to him.

Pippa had been shy about undressing with Jared present, although as time went by, she relaxed. But his fleeting glimpses of her unclad form had fired Jared's already raging desire, and he went nightly to bed in a state of painful arousal.

Jared frowned as Pippa crawled beneath the covers to await him, but he lowered the lamplight before undressing himself. Pippa wondered at this, but the real reason didn't occur to her. He got in bed beside her, but Pippa's heart fell when he simply rolled over on his side.

Pippa knew he wasn't sleeping, and she couldn't let an-other night pass this way. For a long time, Pippa just stared at Jared's broad back, but she gathered her courage and reached to touch his shoulder.

Jared stiffened immediately, but Pippa didn't remove her hand. Instead, she propped herself up on her elbow to gaze down into his face. She saw the frown, but she also felt the quickened pulse as her hair brushed across his shoulder.

"What is it?" he asked in an impatient voice.

Pippa drew a deep breath. "There's something I'd like to ask you."

"What?"

"I wondered if you meant it when you said this was my house, too," she continued.

"Of course. What of it?" Jared asked irritably.

"I wondered if that meant you and I are married . . . forever."

"Yes," he replied slowly. "Why do you ask?"

Pippa hesitated, but then decided there was nothing to do but ask. "In that case, I thought we might have a baby," she said evenly.

Jared's eyes widened, this being the very last request he expected his wife to make. "What?"

"Well, we've been married awhile now," replied Pippa thoughtfully. "It wouldn't be unheard of for a couple married this long to begin having children."

Jared was astounded. "You know how one goes about . . . having children, don't you?"

Pippa frowned. "Of course I do."

Jared stared up at his wife's calm, reasonable face, but his own heart was pounding loud in his ears. This wasn't exactly the way he'd hoped Pippa would approach the subject, but now opened, he couldn't let it be closed. Pippa saw the flash of desire written plainly across Jared's face, and she thought of Lucy's whispered words about "harem arts."

At the time, she had dismissed the notion as overly romantic, but seeing Jared's face, she wondered. To test this theory, Pippa pressed a slow kiss against Jared's shoulder, and he trembled at her touch. Her own long-repressed desires flooded to the surface, and Pippa was enthralled with the idea she had such power over him.

She kissed him again, and Jared closed his eyes. Pippa's fingers traced a line across his lips. Jared's breath came quick and shallow, and Pippa felt intoxicated with her ability to arouse him. She leaned over his shoulder, her barely covered breasts brushing against his arm, and she kissed the side of his face.

"Kiss me," she whispered.

In a flash, Jared was on his back, drawing her on top of him. Pippa's hands were in his blond hair, her lips parted as they found his. She tasted both corners of his mouth, the delicate tip of her tongue dipping between his lips, and Jared groaned as desire pounded in his ears.

Pippa kissed him leisurely, indulging her fantasies with his taste. She lay half on top of him, and Jared felt the taut peaks of her breasts against his chest. The dam of his restraint gave way and he met the light delving of her tongue with a passionate entreaty.

"Pippa," he groaned, but Pippa didn't stop as she explored every inch of his face with soft kisses.

"Pippa, climb on top," he ordered hoarsely, but Pippa drew away to look questioningly into his face.

"Get on top," he repeated in a ragged, deep voice. Pippa knew what he was asking, but she had no idea how to do it.

Jared had no intention of wasting precious time explaining his requirements to his innocent wife. He pulled her body over his, directing her to a sitting position just below his need. Pippa's breath caught with delight when she felt his aroused manhood between her thighs, but she was uncertain what he expected.

"What do I do?" she whispered, but Jared smiled.

"Love me, little witch," he answered, his voice low and husky, impossible to resist.

His large hands cupped her bottom and he lifted her above his hardened staff, lowering her slowly on top of him. Jared groaned as he met her damp, slippery flesh. Pippa gasped as her body lowered over his, taking the entire length inside her aching depths.

Her eyes on his, Pippa pulled her nightgown over her head and let it fall to the floor beside their bed. She smiled slightly as his blue eyes darkened, but her own heart was thunder in her breast.

Tentatively at first, Pippa moved against Jared, but as she felt him deep and hard inside her, Pippa forgot her embarrassment. Pippa rocked against him, her hips rising and falling until all her reason fled. Jared was wild with Pippa's abandon, and the tautness of his body, wrought by day after day of desire, now tightened unbearably as she moved above him. Her long hair fell down her back to brush his thigh above the cast as she leaned back in the triumph of a pagan queen.

Despite his encumbered thigh, Jared thrust deeply into her soft, yielding warmth. He groaned with ultimate pleasure as she twisted above him, her bare flesh gleaming in the dim light as she joined him upon the rapturous crests of their ecstasy.

The pounding need stilled, and Pippa collapsed on Jared's chest, burying her face against his neck. Jared stroked her tangled hair, but as Pippa reflected on what she had just done, she whimpered with embarrassment.

"What's the matter?" asked Jared.

"Sometimes I think I should be more restrained," she whispered.

Jared kissed her head. "Why is that, when it's obvious now your . . . lack of restraint pleases me?"

Pippa shook her head. "I can't help thinking this is something Miss Honeycastle would never have done."

Jared laughed, a sound Pippa hadn't heard in many days. "That, my dear, is why Miss Honeycastle's fiancé has departed to Mexico with the vixen Ruby!"

Pippa smiled despite herself and kissed the curve of his mouth lovingly. "You were bad to Kim about that, Jared Knox," she said reproachfully. "She admires Miss Honeycastle."

"God knows why."

"Because she is good and a perfect lady," Pippa told him. "As Kim wants to be. If Miss Honeycastle can endure her trials, maybe Kim believes she can too, that what happened to her isn't insurmountable."

Jared frowned guiltily. "I hadn't thought of that. I'll apologize to her tomorrow, though I fear I may then have to endure long chapters yet."

Pippa kissed him. "If you are very good, she may conclude the book tomorrow. And you'll have done a good service for your sister."

"Now that you've been of such . . . service to me, my dear wife, I believe that wouldn't be impossible."

"Will you be pleasant now?" asked Pippa innocently.

Jared smiled. "Have I been difficult?"

"You have," she replied adamantly, but her eyes were shining. "Quite grumpy. Is this why?"

"It is."

"Does your leg hurt now?" Pippa asked hesitantly, but Jared grinned.

"Not at all. In fact, it's much improved. When the good

doctor removes this damned cast, I'll be as agile as I ever was."

Pippa's eyes twinkled and she smiled devilishly. "You were very agile, Jared," she murmured. "Though I find I like you . . . in my control," she added seductively, and she felt Jared's shaft grow hard and stiff within her.

"When have I not been in your control?" he asked. Pippa bent to kiss him and all was forgotten but the desire that flared between them.

Jared's temper did improve, and the next day he called Kim to his room to apologize for ridiculing Miss Honeycastle.

"You must forgive my blacker moods, Kim," he said pleasantly. "I have the highest regard for Miss Honeycastle's virtue," he added, but he glanced to where Pippa stood and smiled.

"Then you want me to finish the story?" asked Kim hopefully.

"I couldn't survive without learning her fate," he said flatly.

"I think I'll leave you two alone," said Pippa as she moved toward the door, but Jared called her back.

"Don't go, my dear. I wouldn't think of depriving you of the end of this story. Sit down," he ordered, and Pippa reluctantly sat beside him on the bed.

Pippa actually found the bits and pieces of Kim's melodramatic novel involving, but the virtuous Emily Honeycastle's character bothered her. Emily reminded Pippa of someone, and as she sat to hear the end of the story, Pippa realized that someone was Christina.

By the story's ripe conclusion, Pippa was leaning forward

as she listened to Kim's tearful voice, though it was all Jared could do to keep from yawning. Miss Honeycastle's fiancé indeed returned, but to find Emily dying of consumption, just as Jared had predicted.

" 'Why have you come back, Cabot?' " read Kim, and her voice choked on the dialogue. " 'I can never hope to win your forgiveness, my darling Emily. But I have learned that my love for you exceeds all else. My life is nothing without you.' "

Kim paused to dry her eyes, then continued in a quivering voice. " 'What about that . . . that Ruby?' 'She is nothing to me, she was a part of my base, animal nature. Nothing more. Please, beloved, marry me, as we planned long ago. My heart speaks truly at last.' "

But Miss Emily Honeycastle wasn't long for the world, so the tender reunion was fatefully thwarted. With her last breath, Emily whispered, 'I forgive you,' but Kim was in tears as she read.

"The end, I presume," said Jared unemotionally, and when Kim nodded, he breathed a muted sigh of relief.

Jared glanced at Pippa, but he saw his own wife's face wet with tears. Kim dried her eyes and left them alone, but Jared stared at Pippa in astonishment.

"Don't tell me Miss Honeycastle's melodramatic end has moved you, my dear!" he exclaimed in disbelief, but Pippa shook her head.

"Not Miss Honeycastle," she said in a broken voice. "I was thinking of Ruby."

"Ruby?" questioned Jared in amazement.

"Yes, Cabot's mistress. She must have loved him, if she ran away with him to Mexico. I imagine they . . . they . . . Well, you know."

Jared's eyes glinted and Pippa blushed. "Indeed. Those

hot desert nights," he guessed. "But why does this sadden you, angel?"

"I don't know. I just felt sorry for her, that's all. She must have thought he loved her, and then to have him go back to his old love, because she was more virtuous."

"Oh, for God's sake, Pippa. It's just a book, and not a very good one."

"I know," said Pippa, but she realized why the story troubled her so.

She was Ruby, running off with the man she loved, defying society's requirements, and she had paid for it. She and Jared shared passion, yet one day he might wish he had married his first sweetheart—Christina, wronged by Jared, abused by her husband, yet still virtuous and good.

Jared's cast was removed, and in a short time, it was apparent that his recovery was complete. He took long walks along Richmond's streets, and his leg regained much of its former strength.

"You're going back, aren't you?"

Jared sat looking out the window in the sitting room, and a light snow fell upon the streets outside. He turned to see Pippa watching him, but there was no point in denying the obvious.

"I must," he told her quietly. At his admission, Pippa knelt before him, her face a plaintive appeal to his heart.

"I know," she whispered. She knew this day would come. As the weeks dragged on, the Confederacy stubbornly refused to yield to the greater force. Men starved in Petersburg, desertions tripled, yet the heart of the Army of Northern Virginia beat on. Jared Knox was part of that heartbeat. Pippa understood this now, but she couldn't bear to be parted from him.

"If you must go, Jared," she begged, "then take me with you."

Jared smiled sadly, but he shook his head. "No, Pippa. I won't drag you to Petersburg again."

"I survived well enough before," she maintained adamantly, but Jared wasn't convinced.

"No, Pippa. The siege in summer was one thing, freezing in the midst of winter is another. I would leave knowing you are safe and well here."

"I'm accustomed to the cold, Jared. I could help as I did before. Jared, please," she pleaded, but Jared touched his finger to her lips.

"No, Pippa." Jared saw that she didn't intend to relent, and it occurred to him that she might attempt to follow him.

"Pippa, if Richmond is overrun, and I believe that will happen, you'll be needed here."

"Why?" asked Pippa doubtfully. Her sojourn in Richmond's hospitals had been less than rewarding.

Jared paused to consider this. "You know that Kim is terrified the Yankees will come, and it's true that they often seize homes such as this to house their officers."

"What can I do about that?" questioned Pippa.

"You're a Yankee, Pippa. Maybe they'll be more respectful of you."

"A Yankee married to a rebel," she reminded him.

"Be that as it may, I think Kim will feel safer if you are here."

This argument convinced Pippa, but her heart broke to think he would be gone. "When are you leaving?" she asked tearfully.

"In a day or so," he replied, but Pippa's face went white at the answer.

"So soon?" she whispered.

Jared didn't answer, but he bent to kiss her mouth. Pippa wrapped her arms around his neck and he drew her up onto his lap, cradling her head against his shoulder as she wept. But Jared knew there was nothing he could say that would ease the pain of their parting.

Jared returned to his brigade in Petersburg. From the day he left, the winter dragged slow and long for Pippa. Making matters even worse, Pippa had learned just before he left that she wasn't pregnant. Jared's reaction hadn't consoled her. Finding her crying in their room, he attempted to comfort her.

"There's no baby," said Pippa miserably. She thought a pregnancy would distract her from Jared's absence, but now she would be alone without him.

"Perhaps that's for the best," he told her, but it wasn't what Pippa wanted to hear.

Christina came to say a tearful farewell the day Jared left, and Pippa was reminded painfully of Miss Honeycastle. Since then, Pippa had seen more of Christina than she cared to, and the other woman's interest in Jared's letters irritated her.

Christina and Pippa rarely spoke, each having a silent agreement to avoid the other. As Kim was now close to both women, they came in frequent contact with each other. Christina had been at least polite to Pippa when Jared was there, but now Pippa noticed a change.

The women sat in the parlor sewing together, but since Christina and Mildred had joined their circle, Pippa enjoyed the times less. Caroline apparently felt their presence inappropriate while Jared was home, but now she welcomed their help.

"I'd think your son would have returned to his duty sooner, Caroline," ventured Mildred antagonistically, and Pippa glared fiercely at her.

"Dr. Wachtel wasn't in favor of his return as it was," replied Caroline gracefully.

"I think he healed admirably," put in Kim hotly. "Much faster than other men."

Kim turned to Pippa. "Mostly because of Pippa's skill," she added. It occurred to Pippa that, like her brother, Kim also enjoyed irritating Mildred Smith.

"Jared is most remarkably strong, Mother," said Christina, and Pippa glanced her way suspiciously. "He always does the right thing."

Pippa vehemently wished to disagree with this assessment, but she sensed Christina's comment had been meant for her. More and more, Christina made small remarks that Pippa wondered about, but Pippa wasn't certain just what they implied.

Winter gave way to spring, but spring brought little hope to the beleaguered Confederacy. Abraham Lincoln had been inaugurated for his second term early in March, signifying Union steadfastness to their army's goal.

Even when the Confederate Congress authorized the arming of slaves for combat, few held any real hope a Southern victory could ever be realized now. Yet Jared's letters, though grim, held no sense of that defeat.

General Lee would try every door, every path, until none

remained for him to open. But until the last door was barred, Robert E. Lee would not give up his country's cause.

Little more than two weeks later, Federal troops approached Richmond. The rebel army that had waited there to stop them withdrew in hopes of joining Lee's as he retreated from Petersburg. Katy and her husband left the city with many members of the Confederate government who were also fleeing.

"What will we do, Mother?" cried Kim.

Kim's hysteria had been growing as it appeared only a matter of time before Richmond was occupied by Federal forces.

"These are Union troops, darling, not Yankee raiders. I don't think we need fear them."

"Dear God, Mother, they're Yankees!"' cried Kim, and she raced to her room, refusing to leave for any reason.

On April third, Mildred and Christina joined the others for the sewing circle. The socks and blankets they worked on could have little use now as Lee's army pushed west, flanked and outpaced now by the Army of the Potomac at every turn.

Early afternoon was tense, and Mary burst through the door. "They're here!" she gasped as the others met her by the front door. "The Yankees are in Richmond, Mother!" she said again.

"We must remain calm," said Caroline quietly, but her own voice was shaking.

"Mother," said Mary. "There's a group of them coming this way. I had to warn you, but they're right behind me. They're colored troops!"

Mildred gasped in horror. "The devilry of Yankees!" she

exclaimed bitterly. "They would send those black demons down upon us to exact revenge, no doubt. We'll see no mercy now."

Pippa frowned. "I don't know what you think they're going to do," she said calmly. "They're occupying the city, Mrs. Smith, not destroying it. I understand all the burning was done by Confederates, destroying warehouses and ammunition. I don't believe you need fear."

Mildred glared at her. "Of course, your Yankee daughter-in-law need fear no retaliation from her own kind."

Pippa rolled her eyes. "There's no reason to fear colored soldiers, either, Mrs. Smith. They've behaved honorably thus far, and I see no reason they shouldn't now."

Lucy left the room to watch for the soldiers from the kitchen. Pippa had seen the blaze of excitement in her dark eyes. This was a moment long awaited by Lucy, and Pippa couldn't help but share her hope as they heard the sounds of approaching soldiers.

Kim hid upstairs, but the others waited by the windows. Mildred and Christina were loath to leave. Caroline invited them to remain until the situation stabilized. Pippa would have liked to offer them a coach to their own home, but it became obvious there was no choice.

"Look, Mother! Outside," cried Mary in abject terror. "They're here."

Caroline looked out the window and gasped. "Yes." She gathered herself together, but Pippa saw that her face was very white. "They appear to be coming to our own house. We should face them without fear," added Caroline, but she seemed unable to go the door when they heard a loud knocking.

Pippa looked around at the other women, but she didn't share their fear. Nothing she had seen during the war had led her to believe the Yankees were any different from rebel soldiers, and she doubted very much they had anything to fear from these men of the North.

"I'll go," she said calmly, and Pippa went to open the door.

If Pippa felt nervousness when she pulled open the heavy paneled door, it evaporated instantly when she saw the tall soldier on the other side.

"Byron!" she cried, and to the astonishment of the others, Pippa leapt into his arms, and the smiling black soldier swung her around.

"I thought I might find you here, Mrs. Pip!" he exclaimed.

"What are you doing here?" she asked.

"Taking Richmond, of course," Byron replied with pleasure. "They sent the U.S. Coloreds in first. Ultimate revenge, I suppose, but it's fairly calm throughout the city."

Seeing Pippa's familiarity with the colored soldier, the other women dared approach him. Byron respectfully doffed his Union cap to them. Caroline studied his face, and Pippa wondered if she remembered him, though that seemed unlikely.

Pippa turned to the others with pleasure. "You needn't fear. This is Byron," she told them simply. "He lived with my father and myself in Maine. And he's a friend of Jared's."

"You've seen Jared?" asked Caroline.

"We saw each other briefly last summer in Petersburg," explained Byron carefully.

Caroline turned to the others. "You are safe, ladies," she told them. "Byron is known to me." She turned back to Byron. "Is there a reason you've chosen to come here?"

Byron looked uncomfortable as he stated his purpose.

"We're to locate a house for our commander, and I thought of yours, begging your pardon, Mrs. Knox."

Kim came down the stairs, and though Pippa feared the girl would fall apart at this, instead she appeared relieved. "Mr. Byron," she began slowly. "Yours is a colored company?"

"Yes, miss. It is."

"Then I'm certain you'll be welcome."

The others stared at Kim in disbelief, and Mildred sputtered angrily. "I can't think what has gotten into that child, Caroline." Mildred's eyes went to Pippa suspiciously. "Welcome, indeed!"

"Why, thank you, miss," said Byron politely. He turned to Caroline. "I hoped Pippa could convince you we mean no harm. Not many other households in Richmond offer this option. As a matter of fact, we may be able to insure your safety. General Lee's wife has a Federal guard now, and I imagine she's the safer for it."

"Thank you, Mr. Byron," said Kim. To the amazement of all, she appeared relieved by the black man's presence.

"I'll go tell the major," said Byron with relief. "Major Owens is leading my division here. He's a fine young gentleman, and I know he'll behave honorably."

Byron left the others and returned shortly with a young white officer and several other colored soldiers who proceeded to make camp on Jared's front lawn. But if Kim's reaction to the colored soldiers had surprised her family, her reaction to Major Owens was even more astounding.

Seeing the young man's handsome face, Kim blanched and screamed, though Major Owens was stunned by her reaction. Pippa was completely confused by her sister-in-law's behavior. From what she could see, Major Owens was a very attractive man, with dark brown hair and a face that resembled Jared's. In fact, a girl might swoon for such a young gentleman, and Pippa couldn't understand what possessed Kim to scream instead.

"Kimber, darling, what's wrong?" asked Caroline as she went to her daughter.

"He's . . . he's not a colored Yankee," said Kim in a voice wrung with terror.

"No," agreed Caroline.

Major Owens saw the pretty rebel girl's fear and it moved him. He had no idea what frightened her, but he felt it his duty to reassure her.

"You need not fear of me, Miss Knox," he told her, his voice a soft Boston clip that spoke of an exclusive upbringing.

Kim glared at him with deep misgivings, but he removed his cap and bowed slightly. "I am Major Carey Owens, and I assure you, we mean you no harm. As the sergeant has perhaps informed you, we may even be able to offer you our protection. There are many deserters, from both armies, in the city now. Since your Confederate troops have moved from Richmond, it's likely to be an uncertain, lawless time."

"Well, obviously there's nothing I can do about your presence," said Kim hotly. Pippa was relieved to see the girl more ready to fight than flee. Apparently she wasn't all that afraid of Carey Owens.

"My men will be camping outside," said Major Owens. "But we'll replace whatever is damaged, and none of your lovely flowers will be damaged, I promise you."

Pippa smiled at the New Englander's chivalry. His graciousness continued unabated by Kim's frosty glare. "I won't trouble your household. If you have servants' quarters, I might use a bed there." Then Major Owens sighed. "I would welcome that."

"Of course, Major," said Caroline gratefully. She didn't think Kim would take well to a Yankee officer sleeping down the hall.

"Lucy!" Caroline called toward the kitchen, and Lucy appeared at the end of the hall. Pippa guessed she had been watching the soldiers at the other side of the house. Lucy's eyes were shining with pride as she answered Mrs. Knox.

"I wondered if you would escort Major Owens to the servants' quarters. That has been unused for some time," explained Caroline turning back to Carey Owens.

Carey Owens stepped forward, and Byron came from around behind him. Pippa saw Byron's shock, but she didn't recognize it for what it was until she heard Lucy gasp.

"Lucy!" he breathed. As the reality of the situation dawned on Pippa, she turned to see Lucy's face staring in utter disbelief at the tall sergeant who stood before her.

"Byron," she whispered. Everyone in the room recognized that these two had met before, but only Pippa understood the significance of their reunion, and she couldn't believe she hadn't guessed before.

"Lucy?" questioned Caroline, but Lucy didn't hear her. Disregarding Caroline's request, Lucy turned and fled up the stairs.

"What on earth is the matter with Lucy?" asked Mary.

Pippa looked at Byron and she smiled. "I expect she's seen something of a ghost," she guessed. "But I never dreamed it was you."

Byron's eyes met Pippa's and he realized she knew of his old love. "We were known to each other," he explained, and Mildred gasped at the suggestion of intimacy.

"It's strange," reflected Pippa. "But though I've mentioned the men who lived with us, I don't believe I ever used your name."

"Why would you?" asked Mary. "Lucy isn't all that alert."

Byron's brow rose, but Pippa's look silenced him. Mildred saw an entirely new avenue of suspicion to direct at Pippa. "So your father housed contraband slaves, Philippa?" she asked venomously.

"He did, yes," answered Pippa. There was little reason to deny it now.

"Does Jared know this?" asked Christina quietly.

Pippa turned to glare at the other woman. "He does, and he was very understanding." This was true as far as it went, but Pippa left out the method Jared was brought to this understanding.

Byron was staring up the stairs, but now Caroline herself showed Carey Owens to the servants' quarters. Kim watched him go with a tight frown on her lovely face.

"I suppose he'll be taking dinner with us," she said with annoyance.

"He doesn't seem that bad, for a Yankee. He seems to be a gentleman, at least," said Christina, and Mary nodded in agreement.

"He's really quite handsome," added Pippa with twinkling eyes.

"Is he? I didn't notice," replied Kim, but Pippa didn't believe her.

Pippa went upstairs to find Lucy, and as she had guessed, Lucy was sitting in Jared's room staring blankly out the window. Pippa entered and went to sit beside her. Lucy fiddled with a flowerpot on the windowsill and Pippa patted her shoulder.

"It doesn't seem possible," she said. "Byron was the man you loved?"

Lucy turned to her, and all her emotions were bare upon her beautiful face as she nodded. "He is Jared's brother," she said, but though she had expected Pippa to be shocked, Pippa merely sighed.

"Yes, Jared told me that when he let Byron go last summer."

"I knew you housed contrabands," began Lucy. "But I never dreamed . . ."

Pippa nodded. "If I'd only told you his name! To think how often I went from you to him with messages, yet you never knew."

"It would have made no difference," sighed Lucy.

"Why not? Surely now that he's back . . ." began Pippa, but Lucy stopped her.

"Oh, Pippa! You saw him. He's a Union soldier. He's so far above me."

Pippa hugged Lucy. "I doubt he thinks so. In fact, he wants to speak with you, in private. He'll be waiting for you in the servants' quarters while Major Owens dines with the family. I suggest you go to him."

"But he left me," began Lucy as tears formed in her eyes.

"And he has returned. Go to him, Lucy."

Pippa kissed Lucy's brow and left her to consider the man waiting downstairs. But Lucy knew nothing in heaven nor earth nor hell beyond could keep her from Byron's arms now.

Carey Owens did take his dinner with the family, and Kim was in attendance despite her earlier disavowals. She wore a pretty blue dress that set her bright eyes sparkling with a light that captured Major Owens's attention even as he addressed the others. Kim's fair hair was arranged with great care, and Pippa decided the Yankee officer was just the person to free the rebel girl's heart from the bounds of fear.

"Have you been away from your family long, Major Owens?" asked Caroline.

"Since the beginning of the war, yes, Mrs. Knox," replied Carey Owens politely. "Although I've returned to Boston on furlough on occasion."

Carey Owens sighed. "But it's never for long, and then it has the quality of a dream. A dream from which I too soon awaken."

Caroline looked at him sympathetically, and Pippa saw that though she looked away, Kim was also moved.

"Have you a wife?" asked Pippa suddenly, and beside her, Mary smiled.

"No, I have no wife," replied Carey Owens. But as he answered Pippa, his blue eyes wandered to the beautiful Virginian girl who sat across from him. To his delight, he saw the faint rise of color in her fair face.

Abraham Lincoln came to Richmond himself, and Pippa went with Carey Owens and Kim to see him. Pippa had been increasingly restless and anxious, as the days without Jared passed by. Even in his house she felt unsafe, though she couldn't imagine why that should be so. She gleefully accepted the invitation to see Lincoln, for she had long admired him.

What interest Kim had in the Union's President, Pippa couldn't guess, but as Kim's eyes rarely left the major's handsome face, Pippa decided it didn't matter. Pippa only saw the President from a distance as he passed through a crowd of former slaves, and he didn't address them, but she was moved by his presence.

They called him "Father Abraham," and as Pippa watched him pass by, it occurred to her that the Army of the Potomac might have had better success had he commanded it directly, as did Robert E. Lee. The two old men affected her in much the same way.

When they returned home, they were met by another surprising visitor. Burke Mallory had arrived from New York, and though Pippa was glad to see him well, she wondered at his presence. He greeted Kim warmly, but Pippa noted the faint light of fear in Kim's eyes when she saw Burke Mallory standing with her mother.

"Miss Knox, it's good to see that you've come through the war beautifully," complimented Burke, but Kim was quite restrained, and she stood very close beside Carey Owens.

Burke looked at the major with suspicion, and Carey Owens seemed to have no higher regard for him.

"Well, Major. The war appears to be nearing its bitter end. I assume you'll be going home soon?"

Kim looked up at Carey Owens questioningly as he replied, "My duty will be over then, yes. As for where I go afterwards, that will depend."

Carey smiled at Kim, who blushed, but Burke Mallory frowned.

"Why are you here, Burke?" asked Pippa.

"I came to find out what happened to you, cousin," Burke told her, but he been surprised when she walked in the door. "When I last saw you, your fate was, shall we say, doubtful."

Pippa was glad that Burke had the sense and good grace to keep those circumstances to himself, but he was annoyed to learn she had married Jared Knox.

"Well, I suppose you had no choice," said Burke. "It was obvious he wanted you from the day of the dance."

Christina entered the room as they were talking and looked at Pippa suspiciously. Pippa glared back defiantly, and she wished acutely that Christina would leave. There was little chance of that, however. Mildred's home had been looted by deserters and burned badly; thus, Caroline had been obliged to invite them to remain. Mildred lost no opportunity to comment on the Yankees now ensconced around the grand Knox home, and more than once Pippa had to bite her tongue in Mildred's presence.

Burke left the house, but Christina was waiting for Pippa. "Your marriage seems to have surprised Mr. Mallory," said Christina as she followed Pippa into the sitting room.

"But then, Jared's unexpected marriage seems to have taken everyone by surprise."

Pippa turned around to face Christina, but she wasn't at all certain what the woman was getting at. "I suppose that's true," she replied slowly. "What of it?"

"I'm curious what necessitated the suddenness, that's all."

Pippa frowned, thinking quickly. "Jared wanted to bring me to Richmond as his wife."

"According to Mr. Mallory, you met at the Carltons' ball. A brief courtship," mused Christina. "Yet you weren't married until you reached camp," Christina reminded her. "Why didn't you have baggage, if this wedding was planned?"

Pippa wondered if Christina had guessed about her spying, but that didn't seem likely. She was suspicious about something, but Pippa was taken aback to learn what that something was.

"I'd guess you gave him no choice," said Christina, but Pippa's eyes widened.

"No choice?" she asked in genuine confusion.

"Yes," said Christina with a flare of anger. "It's easy enough to guess what happened."

"What?"

"You followed him, didn't you? You threw yourself at his feet. Being a gentleman, Jared was forced to marry you, but it has been obvious to me that it wasn't his choice."

Pippa stared at the other woman in shock. Far from the truth, yet still . . . "I did not force him to marry me, Christina. In fact, I had no idea that was his intention until he brought me to the chaplain."

Now Pippa had said too much and Christina's eyes glittered triumphantly. "Indeed? So much for the romantic elopement."

Pippa's fury blazed and she would have liked to strike the other woman, but Caroline entered. "Have you seen Kim, Pippa?" she asked.

"I believe she's in her room," said Christina sweetly.

"Major Owens has left," said Caroline. "But Kim seemed bothered by something. I hope all is well between them. He's such a respectable young man, and so handsome as well. It's good to see my daughter's eyes shining again."

"I'll see if she's feeling well," said Pippa quickly. She had no wish to speak further with Christina, but the conversation had already weighed heavily on her.

Pippa found Kim in her room, sitting stiffly upon the bed. Pippa went to sit beside her, and she noticed that Kim's hands were tightly clasped.

"Is everything well between you and Major Owens?" asked Pippa hesitantly.

"Oh, yes. Pippa, Carey is the most wonderful man. When

I'm with him, I forget everything. I feel every heartbeat. Do you know what I mean?"

"Yes, I know."

"Of course, you would, with Jared," remembered Kim. "Pippa, I think I love him. Do you think that's possible?"

"I think it's possible," said Pippa softly.

"Did you know with Jared, right at the start?"

Pippa hesitated. "When I first heard his voice, I trembled," Pippa admitted. "And when I first saw him . . . Yes, I knew."

Kim smiled and took her hand. "Carey wants me to go to Boston with him, as his wife," she whispered.

Pippa beamed. "That's wonderful, Kim. He seems a fine man." Seeing the trace of fear in Kim's eyes, Pippa paused. "What's wrong, Kim? What's bothering you?"

"Why is Mr. Mallory here?" Kim asked in a small voice.

"Burke? I have no idea. Some business matter, I suppose. He often came here for that purpose. Why?"

"I don't know," replied Kim quietly. She looked intently into Pippa's eyes. "Has Jared told you about . . . about the night our house in the country was burned?"

"He has told me something of it, yes," admitted Pippa gently.

"Did he tell you what they did?"

"Not specifically, no," said Pippa.

Kim's eyes clouded over, and when she spoke, it was as if her voice came from far away. "Mother and I had gone home to retrieve some of our things. She was desperately worried about Jared. She believed she would learn his fate there before here."

Kim paused, and Pippa squeezed her hand. "The night we arrived, that was when the Yankees came."

"Soldiers?" asked Pippa, but Kim shook her head.

"I don't think so, no. I believed they were at the time. They had Federal uniforms, but I've learned things from Carey that make me believe they were perhaps deserters. They didn't seem official. They only wanted to frighten us, though I've never understood why."

Pippa's heart labored as she saw the other girl's fear at the memory, but she forced herself to exhibit a strength she didn't feel.

"They robbed our house, then set it on fire. Then they bound Mother outside," continued Kim in a toneless voice. "They took me away, somewhere near the peonies. I screamed and I fought, Pippa. I really did. I kicked them and bit them, but it made no difference. No difference at all."

Tears started in Pippa's eyes as she waited for the story to go on, yet she was terrified to hear its conclusion.

"They tore my clothes, touched me," said Kim in a tiny, weak voice. "They said they were going to . . . do things to me. They described these things vividly, and I was terrified. I got sick, but that didn't stop them."

Pippa held her breath, dreading to hear any more, but then Kim sighed. "I've never forgotten the terror of that moment. I was helpless, Pippa. You cannot imagine. Before that night, I had been so sure of myself—the belle at every ball. I was certain nothing bad could happen to me, even with the war. But then, I was very young."

"You are still young," Pippa reminded her, but Kim shook her head.

"Not like that, Pippa. I will never be that young again. I know what would have happened to me. I saw a man tear open his trousers while the other held me down. I heard them laugh, I felt them slap me when I fainted. They tore away my pretty chintz dress. It was my favorite," added Kim wistfully. "Funny, that was the strangest thing. That such a thing could happen to me when I was wearing my favorite dress."

Pippa's tears broke from her eyes, but Kim herself didn't cry. "Did Jared tell you what happened next?"

"No," said Pippa.

"I closed my eyes," Kim remembered slowly. "But I heard a shot. I thought I was dead myself, but then I saw a Yankee fall. And then another. And then the last."

Pippa breathed a sigh of vast relief. "Jared?"

Kim nodded. "He picked me up and carried me away. And, Pippa, he was crying. I'd never seen my brother cry, but he was crying. He put his jacket on me and he brought me to Mother."

Suddenly Kim laughed. "Mother was still tied up, but he had pulled off her gag. She told him to save me, and he did. Leaving her there tied."

Pippa put her arm tightly around Kim's shoulder. "I'm sorry, Kim. But nothing they could have done to you would have destroyed what you are, how much you mean to those who love you."

"I know that now, but it has been a long time," agreed Kim. "After that night, I felt afraid, all the time. I felt weak. If Jared hadn't come back, if he had been a minute later . . ."

"But he did come back," Pippa reminded her.

"Yes, and what you say is true, Pippa. I thought I couldn't love a man, not when they have such desires, such an animal rage. But now I think desire could be sweet, if it were done with kindness and with love. Nothing they did changed my worth. Carey has made me see that."

Pippa sniffed. "You are much braver than Miss Honeycastle," she said tearfully.

"Yes, I know," replied Kim matter-of-factly. "I told Carey. I felt I had to, you see. He had confessed his love, and I didn't think I was worthy of it. I felt dirty, because of what they did to me. But Pippa, he was so kind and sweet."

"I don't understand, Kim. What is troubling you today, if all is well with Major Owens?"

"Burke Mallory," replied Kim. "He was there that night, just after Jared arrived. When he looked at me, I think he knew what happened."

"Perhaps he guessed," speculated Pippa, but Kim was adamant.

"No, Pippa. I had met Mr. Mallory before, and he had been . . . suggestive then. He said he was smitten with me, but though he is attractive, I felt uncomfortable with him. I believe it angered him. One of the men who attacked me said a strange thing—he said that after this night I'd be glad to accept any man's proposal, no matter who it came from."

Pippa's brow knit thoughtfully. "Do you think Burke had something to do with what happened to you, Kim?"

"I don't know. I don't see how he could. But when I saw him here today, I felt afraid. But there, I'm being foolish. Carey is here now, and I'm sure Burke's presence has nothing to do with me. He came to see that you're well, that's all."

Pippa nodded, but inwardly, she wondered. Burke was taken with a Virginian girl, Pippa was certain of that. Looking at Kim's beautiful, fragile face, Pippa guessed easily who that girl might be.

When Burke stopped by the next morning, Pippa's suspicions were confirmed. Major Carey Owens sat close beside Kim, and Burke was heartily annoyed by the young aristocrat's presence. Carey couldn't help but notice Burke Mallory's hostility, but he rose to leave them.

Carey took Kim's hand and kissed it lovingly, and Kim

blushed while Burke glared at the tender scene. Pippa squirmed nervously in her seat, for there was a light in Burke's eyes that she didn't like at all. Surprisingly, Kim remained in the sitting room after Carey left, and she smiled brightly at Burke.

"Major Owens has asked me to become his wife," she told them, and Pippa bit her lip as she saw Burke's eyes narrow.

"I wonder if that's a wise decision, Miss Knox," he said in a voice Pippa considered distinctly threatening.

"Why, of course it is! Carey's family is highly respectable, Mr. Mallory."

"How will the major react when he learns your innocence is, shall we say, compromised?"

Pippa gasped, but to her lasting astonishment, Kim laughed.

"How would you know that, Mr. Mallory? Unless, of course, you're more aware of what happened to me that night than you should be? You came by shortly after . . . You offered to buy the entire property, didn't you?"

Pippa's eyes widened as Kim calmly voiced her accusation to Burke, but when Burke got up from his chair, Pippa leapt up and stood between them.

"Don't you go near her, Burke," she commanded, but Pippa was trembling with fear.

"I believe your mother and sister are at work in the hospital," said Burke in a low voice. "Save for the idiot maid, you ladies are alone."

"No, we're not," exclaimed Pippa just as Kim said, "Yes," behind her.

"Why did you do it?" asked Kim, and Pippa marveled that Kim could remain so calm. To Pippa's horror, Burke went to lock the front door, drawing the shades closed as he came back into the sitting room.

"The size of your father's plantation appealed to me," he admitted. "It seemed a worthy investment."

"You burned Jared's house to buy it?" asked Pippa, much aghast.

"You credit too little romance to my nature, dear cousin. I've always had an eye for a beautiful woman. You might have caught my fancy, but you've always been so cold. But the lovely Miss Knox here, she suited me very well."

Kim laughed, and Pippa wondered how on earth she would stop the girl from provoking Burke further. "There wasn't much chance of that!" exclaimed Kim. "Because, Mr. Mallory, you didn't suit me at all."

Pippa winced, and Burke stepped forward, his face ablaze with fury. "You arrogant little rebel," he said in a voice that trembled with anger. "So proud, yet you were set down from your high horse that night, weren't you?"

Kim tossed her head. "I knew my brother would save me, just as he later took Pippa from you," she said, and Pippa turned in surprise at the outright lie.

"So those men were working for you?" asked Kim casually.

"They were," ground out Burke. "But today I won't need their help to finish the job."

Pippa was horrified. She had promised Jared she would protect Kim, and now a man she had trusted was threatening to destroy the girl's newfound happiness.

"You'll do no such thing, Burke Mallory," said Pippa in a shaking voice.

"No? What, pray tell, do you intend to do about it?" he asked without concern.

"Whatever I have to do," replied Pippa firmly, wondering

what she could use as a weapon against him. Glancing about the room, she saw little to use to her advantage.

With surprising strength, Burke grabbed Pippa and lifted her off her feet. "I think not, Mrs. Knox. In fact, though I might enjoy having you watch the spectacle to come, perhaps it's better that I bind you here. Miss Knox and I will adjourn to the privacy of the upstairs bedrooms where there will be no inconvenient witnesses."

Kim stood passively as Burke restrained the struggling Pippa. "Now, my sweet Virginia flower, I believe I'll sample what those fools were too slow to take."

"Then what?" asked Pippa in disgust. "Do you intend to murder us both with the Union army camped outside the front door?"

"Not at all, Mrs. Knox," replied Burke. "Of course, I can escape Richmond before they learn what transpired here, but I doubt even my father's vast connections could relieve me of such a charge. I feel safe enough knowing the Union is hardly likely to take the word of a bitter rebel girl over a man with my reputation . . . and power."

"I would not count on that if I were you."

Burke whirled around, dropping Pippa to her feet. There stood Major Carey Owens with Byron and several other soldiers at his side.

"In fact, I would imagine such a confession, heard by as many witnesses, should hold good in any court in the land, North or South. I, too, am not without 'connections,' and I'll see they're put to good use when your case comes to trial."

"You see, Mr. Mallory," added Kim brightly, "I'm not as helpless as you imagined. I hope you remember that over the long years you languish in prison!"

Pippa looked from Kim to Carey, and she began to realize that this interlude had been carefully planned.

"You might have told me beforehand, Kim," she said, as the soldiers led Burke from the house.

"There wasn't time, Pippa. But I never would have been brave enough to face him without you. Carey and Mr. Byron were in the back room all the time. So I wasn't afraid when Burke locked the front door."

Pippa collapsed on her chair. "I never dreamed Burke was evil. I thought him weak and lacking in loyalty, but that he could do such a monstrous thing with no remorse . . ."

Kim seemed remarkably calm after the incident, and Pippa looked to her in amazement. Her own hands were still shaking from her terror.

"I shouldn't be surprised, Pippa," said Kim thoughtfully. "After all, Burke has used his father's wealth and position to spare him from his duty from the beginning of the war. He is a coward. Only a coward would threaten a woman that way."

"I suppose that's true," agreed Pippa.

"He told me once he refused to join the Union army because he sympathized with our cause! Can you imagine? But I could never have cared for a man who paid three hundred dollars to send another in his place. Carey would never have done that."

Pippa smiled. "No, I suppose he wouldn't."

Twelve

"Pippa! Pippa, wake up! He's gone, dear God. He's gone!"

Pippa struggled from the depths of her sleep and opened her eyes to see Lucy bending over her. Dimly, Pippa was aware that she was being shaken, but it was some time before she understood Lucy's urgency.

"Who's gone, Lucy? What are you going on about? What time is it?"

Lucy cast her eyes heavenward. "It's past midnight," she said impatiently.

"Couldn't we discuss this in the morning?" asked Pippa drowsily as she lay back on her bed. "I'm so sleepy."

"Pippa!" exclaimed Lucy in distress as she again tried to rouse her friend.

Pippa shook her head and sat up. "Who's gone, Lucy?"

"Byron. Oh, God, I tried to stop him. Pippa, I did. But he's a man possessed."

"Byron? Possessed of what?" asked Pippa as she groggily sorted out Lucy's words.

"A desire for revenge," said Lucy solemnly.

"Revenge? For what?"

"He intends to kill the man who fathered him," Lucy told her in anguish.

"David Knox?" asked Pippa, but now she came to her senses, and her heart pounded with fear.

"Pippa, we must stop him." Pippa looked more closely at Lucy and she saw the other woman was crying.

"Lucy, what is going on? I thought the two of you were . . . were, well, together. I haven't seen much of either of you, and I notice Major Owens has taken the smaller room in the servants' quarters," added Pippa knowingly.

Lucy took an exasperated breath. "We've been together, yes. It's been heavenly—naturally. It would continue so, if only he would forget this mad idea of revenge against his father."

"What can I do about it?"

"You must warn Jared, so he can stop Byron from ruining his own future. You said Jared cares for his brother, and I know he cares for his father. Surely he could help intervene in this madness."

"But the wires are all cut, Lucy," reasoned Pippa. "How could I reach Jared now? He's with the army, and from what I hear they're racing west to escape Grant. How on earth do you expect me to find him?"

Lucy began to sob. "If you don't, Pippa . . . If you don't, Byron will kill David Knox, and he'll die for it himself. He says he doesn't care, it's for his mother. But Pippa, if he dies, I have no reason to go on living. Please, help me."

Pippa lifted her head. Her own strength flooded back into her body and she nodded. She felt like a Celtic queen leading her tiny forces against the Roman army, but Pippa was undaunted.

"I'll find him, Lucy. Now, help me to dress. Did you by chance pack the trousers I used to wear riding? And I'll need my boots. Not the fancy ones, the ones I used to wear running messages. The comfortable ones."

As Pippa spoke, Lucy hurried about the room gathering Pippa's things together. "Yes, I did pack your trousers, as a matter of fact. I didn't know what else to do with them. Here," she said, handing the soft, worn cotton pants to Pippa.

Pippa dressed. "My cape," she said importantly, and Lucy retrieved Pippa's treasured mantle.

"What are you going to do for a horse?" asked Lucy as they headed down the stairs.

Pippa went to the back door and looked toward the stables. "If I steal one of the Union mounts, I could be in big trouble," she said with a half-smile. "But my old carriage horse is there. Wilson brought him with you. I'll take him. We know each other well."

In a short time, Pippa was astride the big, bay cart horse that had borne her often across the Yankee lines. She carried a cryptic map, but Pippa knew the direction she had to take. Her own senses would have to bear her in the direction of Lee's army, but need would find a way. Of this, Pippa was certain.

In fact, finding Lee's army wasn't as difficult as Pippa imagined. Grant's vast forces poured all over the area, and always the miles of his line stretched westward. Pippa herself was taken for a messenger, and with her hair tucked beneath her hood, no one noticed her femininity.

She rode for hours, stopping to steal a fresh grain bag from sleeping cavalry officers, and then to water the old horse. On the whole, the animal seemed pleased to be back at work. *How many times we've ridden together against the Confederacy,* Pippa thought. *But now we ride to save a rebel commander's life.*

Jared Knox led a small brigade along the Appomattox River, though there was little chance their valor could attain victory now. But these worn, ragged men refused to lay down their arms and desert as had many. Major Hallett was there, and young Captain Nicks, and when the Yankee force around them moved in, these men were ready to fight.

Jared had received no orders telling him to surrender, though many had been forced to do so already. General George Pickett had been defeated at Five Forks, but still kept alive was the hope that Lee's army might meet with Joe Johnston's forces and once again do the impossible.

"They're on us, Colonel," cried Captain Nicks, but Jared remained impassive as he considered the terrain around them.

"They'll come in through the open ground," he decided. "We can hold them off for a time, though not for long," he admitted. "We'll be surrounded. Yet if we can reach that crest, we might still escape to rejoin the others."

In this, Jared had been defeated by his own capability. He had led his men more quickly to the westward position, but the others hadn't met him there as ordered. Now he was separated from the bulk of the army, and there was little chance he could cut through the Yankee lines to make it back to Lee's bottled-up forces.

Jared gathered his men together, dismounting from Boreas to join the others. They formed a circle, moving outward, muskets aimed, bayonets fixed. There they waited. "Hold your fire until they're close, men," he ordered. "We can't get any more ammunition, so make it count."

A large force of Union infantrymen moved up the slope as Jared had predicted. Seeing the small rebel company holding out against them, the Yankees came forward recklessly. Jared's men withstood their hasty fire, waiting. When the Yankees came close, the rebels opened fire with surprising success.

The Yankees were driven back with little loss among the

band of rebels. "Good work, men," said Jared, but he knew the Yankees would be back in a larger wave.

"Move on down along the river," he ordered, "but keep your positions, ready to come around and fire."

Three more times the rebels endured Yankee assaults in this fashion, each time a measured success. Slowly, Jared moved them to the crest that had been his goal. As they reached the top well ahead of the Yankee infantry, Jared's hopes were suddenly dashed.

Across the field raced a large group of Federal cavalry-men. If the Union cavalry had begun the war as little more than a joke to amuse the Southerners, now it had developed into a formidable force beneath Phil Sheridan.

Jared was vastly outnumbered now, and as he looked to his men, he knew he couldn't risk their valiant lives further. "I'm afraid they have us, Major," he said regretfully, as Major Hallett readied his revolver.

"Sir, we can knock a few of them off their horses before it's over," said Captain Nicks, and his face was burning with the light of battle.

Jared considered this. "We could make a stand," he said thoughtfully. As he spoke, the cavalrymen galloped nearer. Jared reloaded his revolver and turned to face the oncoming Yankees but he did not fire.

A large bay horse was drawn to a sudden stop before them and in the strange music of war, Boreas whinnied as if recognizing the other animal. The small band of rebels stood ready to fire, awaiting the command of their colonel, but Jared Knox couldn't issue that order.

"We meet again, cousin."

The Yankee cavalryman, a colonel himself, leapt from his horse's back and faced the rebels fearlessly. The rebels looked doubtfully to Jared. They were reluctant to fire on a man of courage and, reluctantly, even Captain Nicks had to admit the large Yankee was such a man.

Jared stared in astonishment at the man who faced him, but then a slow smile grew on his face. He lowered his revolver. In a curious gesture, the Yankee lowered his saber in salute. Jared returned the salute of honor, and Captain Nicks breathed a sigh of relief. It appeared he wouldn't die on a field of battle after all.

"You may lower your arms, gentlemen," said Jared calmly. "I believe we've gone as far as we're going to. It may be the time for surrender has come, after all."

The Federal cavalrymen surrounded the little group. "Surrender!" shouted a youthful Yankee, but his commander looked to him in amusement.

"Calm down, Rogerson," he said with a shake of his head.

Jared was smiling, a strange sight upon the stricken field, but he walked to the Yankee colonel without fear.

"So we meet at the end as at the beginning." The big Yankee stepped forward to shake hands with Jared.

"Garrett," said Jared. "I heard you were out of this last summer. I'm glad to see that isn't so." Jared eyed the marks of Garrett's ranking. "I see you weren't outdone by my title," he observed. "Or did Jefferson not relay my challenge to you?"

"He did," said Garrett. "I couldn't allow your name to pass down in the annals of our family name with a greater ranking."

"But I understood you were with a Massachusetts regiment," said Jared.

Garrett nodded. "I was, for a time. But I transferred to find enjoyment on horseback. It's been a very long war," he sighed. "Though you appear to have come through it well."

Jared shook his head. "I've only recently returned to my

brigade," he told his cousin. "I also was hit last summer," he added as he slapped the thigh that once had agonized him to the limits of endurance.

"Really? You're lucky you didn't lose it," said Garrett.

"It was fairly close," Jared admitted. "I might have relented, but my wife was adamant on the subject."

Garrett's eyes widened. "Your wife?" he asked. "So you finally chose among that vast assortment of Southern belles, and made one your wife?"

"Not exactly," replied Jared. "Philippa is from New England."

"You married a Yankee girl in the middle of war?" laughed Garrett, but Jared grinned.

"It came about . . . unexpectedly. And it has not been without its hurdles."

"So runs the course of love," sighed Garrett, and Jared remembered that Jefferson had mentioned a woman in Garrett's life.

"What are we going to do with them, Colonel?" asked the impatient Rogerson.

"Lee and Grant have been exchanging messages since yesterday," Garrett replied calmly. "I doubt we'll have much longer to wait. Come, we'll ride back to the camp together. Your men appear underfed at best. We'll see what we can do about dividing rations."

"That will be appreciated," said Jared gratefully.

"It will indeed," piped in Captain Nicks. They had gone forward on the barest minimum of food, and hunger gnawed at every rebel stomach. Captain Nicks's eyes gleamed at the thought of sharing the Yankee rations, and he decided surrender wasn't such a bad decision after all.

* * *

Pippa made her way through the Union campsite in confusion. She had been told she might find Jared there, for he wasn't with his own men. Blue and gray mingled easily together, awaiting the official surrender to come the next day.

Lee had ridden Traveller to meet with Grant the day before, and the steadfast Grant's terms had been surprisingly gracious. Thus relieved, the Southern soldiers on the whole were relaxed and at ease among their recent enemies, already discussing old battles together.

Pippa came to a row of officers' tents just as the sun set low beyond the western horizon, and her heart sank with it. She had been unable to find either Jared or Byron, and Pippa was deathly afraid the damage had already been done. It couldn't be easy for a colored infantrymen to locate a Confederate officer, let alone kill him, and she prayed she was not too late to avert the disaster. Pippa looked around, but she saw no sign of Jared.

"Excuse me, Captain," she said when she saw an officer coming towards her. "Do you know where I might find Colonel Knox?"

The captain looked at her doubtfully, but he pointed to a tent at the far end of the row. "That way, ma'am," he told her.

Pippa went to the tent and saw a large Yankee officer standing outside the entrance. "Excuse me, sir," she said in a small voice.

The colonel turned to her, and his brow rose. Pippa was still wearing her old trousers, and her long hair fell about her shoulders. She guessed that she was an unusual sight. The colonel smiled faintly, and Pippa realized he was remarkably handsome. His face was square and strong, his eyes gray and intelligent, and she was sure he must be a formidable leader of men.

"Can you tell me where I might find Colonel Knox?"

The man's smile deepened. "I am Colonel Knox," he told her.

"No, you're not! You can't be. I mean, you're not the right one. Oh, dear."

"Perhaps you're looking for my cousin, also Colonel Knox. Is that right?"

"Jared Knox. My husband."

"Then you must be Philippa. I'm Jared's cousin, Garrett Knox," he told her.

"Oh, have you seen Jared? Do you know where he is?" she asked desperately.

"Come with me," said Garrett. He led Pippa into his tent and gestured towards the corner.

Jared lay asleep upon the floor, covered thoughtfully with his cousin's blankets. Pippa closed her eyes with relief. "Then he's all right?"

"He's fine," Garrett reassured her. "Hungry and tired, but they all were. We were in the midst of conversation when he simply dropped off," he told her. "So I left him there."

Pippa frowned. "I must speak to him," she said reluctantly. Looking back out of the tent, she sighed. "But then, there's nothing he can do tonight. No, I'll let him sleep."

"That's probably a good idea," agreed Garrett. "Though I doubt he'll be displeased to find you here."

Pippa looked to him earnestly. "I hope not," she said, and Garrett realized that Jared's wife wasn't certain of her husband's feelings.

But Garrett could see easily what had drawn his cousin to this slender Yankee girl. Her great mass of golden-brown hair framed an exquisite face, but not only was she exceptionally lovely. Philippa Knox had a mystical appeal, an intensity that was singular for women of her time.

Pippa followed Garrett from the tent, and she sat beside

him on a makeshift bench. He found her some relatively
fresh army rations and Pippa devoured her portion while
Garrett watched in amazement. Seeing his expression, Pippa
smiled weakly.

"I haven't eaten much since I left Richmond," she explained by way of an apology for her unladylike behavior,
but Garrett seemed amused.

"I understand there's an official surrender tomorrow," she
said, hoping to divert Jared's handsome cousin from wit-
nessing her hunger-produced greed.

"Yes," said Garrett. "But I think I'll leave in the morning." He sighed. "It's been good to see Jared again, but I'm
eager to return to Maryland. To be home at last."

Pippa nodded. "I'd think so," she agreed, but something
in Garrett's gray eyes told her more was waiting for him
there than his home alone.

Garrett left Pippa with Jared and, uncertain what else to
do, Pippa slipped her clothes off save for her light chemise.
She slid into the dubious bedding beside her husband. Jared
woke to feel the soft body beside him, but it was impossible
that Pippa could be lying next to him there on the site of
surrender at Appomattox Court House.

A dream, he thought. But one he couldn't resist. Jared
moved closer to the dream figure, his arms encircling her
slender body as he drew her against his burning arousal.
The dream Pippa murmured softly and nuzzled his neck,
but this was the way Jared's nightly dreams often began.

He felt her kiss his neck, he felt her hands run along his
side, leisurely seeking the source of his pleasure. Jared's
dream soared as her fingers traveled the length of his shaft,
slowly wrapping around him. Again she murmured sensually

as she caressed his pulsating arousal. As he had each night when he endured this dream alone, Jared ached with need, but this night was far more vivid.

"Pippa," he whispered, but his words were stopped when her soft lips pressed against his.

Jared didn't move, but her leg slid sensually over his. She squirmed closer against him, her soft whispers urging him to fulfill a need Jared couldn't begin to deny. A low, drowsy moan came from deep in her throat as she felt the heat of his erection between her parted thighs, and she shuddered as he slowly entered the dewy, tight cavern of her body.

Jared was lost in the power of his dream, willing it to continue, fearing he would wake and lose its sweet intensity. He reached to pull her long, soft leg higher over his, and he drove within her as he strove to attain his release before his perfect vision could vanish.

"Pippa, don't go," he murmured as the soft body pressed tighter against him, her leg curved tightly around his as she writhed in her ecstasy.

Jared reached his own crest of pleasure with surprising satisfaction. But as he drifted into a deeper sleep, he noted with wonder that rather than vanishing, his dream Pippa curled up happily beside him and returned to sleep as well.

"Pippa! What on earth are you doing here?"

Pippa turned to Jared sleepily. "A strange time to notice, considering," she said with a drowsy smile.

"It was real!" he exclaimed in amazement. No wonder his body felt pleasantly sated when he woke.

Pippa's face was puzzled, and she looked at Jared suspiciously. "What was real?"

Now Jared smiled. "I thought your . . . arrival was a dream."

Pippa's brow rose, and she looked at her husband reproachfully. But the purpose of her arrival flooded back to her and she sat upright on the bedding.

"Jared, something dreadful has happened, or will happen if you don't do something about it. We must hurry. Where's your father?"

"What are you talking about, woman?"

Jared made no move to rise. Far from hurrying anywhere, it would be most enjoyable to repeat the sequence of last night's dream, this time with the pleasure of knowing it was just as it seemed.

Pippa had already left the bed and was now hurriedly dressing. She pulled on men's trousers and proceeded to don a well-worn pair of high-topped riding boots.

Pippa glanced back at Jared in annoyance. "Jared, you must get up! There's so little time."

"There is indeed," reflected Jared with a yawn. "I had hoped to spend it in a way other than seeing my beautiful wife become a boy before my eyes.

"Maybe I'm still dreaming," he mused. "I haven't slept nor ate in days, until last night. It may be I'm more drained than I imagined."

Pippa found Jared's uniform and tossed it at him. "Jared! Get dressed, please!"

Jared opened his eyes and looked at her. "What is wrong with you, girl?"

Pippa had no choice but to tell him without the gentle build-up she had planned. "Byron is here, Jared. He's looking for your father," she said miserably. "Jared, I believe he intends to kill the general!"

Jared sat up, then without speaking, he dressed in a flash. "Where is he?" he asked as he pulled on his own boots.

"I don't know, I can't find him. But I know he's here. Lucy said so."

Jared stopped and frowned. "Lucy? Did you learn this from her, Pippa? The woman may not be as simple as she seems, but she's definitely addled."

"There's no time to explain," she said impatiently.

Pippa grabbed Jared's arm and tugged him toward the door. "Where is your father?" she asked.

"He was shot an hour before the surrender," Jared told her calmly.

"Shot? Is he terribly injured?" asked Pippa with concern.

"I think not," Jared replied. "I saw him yesterday, and he was refusing to be taken to the hospital. He's at a farmer's house not far from here."

Pippa considered this. "Then maybe Byron wouldn't have found him yet."

"I doubt he ever had such intentions. It's far more likely a product of Lucy's imagination. How would she know what Byron is doing?"

Pippa faced him squarely. "Apparently he told her something after he arrived in Richmond."

"Byron was in Richmond?" asked Jared.

Pippa nodded impatiently as she led Jared from the tent. "He was, and his commander, Major Owens, is staying in the servants' quarters. I think he and Kim are going to get married. Especially after Carey saved her from Burke."

"What?" Jared stopped to stare at Pippa in disbelief, and again he wondered if he was still dreaming.

"Burke instigated the raid on your house, and the attack on Kim, for his own purposes," Pippa told him. "Oh, do hurry, Jared. Where is Boreas?" Pippa was plainly exasperated, for it was obvious Jared wasn't taking Lucy's warning very seriously.

"With Garrett's horse, I suppose. How did you get here?" he asked.

"There," said Pippa, as she pointed to where she had left the old cart horse, but Jared laughed when he saw the heavy animal.

Garrett Knox rode toward them, and saw Pippa hurriedly saddling her horse. "I'd think you might provide your wife with a more suitable mount, Jared. But perhaps Virginia horseflesh has been depleted beyond the point where ladies ride sidesaddle upon graceful palfreys."

Jared grinned. "I've found that Pippa rarely follows the course designated for ladies," he said as he watched his agile wife swing herself upon the horse's back.

"If I'm not quick, she'll be gone without me," he added.

Garrett turned his big horse and cantered off, then returned with an already saddled Boreas. "I'm glad to see you haven't lost my gift," said Garrett as he studied the bony black horse. "Though you might feed him better, Jared," he added seriously.

"Have you seen any fat rebels of late, Garrett?" asked Jared with a faint smile.

"No," agreed Garrett, "but I trust your young wife will see that you're fed properly once you return to Richmond," he added with a nod to Pippa. "Leaving you in her obviously capable hands, I must bid you farewell. It's a long road back to Maryland, but one I wish to ride in peace."

Jared mounted Boreas and again lowered his saber in salute. "I won't have this much longer," he said as Garrett returned the honor. "But it's good to see its final use is one of friendship."

Garrett rode away, and Jared moved his horse to where

Pippa waited. He smiled when he saw her gray cape about her shoulders, her slender legs encased in snug trousers, and his eyes coursed her form appreciatively.

"So we've come full circle, little witch," he said with pleasure. "But now we ride together."

With that, Jared urged Boreas into a sudden gallop, and Pippa followed along though her large mount couldn't begin to keep up with that of her husband's. But Jared didn't leave his wife too far behind. His reasons for slowing the pace of the great, black horse were less chivalrous than his desire to see the woman whose dark hair flowed behind her like a windswept cloud.

The farmer's house where David Knox was recuperating was quiet, but when they entered, Pippa and Jared saw why. The farmer was bound and gagged, as was his wife, and Pippa's heart nearly stopped as she guessed what this might mean. If Jared had doubted Lucy's story, his face grew white as he realized his error. He pulled the gag from the farmer's mouth, and the old man coughed uncontrollably before he could speak.

Jared removed the cloth from the man's wife, but his heart labored as he saw how gently they had been bound. "Colored soldiers, colored soldiers," gasped the woman, though she seemed too terrified to say anything further.

It was enough for Jared. He raced from the front hall and bounded up the stairs, followed by a breathless Pippa, but when Jared pushed open the door of his father's bedroom, she feared they were already too late.

"Byron, no!" Jared shouted, but when he aimed his revolver, his hands were shaking.

Pippa entered the room, and there stood her old friend.

David Knox was still alive, and Pippa guessed she and Jared had arrived only moments after Byron himself.

"Byron, you must not do this," she breathed, her voice quivering as she spoke.

Byron didn't look away from his father's face, but he held a revolver aimed at the general's head. David Knox didn't look frightened, and when Jared moved to stand between his father and Byron, David motioned him away.

"Jared," he said in a voice that was commanding despite the weakness of his body. "Get back."

Jared shook his head, and his eyes met and held Byron's, but Byron didn't relent. "Do as the man says, Jared," he said, and as he ground out the words, his hatred for his father was painfully intense.

Jared didn't move, and without thinking further, Pippa went to his side. "Byron, please. This will do no good."

Byron's chiseled jaw twitched, but his eyes went to Pippa's earnest face. "You don't understand, Pippa," he said in a quiet, strained voice.

"How would she?" asked David calmly. "The girl is only twenty. There is much she hasn't seen."

Byron looked back to his father and his dark eyes flashed angrily. "When the world is rid of you, there will be that much less evil for her to learn."

David laughed, and Pippa cringed at what seemed a deliberate provocation to the man who held a gun. "When you've removed the world of me, it will be restored to its proper balance, is that it?" he asked, still smiling.

"It will be a step in the right direction," replied Byron.

"You know I can't let you do this," said Jared, and looking to him, Byron nodded.

Jared saw Byron cock the revolver, and Pippa's breath caught as his finger squeezed the trigger. Jared moved toward him, but Byron swung round and struck his brother with force. Jared fell to the floor, his lip bleeding, yet he still held his own gun, and with trembling hands he aimed it at Byron.

"No!" cried Pippa. She guessed what Byron intended. He would kill his father, then die by Jared's bullet. But she knew such an act would destroy her husband, and resolutely, she put herself in front of David.

"You'll have to kill me first, Byron Knox," she said without thinking.

"That is not my name," said Byron furiously.

"It is, and there's not much you can do about it, whatever the circumstances of your birth might have been," replied Pippa adamantly. "You are not going to kill your own father, Byron, and so help me God, you're not going to make Jared kill you. I'll die first myself, and then you'll be sorry!"

Pippa's threat brought a reluctant smile to Byron's lips. "And if I decide to pick you up and restrain you with the farmer?" he suggested with faint amusement.

Pippa shook her head. "Jared won't let you."

Pippa paused and glanced down at her husband. "Will you, Jared?"

Jared hesitated and Pippa's eyes widened. "Well . . ."

"Jared!"

"No." Jared smiled himself, and as he rose to his feet and wiped the blood from his lip, he knew the danger to his father had passed.

"The circumstances of your birth," mused David without concern.

Pippa looked at her father-in-law sharply, and she realized he was flushed. His brow showed beads of perspiration, but she realized this wasn't from fear of Byron, but a fever instead.

"Are you ill, sir?" she asked with concern.

"It's nothing, daughter. The wound has turned septic, that's all. Just a little fever."

David's eyes went to Jared, and then more reluctantly he studied the face of his other son. "You look like me," he said, but Byron frowned.

"I curse every drop of white blood that flows in my veins," he said angrily, but David shook his head.

"You may, but it's there nonetheless." David sighed. "All of my doing."

He glanced over at Jared, then nodded. "I was like you in those days, my son," he began. "But perhaps I was not as resolute. I was certainly less likely to travel my own road. Yet that quality in you didn't come about without my help."

Jared wondered if his father's fever was rendering him delirious and he frowned.

"I loved your mother, Jared. She was pure and good, as far above me as the stars. But as she rose higher and higher in my eyes, I was bound helpless to the earthly realm. One day as I rode across our farm, I saw a woman. She was toiling in the fields, her dark skin gleamed with a golden light, and I was spellbound. I stopped to watch her, enchanted by the raw, perfect beauty I saw in her."

Byron's jaw clenched as David went on, but he didn't make an effort to stop the older man's memory. "I watched her as a field worker went to her side. They laughed together, and I knew they were lovers. I was helpless, I burned with a jealous rage.

"That night, I arranged that the man be sold, though I had never done such a thing before. I gave her time then, to be free of him. Then I went to her. She knew why I was there, and she backed away from me in a terror I couldn't fathom then."

Pippa longed to race from the room, but she couldn't

move. Both Jared and Byron stood motionless, and David Knox went on with his memory undaunted.

"I told her she need not fear me, that I meant her no harm. She believed me, and having little choice, she allowed me my way." David paused and sighed heavily.

"From that time onward, I was a man possessed. I thought of nothing else, I saw nothing else." Seeing Jared's face, David sought to reassure him. "Your mother went during that time to Richmond. She was unaware of what I had done, of course. But then, Caroline could never conceive of such an animal nature as I learned existed in myself."

David closed his eyes, and Pippa realized he was in pain. "It's strange. Both women were alike in this."

He looked then at Byron, as if in his son's face he was seeking a reminder of the mother's. "She didn't fight me, she was almost kind. But never once did she give me reason to think she wished me near her.

"Never once could I imagine she cared for me nor felt the slightest portion of what I felt for her. She was, in her way, as lofty and unreachable as was Caroline, and she bore life's injustices with as much grace."

Byron looked away from his father's face, and tears glistened in his brown eyes.

"A day came when I realized she bore my child. It should have been nothing to me. Such things are commonplace on other plantations, where many black faces resemble their master's. Yet I was stunned. There would be a living reminder of what I was, what I had become. That ended my madness. I'm not certain why. I saw that she was cared for adequately, but I never went to her again."

David breathed a sigh of relief, but his face grimaced as he felt a stab of pain. "Caroline had returned from Richmond, and for a while, I dared not approach her. Yet when

I found the courage, she was there as always. Through her kindness, I came to have two sons borne within six months of each other."

David looked to Jared and Byron. "But perhaps in some small way you, Jared, have benefited from my failure."

"How is that?" asked Jared thickly.

"There was a time, I recall, you were set to marry a young lady of estimable virtue."

"Christina?" asked Pippa.

"Indeed, Christina," said David thoughtfully. "But Christina was not Caroline, though they resemble each other. Her marriage to young Charles showed her true character. I knew then my interference with your marriage plans had served you well."

Pippa was puzzled by this, but Jared was angered. "It was Charles who destroyed their marriage, not Christina," stated Jared coldly.

David laughed, then coughed before speaking again. "Oh, really? An innocent young woman, oppressed by the evil nature of man, no doubt," he taunted, and Jared's jawline hardened. Pippa thought of Miss Honeycastle.

"You do have the tendency to be too trusting with women, Jared," said David in a paternal fashion. His eyes went briefly to Pippa, who squirmed uncomfortably.

"That may be," agreed Jared. "But I hardly see how that involves Christina."

Pippa bit her lip and restrained herself from offering her own opinion on the matter.

"Tell me, boy. What evidence did you actually see of Charles's brutality? Or did you merely take the lady's word for his crimes against her?"

"Are you suggesting she invented the story?" asked Jared, disgusted with his father.

David was unmoved by his son's disapproval. "I'm not suggesting," he replied. "I'm telling you now, the girl fabricated every word. Oh, Charles drank, true enough. But not nearly as much as she led you to believe. But he was my aide, Jared. Christina was with him in those early days. I saw from the first it wasn't her husband she adored, but my own son."

Pippa's eyes were wide with David's revelation, but Jared was clearly unconvinced that Christina might be guilty of any wrong.

David struggled to sit up in his bed, and Pippa propped his pillows behind his back. "I remember the day she learned how to win your protection. Yes, a woman was beaten by a drunken husband, but it wasn't she. I, with Charles's help, came to the poor girl's rescue. Christina was there, and lo and behold! Not a week later she had gone to you with the same story, making it her own.

"I tried to tell you at the time not to discount Charles's side of the story, but you were intent on protecting her. I don't blame you. Such stories move even the hardest heart, as should be. But to malign a good man like Charles . . . No, Christina was calculating and manipulative. You were well spared her as a wife."

He looked at Jared and nodded slightly. "I saw myself in your face at eighteen. So certain you'd follow in my footsteps, do your name proud. You would take a wife as I had done, honoring her all the days of your life, no doubt."

Jared frowned, but his father continued. "Perhaps you even thought to correct my wrong. Or do I miss my guess that you've long known of your brother's existence?"

"That is so," replied Jared stiffly.

"But I believe you would have followed in my footsteps. Too closely," continued David confidently, and Pippa's brow furrowed as she considered this.

"I would never do as you have done," said Jared abruptly.

David's brow rose. "No?" His eyes went to Pippa and he smiled. "What would happen when this one came along? And one day, she would have come along, make no mistake.

"Would it really make a difference, Jared? When you saw her face, looked into those tilted green eyes . . . Would it matter if you had a wife, children? Can you honestly say you wouldn't have desired her anyway? That you wouldn't move heaven and earth to have her, no matter what the result? No matter what your passion for her did to those around you, even to the girl herself?"

David laughed. "As it was, you used that same passion to persuade a loyal Yankee spy into your bed, well before you made her your wife."

Pippa's mouth opened, and Jared stared at his father in amazement, but Byron smiled slightly, his face a dark mirror of his father's. David patted Pippa's hand fondly before continuing.

"William Reid had long been part of the Underground Railroad, unbeknownst to Charlotte, of course," remembered David unhurriedly. Pippa was stunned at the rebel commander's easy knowledge of these sensitive matters.

"He and Parson Frederick aided untold numbers of slaves north. It's hard to imagine his niece wouldn't also be enraptured by their cause."

Jared's eyes widened. "Parson Frederick?" he asked in disbelief. "How did he get away with it, if you knew?"

David shrugged. "Both Reid and the parson were gentlemen, men of honor, doing what they believed to be right. Neither flaunted their activities, so those of us who were aware kept the matter to ourselves."

David glanced over at Byron. "I imagine it was they who

aided you north, and arranged your placement with Reid's brother?" he asked idly.

Byron nodded slowly, his dark eyes filled with hesitant wonder. "How do you know of this?" he asked.

"I knew where you were," replied David softly, though he didn't meet his elder son's eyes. "Always."

Jared turned to Pippa. "It was the parson who involved you in the spy ring," he guessed, but though Pippa squirmed uneasily, it was Byron who answered his brother.

"That would have been my doing," he replied guiltily.

"You?" asked Jared, and his eyes were lit with accusation as he looked to Byron.

Pippa said nothing, but stared uncomfortably at her feet, chewing the insides of her lip in agitation.

"Pippa was devastated when her father died," explained Byron. "But perhaps more so when she learned she was to be sent to Virginia."

A slow smile grew on his face as Pippa fidgeted beside him. "As a matter of fact, she was all set to run away to New York City. To be an actress, as I recall."

Pippa winced with embarrassment at Byron's recollection, and she was acutely aware of her husband's eyes upon her.

"She was very young," Byron went on. "And willful enough to take off on her own as well. I didn't like to think what would happen to her in a city like that. But I was able to convince her to accept her father's wishes only by promising to unite her with the parson."

Jared stared at Pippa, but he couldn't speak. He knew the disaster that his brother had narrowly averted. Yet he was powerless to resist the tide of sorrow that washed over him as he gazed at his wife.

"Don't deceive yourself, son," said David. "You knew where this lady's heart was, even if you couldn't admit it to yourself. Being on opposite sides of a war didn't stop you, Jared. Can you honestly say that you wouldn't have taken her to your bed? Even had Christina Smith been your wife already?"

Jared didn't look at Pippa, but he couldn't answer his father.

David nodded. "No, I thought not. I knew you, Jared. I saw to it that you were sufficiently distracted from your marital intentions by your sojourn in Europe with my brother's strong-willed son. When you returned, I knew you were the man I could never be."

Pippa glanced up at Jared, but he didn't look at her. His face was strained, written with an emotion she couldn't read. She longed to know, to understand his heart, but she was afraid.

David looked to Byron and nodded. "Though you might not consider it, I've aided your life as well."

"In what manner?" asked Byron with obvious disdain.

"I believe there's a young woman for you," he speculated knowingly. "If you've been in my house in Richmond, you've seen her again."

Jared looked at Byron, but he couldn't guess to whom his father referred.

"What about her?" Byron retorted abruptly.

"I take it you've been reunited," he guessed with a glance at Pippa. "I assume you found her a virgin."

Pippa gasped in acute embarrassment, but Byron's frown deepened. "Am I to feel gratitude that another beautiful woman of color escaped your attention?"

Pippa winced, but David didn't react angrily. "After you left, I saw your mother, though we didn't speak. She was very ill then, it was only a few weeks before her death. At her feet sat a young girl crying inconsolably. I guessed easily

enough for whom she mourned. As you say, she was a re
markably lovely child."

"What has that to do with you?" asked Byron doubtfully

"I decided she would remain so. Such a girl wouldn'
remain long . . . intact, with a face like that. So I arranged
her placement at the home of a couple who would see she
retained that beguiling innocence."

Byron said nothing further, and Pippa decided it was time
David Knox be left in peace. "If this is over now—and By-
ron, I gather you no longer intend to commit murder—ther
I think you should leave him now to rest."

Neither Jared nor Byron moved, and Pippa drew an impatient breath. "Jared, I believe you are expected at the surrender?" she reminded him, as if he were to be late for tea

"Byron, you'll lose those stripes if you don't return to
Richmond. Carey Owens may have been sufficiently distracted by Kim to have missed your absence . . ."

"Owens?" broke in David. "And my Kimber?"

Pippa smiled happily. "Kim has a suitor, sir. He's a Yankee. But he's a gentleman."

"So there's a Yankee intending to ask for my daughter's
hand, eh?" asked David. "But if you speak for him, daughter, I may yet relent. If he bears my Kimber's heart, that is."

"He does," said Pippa, but already David had closed his
eyes to sleep.

Jared took his place in the surrendering column, leading
the remnants of his brigade as they marched behind General
John B. Gordon. The rebels were downcast as they passed
the blue-clad Yankees now awaiting the surrender of arms.
It had been a long, bitter war, and now it was over. All their

valor had come to this, and their hearts were heavy as they approached this final end.

Pippa rode slowly back towards the site of surrender. Her own heart was heavy, for she had to tell Jared that David Knox had died. She had watched his condition deteriorate over the hours after his sons left him, but there was nothing to be done. His wound had festered badly, and though the doctors had said it wasn't severe, Pippa knew it had brought about his death.

Pippa saw the long lines of surrendering rebels, but then her eyes were drawn to the sweet blue of the Maine flag. She urged her big horse forward, coming to watch the procession as the Union general awaited the final surrender. To Pippa's lasting wonder and delight, that Union general was none other than Joshua Chamberlain, the heroic professor from Bowdoin College. She saw him sitting straight and proud upon his horse, and tears welled in Pippa's eyes.

She had thought he was dead, another brave man who wouldn't live to see the war's end. Yet there he was in the position of highest honor. General Gordon approached, and farther behind, Jared marched with his men.

Chamberlain spoke to his troops, and with a sudden clatter, the Union force shifted from shoulder arms to carry arms, a gesture of final salute. General Gordon's head lifted at the salute of honor, and he whirled his horse around to face Chamberlain.

The horse rose on its haunches, then seemed to bow itself as General Gordon lowered his own sword in salute. He turned to his men, and the rebels too moved to carry arms in return of the unexpected Yankee honor.

Pippa's gray-green eyes misted, for no more fitting end to the bloody war could have been scripted in heaven itself. Twenty thousand men passed to stack muskets and lay their beloved flag to rest, but Pippa found Jared as he signed his oath of allegiance.

"It seems you and I are of the same country once again," he said, and there were tears in his eyes.

"We always were," she answered.

Jared took the news of his father's death calmly. He seemed pleased that Pippa had been with the general until the end, but they rode back to Richmond in virtual silence. They pitched Jared's tattered tent at night, but Jared was deep in thought, and Pippa dared not disturb him as he absorbed the impact of the last weeks of war.

The faint sense of unease began to show itself again as they approached Richmond. Pippa didn't understand it. She had attributed her anxiety primarily to Jared's absence, but it was more powerful than ever when they returned home.

The family was devastated to learn of David Knox's death. Caroline went to her room and was not seen for several days. Byron also returned, and though no mention was made of his visit to David, he and Jared had reached an understanding.

"What's that you're working on?" he asked as he passed Jared in the dining room.

A sheet of paper was carefully arranged on the table, and Jared was copying a design from a discolored, torn paper with great care. Pippa peeked over Jared's shoulder.

"It's his house," she told Byron with pride.

Byron looked closely at the design. "When are you going to start building?" he asked with interest.

"When I can get my hands on the material," sighed Jared. "By the looks of things, that won't be for some time."

"I can get what you need," said Carey Owens as he entered the room.

Jared's eyes brightened and the three young men sat to discuss the details of his plan. Pippa was lost in the specifics, and she left them to hammer it out without her assistance.

Caroline stood watching her son and his companions from the doorway. Pippa saw the strange light in her eyes, and her heart constricted with the knowledge Caroline wasn't as in the dark about Byron's paternity as everyone imagined. Caroline met Pippa's eyes and her smile was sad. The two women went into the sitting room, but Pippa dared not speak as Caroline gazed out the window and sighed.

"He imagined I knew nothing, of course," she began so softly that Pippa could barely hear her voice. "But I knew. I knew when he came home one evening and his eyes looked through me. And I knew when he went to her."

Pippa felt an icy chill surrounding her, and every breath she took was labored as she waited for Caroline to continue.

"I saw everything in his eyes," sighed Caroline, and even over the stretch of years, Pippa felt her pain.

"I went to Richmond in the hope, like a quick flame, it would burn itself out. But when I returned, he was as distracted as before. And so I waited," she sighed sorrowfully.

"I waited, and he came to our bed late in the night. I pretended to be asleep so he wouldn't know I had waited for him. I lay awake, staring at his magnificent broad back until I thought my heart would break.

"All the years I lay with him, Pippa," whispered Caroline, her voice strained with her grief. "All the nights I dared not cry out my pleasure in his company lest he think that much less of me! He admired me, you see. He thought I was the perfect lady, he called me an angel. This was what he loved, I believed, yet it came between us as well.

"When he went to another woman's arms, I was unable to call him back. He still loved me, I knew that, but from a distance. One day when I looked into his eyes, she was no longer there, nor has any woman been in my place since that time.

"I took him back to myself, my body, biting my lip so hard that it bled lest he see how I craved his love, his body in mine."

Pippa's tears fell upon her cheeks, for she knew these feelings well. Caroline understood, and she sighed.

"Yes, Jared is like his father—he wishes to see the ideal in things, the perfect. See how he struggles with his design! He won't rest until it's everything he has imagined."

Caroline paused and looked intently into Pippa's stricken face. "He has done the same to you, I think. Wanting you to be all he considers perfect. I saw that the night he met you. He had found the girl of his imaginings, and he couldn't see any place where you varied from that perfect picture."

"I am not that," said Pippa in a small voice. "I can never be that."

"No," agreed Caroline. "Nor should you be. I tried to be all my husband imagined of the ideal woman. It is my deepest regret, that I didn't go to him and say, 'I'm no angel, I am on no pedestal save where you've put me.' I would tell him I walked the same earthly plane as he, my heart raged with a passion he never dreamed."

Pippa was crying now. "He loved you very much. He spoke of you at the last," she said brokenly.

"Yes, I know that he did," said Caroline. "Maybe in another world, we'll find each other unencumbered by the mistakes of this lifetime."

Caroline touched Pippa's cheek. "But you, my dear, may yet enjoy your time on earth with the one you love. Tell him what you want from him. Open your heart."

Pippa looked at Jared's mother doubtfully. "I want him

to be happy," said Pippa as the tears started again in her downcast eyes. "He deserves that, after so long at war."

Caroline sighed. "He does indeed."

Pippa lay awake in bed waiting for Jared. It had been nearly three weeks since the surrender at Appomattox, yet not once since had he taken her in his arms and loved her. At first, Pippa assumed he was exhausted and distraught over his father's death, but now she was beginning to wonder.

Jared seemed happy enough in the company of his family, yet when they were alone together, he was unusually quiet. Pippa longed to talk to him about it, and more, but she didn't dare. At night as Jared slept, she lay awake longing to reach for him, to touch him. But he had withdrawn from her in some unfathomable way, and though she had news that wouldn't wait much longer, Pippa hadn't found the courage to share it with him when he was so distant.

Jared entered their bedroom, and Pippa saw he intended to speak with her. Now Pippa didn't want to talk, and she made a quick effort to leave.

"Pippa, wait," he said quietly.

"I've forgotten something I needed to do downstairs," she said hurriedly. Pippa started to get up from the bed, but Jared took her arm and his eyes easily saw through her weak excuse to escape.

"It can wait," he told her firmly. "It's time we had a talk."

He sat beside her on the edge of their bed, and Pippa's heart held its beat as she waited for him to go on. As she looked into Jared's face, she doubted very much he was going to say what she wanted to hear.

"There's something I must ask you, Pippa. Do you think of returning home, home where you were free?"

"Home? Do you mean to Maine?" she asked. Jared nodded.

"I miss it sometimes, yes," she replied honestly, but her face was decidedly puzzled as he nodded again.

"Pippa, if you want to go . . . You must know I won't stop you. Our marriage wasn't exactly as it should have been. If you want your freedom, then I will give it to you."

Jared spoke with effort, but Pippa was stunned beyond words. Her breath stopped, and for a moment she feared she might faint, but then Jared rose. "I'll give you the night to consider it," he told her. "But tomorrow I must have your answer."

Jared left without another word and Pippa stared blankly at the door. He didn't want her anymore. He wanted her to leave. All their passion had come to nothing. She, like Ruby, was to be discarded now that his fires had died.

Pippa sat still as stone for hours, staring at the door until her vision wavered with the strain. Pippa wanted to die, but a tiny flutter of life within her forbade it. She would live, because she had to live, but Pippa wouldn't beg Jared to keep her at his side when his happiness depended on her leaving.

In the early morning light of a sweet Virginia spring day, Pippa donned her cape one last time and slipped in silence from her husband's house. Once again, she rode away on the large cart horse. Once again, Pippa was bound for the land beneath the northern star.

Thirteen

Jared woke early and went to Pippa's room to see if she was awake. He hadn't slept for fear of her answer, but when he saw the empty bed, Jared's heart crashed in his chest.

Lucy entered the room and stood beside him. "She left early this morning," said Lucy with a sigh.

"Pippa has gone?" he asked painfully, but he realized Lucy had spoken to him in a markedly clear and intelligent voice.

"Your wife is a woman of unusual honor," Lucy told Jared without fear. Seeing his surprise, her dark eyes glittered. "As I've often had the occasion to witness during our past association."

Jared knew what had happened. It was clearly revealed in the clear, intelligent eyes of the woman who faced him now. Jared understood what his wife had done, and why she had to do it. Yes, it was honor. Honor that would not betray a brave young woman fighting for her freedom.

"Where has she gone, Lucy?" asked Jared.

"She went to take a train from Washington," Lucy told him, but faint glimmer of a smile crossed her face. "She left me a note, so that . . . I . . . wouldn't worry about her."

"Do you know where she was going?" Jared pressed as his heart thundered in his chest. If he hurried . . .

"Yes, I know." Lucy paused and her eyes searched Jared's strained face. "Don't you?"

* * *

Jared hurriedly packed a bag and headed down the stair with purpose. He was a fool to leave Pippa to her own thoughts, not to influence her decision any way he could. He had to tell her how much he wanted her to stay. His pride had stopped him, his desire to know their marriage was what she wanted. Too much was still unsaid between them, and Jared wanted the chance to say it to her face.

There was no time to tell his family where he was going. Jared left that to Lucy. He went to the front door, but it swung open before he touched it, and there stood Mildred Smith.

Jared repressed a groan. "Mrs. Smith," he said coldly. "What brings you here?"

Mildred's face was exceptionally white and strained, and Jared looked at her more closely as she glanced nervously around the room behind him.

"Your wife, Jared," said Mildred in a choked whisper. "Where is she?"

Jared's brow furrowed, and he frowned. He had no wish to discuss Pippa's whereabouts with Mildred Smith, but it was like the old crow to pry into his marriage at such a time.

"I can't imagine how that could be your concern, Mrs. Smith," replied Jared, but Mildred eyed his baggage and she shook her head vigorously.

"You must tell me, Jared. Please, it's of utmost importance. Where is your wife?"

"Pippa is . . . out," Jared told her obstinately.

Mildred drew a strained breath. "Must you always be so difficult?" she complained.

"Why do you want to know?" he asked with decided suspicion.

Mildred hesitated, but there was nothing left but to tell

Jared the truth. "I believe she's in danger, Jared," she confessed, but her eyes were cast from his.

"Danger?" asked Jared skeptically.

Clearly, Mildred had crossed her usual bounds of peculiarity, and Jared sighed impatiently as he glanced to the street beyond. But Mildred now met his blue eyes, and he saw the sudden power of her resolve.

"Has she left you?" she asked bluntly.

"She has gone to Maine, where I will join her," Jared told Mildred irritably, but Mildred closed her eyes in a semblance of prayer.

"Then you must hurry, Jared," she breathed. "There is so little time."

"Why?"

"Christina has gone also," Mildred told him in a pained, hushed voice.

"What of it?" asked Jared, but a cold fear touched his heart, though he couldn't guess the reason.

"Jared, I believe Christina intends to kill your wife."

Jared stared at Mildred, and now he was certain she had taken leave of her senses beyond her usual capacity. "What led you to this conclusion?" he asked, but his doubt was obvious, and Mildred gripped his arm.

"She's done it before," Mildred whispered, but her eyes flooded with sudden tears. "Charles," she mouthed, but Jared shook his head.

"Charles had the typhoid," he reasoned.

"He did," agreed Mildred. "But that wasn't what killed him, Jared. He died long before the illness had advanced to such a point."

Mildred's voice broke with a harsh sob and she leaned against him. Jared's heart froze, but he led Mildred into the sitting room and she collapsed into a chair. She regained herself, but her face was swollen and blotched with tears as she struggled to speak.

"I didn't know for certain, I swear before God," she told him brokenly.

"I can't believe Christina would harm Charles, or anyone," said Jared, but Mildred smiled through her tears.

"You've always been too trusting of women, haven't you?" she said, and Jared was amazed at the companionable tone of his old nemesis.

"So I've been told," he replied darkly.

"She wanted you desperately. Even as a child," said Mildred. "From the moment I first held her, I knew something was . . . missing from her nature. She was different from her brothers and sisters—I saw that from the first. Often I wondered where I failed, yet I came to see there was nothing to be done.

"I protected her, guided her. But when it came to you, she wouldn't heed my advice. She was determined to be your wife, and when you left . . . Charles saved her pride, and I hoped her . . . strangeness would pass. I thought it had. But when you returned, I saw how wrong I was.

"I knew what she told you about Charles, I know that you tried to help her. I know that she confessed her love then."

Jared frowned at the painful memory, but Mildred nodded when she saw his reaction. "You were a difficult child," she mused with the faintest trace of fondness. "How I longed to see you horsewhipped! Yet you always retained that intangible honor, and when Christina saw you wouldn't take her from Charles, then she decided to free herself by . . . other means.

"She was elated at his death," remembered Mildred with agony. "She barely attempted to conceal her reaction. Always she was here, waiting to hear of you, waiting for your return.

"When you brought your Yankee wife the shock was over-whelming. She sat in her room for hours, her face blank, no words. I thought she had accepted it, but I was a fool. When you took your wife to Petersburg, she said again and again how fortunate it would be if Philippa didn't return.

"After your illness, I saw her watching Philippa. I knew what she was thinking. I've kept my eye on her, like a hawk, but I was too late."

"How would she know where Pippa has gone?" asked Jared, but his heart was thundering with fear.

"Christina watches her, Jared. She stares from the attic window of our burned house, stares at your room. She watches you, together." Mildred hesitated, color rising in her pale face. "Christina feels that Philippa bewitched you, that she did . . . things to, well, seduce you from your senses."

Had the situation not been so dire, Jared might have laughed at the conversation he was holding with his old nemesis. "Pippa and I are married, Mildred."

"I was married, too," said Mildred. "But Mr. Smith never . . ." Mildred caught herself. "Never mind that."

Jared breathed a sigh of relief when Mildred returned to the subject at hand.

"There was nothing I could do for Charles," Mildred said painfully.

"I believe he would have died anyway—he was very ill. I love my daughter, and I let it pass. I told myself I was mistaken. There was blood on his pillow, from where she had suffocated him in his sleep. I told myself it didn't reveal the manner of his death, and I burned it. But I can't allow her another life. Especially not that of a young mother."

"Mother?" questioned Jared doubtfully. "Pippa isn't a mother."

"Not yet," Mildred told him. "But soon. Didn't you know?"

Jared stared, dumbfounded, shaking his head as his heart quailed for the misery Pippa must be enduring without him. "Does Christina know this?" he asked weakly, but Mildred's tears flooded across her cheeks.

"She has guessed, but it won't spare your wife, Jared. There is no such remorse in my daughter. It has fired her haste to be rid of Philippa. Now go, for there's no time to lose. It may already be too late."

A southerly wind blew up from the ocean, tossing the summer-warmed waves high upon the rocks. The spray of the sea's savage pounding reached Pippa's face, but she didn't move back from the low cliff. She gazed out across the sea as it raged against the northern shoreline, her dark hair swirling in the ocean breeze, but nothing eased the bitter pain in her heart.

Pippa had given her old cart horse to a rebel prisoner of war in Washington, then taken a train north hoping to find a measure of peace. Joshua Chamberlain invited her to stay in Brunswick with his family, but Pippa chose instead to seek the seclusion of her father's tiny cottage several miles from town.

Her only bright moment since leaving Virginia had come as she passed her old home and saw none other than Darius tending the garden with his little Persian wife, and his children playing in the yard. He had assumed she was merely visiting relatives, and Pippa had let that impression stand. But her heart throbbed in pain when he had asked if her husband would be joining her.

Tears welled in Pippa's gray-green eyes as they always

did when she thought of Jared Knox, and the salt of her tears was met by the fine salt spray of the sea. "Jared," she whispered softly, and Pippa closed her eyes.

"So you think he will come for you? You wait in vain, I think," came a soft voice from behind, and Pippa whirled in astonishment.

Christina stood behind her, her blonde hair bound in a neat chignon, unaffected by the ocean breezes that tossed Pippa's wildly about her head. Christina was dressed in a fashionable traveling dress, respectably attired in every way. With discordant shock, Pippa saw an officer's revolver held purposefully in her hands.

Christina saw the direction of Pippa's astonished gaze and she smiled. "It was Charles's," she told Pippa idly. "One of the few useful items he left me."

"You intend to kill me?" gasped Pippa. "Why?"

"Even you couldn't be stupid enough to doubt the reason," scoffed Christina.

"Jared," breathed Pippa, but then she shook her head. "If you've followed me here, you must know Jared doesn't want me anymore."

Christina frowned. "If he ever wanted you," she agreed. "I know your intentions, Philippa. You are obviously a crafty woman. When Jared learns of your . . . condition, you know he'll take you back, no matter what you've done."

Pippa's throat constricted as she thought of the baby she carried, and her limbs went cold with fear. Her own life might not matter without Jared, but her child's . . .

"Jared will never know . . ." she whispered, but Christina laughed.

"Do you expect me to believe that? You seduced him, for just that purpose. You must have known you couldn't keep him long when his true love was widowed."

Despite her fear, Pippa's eyes narrowed angrily. "If you were his 'true love,' I expect he'd have married you when he had the chance," she replied with vigor. Seeing the fury in Christina's face, Pippa instantly regretted her rash assertion.

"Or not," she added weakly, but Christina lifted her gun and stepped closer to Pippa.

"I could kill you here," she speculated thoughtfully, but then she glanced back toward the cottage.

"But shooting . . . well, the Yankees would make some effort to locate your murderer, I've no doubt. Jared himself might fall under suspicion," added Christina affectionately. "No, we'll go to that cottage. Now," she ordered harshly, but Pippa didn't move.

If she went, she would be killed. Pippa's mind raced in a wild jumble of thought, but her heart was pounding so loudly that she could make sense of nothing save the need to protect her child.

I am not going to die, Pippa thought firmly. *I am not going to let you kill me and take my husband.* Pippa's mind cleared, and she faced Christina with the courage of one who has nothing left to lose.

"The manner of my death means little to me," she said with effort. "If you can be traced as my killer, so much the better. Jared is in Richmond. No blame will come to him."

Pippa was amazed at her own self-control, and Christina hesitated at Pippa's defiance. "I could push you from this cliff," she said menacingly, but Pippa's brow rose doubtfully.

"I'm a very good swimmer," she lied evenly, but she drew a restrained breath of relief when Christina accepted this assertion.

"Then you'll go to the cottage or die here. You may choose," offered Christina with a cruel smile, but Pippa didn't answer.

Christina would pull the trigger—of this, Pippa had no doubt. Yet if she went to the cottage, that would give her a few more moments to escape.

The evening sky darkened swiftly above them, clouds of slate gray racing in from the sea to herald an early nightfall. Christina glanced upward and frowned.

"It might be best to kill you now and push your body to the waves," she said, and Pippa blanched with fear.

"Bodies are pushed to the shore by the waves, Christina. The tide is coming in. Fishermen come here daily. I would be found."

"Then you prefer the cottage?"

"I do," agreed Pippa reluctantly, though how this might avail her, she couldn't yet guess.

Christina seemed in a hurry, but Pippa walked very slowly in front of her, tripping occasionally to slow their passage. Night raced inward, and Pippa sensed this was troubling to Christina. *Perhaps she doesn't want to spend the night alone,* mused Pippa in disgust. Whatever the reason, Pippa had no wish to see Christina satisfied.

Pippa stopped outside the door of the cottage and took a deep breath. One last time she glanced south across the sea. She saw the first stars flickering high above the glittering water, she saw the sliver of a new moon like a jewel in a crown.

I will never see him again, she thought numbly. *I will die here, he will never know the reason. I will never know our child, it will never be . . . No,* she thought, and her mind hardened to find a way for her own survival.

"What are you going to do?" asked Pippa as they went inside, but Christina didn't answer. "I assume you had a plan when you followed me here," added Pippa provocatively.

"Such things don't come about best when planned," replied Christina calmly. "One does best when one follows the easiest route, I've found," she said idly as she looked around the room. "Take what is available. A pillow to the face of a weakened man . . . or a fallen oil lamp to the wood of an old cottage."

Pippa swallowed hard, her mind struggling for some reason for delay, but Christina nodded as she settled on her method.

"Choose a seat, Philippa. It will be your last, so let it be comfortable."

Christina pointed the gun at Pippa, and Pippa knew she would be killed if she resisted. Christina was desperate. Though she would prefer a fire that might be deemed accidental, her desire to be quickly rid of Pippa was evident as well.

Pippa sat in her father's armchair, fighting the tears that clouded her green eyes. Christina looked around for something to bind Pippa to the seat and she found an old, tangled web of rope still attached to an anchor. She bound Pippa tightly, leaving the anchor at her feet, and Christina smiled with satisfaction at her success. Pippa watched with horror as Christina lit the oil lamp, and she glanced out the window for one last glimpse toward the south.

It was already very dark, and a glimmer of hope struck Pippa's thoughts. "A fire will be seen!" she said hurriedly, as Christina lifted the lamp, and Pippa's breath caught as Christina considered this.

"I'll be rescued by a fisherman, you might even be caught," she added hastily, and Christina frowned.

Christina glanced out the window and nodded thoughtfully. "Then we'll wait until the morning," she decided reluctantly.

"A few more hours to prolong your life . . . No, there's no hurry. In the morning, you'll burn like the witch that you are. Then Jared will be free of your spell, free to come back to me, and all will be as it should have been from the beginning."

A few more hours, thought Pippa wearily. *What good will that do me?* she wondered miserably. Yet she might find a way to free herself of the knots, she might yet reason with Christina, though that seemed unlikely. Obviously, Christina had little compassion, but it was worth a try.

Pippa closed her eyes and she saw Jared's face clearly, she remembered each moment since their first meeting. She saw the light of love glimmering in his blue eyes, she recalled his flash of anger, she remembered the passion of his lovemaking.

Why did you ask me to go? she wondered painfully. *Would the baby make a difference? Why don't you want me anymore?* Pippa had no idea, but she knew she had to find out before she died.

Why did I run? she agonized as tears flooded her eyes and touched her lashes. *I should have gone to him, begged him to keep me. I should have promised him anything, if only he would let me stay.*

Jared . . .

Jared Knox rose from his seat as the train ground slowly to a stop, and the attendant frowned slightly as the young Virginian made his way to the doors.

"Impatient, aren't we?" said the attendant, but Jared glared at him and said nothing. "Always in a hurry, folks nowadays. You're in New England now, son," rambled the attendant, but Jared rolled his eyes and repressed a groan.

"Nope, we take things slow here. Think about it afore saying it, if you take my meaning."

"Indeed," replied Jared curtly. The attendant eyed Jared suspiciously at the sound of his voice, surveying his well-tailored wardrobe with suspicion.

"Where are you from? England?" he asked as he opened the door to let Jared pass.

"No," replied Jared coldly. "Virginia."

The attendant's eyes widened dramatically as Jared passed him and hurried away, but then he sighed and shook his head.

"Virginia! Well, that explains it . . . He's a damned rebel."

It was past midnight, the train being late as usual, and Jared had no clear idea where to find Pippa. At the train station, he learned the whereabouts of her father's Brunswick home on Federal Street, but no one knew the location of her cottage by the sea.

Jared had no choice but to try the Federal Street house, but he banged on the door for some time before anyone answered. The door opened, and a small, dark man peered up at him blearily and with decided suspicion.

"Not interested," said the man in a marked accent.

"Are you Arabic?" asked Jared, but the little man frowned.

"American," he replied indignantly. "Before that, Persian. Darius, I am. Who are you?"

"Jared Knox," replied Jared. "I'm looking for my wife, Philippa Knox, and this was once her home. My train was late, and I don't know how to find her."

"Your wife!" gasped Darius. "I know her well," he said enthusiastically, and he forcefully pulled Jared in the door. "She was alone, waiting for you, yes? Sad, I think. Now many visitors. How good, how good!"

"Visitors?" asked Jared, but his heart stopped as he waited for Darius to continue.

"Aye, her sister too came looking. I say she gone to the water, alone. Glad her sister there."

"When?" pressed Jared, but his heart now raced in terror.

"Just the morning of yesterday," replied Darius in confusion. "Well-mannered lady, that," he added, but Jared grabbed the man's arm.

"My wife has no sister," he said. "The woman to whom you spoke intends to kill Pippa."

Darius's eyes widened, and he groaned, clasping his hand to his brow. "No, no . . . What have I done?"

"You had no way of knowing," said Jared. "But maybe I can reach her in time. Darius, I need a horse, badly. Have you one?"

"No, sir, not even for cart. You talk to the general. Up street and to right of school. Chamberlain."

Jared nodded, and he hurried from the house in the direction Darius indicated. A rebel pounding on the door of an esteemed Yankee general might be frowned upon, but Jared Knox had no choice if Pippa was to be spared.

A servant opened the door, himself half asleep, but Jared had no time for formalities. "I must speak with General Chamberlain, immediately. It's urgent," he pressed, as the servant looked up at him blankly.

"Who are you?" asked the servant groggily. "I can't think of anything important enough to wake the general from his sleep. Surely it can wait until morning."

"It cannot," replied Jared furiously.

"Who are you?" asked the servant again, coming to his senses as his suspicions soared.

"I am Jared Knox."

"You sound like an Englishman . . . or a Southerner. Just where are you from?"

Jared rolled his eyes and drew a deep breath. "I'm from Virginia," he admitted reluctantly, and the servant's eyes lit with accusation.

"Ha! Probably some assassin sent by Jefferson Davis. Lincoln not enough for you?"

Jared stepped toward the man in pure exasperation, but the servant backed away in terror, his wild shout ringing through the darkened house. Doors opened from above, and a man appeared at the top of the staircase holding aloft a lantern. Seeing the scene below, he smiled faintly, then proceeded down the stairs.

"What is it, Libby?" he asked, but his eyes were on Jared and revealed no fear.

"A rebel, sir, come to kill ye."

"Jared Knox, General Chamberlain, come to ask your help for my wife," added Jared.

"Jared Knox." Joshua Chamberlain thought a moment. "But weren't you lost at Gettysburg?" he asked. Jared stared at him in amazement.

"So it was thought at the time," Jared told him, but Joshua Chamberlain nodded.

"Your cousin was grieved. I trust he has learned of your well-being since."

"He has."

Chamberlain came to Jared and shook his hand. "Now what's this about your wife? You married Gordon Reid's little girl, did you not? Little Pippa? I asked her to stay here, but she would have none of it."

"Someone has followed her here," Jared told the general, and his desperation was plain to Joshua Chamberlain. "A woman who means her harm, if I can't find her in time. I don't know where to find her cottage."

"I know it well," said Chamberlain. "Wait here, and I will dress. We will ride together, Yankee and rebel. Reid's cottage is down the point aways, but it's no more than ten miles. Longer marches than that have we both taken, have we not?"

"We have," agreed Jared, and for the first time since he left Richmond, his heart lightened with the promise of hope.

Pippa stared out her window, willing morning away, but at the first glimmer of light, she knew her hours were short. Christina was asleep in the bedroom, having no fear for Pippa's escape, and indeed Pippa had no luck whatsoever in freeing herself from her ties.

Pippa heard Christina stir in the next room, and her heart twisted in fear. It was some time before Christina appeared, but she was fully dressed and neatly coiffed when she came from the bedroom.

"Still here?" she mocked, but Pippa said nothing. "God cannot say I gave you no chance," added Christina seriously.

"I'm sure He will be thrilled," replied Pippa.

"He will understand," said Christina with conviction. "It was you who interfered with the Lord's design."

Pippa sighed and shook her head, but there seemed little hope in arguing over God's wishes.

"You seduced Jared, you used pagan wiles to turn him from a virtuous life."

"Miss Honeycastle," murmured Pippa, and a small giggle erupted weirdly from her lips. "I do not see that murder is more virtuous than seduction," argued Pippa, but Christina was unimpressed by this logic.

"Yet witches were burned at the stake, were they not, for their crimes against the virtuous? I would imagine they were such as you, Philippa. Women who appealed to a man's . . . baser needs, who drove them from their minds with acts of wickedness."

"I liked the acts of wickedness," replied Pippa defiantly. If she was to die, she would die unrepentant. "And so did Jared."

This was too much for Christina, and Pippa saw that her hands were trembling when she lit the lantern.

"You are a witch, and you will be purged thus," invoked Christina in a voice that was a chant. "In fire. You'll be returned to the flames from whence you came."

"And Jared's child?" questioned Pippa. "Have you no thought for that?"

"A child of the devil."

"And an angel."

"Jared was blind when he loved you," said Christina, as she made a small pile of kindling with sheets near the wall. "The wind will blow the flames," she told Pippa casually. "From the far side of the cottage to where you now sit. By then it will be an inferno."

"How can you kill me, knowing I bear a child?" wondered Pippa, desperate to reason with a woman who had no reason.

"Death serves its purpose," said Christina calmly. "It's a cleansing, of all that's not as it should be. Charles didn't understand this. He fought the typhoid, he intended to recover, I even saw signs that he might truly defy God's will in this. Of course, I couldn't allow him such defiance."

"You killed your husband?" gasped Pippa, but now she knew there was no hope.

"I redirected his defiance," corrected Christina. "He

blamed Jared for coming between us, yet he guessed in the end. He threatened to tell Jared things that would tarnish me in his eyes."

"Jared knows you lied about Charles beating you, Christina," said Pippa fiercely. "David Knox told him."

Briefly, Christina's pale eyes flashed, but then her unnatural calm returned. "David Knox has died for his sins. It was he that drove Jared from me. But he cannot part us now."

It was hopeless. Even now, Christina appeared so calm, so maidenly—even as she removed the glass plate from the lantern and set it to the kindling. She paused to brush her hair back into place, and then she turned to Pippa.

"If you accept that you are evil, a witch, it will go easier for you," she told Pippa. "But either way, the flames will tear you from Jared."

Christina stepped back from the little fire and watched it admiringly for a moment. Her nose wrinkled at the smell of smoke, and she drew forth a delicate handkerchief to protect herself from the odors.

"You can't take what you weren't meant to have, Philippa," said Christina as she opened the door. "You used the means of a devil to steal Jared from his rightful wife, and only by fire will he be purged from your fingers. Women who use seduction rather than virtue will always perish thus."

Pippa stared at her in disbelief as Christina turned away, shutting the door behind her. She struggled briefly as panic overtook her, but to no avail. She stopped, staring at the growing fire as her eyes watered from the smoke and her anguish.

The little flames crept up the woodwork and found the light cotton curtains, leaping hungrily along the dry cloth. Pippa felt the light breeze in her face, rustling through her hair. Now it worked against her, fanning the flames into a frantic dance. With every second that violent dance drew nearer. Smoke filled the room, and Pippa cried. Her tears fell from her face to her bound hands, running in rivers as she fought for control over her last thoughts.

She wanted to remember every moment with Jared, every word spoken, every touch. She wanted to feel her head against his chest, his fingers sifting through her hair, his gentle kiss as it turned to passion, his body against hers as they loved.

But the smoke obscured her thoughts, filling her lungs with molten agony. She coughed, fighting to breathe, but it was no use. Her thoughts ceased and her soul took wing, lifting from her body. As it rose, Pippa saw the ocean set against a backdrop of the dark green, New England forest.

There along the road came Jared, Jared on a shining gray horse, Jared coming to save her as on the wings of angels she flew above him.

"It's not far now," called Joshua Chamberlain as he raced along down the dirt road beside Jared. He noted the faint hint of smoke carried on the wind, and his heart quailed as he guessed its direction.

Jared, too, caught the ghastly suggestion of fire, and he urged the gray horse faster, beyond its limits. The noble animal lengthened its stride still more and met the urging. They raced past saltwater farms, past surprised farmers who looked up from their chicken pens and shook their heads at the apparent exuberance of the young.

"There!" shouted Chamberlain, as they approached Gordon Reid's little cottage, but both men were sick with fear when they saw the red flames leaping from the windows.

Jared leapt from the gray horse and ran to the door, knocking it inward. A great billow of smoke burst from the house and he reeled before pressing inward. Chamberlain followed him, but neither could see in the gray cloud that choked the little rooms of Pippa's cottage.

"Pippa!" Jared called desperately for her, but there was no answer.

He called again, but then through the fire and smoke, he saw her. Pippa sat crumpled in a chair as flames leapt toward her with the gleeful violence of a barbarian army. The roof shook and cracked, collapsing between them as the fire raged, blocking Jared from her.

"Not that way," yelled Chamberlain as Jared forged ahead, but he had to forcibly drag the young Virginian back.

"We can go in through the back window," he suggested, and Jared accepted the general's suggestion.

They raced around to the far side of the cottage and smashed the window. Chamberlain knocked away the glass and Jared climbed in, jumping to the floor beside Pippa. She was very pale, her eyes closed, but Jared had no time to check for life. His hands were shaking as he untied her bonds. As he lifted her limp form into his arms, another portion of the roof collapsed around them.

A burning beam struck his back, and Jared lurched forward, but he managed to reach the window. Chamberlain was waiting, and Jared passed Pippa through the opening, climbing out himself just as the remaining beams crashed behind him.

"Get her away from here," he gasped. Joshua Chamberlain carried Pippa towards the ocean, where the clean, salty wind blew the smoke inland.

The general lowered Pippa's body to the earth, but as he looked toward the forest, he saw the slim figure of a woman watching them before she vanished beneath the trees.

"A woman," he murmured, but the perpetrator of such a crime deserved no mercy whatever her gender.

"Give her air," he told Jared, but the general ran after Pippa's assailant.

Tears coursed across Jared's face as he knelt beside his wife, but he bent over her, blowing air into her smoke-filled lungs and pressing upon her chest to revive her. For an eternity, there was no reaction, but finally Pippa coughed and sputtered, fighting for air.

"Pippa," murmured Jared, his limbs weak from the force of his relief.

Pippa didn't wake, though her breaths came with increasing power and regularity. "Pippa, my love," he whispered as he cradled her head in his lap, drawing her slender body against his as he cried.

Christina saw Jared go into the house, into the flames. She saw the Yankee pull him away, but maybe Jared needed to see his wife's end firsthand. Maybe now he would see her for the witch she was. When the Yankee emerged again bearing her body, Christina froze in fear herself. The flames had no time to immerse Philippa in their midst, to devour her. Then in Jared's arms, she came back to life.

The Yankee had seen her! Christina retreated into the thick woods, but her new dress caught and tore on the grasping shrubs. Yankee trees seeking to avenge one of their own. Witches have familiars, after all.

Christina knew the Yankee would come after her, and she hurried, though the trees purposefully delayed her progress. She heard his shout, and she began to run. She saw the forest's end, she saw the rocks beyond. He would never reach her there.

"Stop, wait!" shouted the Yankee, but Christina laughed as she ran.

Does he think me a fool? she thought wildly as she glanced back at the man following her. She ran faster, but she reached the rocks to find they were covered with slippery, green seaweed. Christina picked her way across the jagged rocks to where the ocean slapped violently.

Pippa had told her the tide was coming in the night before, but now Christina realized it wasn't so. It had reached its peak, and was retreating now, retreating with violence. Again a great swell met the jagged rocks, crashing high, unseen fingers reaching to grab Christina's ankles.

Christina looked back, and the Yankee was nearly upon her. She turned to the tide, and she smiled. A fitting end, bittersweet as befit a noble heroine, defeated by evil, yet virtuous to the end.

Christina stepped to the edge of the rock, and just as Joshua Chamberlain reached to stop her, she threw herself into the foam below.

The great tide pulled her under, dashing her against the rocks below, and Chamberlain searched in vain for her body. He shook his head sorrowfully, but when he turned to see the young rebel holding his wife tightly, he knew it was a better end than might have been.

Pippa woke and peered around the strange room, but nowhere could she attach familiarity to her surroundings. It was homey, rustic . . . like a farmhouse, she considered happily. As she lay, the pleasant aroma of roasting chicken wafted into the room and she drew a deep, hungry breath.

"Where am I?" she said aloud, but she startled when a woman answered her.

"You're at the Neils', dearie."

Pippa looked over to see Annie Neil enter the room. "Feeling better, then?"

"Yes, thank you," said Pippa, but her face clouded as she struggled to sit up.

"You just rest, honey. I'm starting on your supper now."

"What happened?" asked Pippa. "How did I get here?"

"General Joshua Chamberlain himself brought you here, honey," said Annie Neil. "Said I was to take care of you, until you're well enough to go back to Virginia."

"Virginia," murmured Pippa, but her chest constricted as she realized how much she longed to do just that.

"You'll be wanting to go soon, I'd expect," mused Annie Neil as she drew back the curtains. "What with the fire and all."

"The fire," said Pippa, as the bitter memory flooded back to her.

"Now don't you be thinking about it," advised Annie Neil. "It's over now. Dinner will be ready in an hour or so, but I expect you'll be wanting your privacy until then," she suggested with twinkling eyes, though Pippa watched her doubtfully.

The farmer's wife left the room, and Pippa closed her eyes. Over indeed. She had been filled with dreams of Jared—that was why she was happy when she woke up. But no, Joshua Chamberlain had saved her. Perhaps he was coming to call, or a fisherman had spotted the fire. What became of Christina, Pippa couldn't guess, but for the time being, she felt safe enough. She rose from her bed, somewhat lost in the nightgown she found herself wearing. Annie Neil was a large woman.

Pippa gazed out the open window toward the sea, and she

sighed heavily as the loose gown fluttered around her slight form.

"You look south. Can it be your heart lies in that direction also?"

At the sound of the soft Virginian voice, Pippa's heart stopped, then leapt into activity of such resounding force that she couldn't begin to urge her trembling body into the slightest motion.

"Pippa," he said gently, and Pippa turned her head in utter disbelief to the man who spoke behind her.

Jared smiled, the slow, sensual smile Pippa adored, and he came toward her. His eyes searched Pippa's stunned face, but his own throat was constricted with the force of seeing her well.

"Jared," she said, but Pippa's voice was a mere whisper. "Why are you here?" she asked with effort, but her heart was racing and Pippa began to tremble.

"Why do you think, angel?"

Pippa caught her breath, fighting the hot tears that threatened, but her hope had risen so powerfully that it wouldn't be denied.

"I don't know," she whispered, fearing to utter her hope lest it be destroyed forever.

Jared reached to brush her hair from her face, touching her cheek, but Pippa cast her eyes from his. "Don't you?" he asked quietly. "Did you really think I could let you go, when all my life depends on having you near?"

Pippa's eyes met Jared's, but she could barely believe what she beheld there. "But you said I was to go," she said in a small voice.

"No, angel. I asked you if that was what you wanted."

"I thought you were just being . . . gentlemanly," said Pippa, but Jared's brow rose doubtfully.

"That hardly seems likely."

"I thought you didn't want me anymore," she added painfully.

"How could you ever think that, Pippa? When it has been plain from the beginning how wanting you has directed every portion of my life."

"But you didn't, you weren't . . ." fumbled Pippa.

"I didn't avail myself of that wanting when we returned to Richmond," he finished for her.

"I don't understand you, Jared," said Pippa, but she longed to believe their parting had been no more than a dreadful mistake.

"Don't you, angel? How could you not after hearing my father's words?"

"Your father?" asked Pippa in growing confusion.

Jared nodded, and he looked out the window over the endless blue-gray sea. "What he said about me was true, Pippa. My passion for you exceeds all else. After he died, I came to realize how much of this life I had forced upon you, all because I was mad to keep you near me."

"I wanted to be with you!" exclaimed Pippa.

"Did you? But I gave you no choice. I had to have you, from the first, and as my father said, I used our . . . passion to convince you."

"I was easily convinced," replied Pippa with a smile, and Jared smiled, too.

"Yet I never asked if it was what you wanted, Pippa, for I feared to hear your answer. I forced you from Fredericksburg, I dragged you with me into the Wilderness, I gave you no choice whether to marry or not. Then, in Petersburg . . ."

Jared faltered, drawing Pippa's shaking hand to his lips and kissing her fingers tenderly. "Pippa, I made your life hell. In the madness of my desire, I forced myself on you. I placed you in danger at the Crater. Had I lost you, knowing your death was my own doing . . ."

Pippa's eyes widened at Jared's painful sentiment. "I can't say those weren't bleak days, Jared, when I lost your love," she began with effort. "But the night you came to me . . . I've never wanted anything more than I wanted you that night."

A quick blush touched her cheeks, and Pippa smiled weakly. "I placed myself in danger at the Crater," she admitted guiltily. "I was afraid to learn that you regretted our night together," she added shyly, but Jared touched her cheek and wouldn't let her look away.

"I should have assuaged your doubt, love. But my own remorse was too great to face you when I had taken you against your will."

Pippa's heart thudded with hope at Jared's words. "You did no more than I desired," she told him, but then her face clouded. "But when the war ended," she ventured hesitantly. "When we were of the same country again, then you were so distant."

Jared sighed and nodded. "When the war ended . . ." he repeated wearily. "From the beginning, I tried to bend you to my will, Pippa. Yet it was I who could not remain unchanged. Like the South itself," he finished thoughtfully.

"How is that?" Pippa asked.

"Perhaps it was my surrender, as well," he told her, "to offer you your freedom. Or maybe I wished to reassure myself that our marriage was what you wanted. But when I woke to find you gone, I knew I would do anything to bring you back. When I spoke with Lucy . . ."

Pippa's eyes widened. "Lucy? What did she tell you?"

Jared smiled. "It wasn't so much what she told me as
how she phrased it," he said knowingly.

Pippa looked nervously to her feet, but Jared cupped her
chin in his hand and lifted her face to look into his eyes.
"She is a woman of exceptional courage, I see that now. It
grieves me that such a woman needed to wear the cloak of
an idiot to survive in my land. But Pippa, that I forced you
to abandon what you held dear—this grieves me most of
all."

The tears fell to Pippa's cheeks, and Jared gently brushed
them away. "You were what I held most dear," said Pippa
with an intensity of feeling that brought fire to her eyes.

Now Jared's own eyes glistened. "Pippa, I love you so.
When Mildred told me of your danger . . ."

"Mildred?" asked Pippa, and Jared nodded.

"Perhaps I've misjudged her, somewhat. I certainly never
dreamed I'd be discussing pleasures of the flesh with Mildred
Smith."

Pippa eyed Jared doubtfully. "Pleasures . . . ?"

"Don't ask." Jared grinned and kissed Pippa's hand.
"Mildred's confession saved your life, my love, for had I
been but a moment later . . . I wonder now if her sour nature
wasn't because of her anxiety over Christina."

"Christina," breathed Pippa.

"She's gone," Jared reassured her. "General Chamberlain
tried to stop her, but she threw herself from the cliff. A
fisherman found her body this morning."

"She was so calm, through all of it, Jared," Pippa remembered with a shudder. "So certain I was evil, that she was
merely righting a wrong with my death. She said I had seduced you," Pippa added uncomfortably. "That by my lack
of virtue, I ruined your life. I inspired . . . well, lust, when
you deserved a respectable wife."

"Such as a murderess? I think not."

"At times, I thought much the same as did she," Pippa confessed, but Jared touched her face and she met his eyes hesitantly.

"I don't deny your . . . inspiration, Pippa. But desire is only a part of what I feel. Can you doubt my heart when I look at you?"

Jared took her small face in his hands. "When I first saw you across that ravine, my heart leapt in recognition. When we met in your aunt's library, I couldn't help but love you. Yet I held an image of what you should be, and when I learned you had your own purposes, I was furious."

Jared paused and his hands went to her shoulders. "But Pippa, hear me now. From the time you came to my room bearing morphine bought with your dearest possession, from that day, I have loved you for nothing save for what you are."

Pippa caught her breath and her lips parted, yet she couldn't speak. "And whatever you want, angel, that I will do if it will bring you back to me. But know I will not leave this place without you."

Pippa smiled through her tears. "You've done what I wished you to do, Jared. You've come for me, as I dreamed you would do night after night."

Pippa's eyes brightened, and Jared knew her heart was healed. "But I think I'm unwise to answer you so easily," she added.

"Why is that, love?"

"It would be good to have you . . . convince me further, I believe," suggested Pippa with sparkling eyes.

"How would I do that, my sweet wife?" questioned Jared, but his own eyes were blazing with her veiled suggestion.

"You will lock this door, Jared Knox, and you'll love me

as I've longed for you to do. When I'm satisfied that your promise is in earnest, I'll tell you a secret."

"What secret?"

Pippa touched her stomach and shook her head. "That you must earn." Jared's grin widened as he drew her into his arms and kissed her forehead.

"Now that you are mine again, my love, I will with pleasure spend my life earning your favor," he said, as he lifted her and carried her to the bed.

"All I have is yours," she vowed. "I've loved you since I first saw you. If you hadn't come for me, I would have returned to you, to offer you anything if you would only love me again."

"I never stopped, angel," murmured Jared as his lips brushed against hers. "But your offering is accepted, and returned in force. We are one, my love. We cannot be parted."

"But we're better for our differences," added Pippa as Jared laid her upon the bed.

The curtains rustled and lifted as the ocean's strong wind blew in from the cove. The wind swirled around the little room, dancing in celebration of a union that wouldn't be sundered, even when death had come so close, so many times.

The wind touched upon the fear and the doubt, lifting them from the two who now loved in abandon, and from the ravaged land in which they lived. On the wings of love, Jared and Pippa were free at last from the bitter years of war.

Epilogue

"Except for her hair, she looks like you, angel," Jared murmured as he sat down on the bed beside Pippa.

Pippa looked up from the sleeping baby and smiled at her husband. Jared brushed Pippa's long hair from her face and, as their eyes met, Pippa felt a tremor of anticipation.

"Here, give her to me, love, and I'll take her to the nursery."

Jared took the tiny, bundled form and kissed her little forehead tenderly. With utmost care, Jared carried the baby to the next room and laid her gently in her cradle. Pippa was lying back on her pillows when Jared returned, and she was smiling as she considered how very well her life had gone since Jared had come to her in Maine.

Jared sat beside her, but he touched her shoulder gingerly as if he feared she might break. Pippa looked at him in wonder, but her eyes lit with a devilish gleam.

"I'm perfectly recovered from Elizabeth's birth, Jared," she told him suggestively. "You needn't be so careful, if you please."

Jared's brow rose. "It hasn't been that long, angel," he answered doubtfully, but Pippa sat up to nestle close beside him.

"It has been long enough," she purred, and to convince him of this, she pressed a soft kiss along the firm column of his neck.

Jared shuddered, turning his face to find her lips. He kissed her slowly, savoring the sweet taste, but as Pippa drew him down upon the bed, Jared knew his wife wouldn't be denied.

"I've never been able to resist you, my love," he murmured against her hair.

"But it's been awhile since you were able to reach me," giggled Pippa as Jared ran his hands along her side.

"That's true, but at your very roundest, I still found you amazingly desirable."

"That is fortunate," said Pippa earnestly. "Because at my very roundest, I found myself often wishing for you."

"A wish I too easily granted," groaned Jared. "It's a wonder Elizabeth's birth went so easily."

"Easily for you!" exclaimed Pippa, but she had borne their first child with a minimum of discomfort. "I hope Lucy's is no more difficult," she added thoughtfully.

Jared drew back from his wife's arms. "That reminds me. What would you think of having Byron and Lucy as overseers on my estate? The house will be finished in a few weeks," he told her. "I'll need someone. Byron has been an enormous help during the construction. He'll need work when it's finished."

"I think that's a very good idea." Pippa paused. "Do you think your mother would approve?"

Pippa had never divulged Caroline's confidence about Byron's paternity to Jared, and she was afraid his presence would be a constant reminder of the pain Caroline had endured.

"Of course not," said Jared. "As a matter of fact, it was

Mother who suggested the idea, though I also thought of it."

"Then I think that would be perfect," said Pippa with relief.

"When you are finished with this house, will you design a pretty, little house to replace Father's cottage in Maine?" she questioned.

"As you wish."

Pippa sighed. "It will have to wait, I know. There are many who need your gifts here," she said with unrestrained pride. "Kim and Carey will need a house in Massachusetts, too."

Jared groaned. "One house at a time, angel."

"There's no hurry," agreed Pippa. "But I think it would be pleasant to visit Maine during July and August when it's so hot in Virginia."

Jared smiled and got up from the bed. Pippa watched him as he found a sheet of paper on his desk and brought it back to her.

"Here, what do you think of this?" he asked as Pippa examined it.

Pippa's eyes widened and shone with love when she recognized the perfect replica of Jared's own little house in the woods.

"Do you like it, Pippa?"

As an answer, Pippa flung her arms around Jared's neck, kissing him wildly as they fell together upon the bed.

"Jared Knox, I love you so. When did you have time to do this?" she asked as she lay on top of him.

Jared grinned. "Well, over the last few weeks I found I required a distraction," he admitted. "It's a good thing I finished the task before your recovery was complete," he added. "I doubt I'll want to spend my time designing houses for some time to come."

Pippa looked into his shining eyes and saw there the unrestrained power of Jared's love. It was the same look, but better, that she had first seen when she turned around in her aunt's library and beheld his handsome face.

Yet now Jared's eyes were free of all doubt, and as she kissed his mouth, Pippa knew they had attained a freedom together neither would have known apart. In this, the freedom to live and love fully, their love soared on gossamer wings and carried them upon the blissful crests of the wild, rebel wind.

Dear Reader,

Jared Knox walked into the first story I ever wrote, smiled that teasing smile, and promptly stole the show. I put aside everything to write his book. He proved a demanding hero, too. He wanted nothing to do with the sweet, innocent heroine I first provided. When I found Pippa, set with Yankee determination to forge the future she wanted, Jared met his match. Pippa's own integrity threatens the thing she loves most—Jared.

During the Civil War, men and women behaved with an innocence and honor that seems inconceivable in today's world. I wanted to meet the historical figures I admire most, so I invited two into my story. I respect Robert E. Lee, more because of his love for his troops than because of his brilliance as a commander. Joshua Chamberlain's gentle intelligence and soft-spoken dignity touch my heart beyond any war hero of any time.

When I finished *Rebel Wind* and left the Civil War behind, I took something from that time with me. What was true for them, what was good in them, still exists in us today. Maybe we're not so innocent; I hope we won't allow ourselves to be drawn into bloodshed ever again. If, like Jared and Pippa, we can learn to love our enemies, we'll have lived up to the promise of both North and South.